D1016002

ABOVE THE RAIN

"A meditation on family, circumstance, and violence, both political and personal."
                                                    —*Publishers Weekly*

"A quality of grace, hope, and forgiveness fills [Del Árbol's] books, propelling readers forward amid intricate plotting with any number of possible outcomes. [He] is equal parts painfully realistic and playfully mystical in writing about the way humans have of helping and destroying each other . . . As William Faulkner famously said, 'The past is never dead. It's not even past.' He might have found a kindred spirit in Víctor del Árbol."
                                                    —*Houston Press*

"*Above the Rain* is an exceptional novel about the present's inability to deny the past, a clear-eyed examination of the cultural clashes in modern Europe. It's also a novel about love, the different kinds thereof and how they offer their own various sorts of healing and redemption."
                            —Scott Phillips, author of *The Ice Harvest*
                                and *That Left Turn at Albuquerque*

"Víctor del Árbol's *Above the Rain* is a heartrending tour de force about mortality and chance and learning to live with ghosts. Rich with noir atmosphere, the book begins in 1950s Morocco and then brings us to contemporary Spain and Sweden. A sprawling ensemble cast drives the narrative, making for an epic unknotting of voices and experiences. It's expertly plotted, suspenseful, and immersive. Lisa Dillman's translation is crisp and elegant. Just extraordinary."

—William Boyle, author of *Gravesend* and *City of Margins*

"Haunting and provocative, *Above the Rain* is a novel of devastating, heartbreaking beauty. It demands your bravery, fires your imagination, and challenges your heart and soul. The rewards are rich. I will carry Miguel and Helena with me for a very long time."

—Bill Loehfelm, author of the Maureen Coughlin series

"A dark, vividly descriptive tale of two complicated people whose troubled pasts motivate a road trip full of winding turns, unexpected plot twists, and retribution. Adeptly plotted, an examination of our own pasts, of what we cannot change about them, and what we do with the time we have left."

—John McMahon, Edgar Award–nominated author of *The Good Detective*

"A sweeping and devastating historical novel, full of suspense, Del Árbol's *Above the Rain* is a masterclass in the way that trauma is reinforced and repeated throughout generations, with deadly consequences. In Del Árbol's noir-inflected masterpiece, the past is always present, the political is always personal, and love, however fleeting, is the only redeeming grace. I loved every moment of it."   —Halley Sutton, author of *The Lady Upstairs*

ABOVE THE RAIN

ALSO BY VÍCTOR DEL ÁRBOL

Breathing Through the Wound

A Million Drops

The Sadness of the Samurai

ABOVE

── *the* ──

RAIN

Víctor del Árbol

Translated from the Spanish
by Lisa Dillman

OTHER PRESS
New York

Originally published in Spanish as *Por encima de la lluvia*
by Ediciones Destino, Barcelona, Spain, in 2017.
Copyright © Víctor del Árbol 2017
Translation copyright © Lisa Dillman 2020

AC/E
ACCIÓN CULTURAL
ESPAÑOLA

Support for the translation of this book was provided
by Acción Cultural Española, AC/E.

Production editor: Yvonne E. Cárdenas
Text designer: Jennifer Daddio
This book was set in Filosofia and Helvetica Neue
by Alpha Design & Composition of Pittsfield, NH

1 3 5 7 9 10 8 6 4 2

All rights reserved. No part of this publication may be reproduced or
transmitted in any form or by any means, electronic or mechanical, including
photocopying, recording, or by any information storage and retrieval system,
without written permission from Other Press LLC, except in the case of
brief quotations in reviews for inclusion in a magazine, newspaper, or
broadcast. Printed in the United States of America on
acid-free paper. For information write to Other Press LLC,
267 Fifth Avenue, 6th Floor, New York, NY 10016.
Or visit our Web site: www.otherpress.com

Library of Congress Cataloging-in-Publication Data
Names: Árbol, Victor del, author. | Dillman, Lisa, translator.
Title: Above the rain : a novel / Victor del Árbol ; translated from the Spanish by Lisa Dillman.
Other titles: Por encima de la lluvia. English
Description: New York : Other Press, [2021] | Originally published in Spanish as
Por encima de la lluvia by Ediciones Destino, Barcelona, Spain, in 2017.
Identifiers: LCCN 2020040743 (print) | LCCN 2020040744 (ebook) |
ISBN 9781635429954 (trade paperback) | ISBN 9781635429961 (ebook)
Classification: LCC PQ6701.R364 P6713 2021 (print) | LCC PQ6701.R364 (ebook) |
DDC 863/.7—dc23
LC record available at https://lccn.loc.gov/2020040743
LC ebook record available at https://lccn.loc.gov/2020040744

Publisher's Note: This is a work of fiction. Names, characters, places,
and incidents either are the product of the author's imagination or
are used fictitiously, and any resemblance to actual persons,
living or dead, events, or locales is entirely coincidental.

For those who love life more than loss

AND OF ALL OF THOSE,
FOR EVA

I have discovered that all the unhappiness of men arises from one single fact, that they cannot stay quietly in their own chamber.

How can I bear this sorrow that gnaws at my belly; this fear of death that restlessly draws me onward? If only I could find the one man whom the gods made immortal, I would ask him how to overcome death.

Gilgamesh, Book IX
TRANSLATED BY STEPHEN MITCHELL

PROLOGUE

Tangier, July 1955

The presence of Enrique's things was testament to his absence: bags piled up in a corner containing the clothes he hadn't taken with him; an ashtray full of American cigarette butts that Thelma refused to empty; the wooden bookshelf buckling under the weight of old books; filing cabinets containing folders full of papers written in his hand, bearing his signature; a shoebox with no shoes; and Enrique's favorite record, *Angel Eyes*, by Matt Dennis, which she listened to over and over, like a disease she'd caught that made her sicker each day. The incurable disease of memory.

Thelma should have thrown all his things onto a pyre and watched them burn, should have painted the walls a different color, should have at least opened the bedroom window to clear the air. But doing any of those things would have meant accepting that this time Enrique's absence was definitive, that this wasn't like other times, when he'd leave but then come back. And she wasn't ready for that. She still needed to mourn him, curse him, hate him, and forgive him.

Every night, she stayed up until late, and like a monkey repeating a game it's been taught without understanding the rules, dragged herself to the bathroom to stroke Enrique's shaving brush or lovingly put on his bathrobe, to use his comb on her hair, brush her teeth with his brush and tune in to the radio station he listened to while getting dressed in the morning. Sometimes, Thelma simply sat on the toilet staring vacantly at a white tile until her legs went numb and her eyes hurt from not blinking. She'd be overcome, then, by the sense that it was all unreal and distant. When she came to and realized that he wasn't coming back, she would scream and break things, scratch her face so that the pain could be expressed via skin under nails and stinging flesh, because that was the only way to escape her living death.

Nothing changed her routine of abandonment. That night she sat on the edge of the bed and poured herself a generous tumbler of London 40. She was drunk in the usual way, a sick woman accustomed to her sickness. Though alcohol no longer helped her forget, at least it deadened the pain, and her thoughts dropped like pebbles onto the sandy bottom of her mind and lay there quietly, rocking gently in the emptiness. She stroked the dirty sheets she'd refused to change and relived the memory of Enrique, head against the pillow, cigarette in his right hand, glass of gin in the left, lightly clinking the ice cubes. This was a sign of his impatience, a way of saying Thelma wasn't convincing enough in her fake orgasm as she masturbated for him.

"Fucking bastard," she whispered, head lolling to one side, ashamed at the memory of how vile it had felt to be used that way. And yet she missed Enrique's unequivocal expression, his ruthless green eyes that judged her with infuriating condescension, like a god judging its creations. When his brow furrowed in that withering look and he took his eyes off her, it was like Thelma no longer existed. Like she'd been expelled from his thoughts. And it was the worst thing in the world.

Gin in hand, Thelma went to the window. Day had not yet dawned and already the heat was oppressive.

Tangier was still there. As unrelenting as it had been in the Delacroix paintings her father collected in his London home, the ones that had made her love this land even before she was capable of imagining it. *Wa fiki barakat allah*, the air seemed to chant. That was the first Arabic she learned: Allah has brought us this blessing. Ramadan was coming to an end, and she could smell the aromas accompanying it: *harira*, the soup that broke the fast, and the sweet bread and dates eaten with it. In a few hours the hustle and bustle of the market would start up, and with it would come the scent of lamb, spices, and coffee in the old souk; the hotels and little shops would once again be filled with the to and fro of colored jellabas and slippers, European suits and leather shoes, all intersecting with no apparent friction.

Perhaps what she missed most were their Sunday walks through the medina, Enrique with his arm around her, looking so handsome and gallant in his Regular Forces Battalion uniform, a red tarbush on his head. Women would turn to look at him as he passed by on the street, a handsome Spanish captain with green eyes and dark hair, but she wasn't jealous. On the contrary, she felt happy and proud.

When they'd first arrived as newlyweds in 1944, Tangier was unprejudiced, and they could visit their Moroccan friends, who lived in houses with roofs so low they had to bend down to get from one room to another. They soon made other friends, famous and important ones: Boulevard Pasteur tycoons, with their shady business deals; extravagant American painters and writers; Canadian, Australian, French, English, and Dutch adventurers looking to make a fresh start in a land where no one asked questions. It was all perfect, and no one thought it would stop being that way. They lived in the knowledge that happiness was fragile, but refused to accept its ephemeral nature and instead held on with both hands. Thelma was twenty-five, and Europe was at war. The moment she set foot in Tangier, she had the feeling she'd disembarked in an unsettling and dangerous world, but one full of incredible energy and passion. It was just what a pregnant English newlywed from a good family needed—to discover the exciting side of life. She was immediately seduced by the beautiful *riads* of Petite Place, the many cafés and the Mendoubia Gardens, where she spent entire afternoons sketching in her sketchbook, capturing faces she found exotic. She fell in love with everything she saw, touched or tasted, her senses surrendering to adventures at Malabata Beach, where nights lasted well into morning around the embers of a bonfire, smoke drifting up to a magnificent, all-encompassing black sky, eating fish tagine and listening to Jajouka music.

Eleven years later, where had that world gone? The sounds, flavors, and smells had vanished, and the streets that once beguiled her were now like a desiccated snake skin, something that once had been but no longer was. Religion, nationalism, politics, and mutual hatred had plundered the soul of the place that once belonged to everyone and no one. In the mornings, storefronts were covered in graffiti in support of Mohammed and annexation to an independent Alawite kingdom, as well as slogans full of hatred for the colonizers. Week by week the atmosphere became more stifling for Europeans. All of her friends were leaving, even those who'd held on until the end. And she would have to leave too; everybody was advising her to go. Tangier was no longer a safe place for a woman alone with an eleven-year-old daughter.

That very afternoon, Thelma had been paid a visit from the British consular secretary, an old-school diplomat and friend of her father's who was careful with his words but unmistakable with their meaning. He was delivering a message from her father.

"You've still got a family in London willing to take you in, a home, an income, and friendships that have survived the distance, friends who would bring you back to the world you and your daughter belong in."

Thelma had listened to her father's words, spoken from this old diplomat's mouth, with polite reserve. He couldn't possibly understand that at thirty-five, Thelma was no longer the young woman who'd run away from the asphyxiating atmosphere of the old mansion. Her response was laconic and categorical.

"The world where my daughter and I belong no longer exists. There's no place to go back to."

She knew what she had to do, and had only been postponing it for one reason. That night she took the bottle of London and a glass and went up to the attic she once used as a studio. In one corner stood the easel, covered with a sheet. Gently, she pulled it off and uncovered the painting. Thelma took a slow walk around the easel, stepping back for perspective, and looked at it sidelong, as though fearing she'd ruin the portrait if she looked at it straight on.

This was her masterpiece. Thelma told herself that even Enrique, who had hotly forbidden her to paint this portrait, would have to acknowledge the talent and effort she'd put into it, harmoniously integrating the light of the landscape and shadows of the man's young dark face. The model's beauty was unquestionably masculine, rugged and at the same time haughty; Thelma had used the beach as a backdrop, and dressed the young man in a white gandoura robe. The effect of motion had turned out exceptionally well: the wind in the folds of his clothing, the waves dissolving into churning foam, the branches of a carob tree in a distant corner. The only thing not moving was the fierce expression on the model's face: the stillness of his lips full of things about to be said, and a smile that was not an invitation to joy but a poorly healed scar. He looked so alive.

"It's all your fault," she said, blaming the portrait and bringing the gin to her lips.

She should destroy it, now that she'd finally finished. Wasn't that how exorcism worked? You got something out of your system, made it real and then let it go. But every time she tried, something stopped her; it was like a hand grabbed her wrist.

"Damn you!" she shouted, her hand shaking violently. The gin slipped from her fingers and the glass hit the floor, shattering. With a strange expression, Thelma observed her bare feet. A shard of glass had pierced her right arch, and blood trickled out from between her toes like a worm that knows where it's headed. Wracked by sorrow, she bent double, then fell to the floor and curled into a ball, hugging her knees to her chest.

There was nothing else to do. She could surrender to immeasurable despair, each minute thick as oil, or put an end to the pain. There was no tone to the darkness, nothing to cling to, no more lies. Only death as a feeble reprieve, and also a cry for help and, ultimately, a kind of revenge. Death, only a few centimeters from life, one step away, a step she'd decided to take that night.

But she couldn't do it alone. She couldn't let Enrique have the final victory.

Thelma walked downstairs, leaving a trail of blood that the carpet soaked up like a sponge. She opened her daughter's bedroom door carefully and approached the girl's bed. Her daughter was asleep, face to the wall, one hand resting on her hip and the other beneath the pillow. Still safe from the clutches of disillusionment and betrayal. Her small body unscarred; her soul, her heart still safely inhabiting a world of made-up games played outside, childish adventures and boundless dreams. Everything about her said innocence: the tiny moles on her back, the bony shoulders and clearly demarcated spine, the colored underpants with girlish designs. Her pelvis still bore the perfect curve of the pure, and her breasts, just beginning to develop, aroused nothing but tenderness. She was so perfect it was frightening to contemplate the horrors to come. One day, not long off, someone would gaze at her with desire, the childish games would disappear, she in turn would learn to desire others, her dreams would take on another dimension, and then her eyes, now serenely closed, would see the world in another light, one lacking in innocence. She'd find love and feel both blessed and cursed, she'd be swept away by a current of emotions and drown in them. And nobody would be able to protect her from the pain that would break her heart, smash it to pieces.

Thelma couldn't let that happen.

"Are you awake?" she asked, sitting on the edge of her daughter's bed and stroking her bare shoulder.

Helena heard her mother's thick voice but didn't open her eyes. She sniffed and could smell the gin and knew what that meant. Her mother was about to launch into a series of lamentations and monologues, sobbing and laughing hysterically. She would refuse to stop trying to rouse Helena, then talk and talk until dawn. She always did this in English; that was the language the two of them spoke to each other. Her mother often slept until noon after one of those sessions. Then she'd appear wordlessly in the kitchen, her eyes dead. She'd sit at the table, half-dressed, her hair a mess, and then look up, light a cigarette, and observe Helena through the spirals of smoke. Sometimes she smiled sadly, took her daughter's hand, pulled her into her lap and asked Helena if she loved her. Helena would shrink from the contact and nod silently, not daring to look up. Only when her mother forced Helena to raise her chin and look into her eyes was the lie unsustainable. Thelma would know. Would think: *You hate me too, don't you? You all hate me.*

"You know I love you, don't you, darling? You know that, right?"

Sitting on Helena's bed, her mother stroked her hair. Helena hid her face between clenched fists to protect her cheeks from being kissed or stroked. But her mother wasn't going to leave her alone.

"I know you're awake. Come on, no more faking. Open your eyes."

With a groan, Helena sat up in bed. She saw the shaken look on her mother's face. She also saw the blood on her foot.

"That's it, little one. You know what?" her mother said, eyes gleaming feverishly, "we're going to go to the beach. We can go swimming and watch the sunrise."

"You know I don't know how to swim."

Thelma jumped off the bed with a nervous jerk and began searching for Helena's clothes.

"Oh, don't be silly. You swim perfectly. Besides, I'll be with you. Don't you want us to be together?"

"I'd rather stay in bed."

Her mother pulled off the sheet with one hand, tossing Helena's clothes at her with the other.

"Can't you obey without complaining, just once?" Helena was so like Enrique it was infuriating. Every gesture—the way she held her fork, kicked a pebble, dropped onto the sofa in a sulk when she got back from school—all of it was so like her father. She was just as unpredictable, and as haughty in the way she furrowed her brow when something annoyed her. Sometimes Thelma hated her daughter for what she represented, and though she tried to fight the feeling, it was impossible to overcome. Helena's hard features lent her an odd sort of beauty, one being slowly chiseled, a promise of what was to come, a great change on the horizon. Maybe life wouldn't cast her in the role of scapegoat; perhaps she'd be like Enrique, a destroyer of lives and dreams, a perverse human being adept at betraying the love and loyalty others offered her unconditionally.

Helena refused to budge. Thelma gave her a hard stare.

"Don't be a child! Can't you see that I need you? Could you not act grown up once and for all?"

Helena felt guilt-ridden anguish tighten in her chest. She wasn't grown up, she was eleven years old, and no matter how anxious she was to grow up there was no way to simply skip the years it would take before anyone thought her worthy of being told the real reason her whole world had disappeared.

"Where's Papá?"

Where is my old life? asked her eyes—as green as Enrique's—while her mouth frowned in the same definitive way. Helena missed having her father scold her for a messy room, coming in each morning to check and see that her bed had been made with military corners, sheets turned down evenly, not a single wrinkle. She wanted to go back to the days of complaining about her mother tugging too hard when she brushed her hair, squirming as Thelma searched her scalp for nits, crying when she scrubbed behind her ears so hard that they felt hot as bread fresh from the oven. She longed for arguments at dinner over refusing to try brussels sprouts, longed for her father to lecture her about children going hungry just two blocks away. Now she felt lost. Had she wanted to, she could have raided the pantry and stuffed herself silly with sweets without arousing so much as an apathetic look from her mother. Every night she climbed into an unmade bed, and nobody scolded her for the jumble of clothes on the floor. She went to school without anyone getting the tangles out of her hair, some mornings having had breakfast and others not, and no one cared. Even the tedious daily bath-time ritual had vanished.

Thelma went very still, looking at the open door. She bent to pick up the sheet and stroked it like it was a dead man's shroud.

"He's never coming back."

"Why?" asked Helena.

Thelma dropped the sheet and stood trembling. Her voice was like ice.

"Because those we love betray us, they cause us pain. They take everything from us and then go off someplace else in search of what they think we can't offer them."

Helena shook her head stubbornly.

"My father loves me very much. I know he's coming back for me."

Thelma turned to her daughter, face like a statue.

"The truth is that your father cares only about himself. We're alone, you and I. Now, behave. Get dressed and come with me."

Few women drove a Renault the way her mother did. Helena used to puff up like a peacock when Thelma came to pick her up in that black car with its big tires, honking the horn as she drove up to the English school so all her friends would turn and look enviously. Thelma would offer to take them for ice cream, or for a drive around the port. Helena's friends, sitting in the back seat, would be astonished to see Thelma smoke, and cover their mouths to titter as she shouted insults out the window at other drivers. They all thought Helena had the best mother in the world. And for a time, Helena did too. Those were happy times.

But Helena wasn't having fun that night. Her mother was driving too fast, and the tires screeched dangerously on every curve.

"Where are we going?" she asked, frightened.

Thelma smoked with one hand and touched the wheel only lightly with the other, letting it slide beneath her fingers. She had her eyes on the road but gave the impression that she wasn't seeing it.

"To Merkala."

The beach, surrounded by mountains, was in the east, close to Merchan, a seaside neighborhood that was deserted at that time of night. Close by, a small river flowed into the sea, and the beach had a gravel parking lot. Thelma stopped the car but didn't let go of the steering wheel for some time. She lit another cigarette and exhaled thick smoke slowly. Helena watched her face light up and grow dim with each puff. Out past the car was the sea, and beyond that, farther off, the dark hazy contours of Spain. A few rowboats rocked in the water, and the pebble beach, still wet from the tide that had just receded, was ash gray.

"Let's go," Thelma said, opening the car door suddenly. The wind was blowing, and her white dress stuck to her like gauze, revealing the outline of her body. Her hair blew wildly, obscuring her face. She walked a few meters, rubbing her arms, and looked back at Helena, who'd remained in the car. Thelma's expression was totally blank.

"Come on, get out. Let's go."

Helena cowered. Something was wrong. Her mother was acting even weirder than usual. Maybe she was just angry, testing her. Sometimes she punished Helena for talking back or being defiant. Maybe her mother was mad because she'd been surly, back in her bedroom. If that was it, there was a solution. She was prepared to submit to her mother's protective embrace, to let herself be kissed.

"Let's go home, Mum. I'll clean up my bedroom and behave, I promise."

Thelma looked up at the sky. The stars were slowly fading away, and there was just starting to be a hint of light, the distant break of day still but a suggestion.

"Come," she repeated, robotlike.

Helena whimpered.

"I don't want to."

Thelma retraced her steps to the car and opened Helena's door.

"I said, let's go."

Helena shook her head. Without another word, Thelma slapped her, hard. The blow knocked the girl's head back, and she covered her cheek, eyes wide in shock. It was the first time her mother had ever laid a hand on her. She began to weep silent tears. Thelma didn't bat an eye, simply grabbed hold of her daughter's wrist, pulled her from the car and dragged her to the shore.

Waves rushed in and out playfully. Thelma wet her feet. Suddenly she felt fine. The breeze felt sensuous, quick and urgent. It was as though the air, more than cheering her, was beckoning her insistently into the sea. She'd spent months beating back the pain that stifled her and now saw there was no need to keep fighting it.

Helena began to thrash forcefully when the water was up to her knees.

"Please, Mum. I'm scared."

Thelma inhaled forcefully, a contemplative glimmer in her eyes.

"There's nothing to be scared of. We'll do it together, see?" Thelma made her way deeper without releasing Helena's hand.

The bottom was rocky at first, then turned to squishy sand. Slowly the water crept higher. When it reached her waist, Helena stopped, refusing to go any farther. She was crying, and struggled to break free from her mother.

"Mother, please, stop!"

Thelma paid no attention. Suddenly, Helena realized there was nothing but water beneath her feet. Terrified, she began batting the surface with her free hand. Rather than help her stay afloat, Thelma grabbed her daughter's shoulders and pushed down, submerging her. Helena began to scream. Her head went under and she swallowed water, grabbed her mother's wrists and tried to wrench herself free. But Thelma would not let go. Though Helena thrashed furiously, the weight of a full-grown woman was too much for her.

It was almost impossible to break the surface and get a breath of air. Her lungs were about to explode, and everything seemed murky and muddled. Her ears hurt, and she could feel hair in her nose, in her ears, could feel hair getting in her mouth. In a final desperate attempt to free herself, she managed to twist to one side and knee her mother in the stomach. The pressure of Thelma's hands on her shoulders subsided for a second, and she managed to escape. Her mother's fingers reached out to grab her ankle, but Helena moved farther. After what seemed an eternity, she finally touched the bottom and then, crawling desperately, ignoring the stones hurting her knees, she made it to shore, coughing and spitting snot and seawater.

Helena thrashed like a wounded animal and looked out to sea. Thelma hadn't moved, staring at her like a madwoman, divorced from reality. Then turning away from the beach, she began swimming gently out to sea, getting farther and farther from shore.

"Mum!" Helena shouted.

Thelma heard her daughter's cry over the sound of the waves but did not turn to look. She closed her eyes and kept swimming.

For several minutes, Helena watched her go. She called, screamed for her to come back, and then she saw her mother disappear under the water's surface.

When the sun had turned into a bright shining sphere, Helena was still there. Her mind said that her mother would come back. Her father too. That everything would go back to how it had been, that they'd all walk together through the dried fruits and sweets stalls at the market, that in winter they'd go to London to visit her grandparents, that she'd go horseback riding, and then they'd come back home and Thelma would paint her paintings and her father would listen to Matt Dennis on the record player as he waited for her to grow up.

PART ONE

February 2014

1

Sevilla

Miguel had no way of knowing, on that freezing February day, that the last of his lives had just begun. The final one. He was a logical man, and logic dictated that this would be a day identical to all the others, the same passing of hours since Águeda's death.

At six a.m. the clock radio went on automatically, as if he still had reason to get up early. For the last fifty years, Miguel had risen at the same time and to the same song: Domenico Scarlatti's Sonata in B Minor, L. 33. He liked Scarlatti because his compositions were devastatingly tidy, the notes predictably arranged: they uniformly rose, fell, and rose again. Unlike his daughter Natalia, Miguel found nothing aesthetically pleasing about chaos.

With the sonata on in the background, he went to the bathroom and saw that his personal hygiene supplies were carefully lined up on the marble surface. He took a brief shower in water that was warm rather than hot, used a neutral soap, dried himself meticulously, and sniffed the towel to make sure that it didn't yet need to be thrown in the laundry basket. With small scissors and a metal comb he spent the next fifteen minutes examining his impressive Prussian-style mustache. The trick was to be methodical, to measure the hairs with the comb and then trim from the right to left, top to bottom. He'd never changed this method since beginning to grow a mustache at age eighteen, which he'd done as a sort of declaration of intent: he was determined to occupy the place in the adult world to which he was entitled, and to do so with unfaltering poise.

The thick curl over Miguel's upper lip, white now that he was seventy-five, was still his foremost calling card, the thing about himself that he wanted to communicate to others: order, solemnity, equanimity. To those who didn't know him, his bearing might seem comical, but he'd never worried much about other people's opinions, especially not value judgments anyone might make about his person. Miguel's secret verdict about his fellow human beings was resolute: he saw the vast majority of the public at large as utter morons. He had no scientific data to uphold this belief, but based it on a lifetime of experience in the banking sector. With a few honorable exceptions, the people he'd met were unrepentant dreamers who not so much allowed themselves to be deceived as demanded it; they were people who couldn't stand hearing the truth when it contradicted their illusory aspirations. People who possessed not the slightest capacity to analyze their options in life realistically, who imperiously demanded privileges to which they were unentitled, unable to fathom that what they saw as unfair—that some had more than others—was the natural order of things.

Once he'd finished trimming his mustache, Miguel clipped the few hairs sticking out beyond the bushy line of his eyebrows, examined his ears and nose, and gave a satisfied look in the mirror. Routines restored a sense of control and autonomy, and getting dressed was part of a ceremony, a protocol strictly adhered to. Choosing a matching shirt, pants, tie, and jacket; shining his shoes; selecting argyle socks, cuff links, tiepin, and watch. Once this was all done, he laid it out on the bed to visualize the overall effect before getting dressed. It was important to broadcast the correct image of one's identity, and appropriate clothing gave the impression of self-assurance.

There was little more to do at home: smooth any wrinkles in the bedspread, ensure that the labels on the canned goods all faced out, adjust the folds of the towels on the rack, and run a dustcloth over Águeda's old books, which he hadn't had the heart to dispose of after she died. Natalia had promised to come over one day and look through them to pick out a few volumes, but like almost every time his daughter made a promise, she hadn't kept her word. He ate breakfast at the kitchen table with the TV news on in the background as he read an old newspaper, then cleared the table, washed the dishes—he refused to use the dishwasher Natalia had given him—and dried them meticulously.

Once he felt everything was in order, Miguel could embark on the task that took up most of his time.

He opened the door of the only room in the apartment he always kept locked, and it greeted him with the familiar smell of absence. A wooden trunk, next to the window with the blinds drawn, and a table and chair were the only furniture. The walls were bare. Sunlight streamed in through the gaps between the slats, casting thin lines on the white terrazzo floor. This was to have been their second child's room, the child he and Águeda never had. They'd always wanted a boy. When they married in 1967, they decided that their lives would follow the proper path: they'd have two children, a boy and a girl, spend summers in Tarifa, pay off the brand-new Datsun in installments, and use Miguel's bonuses to make extra payments on the mortgage they would need in order to buy a three-bedroom apartment with kitchen, bathroom, and living room in the San Bartolomé neighborhood; Águeda would give up her apprentice position at the hairdresser's in Triana, and Miguel would support the family so that his wife could devote herself to the children and to reading, which was her true passion. Only half of the plan they'd envisaged had come to pass, so the room had never had a true purpose until Águeda's death. After the funeral, Miguel decided that this would be his place of silence.

On the table was a silver frame with an old photo of Águeda and Natalia, taken on Playa Bolonia in Tarifa, during a vacation of uncertain date. Natalia, just out of the water, was tanned and wore a striped bathing suit; she was twelve years old and her unruly, very blond hair partially covered her freckled face, eyes squinting into the sun and a big-toothed smile. Águeda, too, was smiling, though in a more restrained way, looking forced. No doubt she was having a migraine, and in her right hand she clutched a gold crucifix, commending herself to Jesus, asking him to relieve the crippling pain that afflicted her. Every night, Águeda prayed with Natalia in bed, "Dear baby Jesus, you're a child like me, this is why I love you so and give my heart to thee," and gave her the crucifix to kiss. Miguel would often tease her for these displays of piety and say it wasn't good to fill the girl's head with such mumbo jumbo, but Águeda had no sense of humor when it came to religion. In fact, she had no sense of humor at all. You could see as much in her severe face: thin lips pursed, daunting expression, high cheekbones and pointy chin, no jewels to adorn her neck or ears, hair always cropped short. Águeda was only forty in the photo, but looked much older.

Next to the picture frame were several crumpled papers and a hardback book on origami. Miguel had come across it by chance, in among Águeda's other books. It had intrigued him, and he'd taken it up, though he was yet to master the technique. He was trying to make a figure, a bird, but so far the results were mediocre.

He observed his meager progress in frustration and fixed his gaze on the trunk. Miguel couldn't remember how many years he'd had that old thing. It was in all of his boyhood memories and was the only piece of furniture he still had from a life that seemed never to have existed. He took out a bag containing wax and polish, a brush and cotton rags, and set about carefully oiling the wood grain—eucalyptus that had been stained dozens of times before taking on the dark hue that created a false impression of nobility and distinction. The lid had a gold-colored tin latch ringed with blunted nailheads.

Caring for the trunk calmed him, especially recently, when he'd been feeling rather odd. Sometimes Miguel almost felt like he'd lost consciousness. He would be sitting there, and all of a sudden, he'd be startled, as though he had fallen into a brief dream with his eyes open but recalled nothing of those lost empty seconds; they had vanished somewhere. Lately he'd found himself going from room to room like a sleepwalker, with the sense that his house was a place of exile: he didn't recognize the furniture, the canopy bed, or the crucifix on the wall, which he hadn't dared to take down, in part out of respect for Águeda and in part out of a vague superstition.

Loneliness was not a good companion. That's what his daughter said every time she visited: *You should get a pet, Papá. A cat, maybe. They're as independent and antisocial as you. I'm sure you'd get on great.* "Utter nonsense," Miguel murmured as he polished one of the latches with a rag, the tip of his tongue poking out between his teeth as it always did when he concentrated. Didn't Natalia know he was allergic to cats? Besides, who said he was antisocial? Sure, he'd always been surly and impatient, but he'd never treated his subordinates unfairly, and if he was demanding of them it was only because he was demanding of himself as well: punctuality, neatness, order, pragmatism, and professionalism. What was the matter with any of that?

It was midafternoon. He'd have to get going, stop killing time with paper figures and shining a cheap trunk of no value whatsoever. Making decisions, that was what he missed most: doing things that mattered.

Miguel walked out of the room and locked the door behind him, inspected the contents of the refrigerator, and made a mental note that he needed milk and lemons. He donned his coat and inspected himself in the hall mirror, stroking his mustache. If he'd been holding the briefcase with the metal buckle in his right hand, he would have looked no different from any normal workday: Águeda would have come out from the living room to give him the once-over, picked a stray hair from his shoulder, and straightened the knot of his tie. "Your glasses are dirty, as always," she'd have said, before taking them off and polishing the lenses. Then she would have given him a quick kiss on the lips and stroked his cheek, leaving the scent of her hand cream on his skin to remind Miguel of her presence throughout the day.

Miguel turned to look, waiting for her to appear, walking purposefully, wiping her hands on a dish towel, a rebellious lock of hair on her forehead. But absence was all that appeared. This was the price to be paid for living longer than others.

Two afternoons a week, Miguel met up with his old co-workers from the bank at the Equestrian Center bar. They'd get together for a sherry and talk about all things banking, as if they still had a say. The stock market, the financial crisis, interest rates, who got fired, who took early retirement. Essentially, they were lying, reminiscing that things back in their day had been different—better, naturally. But the truth was that the world was changing quickly, and none of them could keep up with the fast-paced rhythm. Secretly, they felt disconcerted, insecure, and excluded. Soon they'd stop pretending to be up on the rules of the game and move on to the same old topics: their kids who were too busy, grandkids who were spoiled, friends and acquaintances who were dying off, real or imagined inconveniences, the aches and pains of old age. In general, Miguel felt bored by these get-togethers, but he found a way to fake it, and from time to time make some relevant comment, as if he were actually interested in whatever topic was being discussed.

That afternoon, however, Miguel felt particularly scattered. First, he lost several rounds of dominoes after making beginner mistakes, and later when doing crossword puzzles he couldn't concentrate. He seemed absent during the conversation as well. He didn't feel well, had the unpleasant sensation that his clothes were uncomfortable, that his skin was hypersensitive, and things were washing over him: voices, friends' faces, even the space around him at the Equestrian.

"I've got to go," he said suddenly, earlier than normal, giving no further explanation. He walked out of the Equestrian almost without saying goodbye, drawing perplexed looks from his old coworkers. Miguel knew that he'd be the subject of their gossip and sniping now. They'd say he was getting old, that he was a shadow of his former self, and his wife's death had taken too great a toll on him. He didn't care. His old workmates were a bunch of layabouts with too much time on their hands, waiting to tear a man to pieces the moment he turned his back.

On the way home, he stopped at the greengrocer where he always bought his produce. Miguel didn't like the pre-packaged fruit sold at supermarkets, preferring to select it piece by piece, to touch it and smell it before making up his mind. The shop assistant asked him how things were going, and Miguel found that he couldn't remember the man's name despite having known him for years.

"Fine, thank you," he said, nearly ashamed. He paid quickly and forgot to take his change. The man had to chase after him to give it back.

"One of these days you'll lose your own head, Don Miguel."

Somewhat embarrassed, Miguel nodded. Lately he hadn't been sleeping well; his mind had been on other things, he said by way of excuse.

He decided to take a walk before returning home. The cold air would do him good, help him shake off this unpleasant bewilderment. He'd bought oranges and planned to squeeze them and make himself a nice juice, or maybe slice them up to eat sprinkled with liqueur.

Suddenly Miguel became disoriented, as though he'd been walking for too long. His house couldn't be this far. He stopped in the middle of a crosswalk, glancing left and right, and didn't recognize the houses, or even the street. He had no idea where he was, or how he'd gotten there.

"What in the world is the matter with me today?"

He began to panic and set his bags down. He needed to call Natalia. The phone his daughter had given him for his birthday was in his jacket pocket. "So we'll be connected, Papá," she'd said. But the truth was, when Miguel called his daughter, she never answered. Besides, he didn't understand all of the modern apps that phones had on them nowadays. What the hell did he want a camera with who-knows-how-many pixels on his phone for? It was an unworkable application that did nothing but go off in his jacket, snapping marvelous photos of the lining of his pocket. Natalia had shown him how to unlock the phone, but now he couldn't seem to remember the passcode. Was it the year she was born? That was easy: 1-9-7-2.

His fingers trembled, hovering over the keys. No, that wasn't it. He decided to try the year he'd gotten married—and that was when Miguel became truly afraid. He couldn't remember. He couldn't remember what year he'd gotten married.

An orange rolled out of the bag toward the jowls of a dog, who sniffed at it. Miguel reached out, about to pick the orange up, but a hand beat him to it.

"Dogs can't peel oranges," said the hand's owner, giving it back to him. The man was young, very tall, and stocky, probably thirty years old, with messy black hair. His eyebrows were thick, and his deep-set eyes brown. The top three buttons of the man's shirt were undone, showing off a muscular chest. He looked like one of those day laborers who worked the fields. Miguel thought he seemed vaguely familiar.

"Do I know you?"

The young man gave a wide smile, displaying healthy teeth. His eyelid folds fanned into a bouquet of wrinkles.

"Of course you do, Miguel. We've known each other forever."

Miguel blinked in confusion.

"Really? I can't seem to remember . . . I . . . I can't seem to . . ."

Suddenly he realized that the words wouldn't come. They were clear in his mind, all laid out in the correct order, but in his mouth, they fluttered around like a bird batting its wings against the walls of a cave, unable to find the way out.

"What's the matter with me?"

"You're just fine, don't you worry."

Miguel began to feel a strange tingling on his face, which quickly spread to his arms and hands. Terrified, he looked at the young man, who was still smiling, although now with no joy. It had morphed into an encouraging smile, tinged with sadness.

"It's okay. I'm right here."

Everything went blurry. Miguel's head spun faster and faster. And then he fell flat on his face, his head hitting the ground.

I t was just low blood sugar, that's what the doctor had said at first. And that should have been the end of it: a little scare, a bump on his forehead, and a dramatic gash on his cheekbone. They should have taken his blood pressure and sent him home. But the bang on his head had occasioned a CAT scan, which had revealed the presence in Miguel's brain of senile plaques and neurofibrillary tangles. The very words were enough to instill terror.

"What does that mean?"

"It means we've detected the early stages of senile dementia."

Senile dementia.

The two words hit Miguel, a double blow. Hearing them triggered sudden nausea, which he concealed in the presence of his daughter by looking instead at the pathetic still lifes on the wall in the hospital's consultation room.

"I see," he mused, opening his mouth to get a breath of air.

"Are you really sure you see?"

In truth, he did, he saw perfectly what this meant. All he had to do was think back to his childhood, when he was eight years old, sitting in a corner as his mother wandered around the house half-naked, smearing the walls with her own feces. Miguel had spent years shaking off that ghost, convinced that the odds were in his favor: one lunatic in the family was enough. But he'd just learned that insanity wasn't something that happened only to others.

Natalia swallowed. Her eyes darted wildly, filled with a rage she didn't know how to unleash.

"How is this possible? My father has never smoked or drunk in his life, he's never overindulged; he's not even that old. He's only seventy-five!"

The doctor clenched his jaw like a seasoned boxer who was used to taking left hooks.

"The symptoms of this type of illness frequently appear as early as sixty. Had it not been for the fall, we wouldn't have discovered it at all until the deterioration was much more evident. Your father has Alzheimer's, one of the most common forms."

Natalia clutched her father's hand as though afraid she might fall and denied it obsessively.

"That's impossible. He's completely lucid. Those tests are wrong."

The doctor waited for her to calm down. His voice had a sedative effect, as though he'd learned to modulate it so as to give a lasting impression of certainty: although they had to confirm the diagnosis with a few more tests, the conclusion was that the protein structures in Miguel's brain were abnormal. This was a roundabout way of saying that his mind was shutting down. It would be a gradual process, and what mattered was to realize when it became definitive.

"This is still an embryonic stage."

"How long?"

"It's different for everyone. Maybe a year, two at most."

Miguel closed his eyes. It hadn't occurred to him that his death would be so long and drawn out. He'd always assumed that it would be unexpected, something that just happened. No prolonging the agony, no shouting or lamentations, no filth or dependency on others, no slobbering or stench. No ruining other people's lives for decades, as his mother had done. She'd spent her whole life dying, first on the inside and then on the outside; she'd even had enough time to be aware of her own decline and, in the end, when insanity would have been the most use, regained enough lucidity to know she was going.

Now it was his turn.

The doctor took pity, seeing how disconcerted he was.

"Neurodegeneration is irreversible, but there are palliative treatments. We'll keep an eye on your sodium, calcium, and sugar; we'll administer vitamin B_{12} and memantine and inhibitors. For a time, at least, you'll be able to lead an almost normal life."

Next, the doctor gave them a long list of recommendations and prohibitions, foods he couldn't eat, and the addresses of a few private specialized clinics where they could teach Miguel to adapt to this new reality. Then the doctor stood, which was his way of saying that the time he'd allocated to them was over. His face took on well-rehearsed solemnity.

"Try not to be overwhelmed."

Miguel frowned. It struck him as an idiotic remark.

———

t was the middle of the night by the time they got home. Natalia insisted she'd spend the night, but Miguel convinced her to go so that he could be alone. He needed to think. After arguing at length, Natalia gave in. She knew what her father was like, how stubborn he could be when he felt weak. He didn't want her to see him falter.

"Fine, but I'm calling you first thing. Is your phone charged?" Miguel held his phone up wearily and promised to sleep with it on his nightstand. His daughter gave him one final look, on the verge of tears, and he managed to feign composure, even make himself smile.

"It's not that serious, Natalia. Besides, the doctor said they still need to do more tests to confirm the diagnosis. I'm sure they're wrong."

Not even he believed his words. But he had to say them so his daughter would leave him in peace for a while. He needed to collapse, to sink into distress and yield to the fear coursing through his body. And he had to do it his way, not by giving in to the temptation of chaos, crying and shouting, tears and protestations.

Miguel went to the locked room. He flicked the switch, and the bare bulb hanging from the ceiling cast a pale circle of light. Miguel saw his shadow on the wall. He felt as though it belonged to someone else, with its slumped shoulders and lifeless arms dangling beside the body. He reached out a hand and touched the dark shadow projected onto the white of the wall. That was him, like it or not. And sooner or later, the whole of him would be a shadow. He dragged the chair over to the trunk and stroked the lid. The wood was smooth, still moist from the wax he'd applied that morning. It smelled good, like cleanliness and certainty. Gently, he unlatched the buckle and tugged it open. Not a single squeak. Who said memories had to sound rusty?

Miguel looked inside, void of emotion. He wasn't expecting anything, apart from what he already knew was there. His mother's things were nothing without her. The trunk was like a sarcophagus. He riffled through the newspaper clippings his mother had compulsively amassed over the course of more than thirty years. Anything to do with Valle de los Caídos—the Valley of the Fallen, Spain's massive Francoist monument: the transfer of dictator José Antonio Primo de Rivera's mortal remains, the monument's official inauguration, photos of its construction, interviews with the sculptor, Ávalos, and old index cards with hundreds of names and dates typed on them. All of it catalogued with the feverish precision of a disturbed mind obsessed with trivial details. There were copies of the letters his mother had spent years writing to various ministers, law firms, and associations for the recovery of historical memory.

Also in the trunk, filed by date, were the reports Miguel had lodged with the police every time his mother ran away, as well as subsequent intake reports from various mental health clinics, temporary leaves, and notices of relapse. The documents were a chronicle of years of derangement.

Beneath these strange souvenirs, wrapped in a cloth, was the urn containing his mother's ashes. Miguel picked it up and looked at it for a long time, as if he could see inside, see its contents. He brought the urn to his nose and sniffed. It no longer smelled of anything at all.

With the urn under his arm, Miguel went to his bedroom, set it on the nightstand, and lay down on his bed. He stared at the ceiling, which seemed to be getting lower and heavier, like a tombstone. As if he were already dead. He had to do something, he told himself. He couldn't just lie there, accompanied only by his mother and his fear. Giving in was not part of his character. Miguel got up and opened the top dresser drawer, where Águeda had once kept her underthings.

There it was, the bundle of letters tied with twine. Carmen's letters. He'd promised Águeda, when she was on her deathbed, that he would destroy them. Two years later he had yet to fulfill his promise. He hadn't held them in his hands again since the day Águeda found them and kicked him out. Miguel untied the bundle, adjusted his glasses, and dragged the chair over to sit it beneath the bare bulb hanging from the ceiling. He was in need of a friendly voice, a happy memory.

Sitges, April 1980

My Dearest Miguel,

You've only been gone a few hours and I can't let you disappear. I'm holding on to you, what's left of you, in these sheets, in the towel you left by the shower, the moisture from your body, two of your hairs in the sink where you were just combing your hair, the bar of soap that contains something of your hands. You forgot to say you loved me on your way out. I don't mind (though if I didn't, why would I bring it up?). On the little table where we ate, the plates remain untouched beside your wrinkled paper napkin, your half-drunk beer, the scrupulously aligned silverware to the right of the plate. I don't want to move anything so I can keep picturing you there at the open window, your back to me, contemplating the sea. I know it's different from the horizon you told me about, the one you discovered with your wife so long ago in Tarifa. But this one is ours, yours and mine, and we don't have to share it with anyone. I can still hear you talking about your past, interrupting yourself to tell me that even though you don't smoke you don't mind if I do, that in fact you like the spicy taste of my nicotine kisses.

You won't even have made it home by now, to Sevilla, to your life, your family, the wife and daughter you talked so much about. The ones whom you belong to and who belong to you. When I think about it, we spent hours in bed talking about them but said very little, almost nothing, about us, about you and me. I don't mind that, either. At our age, there are things you accept with no drama. But I'd like to imagine that as you fly across the now-darkening sky, anxious because you hate airplanes, you might distract your fear by thinking of me through the window, perhaps smelling your clothes, your hands, so that you too can keep something of me. Something of us, of our wonderfully unexpected weekend.

I'll have to go soon as well, to return to Barcelona. Routine awaits, to wrench away the fragile bonds of happiness. Someday maybe I'll want to tell you of the ties that bind me, ones that have nothing to do with you.

Housekeeping has already called twice; they need to come in and clean, to take what remains of this weekend and erase it—the sheets, the ashtrays, the glasses. They need to air out the room so the scent of your body and mine fade into the air. It will be as though this never happened. That's why I want to stay a little longer, here in this house that was ours for a few hours, too few, this place where I can see the church and a little corner of tranquility from the window, the storm battering the edge of the walkway, and the apple tree whose leaves are falling into the pool. Something inside me is fighting the fact that when I close this door, everything we said, all that we did and felt, will be lost when another pair of lovers come to this bed with the same urgency, the same need to devour each other that we felt.

I'm not fooling myself, I have to accept it as it is, process it, forget about it, and carry on my way as if it never happened; but here I am, naked in bed, writing you a letter and listening to Sting on the radio, his voice blending with yours and with the sounds of the sea as you quietly told me about the father you almost can't remember, your home in Extremadura, your mother who did sewing for other people, as I stroked your messy hair and half listened. I've never seen a man cry the way you did. For others, wanting for them to drink of your sadness.

Can we ever really break free from what holds us back? I feel jealous of a woman I don't know. I imagine it was me accompanying you to Tarifa that summer. And you teaching me to swim, and it was us making love while looking at the Strait of Gibraltar. I want to believe that one day you'll drive me to Casablanca in that car you love so much, that we'll stop for a bite at some random spot, dance in places we can't even picture in our imaginations, buy a pair of those handmade sandals, and the night will envelop us the way it does in those silly movies you like so much. Yes, we will, I tell myself. No, of course we won't, I repeat.

In the meantime, I'm going to send this to you at your bank address. We have to be prudent, you stressed repeatedly. I only hope and pray that prudence is not a shadow of fear. Fear of being happy.

Write to me soon, now, before tomorrow.

Carmen

2

Tarifa, Setting Sun Senior Residence

For Helena, nighttime was a worthless yet inevitable waste of time. She'd inherited her mother's insomnia, and her gift for seeking refuge in gin. The rest had been passed down from her father. But neither of her parents was responsible for her sense of humor—overly abrasive and somewhat impertinent. This she'd cultivated all by herself, starting when she was a girl. Poor little Helena, the traumatized child abandoned to her fate, grew up believing herself to be the most unfortunate girl of all, and for that very reason the one deserving every whim and comfort conceivable. The world owed it to her as compensation.

But the world owed her nothing.

Grandfather Whitman, of course, would not tolerate her victimhood or be bribed by it. It was more than enough, he felt, to have traveled to Tangier personally to pick her up and arrange for her move to London after Thelma's death. Grandmother Alice, on the other hand, was more easily swayed by emotional blackmail. Helena had managed to perfect certain vacant looks in order to get what she wanted. Thelma's death had sunk the old woman into a kind of silence less ominous than that of her husband; on occasion she broke down, and Helena could hear her weeping in the bedroom or would find her going through Thelma's wardrobe, where her country dresses still hung. Grandmother Alice's love for Helena was tainted by loss and regret. *It was our fault, we shouldn't have let her marry that Spaniard when she was so young.* Alice burdened her granddaughter with her sorrow, as though expecting the girl to provide an explanation as to what had really happened to Thelma in Africa. An explanation she could accept. In exchange for this, she let Helena bathe in the lily pool, eat sweets, and ride Isis—Grandfather Whitman's prized mare—when he was away from the estate. She was always solicitous when it came to covering for Helena when she'd been mischievous, and if it was impossible to hide then she bent over backward making excuses for the girl. There was only one time when Grandmother Alice proved inflexible, and that was the morning Helena started speaking Spanish and mentioned her father. Her grandmother gave her an icy stare.

"You will never again speak that name in this house."

Helena nodded, afraid of the possibility of losing her one loyal ally in the enormous old country house.

Despite Grandmother Alice's affection, Helena was relieved when she learned they were sending her off to boarding school, one for high-society girls on the outskirts of London. It had been a unilateral decision on Grandfather Whitman's part. Grandmother Alice was opposed to the idea, arguing that the girl wasn't ready, but he proved unyielding. It had been nearly a year since Thelma's death, the girl was too wild and needed the kind of discipline that, evidently, Alice was in no position to impose. And the weak protest offered by Helena, who in fact couldn't wait to escape her life of silence and shadows, in the end made Alice realize that perhaps her granddaughter was not only ready but in fact needed to get out of the old Whitman mansion. Living far from its cold rooms and her grandparents and returning twice a year for holidays could be no worse than staying there, slowly languishing.

Within the walls of that boarding school, little Helena met Louise, and the two of them became inseparable. And thanks to this chance encounter, her childhood began to vanish without anyone noticing. When she went back to her grandparents' estate, she was outwardly the same, but from the moment Helena got there she ached to go back and be the other Helena, the one Louise was teaching her to be.

This other Helena, built in the image and likeness of Louise, disappeared over the course of time as well, as did each successive version, until she ended up as the shriveled empty shell she'd become at age seventy.

On the table lay what was left of a cake that her friends at the residence—she had to call them that even though they weren't—had ordered from a bakery in town: lemon with chocolate frosting, dusted with powdered sugar. "The gluttony and vice of old folks," she said to herself. The remains, strewn on the rimmed paper tray, looked like they'd been gnawed by hungry rats. Helena had only tasted a few crumbs, which she secretly crumbled between her fingers, to be polite. Real friends would have known that she hated sweets, especially chocolate. She hadn't paid much attention to the ridiculous card bearing a dozen illegible messages, some childish thing that someone must have seen in a stationer's window and thought was cute: "Today is an important day to say how much you matter to us. Happy Birthday." A teddy bear surrounded by golden stars. As though rather than seventy she'd turned twelve, fifteen, or twenty and was still receiving the postcards her father sent every year to the Whitman mansion.

Those postcards, now strewn across her bed, had stayed with her through each of her lives, stored in an old shoebox like an unfulfilled promise. "Until we meet again, little one!" her father jotted on the first one when Helena was eleven, and she'd cherished it. Postcards bought and quickly mailed from any number of train stations—Rome, Porto, Bordeaux, Nîmes, Munich, Dublin, Amsterdam—and sent just before boarding a train to go someplace else.

Helena went through them in a futile search for consolation; she reread them and stroked a finger over her father's writing, always so immaculate, even when expressing the most gruesome of things.

"Why would I think about that now?" she wondered aloud, opening her nightstand drawer and glaring at the little gold flask she kept there as though it was an enemy. She shook her head in resignation and took a long swallow. "You got old. Not a damn thing you can do about it. Stupid old woman," she said, clucking her tongue.

As though surprised, she narrowed her eyes, prepared to disagree with the image she saw in the light coming in through the window from a lamppost in the garden, infiltrating the shadows of her room. She cast her gaze slowly over her ear, right cheek, chapped and parted lips, proud chin; she slid her fingers across her wrinkled neck, stopping at the collar of her shirt. Unbuttoning it she examined her chest, milky as phosphorous and dotted with moles and freckles. She touched her small breasts, the nipples cracked and dark. There had been a time when her fingers ran smoothly over her skin, finding no obstacles, a time when her body drew glances. Some truths were so heartrending. Was this what getting old came down to? Losing all that you'd once been? Far beneath Helena's skin, her heart whimpered and moaned. Perhaps getting old meant being powerless, and having others mistake your surrender for wisdom.

She rubbed a temple with her fingertips. *I'm drinking too much.* Limping openly—something she only did when alone—Helena opened the window overlooking the gardens and lit a cigarette, attempting to blow the smoke out the window. Lying, feigning happiness, and stuffing yourself with sweets were allowed in the residence that was now her home. Drinking and smoking were not.

She concentrated on the vast silence looming over the place. A silence that was intermittently broken. Through the walls she heard a toilet flush, coughing, doors opening and closing. There were others like her, insomniacs who stared at the white ceilings of their rooms all night, unable to sleep even a few minutes. They were easy to recognize in the morning: the first down to breakfast, hair done, well groomed, as if they'd been waiting quite some time for the world to get moving.

She trained her ear and then smiled, recognizing the footsteps that had just stopped at her door. Right on time. Next came the ritual rapping of knuckles.

"Come in, professor," Helena said, slipping the flask into her jacket pocket and moving away from the window. It was a purely formulaic invitation: her door had already begun to open and a messy head of straw-colored hair peeked through the gap.

"Good evening, my lady. Difficult night?"

Now away from the light in the hallway, the head disappeared into the darkness of her room. Helena turned on the reading lamp on her desk.

"You know I can't stand it when you call me that, Marqués."

Professor Marqués's tiny eyes blinked repeatedly, like a cornered rat trapped in the light.

"Interrupting a booze and cig fest, am I?" he inquired maliciously, sniffing the air.

"I was just contemplating a thousand forms of suicide, in honor of my birthday. Any ideas?"

Marqués gave a hearty laugh. He was too small to look like a man, but his expression was too old to pretend he was a boy. Beset by a deformity that could have made him a circus freak, he'd fended quite well for eighty years with his bowed legs, granitelike head, and diminutive stature. Anything about him that might have invited jest was counteracted by the unsettling gravity of his face, so full of humanity. One had to think hard whether it was wise to laugh at a man with eyes like his.

"Celebrating birthdays has become a real tragedy, hasn't it?"

"What do you want, Marqués?"

"Not much: company, complicity, my standard dose of friendship . . . You could offer me one of the cigarettes you smoke in secret," he said in the mournful tone he used when about to break a rule, which was quite frequent.

Marqués—"the professor," as he liked to be called—was the enfant terrible of the residence, the sort of patient feared by doctors, nurses, and aides alike. The staff constantly did battle with his wrathful character, and the other patients tried to avoid him. Helena, on the other hand, was amused by his constant rebellions, which often withered into pointless conflicts.

"I don't know what Director Roldán would say, considering your state of health." Marqués had severe emphysema, which made the way he opened his mouth and nostrils wide to fill his lungs with smoke even more painful.

"She'd say what they all do, which is the only thing they know how to say when confronted with old age: 'Marqués, climb into a closet full of mothballs and try not to move. That way you'll live to a hundred.' And I say, who the hell wants to live forever? Only someone with no bloody idea what life is."

"So, what is life?" Helena asked, for the sheer pleasure of provoking her friend.

"Life is bloody stressing to death! The point of living is to die."

Helena let out a little giggle. When Marqués got angry, the bags under his eyes turned violet.

"Damn it! Are you going to smoke alone or are you going to ask your poor, helpless friend to join you so he doesn't make a scene?"

Helena shrugged and offered him a cigarette. That night, Marqués was wearing cream-colored pajamas that hid his hands. He kept tugging at his sleeves to free his fingers.

"Shall we round it off with a sip of London? Wasn't that what your father used to drink? I know you've got your little American friend's flask hidden in there somewhere."

"Louise was from Bristol."

"Whatever. I'm sure you've told me that countless times, but one of the privileges of old age is not having to pretend you're paying attention to details you care nothing about."

"Marqués, doesn't it seem to you that being overly demanding risks not getting what you want? You're being quite discourteous."

He stared at her unwaveringly.

"It's only the milquetoasts who call sincerity 'discourtesy,' and you've never struck me as the type. Besides, if I didn't take risks, you and I would never have become friends. You're as bored by spineless idiots as I am, admit it." Marqués's face looked ghastly and beautiful at the same time.

Helena nodded and smiled condescendingly. There was a rumor going around at the residence that Marqués had once been a great composer whose career was cut short when an affair ended in tragedy. Helena thought it all sounded overly tragic and romantic, but she'd accepted his eccentricities in good faith from the start because she'd always liked people who colored outside the lines. He was the only one who dared to defy Director Roldán's authority, strolling naked through the grounds on visiting day, spending hours at the piano in the library, staring at the keys without touching them or allowing anyone else to do so either.

"Well? Are you really going to drink alone on your birthday?"

Helena gave up and offered him the gin. Marqués drank calmly and examined the flask, which had an inscription on the bottom: "Life is what happens to you while you're busy making other plans," he read aloud, as though it were a question. "Quite the optimist, this Louise."

Helena reached out and snatched it back from him. She was beginning to regret her generosity.

"You know nothing about Louise."

Marqués adjusted his pajama lapels theatrically and stood up, then removed a carefully folded sheet of paper from his pocket and handed it to her.

"True. If you think about it, I don't know much about you, either. But that doesn't mean I don't know you, does it? Happy birthday, Helena. My gift to you."

Helena unfolded the paper and gazed at it. It was a piece of sheet music.

"It's based on Satie. A piano solo, no orchestra. Look," said Marqués, pointing to the sheet, clearly excited, "there are pauses and low tones for a soft, soothing opening, but then it changes here, getting louder and with a more anxious tempo. I wrote it for you, Helena. It's called 'Helena and the Sea.' It's a portrait. Of you."

"A portrait?"

Marqués nodded emphatically. He'd composed the piece as a portrait, sneaking looks at her to capture expressions and gestures when she didn't realize he was watching.

"Here, in the notes and scales, are the drooping wrinkles on your face, the hands clenched on your lap, the hair falling over half your face and accentuating that distinctive nose of yours, with its pronounced bridge. But also the placid intelligence seen in your expression, which makes you look like one of Leonardo da Vinci's Virgins. And yet the magic resides not in your face but in your eyes: those green eyes overflowing with nostalgia, full of images and memories that you try to hide."

Helena listened, captivated.

"Is that really what I'm like?"

"I don't know what you're really like. That's how I see you."

Some people at the residence were of the opinion that Marqués was a phony, that he'd never composed a thing in his life, that his supposed wisdom was just childish drivel. Others were full of spite and claimed to have it on good authority that, in truth, the supposed professor had spent his whole life fixing cars and motorcycles at his father's shop in Soria, that his wife had left him for a stationery salesman and run off to a town on the Costa Brava, taking the kids. But Helena didn't care what they said. She cared about what she saw. And even if she'd never heard anything about Marqués's success, she had witnessed his passion, the desire that overcame him and sent him into a trancelike state.

"A man is defined by his passion, my friend, the most private of his passions. Everything else is but a shell."

"Would you play this piece for me?"

Marqués was a boy forced to invent his own refuge, to imagine places where he could hide from people. He'd done it all his life. And his desire to be loved, accepted, and seen was moved by Helena's imploring look, inimitable and true.

"But of course." With deliberate ceremony, he rolled up his sleeves and sat at the desk, pushed aside the remains of Helena's birthday cake and placed before him the score. He sat up tall, raised his chin, closed his eyes, and then came the miracle: his entire body, hunchbacked and diminutive, began to sway to the rhythm of his hands, spread over an imaginary keyboard, and he seemed to grow, taking on the stature of a giant. His face was transformed by ecstasy and concentration, his lips pressed into a thin line creating a horizon only he could see. Marqués agonized and rejoiced in the music and its tempo, dancing with the notes that rang out in his head and cascaded perfectly to create something thrilling and true.

It went on for several minutes. Helena couldn't take her eyes from his hands, which moved fluidly over the desk as if he were actually creating sound; his fingers were gentle streams, all flowing into the same sea, each with its own nuance, color, and voice. It was marvelous. Anguished, Helena turned to the window. Far off, at a distance that seemed infinite in the night, lay Africa; some of the lights flickering like fireflies were Tangier. Helena felt a sense of pity. Not for herself but for the girl she'd once been. She could see her through the night, on the other side of the straits, on her knees in the sand, shouting for her mother to come back.

"Stop, Marqués . . . Please."

Marqués stilled his hands and opened his eyes, visibly spent. He was perspiring.

"Don't you like it?"

Helena returned to his side. Her green eyes had closed.

"It's magnificent. One day, you'll amaze the world."

Marqués gave a characteristic shrug.

"Amazing the world no longer interests me—supposing, that is, that the world still has the ability to be amazed, which is something I question."

Helena disagreed, telling him that music was immortal. Numbers transformed into sounds and sounds into images. And images into life and emotion.

"You're too optimistic, Helena. Immortality no longer exists. Nothing lasts more than a second, it's all just a fleeting exclamation and then on to something else. I'm from another time, my lady. One when dreams were built slowly and seeing them crash wasn't cause for desperation. You just picked up the pieces and started again, armed with infinite patience. You didn't simply exchange them for new ones."

"You're very gloomy this evening."

Marqués had a violent coughing fit that made him turn red. Once finished, he wiped the saliva on the back of his hand and gazed at Helena through watery eyes.

"The world and I are riding different trains. All this speed overwhelms me." He shook his big head slowly, like a muscleman trying to make it budge. "Alas, I'm off. Thank you for the nip of gin and for helping me suffocate myself even more with the cig. That's what I call friendship."

He headed for the door, tiny and deformed yet looming above the shadows in the room. At the last moment, he stopped and gave Helena an impish smile.

"Try to air out the room. If Director Roldán smells cigarettes, you'll be in hot water."

Helena rolled her eyes.

"Is that what it's come to? Being watched over like small children?"

Marqués spread his hands and then dropped his arms, clapping once.

"That's exactly what it's come to. Good night."

The professor had left his score on the desk. Helena stroked the smooth surface of the paper. Then she glanced at the postcards from her father, spread out across the bed. Like Marqués, she too was of another era, one that wasn't coming back.

The following morning, the IT instructor was waiting for Helena. A good-looking, jovial young man, he greeted her with his standard gallantry. They both laughed—Helena, less enthusiastically. She liked gallant men, although she no longer believed in them, and thus couldn't help but smooth her bangs with a certain flirtatiousness.

"You look perfect."

"Perfect in what sense?"

"Perfect in the sense that everything is in its place."

She scrunched her nose, sniffing the words.

"Its place being an old people's home?"

He shook his head, eyes shining with genuine affection.

"More like someone who got where they wanted to go unvanquished."

"Well, well, well. A poet." Helena patted the boy's hand. It was the young, strong hand of someone who had no idea what he was talking about. "Thank you. So, then: Shall we begin?"

The library had three computers with webcams. In order to use them, you had to book in advance: the residents had taken a shine to the virtual world. They'd even cast aside their board games to be seduced by social media, which they devoted themselves to as recent converts. They'd discovered they could live longer, reinvent themselves with a simple click of the mouse—and no one wanted to be left out. Helena did okay with the computer itself, but she didn't have a clue when it came to the classes. She was bored by all the abstract concepts: hardware, software, the cloud, files, interface . . . What she liked was the practical side of things. Communicating with any part of the world at any time of day, now that was marvelous. She put on the microphone headphones and, following the instructor's directions, clicked the Skype icon and typed the password she'd memorized: David1968, her son's name and the year he was born. The webcam's little red light blinked in welcome and then turned green.

"Perfect," he said approvingly. The young man patted her shoulder and then moved off to other old people with their noses to the screen.

After a few seconds, a cozy-looking room appeared on her computer screen. On the dark, wood-paneled walls were dozens of paintings, and books and family photos lined the shelves. On the very right, she could see bicycle handlebars. A big dog was barking. Natural light streamed in through a window through which she saw snow-covered fir trees. Apparently, Sweden had nothing but snow. A man with a thick beard and very dark hair greeted her from behind a desk. Helena visually stroked his face, with its white teeth and pink gums.

"Hello, David. You're looking very well."

He thanked her, leaned back in the chair, and rubbed his stomach. Half-joking, he complained about the extra kilos that had crept on over the years. Helena asked after the boys, Neo and Hampus, six-year-old twins with red hair and thick, translucent eyelashes who looked as Swedish as their mother. Like they were straight out of an IKEA ad.

"They're fine. They send their regards."

David was lying. Helena had hardly ever spoken to them, exchanging a few words in English only on special occasions, as she had with Marta, David's wife. Helena knew that Marta didn't like her, and in a sense was glad not to have to feign enthusiasm on the rare occasions when she popped her head into the corner of the screen to ask how everything was going. David and Marta were getting married next year, and Helena was hurt that he'd made no mention of inviting her to the wedding. Of course, he had no obligation to do so: David said they were a modern couple and had decided to marry only for legal reasons; it would grant them certain state subsidies. It was going to be a civil ceremony, obviously, a quick one, with no guests aside from the witnesses and children, on a weekday at city hall. But the engagement ring Marta had shown Helena on the screen a few days earlier made clear that what David said was one thing, and what would end up happening was another.

For a few minutes they made small talk, mixing Spanish and English. From time to time, David taught her a word in Swedish or explained what a certain expression meant, or told her a joke about Danes and Norwegians, and although normally their conversations amused and entertained Helena, her stellar sense of irony was nowhere to be found that morning. David soon realized this.

"You seem worried."

Helena shrugged.

"The east winds have been blowing hard the past few days. They make you a little crazy."

The young man nodded.

"We've been having bad weather here too."

Helena forced a smile, but it didn't take a genius to realize that something was the matter.

"Is something wrong?" David asked.

Helena shook her head.

"I turned seventy yesterday."

"Oh, I completely forgot!"

"Don't worry about it. Piling on the years isn't a particularly noteworthy achievement. I shouldn't even have brought it up, but I suppose I'm starting to ache for certain things. I've never even met your children."

"One day. Marta and I are thinking of paying you a visit, bringing the kids. Maybe next summer."

Promises that always got canceled at the last minute: Christmas, summers, and birthdays followed one after the other, and her desire remained unfulfilled. Almost shyly, Helena suggested something she'd been thinking a lot about.

"I could come visit you there."

David looked dubious.

"Coming to Malmö isn't like going from Tarifa to Cádiz. It's a long trip. Besides, the kids would wear you out."

She didn't want to hear what those words implied.

"Of course, you're right. It's a silly idea."

Over the next ten minutes, David glanced at his watch twice. Helena could hear Marta and the boys in the background, hear the dog barking.

"Well, I'm going to have to leave you. We're going to Stockholm for a few days and the train leaves in an hour. Talk to you next Thursday at the same time?"

Helena inhaled and straightened her spine, pressing it into the seat back. Under the table, she rubbed her right knee. On days when she was nervous or upset, it seemed to hurt more than usual. She bit her lower lip lightly to keep it from trembling, put on her best smile and said goodbye.

"Next Thursday, of course. Have a nice trip."

Long after the connection had been dropped, Helena sat at the computer screen. She didn't move until the IT instructor came over, looking worried.

"Bad news, Helena? You're a little pale."

Helena responded spiritedly, standing and pretending to feel the kind of energy she didn't have. Her knee was killing her.

"Nothing new under the sun. Just old people and their loneliness."

He looked disconcerted.

"Can I do anything to help?"

"Call your mother on her birthday. Just a bit of advice."

Helena walked out of the library hiding her limp. She saw Marqués in the distance, a bundle of papers under his arm, and looked away. She didn't feel like running into anybody.

She headed to the walled gardens, where a stone fountain tried to spout a jet of water that dribbled weakly over mossy stones, and sat on one of the benches. Gazing at the water, she recalled the day her son had stopped at the corner on their way to school one day, let go of her hand, and, staring at her solemnly, said he didn't want her to walk him all the way to school anymore because he was ten and his friends made fun of him. Helena had watched him cross the street, a backpack full of books over one shoulder, standing tall like a big boy, and felt a foreboding pang of loneliness.

3

Malmö

Gusts of wind lashed the Sound. From the parking lot, they could just make out the headlights of cars on the bridge over the Øresund, the bridge's towers, and the trains going from Denmark to Scania and vice versa, all barely visible through the mist. In the distance, the foghorn on the five o'clock ferry announced its arrival.

Deputy Chief Gövan gazed at the scenery, stroking Yasmina's neck absently. His zipper was still undone.

"It's so beautiful here, with you," he whispered, his voice thick. Gövan's breath, exhaled onto Yasmina's bra strap, smelled of blonde tobacco and the Swedish sausages he loved so much.

Yasmina was looking at the same view—the nearby sea, the gray pebble beach, the seagulls, and the vast hulking bridge—but her eyes weren't seeing the same thing. She couldn't ignore the uncomfortable seat, or the gear shift digging into her leg. Being in a rush had ruined everything, like it did other times: Gövan's urgent desire to get her clothes off, her need to be on alert in case someone passed by walking a dog, his swearing because he could never undo her bra on the first try. Yasmina experienced moments of clarity, when she was able to look down on their entangled bodies as if she were hovering above the Škoda's cramped space: her panties at one ankle, Gövan's white shins with red marks at the sock line, his loose watch strap flapping. This was not how Yasmina had pictured things in her fantasies.

"It's late," she said, putting on her blouse. "Don't you have a happy family waiting for you at home?"

The deputy chief looked at her, displeased. His eyelashes were almost white, long as a canopy, protecting delicate blue eyes; countless freckles covered his forehead, and he had the prominent cheekbones and short, flat nose of a seasoned boxer.

"That was a low blow, Yasmina. Sarcasm hurts, you know."

Yasmina frowned. True, it was a cruel thing to say. But there was no reason to pretend they were anything but what they were.

"What hurts is the truth, Gövan. Here we are, true? You came in my mouth and now you'll brush your teeth and go back home, kiss your wife and kids and pretend to be the perfect husband and father."

"I'm in love with you, Yasmina. I've told you so many times. But I'm in a complicated situation."

Complicated situation was one of the many euphemisms the deputy chief was in the habit of using.

"Which means you don't know how to have it all. True?"

It wasn't just that he had a family he took to church each Sunday at Saint Paul's Cathedral—an attractive, sophisticated wife who worked at Malmö's largest exhibition hall, the prestigious Konsthall, and two kids, aged eight and nine, who he took to the natural science museum in Malmö Castle every Saturday. It was more complicated than that. Deputy Chief Gövan's father-in-law was one of the largest shareholders in Wallenberg Laboratories, which meant he could either boost or sink Gövan's career. In addition to that, there were the season tickets to the hippodrome, the sailboat, vacations in Barcelona, the cabin in Uppsala for weekend getaways, and parties at the home of the minister of the interior. *Complicated situation* meant that Deputy Chief Gövan was unwilling to give up his life for the twenty-three-year-old daughter of Moroccan immigrants who lived in a miserable prefab apartment in Rosengård with her grandfather—a religious zealot—and her mother, who worked six days a week as a live-in maid for a rich family in the suburbs.

"I'm serious," Gövan insisted, stroking Yasmina's cheek and pulling her to him. "I'm in love with you."

Yasmina was trying to maintain her composure, not let his flattery pull her into a land of near impossibilities and future disappointments. Besides, she had to think about the

Turk. Just as he'd been the one to bring them together, he also kept them apart, and Gövan's words, spoken in the heat of a good orgasm, could never bridge the gap that separated their worlds.

"You'll forget as soon as your erection goes down," she said, her cold tone hurting only herself.

Gövan's face changed, just as the landscape did when tide came in and the mist vanished, making everything look unpleasant, almost sordid. He glanced quickly at his cell phone. He had several missed calls.

"We should get back. I've got work."

"The Pakistani at the port that had his throat slit?"

Gövan looked at her in shock.

"How do you know that?"

Yasmina recovered quickly.

"I saw it on the news."

Gövan snorted irritably. He'd thought the case was under investigative secrecy, but the press always found a way to stick their noses in. This was his big case, the opportunity that could launch him into the offices of the commissioner general of Stockholm, and perhaps larger pastures after that. But first he had to solve the case. All eyes were on him and the team he led.

"It's complicated business."

"More complicated than the business between you and me?"

"That's not funny."

Of course it wasn't. Yasmina knew she was treading on slippery ground, but still she pushed her luck.

"On the news they said you found a freight container full of drugs near the body. Lots of drugs. Do you have a suspect?"

Drugs, human trafficking, arms trafficking, corrupt officials, politicians implicated in an international network, Interpol getting involved. This could be the case of the century. Or the deputy chief's grave, if he didn't tread carefully.

"That's work stuff, I'd rather not talk about it when we're together. It's not pleasant."

Yasmina knew she couldn't insist, at least not now.

They finished getting dressed in gloomy silence and drove back to the city. Gövan was serious as he drove. On the radio they were talking about the upcoming parliamentary elections. Gövan turned up the volume. Yasmina would have preferred silence, or music, but he wasn't going to listen to her. So she stared out the window at the passing scenery.

They got to the bus stop, and Gövan asked Yasmina if she was sure she had everything, hadn't forgotten an earring or bracelet.

She shook her head sadly. What the deputy chief really wanted to know was if she was leaving behind any trace of her presence. She knew that Gövan would now go to the car wash, give them precise instructions to hand-wash the upholstery, and leave a good tip so the employees would take care to remove any dark curly hair, any suspicious drops of body fluid.

As though realizing the callousness of his attitude, Gövan tried to apologize.

"See you next week? I could find a nice place for us to spend the night. The whole night."

Yasmina dug the headscarf out of her bag and put it on, gave a quick glance in the rearview mirror and wiped the lipstick from her mouth with one thumb. Gövan's scratchy beard had left little red dots on her neck, like flea bites.

"Sure, you know how to find me."

Yasmina did not turn to watch Gövan's old Škoda turn around and drive off down the road. If you stray from the future, you've got no choice but to stick to the present. She walked to bus shelter and waited until the blue-and-white bus appeared. Yasmina recognized the usual faces, the driver with his sunglasses, the same passengers as always—rowdy kids and silent old folks, men with furrowed brows and women returning with shopping baskets or from the rich homes they cleaned, all of them so like her own mother, Fatima. And like her mother, these women, too, observed her warily, as though she were guilty of something despite the niqab and the lack of makeup, despite having buttoned the top button of her blouse to conceal her large breasts. Wearing jeans and being twenty-three and the Turk's protégé had cast her into the hell of questionable women. Rosengård was a tiny, self-contained universe, a place that had nothing in common with the rest of Malmö, a place where everybody knew everybody. She tried to ignore the accusatory looks and sat by the window with her headphones on, listening to music on her cell phone.

The bus soon reached the outskirts of her neighborhood. Rosengård's concrete apartment blocks looked nothing like the idyllic postcard local politicians tried to peddle, though the green spaces were well cared for, and the children ran through the parks so bundled up and protected from the cold they looked like miniature astronauts. But to understand the reality here you had to narrow your eyes and know how to read the landscape: the broken streetlights, the kids sitting on faded wooden benches, the cars with no license plates, and the stores with signs in Arabic, Armenian, Moldovan; you had to listen to the music coming out of apartment windows, see the clothes hanging and taste the spices of the food floating in the air. There were no dogs barking, no people riding by on bicycles, and almost no old people out on the street. On a wall overlooking nothing at all, someone had done a portrait of the local hero, Zlatan Ibrahimović, wearing the Swedish national soccer jersey, arms raised victoriously to the sky. Slightly beyond this were facades covered in graffiti for the far-right Sweden Democrats, urging the inhabitants of Rosengård to go "back to the pigsties" they came from and leave "Sweden for the Swedes."

The rain was pounding down again. Yasmina got off the bus and ran, taking cover under balconies, until she made it to the Old Sweden Restaurant. Water poured from the awning, buckling under its weight and threatening to collapse, but Sture, the owner, never bothered to retract it. Sture was one of the few Swedes left in the neighborhood. No one knew exactly how old he was, but Yasmina was sure it was at least sixty. When she walked into the restaurant, he greeted her with open arms.

"The prodigal daughter returns to the dump," he exclaimed.

"You're telling me. Every time it rains this place smells like shit."

Sture shrugged.

"Bathrooms get clogged, the plumbing doesn't work. What can I do if the Social Democrats have abandoned us?"

"Not another political speech, please. Not today, I'm too tired."

Yasmina turned to the bar and waved in response to the timid yet ardent smile Sture's stepson Erick had given her. She sat down at the same table she always did, under the *Doctor Zhivago* poster—"best movie of all time," according to Sture. The poster had been hanging on the wall so long that Omar Sharif had yellowed, as if he had jaundice.

"The special of the day is *älggryta*, elk stew. Hearty and invigorating. Raquel made it," Sture announced.

Raquel was Sture's beautiful, young Portuguese wife. When she arrived, ten years ago, and took over the cooking, Old Sweden came back to life. The restaurant's dozen tables were now often full, especially for the daily lunch special. It could be herring, smoked fish, or meatballs. And no one could cook game, whether elk or deer, better than Raquel.

At Old Sweden, there was another kind of dish on the menu too, one much sought-after in the neighborhood: first-rate heroin. This was a house specialty Sture took care of himself. His nickname, the Turk, came from his suppliers in Ankara. No one dared call him that to his face, because everyone in the neighborhood knew which way he voted, and, in case they didn't, behind the bar hung a large signed photo of Jimmie Åkesson, who'd dedicated it to "a patriot." "I'm no racist," Sture reasoned, "but I like order, and for people to respect the society they live in. Anyone who's here to work is welcome. Anyone who's not: to the lions." The words were ironic, coming from the mouth of one of Malmö's biggest drug traffickers, married to a Portuguese woman with skin the color of dark honey, but no one was going to contradict him. To an outsider, Sture was just a guy with the kind of friendly, nondescript, slightly naive face you walk past without noticing, a right-wing voter who paid his taxes religiously, worried about the direction things were headed in and about his teenage stepson's education; an honorable restaurateur who wrapped up leftover food at the end of the day so the homeless at the shelter could have a decent dinner. But those who knew him better knew who was behind the burned-out cars in the vacant lot and the beatings of certain newcomers who didn't yet understand the rules of the neighborhood. Sture had done long stints in various prisons, and each of them had occasioned a tale that he neither confirmed nor denied. If anyone asked, he'd simply pat his leg with a smile, show them a scar on his lower back, or his neck, or his forearm, then roll his eyes and offer a round of Raquel's hot croquettes on the house. "Sometimes things are just as they should be," he'd say like a kindly father, "good friends, good food, good music, and delicious croquettes. And though every source of light has its shadows, no one needs to hear about them."

"Have you had a decent meal today?" Sture came over to sit beside Yasmina, bringing with him a light whiff of fried food and dry sweat. He breathed with his mouth slightly open, a small pink hole that was black at the back, a large cartoon face. His short stubby fingers gripped the edge of the table as if he was afraid he might fall and not be able to get up. Yasmina shook her head. It was ridiculous, but she loved this oversized smart-ass like a father. Loving Sture and hungering in spite of everything for his attentions was as absurd as being in love with Gövan, living in this neighborhood, and dreaming about the many places she'd never go. There were some days Yasmina thought her whole life was a castle in the air and she didn't fool herself about it, but the Turk's attentions were the closest thing to affection she'd ever known.

"I'm not hungry, thanks."

Sture didn't even bother to respond. He went behind the bar, exchanged a few words with an awkward Erick, and returned with a plate of *älggryta*.

"It's still hot."

The penetrating expression in Sture's deep-blue eyes left no room for discussion. Yasmina picked up a fork and stabbed a piece of meat so tender it fell into strands. It was delicious, like everything touched by Raquel's blessed hands. Her stomach purred like a cat. Sex on an empty stomach had exhausted her. Sture nodded in satisfaction, and for a few seconds watched her with pleasure. He liked seeing people eat.

"What's new out there on the horizon?"

Yasmina put down her fork.

"You have to be careful. Gövan's not stupid."

Sture pursed his lips as if he were about to whistle.

"Your boyfriend the deputy chief, of course."

"He's not my boyfriend. We have sex from time to time. Isn't that what you asked me to do?"

Sture feigned bewilderment.

"Did I seriously ask you to do that? I thought good half-Swedish Muslim girls didn't do that kind of thing."

Yasmina had a hard time knowing how much truth and how much fiction lay in Sture's clownish attitude. He acted like he never took anything seriously. He acted as though this was gossip unrelated to him.

"Half-Swedish? My passport and birth certificate say I'm a hundred percent Swedish."

"I was referring to your eyes. What's that called?"

"Heterochromia."

"What a word! Anyway, your left eye is bluer than the lakes of Lapland, and your right as brown as the land your grandfather came from. It's like you couldn't decide what you are."

"It wasn't my choice. My apologies for diluting the race."

"Come now, little one, don't be mad at me. You know everyone loves that about you. It's like having two women look at you at the same time, and both so beautiful."

Yasmina laughed. She had a nice laugh, though she didn't use it often.

"You should laugh more, Yasmina. It lights the place up. And one day you should go out with Erick. That boy's in love with you, you know. But he's too wimpy to make the first move."

Yasmina shot a furtive glance at the bar. Erick was gazing at her. When he realized she'd seen him, he blushed and turned away.

"He's a good catch," she joked, "but he's fourteen. Besides, I don't think his mother would approve. Raquel can't stand me and you know it."

Sture burst out laughing. It was all in jest, and it was all true.

"Raquel is an amazing woman, but she's jealous of any woman who comes near me. I'm not surprised, being the handsome, intelligent man that I am ... Now then, back to the small matter of the Pakistani dealer at the port. What does our friend the unfaithful cop say?"

"I don't want to end up visiting you in jail, Sture. You really need to be careful."

Sture clucked his tongue.

"That's not going to happen. You're the one who needs to be careful. The deputy chief isn't going to like it if he finds out what you do." Sture had put on a very concerned tone, as if he had nothing to do with it.

"I'm not planning on seeing him again," Yasmina claimed. She'd said as much other times, but for some reason this time Sture believed her. He grew serious, not in a threatening way, more like a priest at confession, asking the nature of her sin.

"I only need a little more from you, my girl. I promise ... So, our friend the model cop didn't say anything about the port?"

"He doesn't talk to me about work, you know that."

Sture put on a phony expression of frustration.

"He'd be the first guy I know who doesn't brag about his accomplishments to a pretty girl. So what do you talk about between one fuck and the next? I'm just curious."

Broken promises, a taste of heaven that's there one minute and gone the next. Love, lies.

"We don't talk much."

Sture shook his head.

"I find that hard to believe as well...At any rate, you could try to find out if our friend has any clues."

"If I ask him any more directly than I did today, he's going to get suspicious."

Sture scratched his head with a bemused look.

"There are ways to get answers without asking questions, don't you think?"

Yasmina had finished her food. She looked at the clock on the wall.

"Tell Raquel she's a blessing from God, the stew is fantastic. I have to go, my mother has today off."

Sture's eyes softened. Whenever Fatima came up, he changed slightly.

"How is she?"

"I don't see her much."

"Still cleaning rich people's shit? She shouldn't do it, your mother deserves so much more."

"Why do you still worry about her? She doesn't want anything to do with you. She hates you. And she hates me."

Sture returned to his light tone.

"Well, we can't change what others think of us, right? There was a time when Fatima and I were great friends. And sometimes great friends become great enemies."

"You've never told me what it was that you fought about." Sture smiled.

"True, I never did." Without another word, he went to the bar and returned with a ledger that was all too familiar to Yasmina. To the bottom of a long list of figures he added ten thousand crowns.

"See? We're almost settled up."

She shrugged.

"You've been saying that for years."

Sture closed the ledger and stuck the pencil behind his ear like a chatty, honest shopkeeper.

"When people fall behind on their debts, interest accrues, my girl. It's not your fault, but that's how business works."

"A debt incurred by my grandfather. What favor could have been so big that forty years later he's still in debt?"

Sture stared at Yasmina. Very occasionally, he felt a jolt of nostalgia.

"That's something you should ask him."

"My grandfather spends all day praying, and my mother won't speak to whores. And to her, I am the queen of whores."

Sture clenched his jaw.

"You are no such thing. You're paying off a debt that you did not incur. Your family should be grateful to you."

"Well if it's so important to you, cancel it."

Sture put on a tragic expression.

"The order of things, Yasmina. That's what matters. You can't just change the rules, or the game would make no sense. Compassion might be confused with weakness, you know? And in my world, the weak die."

Yasmina found her grandfather at the living room window, sitting in a wicker chair with red cushions that had formed to the shape of his small body. His cloudy eyes were gazing up at the slice of sky visible between concrete-block apartment towers.

"There's been three," he said, not turning when he sensed his granddaughter's presence. His voice was deep and crackly, saliva at the corners of his chapped lips. Yasmina followed the direction of his words and saw the contrails in the sky, slowly fading away. Planes. Her grandfather spent his time counting the planes that crossed his line of vision. He stank. Yasmina noticed when he shifted uncomfortably. He'd shat his pants.

"We need to get you changed and cleaned up, Grandfather."

She pulled him up by his arms, limp and bony white. His flesh was shriveled, his skin hard as jerky hanging off brittle bones. With slow, tiny steps they crossed the immensity of the fifty-square-meter apartment to the bathroom.

"I'm going to sit you in the shower, grandfather. You have to help me."

"Where's Fatima?" he asked suddenly, jerking his hand away like a little boy having a tantrum, angry at everything he sees. "Where's my daughter?"

"She must be on her way. She'll make dinner tonight and put you to bed. You can talk until dawn, I know you like that. But if you're not clean she'll be angry. And you know how fussy she is."

The threat had a deterrent effect. The old man yielded, bowing his head until his chin rested on his chest, and let her clean him.

One day I will get out of here, Yasmina said to herself, hands covered in soap bubbles, shirt sleeves rolled back to the elbow. And the thought of that day, whose date and destination were yet to be determined, was what she clung to while pouring warm water over her grandfather's trembling body.

"Until that day arrives, I wait . . ." she sang quietly.

"What's that you're whispering? It's not right to whisper. It's a sin."

"I'm not whispering, Grandfather, I'm singing. It's a romantic song by Sofia El Marikh about dreams and love in Paris."

Like a cat on the alert, her grandfather pricked up his ears and regarded her warily.

"Singing is a sin. You must not sing. Fatima needs to marry you off to a good man," he said reprovingly.

Yasmina stroked his wet face. Drops of water slid down his chapped skin and formed tiny pools in the cavities of his cheeks and chest. Life itself was a sin, all of it, for this man who was now waste himself.

"Yes, a good man, a God-fearing man," he went on.

"Anything you say, Grandfather."

Abdul noted a certain mockery in her tone. He'd learned to swallow his shame, but secretly pride burned him up, rotting his insides. He let his granddaughter comb his hair at the mirror, put a clean shirt on him, and dab a few drops of cologne behind his ears, although he hated being in her hands. Yasmina personified everything he most despised: blame, dishonor, shame.

"Leave me!" he said, jerking his head away and standing up.

"What's the matter, Grandfather?" Yasmina asked, disconcerted, comb still in her hands.

Abdul gave her a look full of disgust.

"I'll wait for my daughter in my bedroom. Help me."

Once alone in his room, Abdul wanted to cry tears of rage and self-pity. What would his father, Rachid the Spaniard, think if he could see him now, a miserable old man, reduced to this? What would his countrymen think? How would they mock him in the village? The women would spit at his feet and the men would strike him on the head. He, the arrogant Abdul, now nothing but waste. All of his dreams of grandeur come to this.

His father had attained every glory imaginable. He'd been a soldier in the service of Spain who had participated in the retaking of Monte Arruit months after the Spanish defeat at Annual. He'd helped bury the hundreds of bodies left rotting on the battlefield. He'd been rewarded with a brass medal, wages, and land in his own village. Throughout his boyhood, Abdul had borne the weight of that medal, the hatred and rancor of their neighbors, the fear and envy that his father aroused. Son of the traitor, they called hm. But no one dared call his father a traitor to his face. On the contrary, those who despised him in secret didn't hesitate to ask for favors when they needed them, and his father granted them, like some magnanimous king.

When war broke out in Spain, his father enlisted with Franco's troops and was one of the first to cross the Strait of Gibraltar with the rebels. But his presence lingered on in the village; everyone knew he'd return even stronger, with more medals and privileges. In the following three years, Abdul grew up and became a man while awaiting his father's return. He became a handsome, ambitious young man, aware of his body and what it elicited in others. Desire. Desire in both men and women that he learned to use in order to get what he wanted. Soon he realized that the village was too small, his dreams too big for the place. And yet, he had to wait. The war ended, but his father didn't return for five more years. And when he finally did, one day in 1944, riding in a military vehicle and accompanied by a young Tabor officer, everyone stared at his empty right sleeve, flapping in the wind, stitched to his uniform, and the patch over his right eye. But no one dared think his days were over. Even old and worn out, missing an eye and an arm, his father never stood for condescension.

Someone knocked at the door, and Abdul's memories fluttered away.

"What do you want?"

Fatima's voice replied. Familiar. Warm. Abdul smiled. His daughter was the best thing he'd done in his life, his miracle, the sign God sent him in time to give him another chance. He opened the door and gazed at her tenderly. Fatima took his hands and kissed them. All religions instruct children to love their parents without questioning whether the parents are deserving of such love.

"Hello, Father. How are you today?"

Standing quietly in the hall, Yasmina spied on her mother and grandfather. Her father was missing from the tableau. Though the fact was, he'd never been in the picture; it was as if he'd never been part of this family. Yasmina called to mind his image, exhausted, his feet swollen after traipsing all over the city in search of work, head bowed as he accepted Grandfather's insults and her mother's scorn. Sometimes she missed him. Yasmina went back to her room and lay down on the bed. Sofia El Marikh's face, on the poster on the wall, was painfully indifferent. Yasmina looked at the rag dolls on the chair, the childhood photos in their cheap frames. It was the room of a girl who'd grown up intending to fulfill her dreams. Outside, Rosengård sank into the shadows. And the rain did not let up.

Her castle in the air seemed more fragile than ever.

4

Sevilla

The harlequin on the wall bore witness to Natalia's performance, on her knees with her head in the toilet bowl. Nothing solid remained in her stomach, but she kept retching, and each contraction was followed by a string of saliva and gastric juices. When the last spasm ended she struggled up and looked in the mirror. Her face was flushed and her eyes bulging. This was nothing like the drunken vomiting of her teenage years, when she'd developed a technique for throwing up silently so as not to wake her parents sleeping on the other side of the hall—though even then, inevitably, her father would sometimes hear her and come in to cradle her head and hold her hair back as she puked her guts up.

Still grimacing, with both hands on the sink to keep from getting dizzy, she gazed at the harlequin. She'd drawn it in colored pencil when she was twelve, and though it was no masterpiece, it was by far her greatest work. After that fine achievement—third place in the class drawing competition—she knew she'd never have the talent it took to be an artist. Perhaps she'd held on to it for so long to keep her fantasies in check; on days when she felt frustrated by the monotony of her job, she forced herself to look at the drawing so she'd remember her place in the world: she had a modicum of technical skill but lacked imagination, was efficient but not brilliant, tenacious but not a genius. Ultimately, she was her father's daughter.

Natalia used toilet paper to wipe up the vomit that had spattered the porcelain, then rinsed her mouth and washed her face. She put a few drops of cologne on her neck and made sure she hadn't soiled her pajama top before going back into the bedroom.

Gustavo was in bed, the sheets tangled between his legs. He'd put his underwear back on, though his erection was still obvious, and he was smoking a cigarette that dangled dangerously close to the pillow.

"Are you okay? Sounded like an exorcism in there."

Natalia thought of her father's protective hand on her forehead when she was sixteen. He would never have let her go through that alone.

"The doctor says it's normal."

She'd put her glasses down somewhere, along with the manuscript she'd been copyediting a few minutes earlier. She found them under a heap of clothes on the floor. Some things never change, Natalia thought, climbing back into bed. She had to finish editing the text or they'd end up firing her. She was running out of excuses for being late so often.

Gustavo stroked her shoulder. Half an hour earlier, the same move had turned Natalia on, but now it irked her. She tried to shift slightly away without his realizing.

"Is that interesting?" Gustavo asked, pretending not to have noticed her attempt to escape.

"It's pretentious bullshit, but it puts food on the table."

Gustavo leaned back, resting his head on his right elbow. He was still in good shape, and liked to make sure he was in exactly the right position to show off his serratus and hard biceps. Letting his long gray hair fall messily onto his chest was another old trick. Natalia knew them well, his tricks, but despite that fact she couldn't seem to avoid falling for them again and again.

"You should write your own stories instead of editing other people's shit."

Gustavo's condescending tone, his fake reproach, and phony confidence were all familiar. It was like saying: *Look at me, I'm a real artist who composes his own songs and opened for Tracy Chapman.* Gustavo was convinced he deserved more in life, and the fact that he hadn't gotten it gave him the right to look down his nose on anyone who didn't value his talent. Resentment suited him; it didn't make him a failure, it made him seem accursed. He'd been playing the part for years.

Natalia was not about to let the rest of the night be ruined, so she tried to smile.

"Maybe one day I will."

He fell back onto the pillow dramatically.

"Always putting off what's possible, aren't you? If you don't take risks, you can't lose. Isn't that your father's philosophy? Status quo, make sure everything stays the same."

Natalia dropped her glasses onto a misused subjunctive she'd crossed out in red. She knew Gustavo's approach, how he worked his way around to things. He was a lurker, the kind who needed a drawn out ritual of approach before the attack, and he would only attack when he was sure it was worth the effort. All night, Natalia had been dodging the topic of her father. But here it was. There was no way to postpone it any longer.

"This has got nothing to do with my father."

Gustavo rolled his eyes and rubbed his salt-and-pepper three-day beard with one thumb.

"Of course it does. Everything that's happened between us goes back to your father. He's always coming between us." He sat back up against the pillow and stared at her fixedly. "You haven't told him, have you?"

"He's still recovering. I don't want to worry him."

"What are you planning to do about him? You can't keep going to his house every day. You were just telling me you got a warning at work for being late so often. You hardly sleep, you can't concentrate. You could hire a nurse, someone to look after him twenty-four seven."

Natalia shook her head. This was a cunning conversation, headed straight where he wanted to get to. And she was resisting.

Gustavo slapped the sheets in impatient disdain.

"So what's the solution, then? Sooner or later you're going to have to tell him what's going on."

"He could come here, live with me."

There. She'd said it. Now would come the storm and she'd have to hold tight in order to weather it. She had to show Gustavo that at least a few things had changed. She wasn't the easy-to-manipulate young woman she'd been when she first married him at twenty-two.

But Gustavo's reaction was oddly calm.

"You can't be serious."

Natalia put her glasses back on. She still had a lot of work to do before she could go to sleep. And she didn't want to look him in the eye. She wasn't up to that yet.

"Of course I'm being serious," she replied angrily, because in fact he was right; she was not at all sure that it was even remotely a good idea.

t didn't seem that bad: forgo salt, coffee, lactose, and gluten; walk twenty minutes a day; have a light dinner and get enough sleep; take his blood pressure and follow the medication schedule that Natalia had hung in the kitchen; have a weekly checkup. Day and night, Miguel listened to himself, watched himself, on the lookout for any telltale signs. But there were none: the worst seemed to be behind him. He even managed to find some fun in the whole need for constant vigilance. It was a way to kill time, which since Águeda's death had turned into something he simply had to get through.

Natalia came to see him every day, bringing meals she put in the freezer; she cleaned the apartment, made his bed, did the laundry and attempted to make small talk. Miguel tried to respond appropriately to his daughter's attentions, but he'd never been very expressive or given to shows of affection. He came from a time when people were sparing in their gestures, didn't often hug or kiss. Or even speak. He felt uneasy when Natalia sat beside him and for no reason at all put her arm around his shoulders and kissed the top of his head, or when she bent down to lace up his shoe or straighten the hem of his trousers. Miguel responded awkwardly, and Natalia always mistook this for coldness.

"I'm not paralyzed, Natalia. I can fend for myself."

She accepted these rebuffs with a half smile, visibly uncomfortable. She was forty-two years old and felt as if her father still acted like he could manipulate her. Just as he'd always done with her mother.

"Of course you can, Papá. But a little help never hurt anyone, not even you."

One morning, Miguel locked himself in the bathroom. He needed some privacy and some time. He pulled down his pants, sat on the toilet, contemplated the crack zigzagging its way across the ceiling, and waited. The minutes passed but nothing came out, not even a tiny bit. There was no way to fight his constipation. It was the damn medicine. Sometimes he felt as if his guts were full of stones, and others he lost control of his body at the most inopportune moments. He had to concentrate. His buttocks clenched and Miguel let out a cry of pain. Finally, a tiny bit of relief. Not much, just a few goat pellets.

Old age is so sad, he thought as he wiped, afraid to examine his own feces as the doctor had recommended he do. Miguel felt betrayed by his body, subjected to tiny humiliations, like sticking his hand into his own excrement in order to put samples in a test tube to send to the clinic, spending five minutes per morning trying to determine the message hidden in his poop by noting its color, its texture, its smell.

Emerging from the bathroom, he found Natalia at the window hanging out a sheet. His daughter turned to him with a clothespin in her mouth, then left it on the windowsill and tucked her hair behind one ear.

"That just arrived," she said, pointing to a certified letter from the DGT—the national traffic authority—that lay on the table. Is it your new driver's license?"

Miguel didn't reply. He opened the envelope, concealing his anxiousness, and quickly scanned the letter. Then he folded it up and slipped it back into the envelope.

"Everything okay?"

Miguel remained pensive.

"I made something for you—a present," he said, changing the subject.

"A present?"

Miguel opened a drawer and handed his daughter a bouquet of carnations made entirely of four layers of tissue paper; he'd even made the leaves and stems. It had taken several hours, he'd even painted the edges and dusted the petals with blush to make them look more realistic. Natalia gave a quick smile and set the paper carnations down on the table. Miguel knew that from there they'd find their way to the trash in a few days.

"Is something the matter? I know I'm no great artist . . ."

She shook her head emphatically.

"It's not that; they're lovely."

"Then what's wrong?"

Natalia looked away. She shook her head as though debating with herself.

"There's something I want to talk to you about, something important."

"Go on, then. Just say it."

"I'd rather we go somewhere. We could go out to that restaurant Mamá used to like so much, out on the Badajoz Highway. You're always complaining that the Datsun never comes out of the parking garage anymore, and it's a lovely day for a drive."

"Now?" Miguel asked in surprise.

"Why not?" Natalia asked, overly enthusiastic.

Miguel didn't plan on telling her that he'd just had his license suspended for failing his driver's test.

"Okay, then."

The old car sat dormant in the parking lot. It was a Datsun 280Z with leather upholstery that Miguel had bought with his first big bonus at the bank. He'd always treated the car with the kind of care he rarely showed human beings: it had the original hubcaps, the hood didn't have a single water spot, and the body was in great condition, the white paint job still impeccable. There was a time when he'd dreamed of driving across Spain behind the wheel of that car. But he'd never made it past Tarifa.

They drove out of the city and took the bypass, heading for the Badajoz Highway, as they'd done so many weekends when Natalia was little and Águeda sat in the passenger seat telling Miguel not to tailgate, to slow down, to put on his turn signal. Now Miguel drove in silence, concentrating on the road, not passing the speed limit. His daughter was quiet too, but her silence was loud; Miguel could almost hear her chewing over the words that couldn't quite make it out of her mouth. He sensed something was wrong.

"What is it that you didn't want to talk to me about at home?"

A flash of pain gave Natalia's eyes a terribly beautiful shimmer.

"I live more than fifty kilometers from you, and I can't keep missing work. They gave me a serious warning; if I'm late again, I'll be fired."

"I never asked you to. I told you I can fend for myself. I've been doing it since your mother died," Miguel replied defensively.

Natalia looked at her father anxiously.

"Please, Papá. Your invincible days are over. You know it's going to get worse."

Miguel remained quiet. He'd read enough about the incipient disease to know what would happen in a year or two, the progressive decline that would accelerate at the end. His daughter was right, and there was no use denying it. In a few months the blathering would begin, the vacant looks. He'd end up a vegetable, sitting by the window, unable to feed himself or wipe his own ass. But he refused to accept it.

"I've never been a burden to anyone, and I'm not going to start now."

Natalia lowered her gaze. She felt sad and ashamed.

"I'm not going to abandon you, Papá, if that's what you're worried about. What I'm saying is, I think you should live with me. Move in. It will all be so much easier."

"Live with you? We tried that before your mother died, when she kicked me out. In case you don't remember it was a complete disaster. It didn't work then, and I doubt it would work now."

They'd barely managed to tolerate one another for four weeks after Águeda had kicked him out. Miguel recalled the argument with his wife. They'd arranged to meet for hot chocolate and churros. Águeda, sitting on the edge of her chair, staring out at the street the whole time, wore a heavy coat that she refused to take off at any point. The hot chocolate had gone cold, like Águeda's expression, as she began anxiously rummaging through her bag. Finally, she found what she was looking for and tossed the dozen letters from Carmen onto the table as irrefutable proof. Miguel never knew how she'd found them. He tried to explain, but she wouldn't let him.

"Your daughter and I have never mattered one shit to you. You're a selfish, arrogant son of a bitch, and you will be until the day you die. I want you out of the house, I can't stand you there one more minute."

That morning Miguel had been shocked to see how much his wife hated him after nearly fifty years of marriage. Águeda never recovered from that painful discovery. No one, not even Águeda herself, suspected that that she was already dying at that very moment. The disease hadn't made itself known until victory was certain. Natalia was the only one to side with Miguel in those days of harbored resentment, and she worked hard to get her mother to reconsider. But then Águeda was admitted to the hospital for the first time. The cancer acted as glue, sticking them back together, and Miguel moved back in.

"The circumstances are different now, Papá."

Miguel shook his head emphatically.

"The circumstances might be. But you and I are the same, and we both know how it ended last time. Both of us angry."

"Couldn't you at least think about it?"

Miguel was about to reply that there was nothing to think about, but suddenly he winced and instinctively let go of the wheel, clutching his stomach. Natalia reacted quickly, grabbing the wheel and turning it just as the Datsun was about to veer into the oncoming traffic.

"Papá, what is it?"

Miguel inhaled. He was pale. He took the wheel again and pulled over on the shoulder, then wiped his lips on the back of his hand and cleared his throat.

"I'm fine, it's that damn medication. My stomach is in knots. I need to go to the bathroom."

Natalia's eyes swept the terrain.

"We're almost to the restaurant. Can you hold it?"

He nodded weakly.

But by the time they got to the restaurant, it was too late.

Taking slow steps, attempting not to hunch over, Miguel crossed the dining room, where only a few tables were occupied, and managed to lock himself into a bathroom so tiny that his knees banged against the door, which was covered in lewd drawings and profanity. He unbuckled his belt and pulled down his trousers as though yanking a bandage off a wound. Shit had already stained his underpants, and liquid ran down his leg. He was overwhelmed by the urge to cry. "Damn it." Distressed, he took off his shoes, his pants and then his underwear, wiped himself carefully with toilet paper, rinsed the stain on his trousers and looked for a nonexistent hand dryer to dry the wet spot. His undershorts were a mess, so he wrapped them in toilet paper and looked for a trash can, which also did not exist. In the end, he hid them behind the cistern as best he could. The tiny room reeked of sickness.

Twenty minutes later, Miguel had managed to get the smell off his hands using liters of soap. He felt his testicles, loose and flaccid under his trousers. He smoothed his hair in the mirror, which was covered in water spots, and took a deep breath. When he emerged, he avoided the puzzled look of the man who'd been waiting his turn for so long.

"About time, grandpa. I was ready to call the Guardia Civil."

Miguel didn't reply. Natalia had taken a table by the windows and already ordered for them both: a salad to share, grilled monkfish with lemon, bread, and a beer for herself and mineral water for him.

"Does that sound good?"

Miguel nodded absently. When he sat down, his gaze fell on the outdoor tables on the patio.

"I remember when we used to come here with Mamá. She loved their cuttlefish," Natalia said, pretending not to have noticed the wet spot on the back of her father's trousers.

Miguel grunted irritably.

"The one who really liked cuttlefish was you."

He turned and accidentally caught the eye of the man emerging from the restroom, who shot him a disgusted look. Miguel felt the burn of shame. He took some bread from the wicker basket and drank water. The monkfish was cold, his fork was dirty, the glass too small: the world was conspiring against him.

Natalia placed one hand over his on the table, and he pushed it off. His daughter's eyes stared in pain at the space where her hand had been.

"Will you at least think about my idea?"

Miguel massaged his temple. He had a headache.

"I'll think about it."

For the time being, that was enough. They ate in relative tranquility, and by the time dessert arrived, Natalia had recovered some of her enthusiasm. Enough to tell stories about her childhood and get nostalgic. Halfway through one anecdote, she interrupted herself and looked at her father tenderly.

"Can I ask you something, Papá?"

Miguel knew his daughter well enough to know that she would ask, regardless of what he said.

"Were you still in love with Mamá when she died?"

Miguel hadn't been expecting the conversation to take this turn.

"You know I loved her."

"That's not what I asked you. I'm asking if you were in love with her."

Miguel shook his head. Life bulldozed one's feelings and put them back together in different configurations. What the hell was "being in love" anyway? Nonsense that made people who wanted more than they had miserable.

"I loved your mother, I loved her to the very end. That's what matters."

Natalia dug in her bag for a pack of cigarettes.

"You can't smoke here," Miguel warned.

She lit up with a flourish.

"I don't give a shit." Her hand was shaking. "What about that woman who wrote all the damn letters, Carmen, were you in love with her?"

Miguel turned red.

"That was all so long ago."

Natalia had yet to exhale.

"Time is no excuse. Tell me the truth."

Miguel thought his daughter was wrong. Time was an unfailing alibi. And as for truth, it depended solely on those concerned.

"The idea of leaving you and your mother never even entered my head."

"That still doesn't answer my question."

"People's lives are full of things that could have been but were not, Natalia. I made my choice and I never regretted it. It makes no sense to think about anything else. I was never disloyal to your mother."

"There are lots of ways to be disloyal. Why didn't you get rid of those letters? You promised Mamá you would, and it's been two years."

Miguel's mouth tensed.

"How do you know that? Have you been spying on me?"

"No, I've been observing you. Answer the question. Why have you held on to them?"

Why had he? Out of a vague sense of longing, fear of closing that door all the way. Back in those years of his marriage, some mornings he'd find himself seized by a deep and inexplicable sadness. Miguel would stare at his breakfast, listen to Águeda shuffling around in the kitchen with the television on low, and feel that his sense of tranquility was a betrayal. Then he'd lock himself in the bedroom and re-read Carmen's letters, remember how they met, think of her face, and feel better. Reading her letters was like consulting a life plan that never came to pass, the tale of something that could have been but never was. And speaking to his daughter all these years later about the promises he and Carmen had made between the sheets—promises that were never kept—wasn't going to add anything to the story.

"I don't want to discuss this with you, Natalia. You're my daughter, but that doesn't give you the right to judge me. I never replied to a single one of Carmen's letters. I made my decision and followed through on it to the end. That's what should matter to you."

They ate their dessert, protecting themselves behind a wall of silence. When they were finished, Natalia got up and went to the bar to pay. Miguel followed with his eyes. He saw the waiter address her; the man seemed angry and pointed to the bathroom. The customer Miguel had encountered was nodding and gesticulating emphatically.

Natalia turned to glance back at the table. Miguel looked away in shame.

After a few minutes, during which she seemed to apologize profusely, Natalia returned, circled the table, touched Miguel's head and, putting her lips to his ear, whispered quietly as if he were a frail little boy.

"It's okay, Papá, don't you worry. Come on, let's go."

Miguel nodded. Defeated.

When they got to the car, Miguel stopped, staring at the ground.

"What is it now?"

Miguel took a deep breath.

"I'll move in with you."

Moving into Natalia's was like moving to a foreign country and bringing just a few clothes, his old trunk, and the urn containing his mother's ashes. Her basement apartment was cryptlike, a subterranean cave, not terribly deep; it would have made a good grave. The only bonus was that there were no stairs to climb, just a few steps down and the view of people's feet as they walked by on the sidewalk. Miguel glanced around forlornly. The apartment seemed smaller this time, jumbled and disorganized. It was clear that Natalia had tried—organizing the bookshelves, washing the carpet, and cleaning the kitchen counters and appliances. The whole place smelled like a sickly hodgepodge of detergent and Oriental air fresheners, with a slight undertone of black tobacco. But nothing could help how stifled he felt.

"What do you need so many books for? Couldn't you give them to a library once you finish reading them?" He might as well have just suggested, in that morose tone of his, that she throw them into a heap and set them on fire.

Natalia gave her father a cryptic smile.

"How many years has it been since you retired from the bank? Eleven? And you still have all your old accounting records from when you were bank manager, don't you? I remember Mamá used to tell you to get rid of them every day, and you said it would be like getting rid of a part of your life."

As the days went by, clutter proved to be the least of the inconveniences: Natalia insisted on controlling her father's diet and making him try all manner of organic and supposedly healthy foods, but they basically all tasted like cardboard. Plus, Miguel had a hard time getting used to sleeping on the sofa bed they pulled out each night. Despite the curtains in the living room, the bright light of a streetlamp streamed in. Still, the worst thing was the feeling that he was a burden to his daughter. To rid himself of this sense, he tidied up papers, organized figurines, and cleaned the closets, which upset Natalia enormously. It was inevitable that they clash, exasperate one another, and in a sense invade the privacy it was impossible for them to have. Every time they had a run-in, Natalia would downplay it, force a carefree smile, and pretend to concentrate on whatever manuscript she was working on at the computer. Everything was fine.

"Why don't you stop worrying? We'll work it out."

But Miguel couldn't help but feel that his daughter was hiding something, that she had concerns she didn't want to discuss.

t all came to a head in the most surprising way. One morning, Miguel heard the key in the lock and assumed that Natalia had forgotten something, since she'd only said goodbye five minutes earlier. But his daughter was not who appeared in the door with a triumphant smile.

Miguel's stomach turned on seeing Gustavo, his ex-son-in-law.

"What are you doing here?" he asked, not even attempting to hide his hostility. He hated Gustavo as intensely as he'd once loved him, years ago.

Gustavo smiled in phony cordiality.

"A hug would be nice, Miguel. It's been a long time."

Miguel had trouble finding his words, had to chew them up and let them out like mush.

"You are no longer part of this family."

Gustavo shrugged. It was his most characteristic gesture. Basically, he didn't care about anything not directly related to him.

"I think you're wrong. Natalia hasn't told you, has she?"

"Told me what?"

"Your daughter and I have decided to give it another chance. We're seeing each other again."

Miguel swallowed.

"That's not true. Natalia can't be back with you."

Gustavo swung the handful of keys with which he'd just opened the door.

"That's not your decision to make, Miguel. Your daughter and I still love each other."

"You can't even spell the word. You're nothing but a trickster."

"Really, can't we just forget the past?"

"Well, it's clear that you have. But I can't forget what you did to my daughter."

When Natalia first brought a polite, good-looking young man home, in her last year at university, Miguel and Águeda breathed a sigh of relief. Natalia had been through a lot of heartbreak and suffered bouts of depression; she took failure hard and was too fragile for this harsh world. And Gustavo seemed like a nice kid: he had a good head on his shoulders and a clean look about him. They both thought he'd make their daughter happy. But long before they could have suspected, it all turned into a nightmare. As newlyweds, Natalia and Gustavo moved to Barcelona and started coming back to Sevilla less and less. At first this seemed normal for a pair of newlyweds, and Águeda was forever making excuses for them: they needed to be alone, to live in their own bubble. But slowly the explanations became less plausible, and a series of strange accidents began to occur. One day Natalia showed up with a swollen lip and said she'd tripped; weeks later, she had a black eye that she blamed on some kids who'd been playing ball and hit her. She had bruises on her forearms that she hid by wearing long sleeves even in summer, claiming she had very sensitive skin. Gustavo's insolence started to come out at their rare family reunions; he'd make fun of her in public, treat her as if she were an idiot, and be condescending. And Natalia flinched, as though skittish. She quit work, stopped seeing the friends she'd known her whole life, and almost never picked up the phone. This went on until the day she was admitted to the hospital. She claimed it was an accident, that the car had run her down. But the witnesses' testimony differed: Natalia and her husband were arguing in the street, he shook her violently, and actually grabbed her by the hair. She tried to wrench free, and he shoved her into the street. The car dragged her for several meters, breaking her humerus and causing multiple injuries. She could have died, but still refused to press charges against her husband. It took two more years for her to be free of him, but it wasn't Natalia who made the decision. It was her husband, who decided to move on to a younger victim. Since then, Natalia hadn't had a stable relationship.

"If there were any justice in this world, you would be in jail."

Gustavo scratched his beard. He had that phony carefree attitude that some artists tried to cultivate. He was over forty, but tried to appear under thirty, with his mop of hair, trendy clothes, and a stupid smirk that was always plastered on his face.

"We should just wipe the slate clean, Miguel. Kids change everything."

Miguel blinked as though someone had flashed a red-hot knife before his eyes.

"What nonsense are you talking about?"

Gustavo regarded his ex-father-in-law scornfully. He gave a little tut and then nodded.

"I suppose Natalia also forgot to tell you that you're going to be a grandfather. Too much good news for one day?"

Miguel opened his mouth to get a breath of air. He felt an anvil pressing down on his chest.

"You're lying."

"Ask her. Your daughter is pregnant, and believe me, it wasn't the Holy Spirit who did it."

Like a bull struck with a hammer, Miguel cocked his head with his mouth half-open and his eyes in a blank stare. Gustavo used his advantage to go in for the kill. He'd always hated the old fucker.

"I just hope you don't dare try to meddle in our lives. Natalia told me about your illness. I'm sorry—really I am, it's a bitch. But you have to think about her, Miguel. Your daughter is going to be a mother, and she doesn't need you burdening her. It would be best for you to go, move into a home. I hear they're like five-star hotels, and you've got plenty of cash."

Miguel let his head drop heavily. If anyone pricked him with a pin, not a single drop of blood would have come from his veins at that moment.

"You will not be with my daughter as long as I'm alive."

Gustavo clenched his jaw. His eyes glinted in hatred; he could have snapped the old man in two like a straw. But that wouldn't have served his plans.

"We'll see about that, Miguel. We'll see."

That night, when Natalia walked in, Miguel was waiting for her on the sofa. She realized immediately what had happened: the smell of Gustavo's cologne still lingered in the apartment.

"When were you planning on telling me?"

Natalia set her purse and keys down on the table.

"I don't know. I was waiting for the right moment."

"The right moment? Are you trying to tell me you think that there's a right moment to tell me you're going back to the man who almost killed you, and that you're pregnant with his child?"

"It's hard to explain."

Miguel exploded.

"Hard to explain? Have you lost your mind?"

Natalia flushed. The words had been festering inside her for some time, and when she let them out, it was like opening the floodgates, a torrent of blame, justification, and resentment for her father.

"Don't you treat me like a child. I'm not a little girl, despite what you think. You never loved Gustavo, and you're not willing to give him a second chance. You're so harsh, and you judge other people, unable to accept their mistakes. But when it comes to judging yourself, there's a different standard."

"Mistakes? The man beat you every week. He put you in the hospital. You asked me to come get you in Barcelona, and I did."

"But people change. And I love him."

"You cannot love the man who almost destroyed you."

"I do, I love him, and I don't care what you think. He asked for my forgiveness, and we're back to the beautiful things that made us fall in love to begin with. He stopped hanging around those old friends, the ones who got him into coke—the cocaine was what made him have those violent outbursts; he's better now, for months he's been seeing a psychiatrist who specializes in anger management...And now I'm pregnant."

"How could you be so senseless?"

Natalia glared angrily at her father.

"I plan to take care of my baby and have a good life and a good family. That's my right, my decision, and no one is going to stop me. You can accept it or not, but I won't let you decide what is or is not in my best interest." Natalia would have kept going, but a knot of anguish caught in her throat and she burst into tears.

Miguel listened to her reprimands and sobs unmoved, stupefied.

"If that man comes back into your life, I'll walk out of it. Forever."

"Don't threaten me, Papá. I'm not the girl who'd do anything to keep from disappointing you anymore."

"You have to make a choice, here and now."

Natalia stared at her father in shock. He held her gaze, unyielding. Then she nodded slowly. Her voice had turned cold.

"If you can't accept me living my own life, then . . ."

"Then what?"

"You'll have to go, Papá."

Miguel felt a hand reach through his body and wrench out his insides.

Miguel only managed to fall asleep when the dawn light was filtering in through the blinds. His sleep was deep and restless, full of strange images. He dreamed of the young man he'd seen on the street that day, in the minutes before his attack. He was sitting under an apple tree in bloom. Everything else around was desert, and the sky was black, with low clouds almost touching the treetops. The young man was elegantly dressed, and Miguel, at his side, was a young barefoot boy. The man took his hand and led him to a pool. Leaning over it, Miguel could see his own reflection but not the man's. Then the water turned cloudy, as if something at the bottom were churning it up. It turned bloody, and from underneath it a woman's face emerged. She, too, was young, and her eyes were closed, her mouth full of branches and mud. Miguel recognized her. It was his mother. He called her by her name, and the woman opened her eyes and said something unintelligible.

Miguel awoke gasping. For one long minute he lay there in the dark, staring at the ceiling. He couldn't get the image of his mother, dead and alive at the same time, out of his head. He got up and went to the shelf where Natalia had let him put his mother's ashes and unscrewed the urn carefully. There she was, his mother, turned into a pile of ashes. Miguel reached out and traced a finger through them, writing the name he remembered her smearing onto the walls in her own excrement: Amador. His father's name. The name of the young man he thought he'd seen before fainting in the middle of the street, the same man who'd taken his hand in the dream.

He put the lid back on his mother's urn, ashes still on the tip of his finger. Miguel glanced to the right. A shadow moved in the darkness. It was the young man from his dream, smiling at him as he had the first time.

"Hello, Son."

Miguel shook his head. *This is it: dementia*, he said to himself. His bastard ex-son-in-law was right after all. What would happen now? How was his daughter going to take care of him and a newborn baby at the same time?

He could not let himself become a burden to her, and even though she'd never admit it, he was sure she'd feel relieved when he left.

It was time to go. From now on, he'd have to learn to live with his ghosts.

PART TWO

March 2014

5

Tarifa

Director Roldán pictured the creature in her head as a nervous, insatiable mouse eating away at her brain. A migraine could knock her out for a whole day, and the only thing she could do to keep the pain bearable was lock herself in her office. She'd turn out the light, lower the blinds, drink herbal tea with riboflavin and—most important—not cede to the temptation of lying down, or she'd never be able to get back up. It was also important to banish negative thoughts, though that was not easy. Being in charge of a retirement home brought many concerns. People depended on her, and she was not the kind of woman to shirk her responsibilities. She couldn't let down the shareholders, who'd placed their trust in her when no one else was willing to give her the chance to prove her worth as director. After running the whole show for two decades, the residence had become her life's work.

Director Roldán could occasionally find a little respite using a meditation technique she'd been practicing for a long time. She simply stood before the framed picture of a marina on the wall, contemplating it with a soft gaze, not forcing her mind. Slowly, the effects of the painted waves embraced her and rocked her gently, hypnotizing the mouse. Unlike the actual sea on the other side of the windows, the painting offered the refuge of silence and controlled relaxation. There was no way for a gust of wind or splash of sea-foam to disturb her. There were no seagulls—which she was afraid of, an incomprehensible fear she'd harbored since childhood—and no unpleasant feel of sand between her toes.

Her sense of uneasiness that morning wasn't solely due to her migraine, and she knew it. Roldán glanced at the stack of papers piled up on her desk and felt despondent. She observed the stapler, the calculator, the jar of pens and metal clips, the multiline office phone and flat screen of her computer. Aside from the understated marina on the wall, there was not one plant or memento or photo. Not a single personal detail. Roldán was sixty years old and this was it: emptiness, wasted time, the absence of experiences worth remembering. Not one object of affection. For a moment, she pictured a big country house away from the office, imagined being a wife, mother, grandmother. The phone rang, startling her from her daze, and she felt the rodent skitter from one side of her brain to the other in fear. She squeezed her eyes shut.

Peace, serenity, she murmured. She cast aside the ridiculous image of happiness. Roldán couldn't waste time on impossible fantasies. She rubbed her hands together as if she felt cold, a chill coming from within, and picked up the phone. The anxious voice of the personnel officer was on the other end of the line.

"Director, we need you in the chapel right away. We've got a serious problem with Marqués."

The pipe organ was one of the greatest treasures at the residence. A pneumatic gem dating back to the eighteenth century, it was the sole reason that Professor Marqués had chosen to retire there, depleting what meager savings he had. Marqués felt the need to be near those pipes so as to ensure that the keys and pedals were used properly, but the stupid woman that Director Roldán had put in charge of its care and instrumentation profaned the organ's very soul, day after day. Marqués couldn't take it anymore. The last straw, the one that broke the camel's back, had been an offensive rendition of Bach's Toccata and Fugue in D Minor, BWV 565. It was quite a complicated piece, and yet this ham-handed, flat-footed witch had insisted on mangling it again and again, at no point hitting the low notes and ruining the sharps entirely. And not a single person even so much as noticed during mass. In fact, the parishioners' display of ignorance and indifference was what had most irked Marqués. No one realized what an aberration it was; what's more, he'd actually seen faces looking rapt and heads nodding. Stupidity and negligence together, defiling a work of art. It was too much!

In a fit of rage, like Jesus whipping the bankers to cleanse the temple, Marqués had exploded, shouting and hurling insults in the middle of the service; he'd taken off his belt and gone after the soulless woman. When the others tried to restrain him, things got worse. Marqués writhed in fury, lashing left and right, causing a stampede of not only the churchgoers but the priest himself. Prisoner to his rage, he'd holed up in the chapel, and there was no way to get him out. Sitting at the organ, he stroked the keys as though they were a wounded animal to whom he offered succor. When Director Roldán arrived, he was gripping the belt firmly in his left hand, to keep the guards attempting to trap him at bay. Her desolate glance took in the overturned chairs, books of psalms on the floor, and the altar's toppled candelabra. This had gone too far.

For twenty minutes the director tried to mediate, pressing Marqués to cede, but the professor held firm. He was out of control, blathering that it was all Roldán's fault. Had she listened to him and allowed him to be the one in charge of the organ, none of this would have happened. Was no one aside from him capable of seeing the irreparable damage that the instrument was suffering? Did no one care?

Director Roldán was really beginning to lose her patience. Twice she glanced at the time. She had to go greet the new patient about to arrive. And she could not allow the man's first impression to be this debacle, more befitting an insane asylum than the prestigious residence she was supposed to be running. Finally, pressed for time, Roldán bit the bullet and gave the order she knew would put an end to his ridiculous performance.

"Call Señora Scott. She knows how to handle Marqués."

The metal gate opened as Frank Sinatra was singing the final notes of "Can't We Be Friends?" Natalia pulled into the gravel roundabout and drove up to the marble entrance stairway. Then the music and engine stopped simultaneously, and all that remained was a slow sigh of resignation coming from the passenger seat. Natalia was still angry. Miguel was still angry. They'd had no more than a few monosyllabic exchanges on the drive from Sevilla, and it was a relief to put an end to this situation.

"It looks like a nice place," Natalia said, sounding unconvinced.

Miguel nodded, taking off his seat belt and adjusting his herringbone jacket. For years he and Águeda had summered in Tarifa, but until this moment he had never paid any attention to the neoclassical architecture of this building. He didn't so much as glance at the huge flower-filled ceramic planters lining the marble staircase. His attention went to a group of old men who sat chattering around a summer table, by an artificial lake surrounded by benches. *So this is my future*, he thought.

Miguel preferred to say goodbye right there. After all, they'd already argued over everything they'd had to argue over, and their positions were irreconcilable. It was a cold goodbye, as were Natalia's lips when she pressed them to Miguel's angular face. He never kissed, only offered his cheek. He got out of the car and headed for the marble stairway, not turning when his daughter tooted the horn twice in farewell. Instead he simply gripped the handle of his suitcase more tightly.

A nunlike woman came out to meet him with a smile stitched onto her face; she introduced herself as Director Roldán.

"But everyone calls me Mercedes. Welcome to our home, which is now your home as well."

"I had my things couriered over . . ."

"They've all arrived: your books, clothes, and that lovely trunk. Don't worry. We're very efficient, you'll see."

She had a gratingly shrill voice, like an ambulance siren that makes dogs howl, and she talked too much. Miguel didn't trust people who squandered their words on such pointless blather. He'd have preferred the director simply show him to his room, but the woman insisted on giving a guided tour of the building while singing the praises of the residence. Her words blended with the sound of her low, wide heels as she walked along the long marble-tiled corridor, which bordered a walled garden with a fountain at its center. She was taking short little steps because her narrow skirt, which fell below her knees, prevented her from having a normal stride. Her arms were crossed over her chest, protecting her ample bosom in a blue cardigan. Miguel noticed a run in her stockings, on the right calf. It struck him as a disagreeable detail, the kind of thing he found sad. As they walked, Roldán told him about the illustrious people whose portraits lined the walls—for the most part contrite-looking nuns and priests, waxy-looking mystics and martyrs, their mouths ready to rail against infamy, with pompous habits and long-suffering, judgmental eyes. The paintings were grim, and their baroque frames gave the hall the feel of a museum filled with seventeenth-century sacred art.

"Until the last century this was a convent, then it became a retirement home for nuns—which explains the monastic architecture and look of the place. In the eighties it was remodeled, thanks to a generous donation from a wealthy family; they were religious, so they gave us the resources to convert the space provided we maintained the original features wherever possible and restored the treasured paintings that had been languishing in the basement. Some of those you see now are quite valuable. Are you interested in pictorial art?"

Miguel shook his head without speaking, but Roldán was not deterred.

"Anyhow, they invite tranquility and reflection, don't you think?"

More than tranquility, what the supposed invitation suggested to him were sadness, swishing habits, people huddled together whispering the rosary, and wracking tubercular coughs. Religion had always invoked more fear than faith in Miguel. Still, Director Roldán went on about the architectonic and decorative marvels of the place.

"The fountain dates back to the sixteenth century, and there's a sculpture of Christ by Pedro de Noguera, the architect who did the masonry for the cathedral in Lima. Are you interested in architecture?"

Miguel disappointed the director once more. He was too tired to pretend. All he wanted was to lie down. Director Roldán stopped short, as though she'd just remembered something important.

"If you look to the right, you'll see the chapel, which houses an eighteenth-century *realejo* organ. Unfortunately, something has come up and I can't show it to you at the moment, but I'm sure you'll have a chance to admire it tomorrow. The chapel is open every day. Are you interested in sacral music?"

Miguel shrugged. Director Roldán gave him a sidelong glance. "To live here, is it required that I have particular interests? That wasn't mentioned on the website."

Roldán made a show of apologizing profusely, and Miguel shook his head.

"I'm interested in numbers, logic, mathematics. I am— or was—a banker. I also value silence and discretion."

"I didn't mean to upset you."

"Nor have you. I'm just a bit tired. Could you show me to my room, please?"

Vexed, Roldán resumed her tiny steps without opening her mouth again, for which Miguel was thankful. They skirted the common areas without stopping and went up to the second floor, where she handed Miguel a key with a self-assured air.

"You'll find that we integrate the best of two worlds: tradition and all modern conveniences. Central heating for the winter, air-conditioning for the summer, wireless internet connection, cable TV..." She couldn't help but shoot him a mocking glance. "We take care of the tangibles as well; I trust that will reassure you."

"It does, most certainly."

Miguel opened the door and made a quick mental calculation of the space, like a prisoner seeing his cell for the first time. On the virtual tour he'd done, the rooms looked bigger and more comfortable. There was a single nightstand—the unmistakable sign of those who sleep alone—with a reading light, a dresser with three or four drawers, an 18-inch television and a double-sided wardrobe. All very spartan. No pointless decor. *At least there are no Inquisitorial torture devices or hair shirts*, he thought. Miguel's mood lifted on seeing his trunk.

A guard appeared, whispering to Director Roldán from the door. Despite the guard's attempt at hushed tones, Miguel managed to overhear what he said: "Helena has caged the beast." Roldán closed her eyes and nodded. Miguel couldn't tell if the sigh she let out was one of relief or exhaustion. The director glanced anxiously into the room.

"I'll let you settle in. There's a matter I need to attend to."

Miguel was thankful for the solitude. He spent the first few minutes pacing his new room, trying to come to terms with it. He opened the curtain and was greeted with an ocean view, just as he'd requested. There was a small balcony with a wooden table and two chairs, and from the railing he could make out the roof tiles of the city's old quarter, the castle's flags being whipped in the east winds, and beyond that, the coast of Africa.

He opened his suitcase and took out the urn with his mother's ashes, looked around for the ideal place to put it, and settled on the shelf above the television. He stepped back, sat on the bed—whose mattress springs creaked—and contemplated his new life with a vague sense of failure. It was so much colder and more desolate than he'd imagined. Miguel wondered how many people had slept in this strange bed, how many had died seeing the view out this window. That thought added to the gloomy feeling he'd been unable to shake since arguing with Natalia.

"Not very luxurious, is it?" he heard behind him.

The spirit of the room altered, growing darker, as if all the light were sucked up by the place the voice emerged from.

Miguel turned. It was the young man. He examined the room with a circumspect air, opening dresser drawers and wardrobe doors, running a finger along the bone-colored shelves on the wall. Tall and strong, he wore a modest yet elegant suit typical of country folks who wear the same clothes to weddings and funerals alike.

"Why are you looking at me that way?" the man asked Miguel.

Miguel didn't know if the dead were ghosts, spirits, souls, or penitents. For the time being, the young man was unable to clarify the terms of his nature.

"I don't know if you're real or simply evidence of the fact that I'm losing my mind."

The young man pulled a cotton handkerchief from his jacket pocket, brought it to his mouth before coughing—a horrible, hacking cough that belied his healthy appearance—and spat out a dark clump of blood. One strand stuck to his chin, and he wiped it off with a resigned expression. Looking closely, Miguel could tell he was hardly more than a teenager, with shiny cheeks and a sparkle in his eye. Miguel pictured him as a normal fellow who played sports in outdated gyms, went out with girls, and was carefree; a charming, handsome young man who glanced at his reflection in shop windows.

"You're a rational man who believes in nothing that can't be proven, so you need a logical explanation for my presence, and I'm sure you'll find it eventually." The ghost, or whatever he was, focused his attention on the trunk, crouched to examine its contents without touching anything, and then looked up at the urn on the shelf.

Miguel took off his glasses and began tapping the arm against his palm. Perhaps this was a vision that had slipped in through a crack in his brain by using one of those spots his disease caused, spots that were like deserts expanding across his gray matter. Deserts are full of mirages so real they can cause even the most experienced guides to lose their minds, go off course, walk into dunes that swallow them up forever.

"You're not really here. My mind has begun to betray me, that's what's happening."

The young man frowned.

"As you wish. I haven't come to discuss the nature of my being."

"I thought I recognized you when I had my first attack. But I wasn't certain until I had that dream, at my daughter's house." Miguel drew his attention to the urn. "And then I remembered the name my mother used to write on the wall in feces: Amador."

Amador—if ghosts can be summoned by their names—stared down at the tip of his shoes. They had no laces.

"And where does that get us, Miguel?"

"If you're Amador, you're my father, but I'm sixty-five years old and you look under thirty."

"The dead remain at the age we remember them. A strange paradox."

The young man went to the window and looked out at the view. Miguel went and stood to his right, also looking out. He could almost feel the sweat coming through Amador's clothes, almost smell the loose tobacco on his fingers. Everything in his being fought the possibility of this mirage existing, yet he couldn't escape its attraction.

"My mother used to talk to me about you. She said there was a Raquel Meller song you used to sing to her, she liked that."

Amador nodded nostalgically.

"'La violetera,'" he said. "Our first dance was to that song, at an open-air dance. Did she ever sing it to you?"

Miguel shook his head slowly.

"Only to the strangers she brought to bed, men who left behind a vile air and a few coins."

"I see."

"No. You can't possibly see because you weren't there. You left us. She always told me you were a good man, that you did what you did for us, for me. But I never believed her."

Amador examined him carefully. He didn't know how to speak to his son about a time and man he'd never really met.

"And now, Miguel? What do you think now?"

Throughout his childhood, all the way until his mother died, Miguel had been jealous of a ghost. Miguel became the man of the house, having to be one from a very young age, but his father's shadow was always there hovering, a presence that would neither come nor go. The presence of an absence. How could he compete with that?

"Now I think I'll just close my eyes, and you won't be here when I open them up again."

"That's how it was before. Too often. When you were a boy and you'd call me. You couldn't see me, but I was there. With you. It's not much consolation, I know. But it's the truth. I was always by your side."

Miguel looked out, contemplative, as night fell, layering different shades of darkness that made it impossible to see the lights in the distance.

"Does it hurt?" he asked.

His father looked at him out of the corner of his eye.

"Does what hurt?"

"Being dead."

Amador let himself be carried off by the sight of a fisherman slowly crossing the strait, a flock of seagulls trailing behind.

"Only when you think about the living."

6

Tarifa

Walking down the long corridor on her way to Director Roldán's office, Helena thought of something Louise used to say: "The shortest distance between two points is a straight line." It wasn't a particularly original thing to say, and might not even be true in every circumstance, but Louise could make even self-evident truths take on a hint of mystery. She knew how to cultivate the darker side of her personality. Helena could still recall the first impression she got on meeting her, the day she arrived at the boarding school in Mayfield, in the winter of 1956. Louise was lying on the bed in her underwear—lace panties that Helena immediately envied—and smoking as she read Conrad's *Heart of Darkness*. Girls usually want to be the same as other girls their age, but Louise was different: she wanted to be different and to flaunt her difference. Nobody smoked at fifteen, or read Conrad, or Henry Miller, or Céline. But Louise did. Nobody gazed out so shamelessly from under a bold stripe of cobalt eye shadow, or challenged norms and discipline as skillfully as Louise. She was only three years older than Helena, but it may as well have been fifteen. Louise educated Helena, in a grave tone, to stress the impact of her words: "Wise up, we are prisoners here. We're in a dungeon, and Miss Clark is senior warden—you'll meet her soon enough. Our job is to find as much pleasure in our captivity as possible, and to drive the old bat as crazy as we can. And I know how to do it. Just watch." Louise seemed to forever be on the verge of revealing some amazing secret; it was as if she discovered things before anyone else. Compared to Louise—sophisticated, with exactly the right comment always at the ready, and a defiant, self-confident air—Helena had felt like a little prude, an untamed shrew who knew nothing of life. Now, she had the feeling she'd jumped from childhood to old age without taking in the seasons in between.

Helena guessed why the director had asked to see her. The two women had taken an instant dislike to one another when they first met; something about the director made Helena think of Miss Clark playing the role of the mystic poet Saint Teresa of Ávila—always *dying because she did not die*—on bended knee with her transcendent dreams. Poor Miss Clark! How they mocked her, she and Louise, for the way she railed against the secret pleasures that the pair of them had discovered. Louise was ferociously voluptuous, and her eroticism drove Miss Clark to despair. She saw everything about Louise as sinful and vile. Helena wondered if the old woman, who'd hated all manner of spontaneity and impertinence, was not somehow distantly related to Director Roldán. They were like Siamese twins: same overripe grapefruit face, same languid manner of an animal in a permanent state of hibernation.

She knocked on the door and heard Roldán's shrill voice inviting her to come in.

The office was soulless and damp. Sometimes it gave off a bilgewater smell, like a ship, perhaps due to the ugly marina painting that hung on the wall. Roldán was on the phone; she motioned to Helena to take a seat at the desk but didn't hang up; she kept talking and massaged her forehead as though the call were bringing on a headache. When she finally put down the receiver, Roldán looked exhausted.

"Thank you for coming, Señora Scott. What we need to discuss is not pleasant."

Helena sucked in her lower lip. Roldán insisted on addressing her by her married name despite knowing Helena hated it. Or perhaps *because* she knew. *The little witch thinks she can hurt me,* Helena thought.

"What is it?"

The director weighed her words carefully, forming a triangle under her chin with her hands, joining her fingers and, finally, came up with a way to say it.

"The little number your friend Marqués pulled in the chapel a few days ago went too far. I think it would be fair to say that we've been very patient with him. I put my trust in you to keep him in check, because you're the only one he listens to, but clearly we both failed."

Helena tried to hide her smile thinking of the shrieking nurses, the flushed and indignant priest, and the organist flapping about hysterically. It was true, the professor had done a real number.

"Marqués won't listen to anybody, and I am not his mother, I'm his friend." Her derisive tone was evident, as was the director's growing discomfort.

"Do you find this amusing, Señora Scott?"

"What I find amusing is that you insist on calling me by my husband's name. I'm a widow and my maiden names are Pizarro Whitman. Helena Pizarro Whitman—it's not that hard if you think about it. And now that you mention it, another thing that amuses me is that you insist on running this home like a boarding school for teens. We might be old, but we do have the good sense and disposition to make our own decisions, can't you see that? I believe the term is 'legal age.'"

Director Roldán went to say something but thought better of it and stood. She contemplated the marina on the wall. The damn rat was running riot inside her head, gnawing away at her ocular nerve. This was her home, she was happy here and had everything she needed. She was not about to allow anyone to undermine her authority. Especially not a woman she detested, so attractive and worldly, with a life full of travel, people, and experiences. It was hard to admit that Helena intimidated her; the idea made her seethe.

"I understand that you don't like my way of doing things. But communal living is governed by norms."

"And do the norms prohibit eccentricity? Must we all reject everything we were before entering these gates?"

"There are seventy-two people paying quite a tidy sum to live here in peace and comfort. They have no reason to stand for the eccentricities of one misfit."

"Marqués is a good person. A bit excessive, like all geniuses, but harmless."

"Harmless?" Director Roldán snatched a piece of paper from her desk and showed it to Helena. "This is the medical report for the people who suffered from your friend's attack. One suture, multiple contusions, blows... not to mention the panic he created. And there could have been far more serious consequences."

Helena shook her head slowly and raised her palms.

"I told you, I am not Marqués's mother. Speak to him yourself if you want."

"I've tried, but he refuses to come out of his room."

Helena pictured her friend holed up in there, engrossed in composing, his fingers moving intricately across an imaginary keyboard.

"I don't see what I can do."

"You have to understand the situation: I run a private institution and report to the shareholders. You know our home has very few spots, and they're in high demand. We have a long waiting list, and I don't see how I can justify Marqués occupying one of our valuable rooms when he doesn't meet his contractual obligations. Honestly, I think he'd be better off in a different type of institution."

"A different institution?"

A rash conclusion played at the corners of Roldán's lips.

"I think your friend needs a psychiatric evaluation. Given that he has no family or anyone else who can make decisions on his behalf, and in view of the fact that Marqués himself does not appear to be in possession of his faculties, it's been recommended that he be transferred to the hospital in Málaga so they can assess having him admitted someplace more suited to his needs. I was hoping you'd help me convince him."

Helena leaned back in her chair and raised her chin.

"You want me to convince Marqués to agree to voluntary admission to a psychiatric center. Is that what you're asking me?"

The director circled the desk but did not sit down. Helena sensed something uncertain in her expression. She couldn't tell if Roldán was relishing this or suffering through it. Most likely the spiteful side of her was enjoying it, and the would-be saint part was racked by guilt.

"I'm just informing you of the board's decision. Believe me, there's nothing I can do about it."

Helena stood slowly. Inside she was trembling but refused to let Roldán see her flag.

"Pontius Pilate said something similar."

"Listen, Señora Scott, believe me, I—"

"My name is Helena, damn it! And you most certainly cannot count on me. If you want to put Marqués in a straitjacket, you'll have to go and do it yourself."

"There's no need to be dramatic."

Helena shot daggers at the director.

"There's a fine line between dramatic and pathetic, and I think you crossed it a long time ago."

She turned and left, making sure not to slam the door on her way out.

Time can become a matter of finding ways to squander the hours. Miguel began to see this after a few days at the home. To avoid it, the secret was to conceal your tedium by paying undue attention to tiny details. He observed his new neighbors: some became engrossed in games of chess, read books, or strolled through the gardens; others chatted in small groups, told jokes, argued over the TV news, or languished on sofas staring at the bougainvillea while awaiting a family visit—and then hiding their disappointment when nobody came.

Miguel was now one of them, so everyone tried to make conversation with him: they asked about his life before the home, as though tacitly recognizing that once you walked through the residence doors, the past was all that mattered. The first few days, people turned to look whenever he entered a room, and he gave a fake smile, like a boy at his first day of school. Everybody took note of each of his gestures. There was something perverse about it, the gossip of the day. New arrivals aroused interest, altered the residents' mind-numbing routines, brought in fresh air, things from the world outside—although generally this interest was short-lived. After all, everybody was there for the same reason: they were alone, or may as well have been, and had arrived full of memories, ailments, and quirks that all turned out to be very similar. Soon people had gotten used to Miguel's presence and no longer paid such close attention.

He could now walk into the dining room at breakfast without feeling dozens of eyes boring into him. That morning, the smell of toast and fresh coffee floated over tables covered in embroidered tablecloths. There was a continental buffet: Spanish tortilla, cold cuts, fruit, yogurt, juice. Off to the side were the pastries, reserved for the privileged few who'd obtained a doctor's consent. Classical music was piped in, which helped lull conversations and turn them into murmurs. You could say it was a pleasant environment, conceived to muffle inopportune sounds—someone laughing too loud, a fork clattering against a plate, or a glass falling to the carpeted floor.

Miguel took a seat at a corner table and was preparing to hide behind a book on economic theory he'd found in the library when he and Helena crossed glances. They greeted one another cordially. Miguel barely knew the woman, but had heard things about her and her friend Marqués, the extravagant music professor everyone was talking about due to the chapel incident on the day Miguel arrived. As far as he could see, Marqués was some kind of urban legend who never showed his face. As for Helena, her enigmatic air had caught his attention from the start; she had a sort of effortless presence, a lofty, aristocratic bearing. Though she may have been as eager to learn about Miguel as all the rest, she hadn't tried to wheedle details out of him in the standard, invasive way—to fuel gossip—and instead showed a touch of eccentric curiosity.

That morning, as was her custom, Helena was dressed stylishly, confident in herself and her body.

"Do you mind if I join you?" she asked, in fact already taking a seat. She gave off a slight aroma of cigarettes and perfume, a strangely agreeable mix.

"Please, make yourself comfortable," Miguel said sarcastically; Helena, who was pouring herself coffee, paid no attention.

"How's your new life in limbo?" she asked absently. She seemed to have her mind on many things at once, none of them concrete.

"Limbo?"

Helena stared straight at him for a couple of seconds, and then her lips formed a half smile. It seemed clear that she was enjoying Miguel's bewilderment.

"Yes, limbo. The world separating the living from the dead. That's exactly what this place is, in case you hadn't noticed, despite being called 'paradise.' It's a waiting room."

"I see. In that case, I'd say that my wait is going well, thank you."

"Are you serious? Honestly, with your impeccable suit, Bismarck mustache, and plastic frames, you don't look like this is your kind of place. My grandfather would have said you're the kind of gentleman who deserves to see the Isle of Wight one last time, surrounded by chubby grandchildren. And my grandmother would have agreed."

"I'm sorry to disappoint your grandparents' expectations, but I've never been to said island nor do I understand the reference."

Helena wiped a crumb from the corner of her mouth with her index finger and then popped it into her mouth.

"Limbo has its advantages; it would be inconsiderate to refuse them. And you don't look like an inconsiderate person. Didn't Director Roldán sell you on the marvels of this place? They promise immortality: thalassotherapy, hot stone massage, aqua fitness classes, rejuvenating dinners and soirees... Of course, it's all a lie. But we like to believe we'll live to be a thousand. Do you think we'll live to be a thousand, Miguel?"

"I'd say that mathematics and statistical probability are not in our favor."

"A man of science—imagine! Who can resist that?"

Miguel got the feeling he was being subjected to some sort of test, but couldn't fathom its purpose.

"I'm honestly not very comfortable with cynicism. You're unnerving me, do you know that?"

Helena blinked and looked away.

"I'd be careful not to mistake irony for cynicism. But if I've made you uncomfortable, I apologize. I'm a bit out of sorts lately."

"Your friend Marqués?"

Helena nodded sorrowfully.

"Marqués is harmless, an old man with arthritis so bad it makes him walk bowlegged, and lungs and liver in an advanced state of decomposition. It's true that his physical ailment has soured his character, but he's not a threat to anyone."

"That's not what they're saying around here."

"He's just trying to defend himself the only way he knows how. If you spoke to him, you'd see he's got a delectable sense of humor; he's sharp, sarcastic, and intelligent—even if he can sometimes be over-the-top and eccentric. But that's just because Marqués doesn't see the world the way we do: he finds subtle nuances in everything, all that surrounds us, and he won't settle for things as they appear to be. So at times his impatience gets the best of him. And then he feels the need to rebel, to scream and shout in his own way. When he oversteps he might seem dangerous, but nobody wants to admit that the real tragedy is that Marqués and the blues fell in love the moment they met."

Miguel removed his glasses and cleaned the lenses with a napkin.

"That's very poetic. But I heard he physically attacked people attending mass. I don't think it's appropriate that others pay for his inability to understand the world."

Helena shook her head emphatically.

"You don't get it. It's not an inability to understand that makes him behave that way, it's the opposite: absolute un-derstanding. He sees the ugliness, the hypocrisy, the ab-surdity all around . . . and the loneliness. Marqués is afraid; he's very sick and knows his time is almost up. He wants to make the most of every second and feels like others are stealing away the beauty, the harmony. Director Roldán says

Marqués doesn't behave logically, but not everyone operates by the same logic, don't you think? He's only interested in what's exciting. And what's the matter with that?"

Miguel adjusted his glasses and stroked his mustache, frowning. He was attempting to grasp Helena's reasoning but couldn't come to terms with her justifications.

"I'm not interested in what's exciting. I'm interested in numbers. Numbers are the logic of the apparent. Numbers are impartial. The fruit of evidence. They present the facts dispassionately. And the facts say that your friend is unhinged."

Helena shook her head again and looked at Miguel like he was a callow child.

"Have you ever cried tears of joy over a tax balance sheet?"

Miguel admitted that he had not. The last time he could recall having been excited at work was when he discovered that a few bank executives were embezzling from the company. He had spent months comparing data and searching for accounting errors until he uncovered their trick. Nobody thanked him for it. The thieves were fired, and he considered it logical to carry on working as though nothing had happened. Rules are rules, and no one should get a prize for following them.

Helena grew exasperated.

"You do have a heart, don't you? Well, your heart should get excited, feel surprise, leap for joy. And that's what happens when you don't know what's coming next. Aren't you afraid of the unknown? Not every circumstance has a rule."

Miguel expressed what he felt was obvious.

"What's wrong with wanting to have everything under control? Leaving everything to the tyranny of impulse is insane."

Helena looked about ready to throw in the towel.

"Are you always so meticulous? Would you never make a decision without calculating the risk first?"

"Why would I do such a thing?"

"To find out who you really are."

"I know exactly who I am, thank you very much."

"Sure, as long as you're in control of the game. Have you never colored outside the lines? It's very healthy, I assure you, and you find out things about yourself that you didn't expect."

Miguel had only once broken his rule of not yielding to temptation. It was in 1980, the weekend he met Carmen. And he wasn't sure that it had been a good decision.

"Maybe discovering the unexpected means seeing a side of yourself that you don't like, one that should stay buried forever."

"Why would that be? Denying your true self doesn't make it go away."

Miguel finished his coffee, determined to end this conversation. He stood and straightened his jacket.

"Because it leads you and others to suffer needlessly. And now, I must leave you. I've got things to do."

Helena opened her eyes dramatically. They were rather beautiful, large and sparkling with intelligence.

"Things to do...interesting. A purpose to your days. Well, we wouldn't want those pressing affairs to go unattended, would we? Good day, Mister Busy."

They looked at each other for a moment, she seated with the cup in her fingers, and he standing, not knowing what to do with his hands. Finally, Miguel simply headed for the exit.

"Wait," Helena called. Miguel turned. She pointed to his feet. He looked down at his shoes: he'd forgotten to tie his laces. Miguel had never forgotten something like that. He felt naked and exposed to everyone's judgmental eyes. But no one paid any attention.

Conversations like that were repeated over the following weeks. Helena and Miguel were unalike to the core, and yet, against all odds, felt comfortable together and sought each other out. They grew closer effortlessly, like an object and its reflection, discovering that they fit strangely well, complemented each other in the same way light requires dark in order to make sense. Little by little, slowly and smoothly, they grew accustomed to one another's presence in the home's common areas. Soon they found a sort of complicity not based on the excessive sharing of private details but on discussions that nearly always trailed off unfinished. Miguel was amused by Helena's irreverence, her constant insulting of the director, her quick tongue—always sharp, ready to scandalize—and he found her wit stimulating. Every time he was with her and listened to her talk, he tried to determine how much of what she said was true and how much she hid behind her foulmouthed sarcasm.

For her part, Helena assumed that Miguel was fairly boring but also possessed a certain mystery, a rich inner life that he refused to share and that she was determined to unearth. Helena had been inspired by secrets ever since she was a child, and she suspected that Miguel was full of unsatisfied desires never openly expressed. She baited him constantly, but Miguel was a slippery fish. He almost never talked about himself, and when he did it was in a cryptic manner that only piqued Helena's curiosity. His smile was tinged with sadness, his eyes looked out from behind tortoiseshell glasses as though his true self were hiding deep within, and she found an incentive to keep digging.

One morning, Helena suggested they go for a walk around the Roman ruins of Baelo Claudia. It was late, and the red-clay sun cast its rays down on the coast. The rushing waves, thick and cold, made the earth's energy seem to bubble. As soon as they stepped onto the beach, Miguel crouched down and took a fistful of fine sand and let it slip through his fingers, the wind carrying off its grains. Above them, a bird bobbed and swayed in the currents of air. Miguel studied it carefully. The bird looked as if it were about to fall, but then it suddenly soared skyward and flew off. Miguel followed it with his eyes until he lost sight of it over the waves.

"It's always amazed me that things that weigh more than air can fly. Perfect aerodynamics make the impossible possible. I'm afraid of heights, and of flying. And yet I've always been fascinated by it."

Helena followed the direction of her friend's gaze. *Finally, something personal*, she thought.

"We're attracted to what frightens us. Fear is a challenge."

Miguel didn't seem to hear her. He wondered what kind of bird it had been, the one flying off, and without realizing it found himself thinking of his daughter Natalia.

"I used to come here with my wife and daughter every summer. There was an open-air café run by an old Basque couple—just a little prefab place with a metal roof and wooden deck, but they had wonderful fried whitebait. I remember Natalia used to ask me all sorts of questions. There were so many things she didn't know! And she was interested in them all: the names of things, numbers, letters, and places. All the hidden corners of the planet, rivers, mountains, towns and their people, their histories, their way of thinking. She'd point to birds and ask me what their names were, because to her anything that could possibly have a name should have its *own* name, something unique. To get her to stop asking, I'd give them crazy names: 'That blue one with the long beak is called Blue Incantation, the white one diving into the waves is called Arrow of Light.'" He fell silent. *This is what an old man's memories come down to: inventions and ruins.* "I don't know when she stopped asking, when I stopped making up names for her."

Helena stood beside him but was looking much farther off. *The distance between two points.*

"I was here once too. In 1982. With my friend Louise. It was a special trip. I don't remember the beach café you're talking about, but at least the dunes and ruins are still here." Helena recalled Louise jumping in the waves, water up to her knees, rolling her skirt up and tucking it into her underwear. She remembered her laugh. It was incredible, how young they were, even though they weren't, and what they expected from happiness when they should have learned to accept disillusionment.

She took Miguel's arm and patted his shoulder affectionately.

"There's nothing wrong with remembering. It means we lived."

They turned to the childish ruckus being made by a group of retirees at the information kiosk. Miguel found old people's excitement disagreeable—their brightly colored caps, cameras at the ready. Helena, by contrast, smiled affectionately at the scene. Old age was forever in debt to childhood.

In a weary voice, the guide leading the group repeated the same spiel he must have given thousands of times, pointing like a flight attendant to the sites of ancient buildings. He didn't seem to mind that the old folks were more interested in the proximity of the tantalizing blue sea and fine sand dunes than the ruins. Pointlessly, he explained that a pile of dark rocks was the remains of thermal baths two thousand years old, that the paved walkway was the *decumanus*—the east–west road—and that beyond that lay the temples of Minerva and of Juno, the capitol, tribunal, fountain, and basilica.

The group moved off, buzzing toward the *cardus maximus*, the main north–south road. Miguel and Helena walked in the opposite direction, to a rock that had once been the pillar of a solid construction, perhaps a fisherman's house or a storehouse, a place where there had once been life and activity, smells and sounds carried by the sea.

"People didn't used to care about things so much," Miguel noted, a bit removed, since his reminiscing had led him to his argument with Natalia and then to their estrangement. It seemed definitive, although there was nothing he wanted less.

"You gripe and grumble like an old man, I assume you realize that."

"I'm being serious. Fifty years ago, when I was here with Águeda for the first time, nobody was interested in the ruins because they'd always been here. The temples were a pile of rubble covered in weeds; there was no information kiosk, no palm trees or gardens. There were barges on the beach. In a way, it was all more real, less reconstructed. More beautiful."

"What about you and Águeda? What were you like fifty years ago?"

"The same, but younger."

He was lying. They, too, had been more genuine, a young married couple strolling among the dunes, holding hands. In love, still unscathed, open to anything. Each believing that their own happiness depended on the other. And yet his memory of Águeda was fading. Miguel was ashamed to admit that two years after her death he hardly remembered the sound of her voice or the color of her eyes. With effort, he could conjure her image, but when he tried to recall details it all fell apart. What had her hands been like? Cold, he remembered they were always cold, but were they large or small? And which pinkie had been mangled by arthritis, the left or right? He knew her feet had high arches and that her toes were all smashed together, but what was her shoe size?

Helena tilted her head. She looked beautiful like that, her hair pulled back at the neck, the sun illuminating half of her pensive face.

"What about you?" Miguel asked. "What remains of the Helena that was here in 1982 with her friend Louise?"

Helena tucked a stray, windswept lock of hair behind her ear.

"Not much. I actually don't understand the urge to re-create what no longer exists." And, as though attempting to reinforce her point, she spread her arms wide, taking in the entire site of the ruins. "Look at all this. Who says it was ever actually the way it's been made out to be in this reconstruction?"

"Historians, archeologists..."

"And why are those old folks here? I mean, why do people like walking in the footsteps of the past?"

Miguel shrugged.

"They're interested in history, in our common past."

Helena shook her head.

"Those are programmed responses, straight out of your *Life in Order* handbook, Miguel. The first thing you thought of when you stepped onto the beach was your daughter as a little girl. Personally, I think the past is a vanishing point. A place you escape to when you don't want to be here. Everyone always wants to be someplace else, don't you think?"

Miguel felt unsettled, unsure of what to say or how to act; this was something he'd noticed with Helena and it made him feel powerless, just as he had when he was unable to satisfy Natalia's boundless curiosity.

"Not everyone has the urge to flee the present."

Helena lit a cigarette. She exhaled a puff of smoke that vanished instantly, and then she looked away, off toward the sea. Tangier. So far. So near.

"Wise up, we're always running away. The difference, the thing that makes us old, is that *we* run backward and young people run forward."

"So, what are you running from?"

"Distance."

"Distance?"

Helena lifted her chin to the sky.

"Louise used to say the shortest distance between two points is a straight line. But what about the distance that separates us from our dreams? What about the inexplicable fantastic elements that inspire us, the things we let get away, through stupidity or fear?"

"Fantastic elements? Do you not find being here, now, fantastic?"

"I'm talking about things that aren't plain to see, things that are impossible. There's an element of magic hidden in everything. Like you, being afraid to fly yet longing to understand the dynamics of flight. Must we resign ourselves to being who we are, just like that? Deny all of the other people we could be?"

Miguel squinted, a bouquet of wrinkles blooming on either side of his face.

"I'm not sure I understand you."

Helena inhaled deeply and tilted her head back. She smiled and put on a normal expression.

"Then I suppose I can't explain it to you. Something inside of you is atrophied, and I'm not sure I can get through it. This is all Greek to you, isn't it?"

Miguel felt as though Helena had just slapped him and didn't know why.

"Have I said something to offend you?"

"No. Not in the slightest. Some people are made of air and others of earth, that's all. And I suppose they can't understand one another."

They returned to the bus in silence. There was no reason to be angry, they hadn't fought, but it was clear that despite their attempts at goodwill they felt like two strangers who'd randomly chosen each other's company, and it had been a bad fit.

Miguel felt compelled to try to repair the damage, despite not understanding how it had occurred. He felt Helena was slipping from his hands and, for some reason was not willing to let that happen.

"A few days ago, you asked me if I'd ever drawn outside the lines."

"What's bringing this on?"

Miguel cleared his throat. He'd never spoken about this to a stranger.

"I did, once. It was in 1980. I met someone. I was married, and my daughter was eight. I never saw the woman again, but I've never forgotten her."

Helena looked at him in curiosity.

"What was she like?"

"Attractive, intelligent. Free, in her own way. Freer and braver than I was. She had a mole above her top lip. A little dot halfway between her mouth and nose, and her beauty radiated from there. It was impossible not to focus on that tiny exclamation point."

Miguel smiled nostalgically. Lost in Carmen's mole, it was impossible not to notice the sensuous shape of her lips, her subtle lipstick, the way her small teeth crowded together, her pink gums, and the way the tip of her tongue poked out each time she puffed on her cigarette. It was unusual to come across a woman like her in a world reserved for men. She spoke perfect English, and the experiences she'd had in New York, Paris, and London came across in her manner. Her dark eyes squinted slightly when she looked around, never posing or putting on the phony confidence and brusqueness so typical of the bank's other board members. They respected her, she knew this, and it showed. She never hid who she was for a second.

"What was so special about her?" Helena asked, her interest suddenly piqued.

Miguel cocked his head.

"The fact that she chose me."

Why a woman like Carmen had so much as even noticed a man like Miguel was still a mystery. Maybe the night they met at the welcome cocktail party she'd felt pity for him, a man so clearly lost and uncomfortable among the sharks and directors. Maybe it was the dark-framed glasses that gave him a forsaken air, or his unfashionable suit, or his Prussian mustache. Miguel had simply smiled gravely and twisted his wedding ring as though imploring his absent wife to bail him out. Carmen approached. And that night, the world opened itself up in a very unexpected way for Miguel.

Helena gazed at the coastline through the bus window as they drove along. She closed her eyes for a moment, and on opening them, felt the proximity of Miguel's shoulder beside her. A comforting warmth.

"Thank you for telling me something about yourself, something real."

Miguel nodded, slightly discomfited. They spent a few minutes in a silence that was no longer as thick, a silence that trickled and flowed. Helena continued staring out the window, focused on the approaching dusk, but her right hand sought out Miguel's forearm. In the distance, the coast of Africa.

"My mother died when I was young. She committed suicide, and she tried to take me with her. She tried to drown me. Ever since then, I've been afraid of the sea."

Miguel stared at her, eyes wide open.

"I'm so sorry. That must have been terrible."

Helena shook her head.

"Nothing to be sorry about now. It happened a long time ago."

Another silence fell. Miguel had the feeling that he should say something, offer some a posteriori consolation, but when he thought about it, realized that it would be out of place. The only thing he could think to do was squeeze Helena's hand.

"What about your father?"

"He abandoned us when I was eleven. My father was a Francoist officer stationed in Tangier... Why are you making that face?"

Miguel thought of Amador, hiding in some corner of his brain. Waiting to make his next appearance.

"My father fought on the Republican side. He died a prisoner, doing forced labor in Franco's Valley of the Fallen. My mother collected newspaper clippings, anything she could find that might contain any news of him, but I can hardly remember him..."

Only half-joking, Helena asked if this was going to be an obstacle to their friendship. Miguel shook his head. The Spanish Civil War, its sides, meant nothing to him.

"That must have been hard, to find yourself alone at age eleven," he said.

"My maternal grandparents took me to England. I spent my adolescence at an elite all-girls' boarding school, and my friend Louise was the only thing that got me through those dreary years of rules and routines. We spent our time giving the headmistress, Miss Clark, reasons to expel us, but she never did. After graduation, Louise moved to California to pursue her dream of becoming an actress. And I met Walter."

"Your husband."

"My husband. He wasn't the marvel I'd dreamed of, or even someone who met the expectations of the young lady I was at the time; I expected everything from love: passion, desire, adventure—an erupting volcano whose lava would always flow, never harden. And Walter was the opposite of all that: calm, distant, conscientious. He was a law professor at Cambridge who'd spent his whole life doing exactly the same things day after day, a man who saw happiness as virtually the same as comfort. Sound familiar?" Helena added maliciously. Miguel didn't know how to respond, and she stroked his arm. "But he was a good man with a sweet demeanor and beautiful hands. He loved me, in his way, and promised to learn to love me the way I needed. So even though he was fifteen years older I agreed to marry him. I'd just turned twenty and was already closing the curtain on my life."

"You don't strike me as the kind of woman to settle for less than she wants."

Helena gave Miguel a surprised look.

"And what makes you think I settled? I got exactly what I wanted."

Helena dug a photo out of her handbag.

"I got my son . . . David."

Miguel examined the photo and saw a typical-looking eighties London teen: very blond disheveled hair, fleshy lips, on the pale side, and a well-practiced tough look to match his trench coat and knee-high Doc Martens tucked into dark jeans.

"I can see the resemblance."

"The one he really resembles is my mother, and not just physically. David was into art from the time he was a little boy, like it was a gene he inherited. He was a talented painter, like my mother, though she preferred the classicism of Delacroix, and David was more attracted to Hopper and Bacon. He also inherited my mother's extreme sensitivity and tragic outlook."

Miguel handed back the photo. Helena gazed at it melancholically before putting it away.

"You married a good man, had a talented son," said Miguel. "Anyone would call that a full life."

Helena half closed her eyes.

"You could say I had it all. I was a wife and mother, had a good job, a nice house...But some people never really have it all, like my friend Marqués. My father was the same, never satisfied. And I'm like him. I always wanted more, demanded and expected more. Just like him, or Marqués, I thought I deserved what nobody could give me. But one day, suddenly, it all comes to an end. Your life grinds to a halt amid unfinished expectations. And it never goes anywhere else, forward or back. And here I am, unburdening myself to a near stranger lacking in imagination."

Miguel clenched his jaw.

"I'm sorry to be your consolation prize."

Helena objected impatiently.

"Don't be a child. What I'm saying is that my life derailed over thirty years ago, and from that time on, my days became a voluntary confinement with a sick man I no longer loved. I spent my time seeking refuge in old photo albums of my son, listening to the records that Louise used to like, rereading the postcards my father sent from all over the world on my birthdays. When Walter died four years ago, I decided to return to Tarifa, because this is the place where I began to lose it all. I thought I'd find answers, find the straight line Louise talked about that would tie it all together. But here I am telling you these things simply because we're resigned to this being our last stop. Look at us, Miguel: Are we the result of failure?"

Miguel adamantly refused to admit any such possibility.

"We lived our lives as best we knew how, and we've got our children."

Helena took some time to respond. Deep in her expression, Miguel intuited flashes of the past: a young mother searching for mutual understanding with a complicated teen, trying to maintain the difficult balance between what she knows about life and what children must be allowed to discover for themselves.

"What happened thirty years ago, Helena? What was it that stopped your life short?"

"Enough secrets for today," she said apathetically.

The tour bus was pulling up outside the residence.

As soon as they walked into the lobby, Helena knew something had occurred. The slight well-being she'd felt after her chat with Miguel vanished the moment she saw Director Roldán speaking to two nurses, men who were not on staff at the home.

"Did something happen?" Helena asked, instantly on the alert.

The director finished signing some papers and handed them back to the nurses.

"Nothing that didn't need to. We've just moved Marqués to the hospital in Málaga, as I told you we would. The judge authorized an involuntary transfer."

7

Malmö

Raquel had spent most of the morning locked away in the kitchen at Old Sweden, cooking up a lavish feast to treat the newcomer, just the way Sture had requested. She'd gone all out, making a slew of traditional dishes: wheat soup, potatoes with fava beans and corn, *madeirense* tuna steaks and *espetada de louro*—grilled beef on laurel skewers. They were all typical dishes from Madeira, where she was from. But one after the next, they were returned to the kitchen almost untouched. Sture and his sinister companion simply drank, picked at a few things, and smoked. They'd been sitting there for hours, and Raquel wished she could hear what they were talking about. One minute they laughed like old friends despite the fact that they didn't even know each other, and the next they fell silent, staring at one another with an intensity that cut like a knife.

It didn't take much for Raquel to intuit what the stranger's visit was about. His appearance alone led her to the obvious conclusions: his suit and wrinkled jacket—expensive but vulgar—loose tie, shirt messily tucked into his belt, and the bulge in his pocket; his dark hair, over-gelled and combed back to reveal a shiny forehead, oily face, and horselike mouth framed by a carefully trimmed goatee; his unreadable, vacant expression; the silver ID bracelet, gold-chained pocket watch, and signet ring on his index finger; his hairy hands, wide fingers, and broad back; the way he sat, legs spread wide, rearranging his balls from time to time; his twisted half smile. And, of course, his dark skin, terrible English, and Arabic accent. This was one of the heavies Sture euphemistically referred to as "businessmen." She'd never seen him in the restaurant before, and bet he'd been sent by Sture's Turkish associates in Ankara—and that his presence was related to the raid at the port, the guy whose throat had been slit, and the confiscated drug shipment.

Sture had been scared ever since the news broke. He didn't show it, but so many years living with him had taught Raquel to sense when her husband was slipping through her hands. She'd never seen him like this before. Raquel didn't often meddle in her husband's affairs; it was a tacit agreement they'd reached. He took care of her and Erick, and she didn't ask questions. The money came in, they had a good life, and that was that. But the night before, she'd tried—after fellatio—to find out what was going on. If she or her son were in danger, she had a right to know. Sture brushed her off, as usual, with a standard dodge: "Don't think about it; I do the thinking for the both of us, and that includes making sure nothing happens to you." Consciously or unconsciously, Sture always talked about "both" of them; Erick never entered the picture. She pretended to believe him, but this time Sture wasn't as convincing as usual. The port business must have been really serious. Malmö was Sture's territory, and his associates had entrusted it to him, so if a problem arose, it was her husband's responsibility. The newcomer had been sent to clear things up, or possibly to help. But more likely to pressure and threaten.

Maybe this guy was the storm that the fortune-teller had warned her about weeks ago.

Twelve years after Sture rescued her from the miserable hovel in Funchal where she'd been living with her son—Erick was four, still wet the bed, and refused to speak—Raquel continued to wonder why fate had sent Sture to her. She, like her mother—and her grandmother before her—put her faith in the divine plan foretold by the cards, signs, and omens she'd learned to read as a girl. Raquel went to the fortune-teller secretly, since Sture didn't like it—and both women had agreed: the universe was offering Raquel and her son a brilliant future, but not one free of danger. One after the other, Raquel had managed to drive off those dangers: candles, spells, charms to ward off the evil eye, and contact with the other world ensured that the forces of the universe worked in her favor.

It had been a hard fight, but she'd won—though not entirely. Yasmina was still a threat. She wasn't like the others Sture regularly cheated on her with. Her husband felt something special for the girl with two different color eyes—a sure sign of evil—something bordering on paternal affection. He showered her with the kind of warmth and attention he never gave Erick; but he also looked at her with the desire her twenty-three-year-old body inspired. Raquel wasn't afraid of competing with Yasmina for Sture's appetites; despite being almost fifteen years older than the little whore, she felt more than capable of satisfying her husband's instincts, no matter how base or sleazy. Nothing Sture could ask of her was worse than what she'd endured to get by as a single mother in Funchal.

Yasmina might have been no more than another of Sture's prostitutes, like her mother before her, but the girl was a threat. The fortune-teller had warned her: Yasmina was strong, much stronger than the dangers that had come before. At some point Raquel would have to take care of her, but what was critical now was the immediate danger looming over them: the newcomer. Raquel didn't take her eyes off him.

"Look at that guy; Muslims aren't even supposed to drink, and he just keeps tossing them back. Here, go take them the bottle of bourbon," she said to her son, pointing to the tray on the bar with two glasses and an ice bucket.

"Can't you do it?" he grumbled.

Erick was a good kid, and Raquel loved him as unfailingly as Sture ignored him. Her son wasn't like other teenagers in the neighborhood: he didn't smoke or take drugs, and he stayed out of the dealings that went on inside Old Sweden. He lived in a world of books and exams. Erick was a very smart kid, but he was too introverted, weak, and insecure to earn the respect of his stepfather, whose constant jabs he feared. And it drove Raquel mad.

"Stop complaining, they're not going to eat you. Go, do as you're told."

Erick reluctantly obeyed. From the kitchen door, Raquel watched Sture grab hold of her son's elbow when he tried to walk away after serving their drinks, saw her husband say something to the newcomer, and watched both of them laugh as Erick hung his head in shame. Sture put a hand on Erick's neck and gave him a little slap before releasing him.

"What did they say? Did they make fun of you?"

Erick shook his head, downcast. Raquel took his chin and forced him to look up at her. The boy was boiling over inside.

"He told that guy I'm the penance he pays for having fallen in love with you."

Raquel nodded slowly.

"Go into the back to study," she said, her voice icy as she glared at the table where Sture and his uninvited guest were finally standing up.

When the man walked out of the restaurant, Sture dropped the easygoing expression and revealed his true state of mind. For a minute he rested his elbows on the bar, buried his fingers in his hair, and pressed his head between his forearms. Raquel waited, knowing that sooner or later he'd look up and see her there, solicitous. When that moment came, she knew to bring him a glass of beer.

"That bastard is going to screw me. I know it," he said, tight-lipped.

"You'll find a way out of this. You always do."

Sture shook his head skeptically.

"Your faith in me is infinite, isn't it? No matter how I treat the boy. Listen, I'm sorry about what I said. I acted like a jerk."

Raquel didn't hide her displeasure.

"A total jerk. I don't know what you think you're going to gain by humiliating my son that way."

"I just want him to toughen up a little. You protect him too much, fill his head with childish notions—all those books and ideas about going to university and becoming a prosperous businessman. This is the only business I know."

Raquel was not about to argue Erick's future with Sture. There were more pressing matters at hand.

"What makes you think that man wants to screw you?"

"I know what they're like. The Ankara crew got very nervous when the shipment was confiscated. That was millions of dollars lost, and they blame me. I think they're weighing up what to do with me."

"Well you have to convince their emissary that they're wrong, that you're not going to betray your associates and will take care of the whole thing, no more setbacks. Listen to me, it's critical for that man to leave here with a good impression of you; he's got to go back to Ankara happy. You told me to take good care of him, and I can think of something I'm sure he'd love."

Sture looked at Raquel in growing amazement as she explained the idea that had come to her. When she finished, he gave a low whistle.

"You never cease to amaze me, Raquel. Sometimes I wonder what they did to you in that Funchal slum to make you so vicious. There's no limit to your rancor, is there? You could scare fear itself."

Raquel didn't bat an eye.

"This has nothing to do with us, Sture. It's business, and business justifies anything. Isn't that your favorite line?"

Yasmina closed her eyes and concentrated on Sofia El Marikh's voice. When she was dancing and spinning in her room, she could forget about the real world. There was no past or present. Just a future within reach, above her head; it was like the air was a rope she could climb up in order to escape. She'd liked dancing and singing ever since she was a little girl. When she was thirteen she'd promised her father she'd be famous, and her father gave her that look of his, so lacking in ambition and aspiration. "If it makes you happy, that's enough for me," he replied. At that age, Yasmina didn't think of happiness as something so hard to achieve; she saw it as a cake behind glass: something that was always there, just waiting for her to save up enough money to buy it and then gobble it all up.

Perhaps her father should have warned her that the road to happiness was full of missed chances. And her father had missed his chance, which left him wallowing in melancholy. He rarely raised his voice, and his disposition wasn't imposing enough to intimidate, but from time to time he drank, and then his reticence turned into an absurd, exacting severity; he would get worked up and look for someone to order around, but there was nobody to obey—just Yasmina. "I know the truth," he'd say, half-drunk. "And the truth is what I say." Her father's truths were useless. It was true that he and her mother were half cousins, and true that until he died they slept in separate beds and hardly said a word to one another. It was in one of his alcoholic rages that he told Yasmina that things hadn't always been that way, that there was a time when her parents had loved one another. Not when they were first married, of course, because it was an arranged marriage; that's the way things were done back then. Marriages were contracts, family agreements in which the bride and groom's only role was to obey. "Your grandfather Abdul was Rachid the Spaniard's son, and everyone was afraid of him; they respected and feared him, admired and hated him. His word was law, and I was the one he chose as his daughter's husband. I never knew why. He must have had his reasons, but he never explained them to me. All I could do was obey, call things off with the girl I'd been in love with since I was a boy, and marry your mother."

When he talked of those things, his eyes lit up momentarily, as if a piece of the man he once was still remained. But then grandfather Abdul would appear and start shouting, calling him terrible things: a drunkard, a bum, a useless cuckold. "One day I'm going to kill your grandfather," he'd murmur, bubbling over with rancor. But he never did. He simply let himself die slowly, lacking the will and courage to live, and then one day threw himself under the four o'clock express to Stockholm. Yasmina was the only one to grieve.

These days, though, she hardly ever thought of him.

Her bedroom door opened, and Yasmina's arms dropped like a marionette whose strings have been cut. She saw her grandfather's grave expression, the way he watched in a mix of disgust and fear from the doorway. Yasmina remembered, then, that she was dancing around in her underwear. Quickly, she snatched the comforter from the bed to cover herself.

"You should knock."

"I don't have to knock on any door in my house."

Abdul stared at the dress on its hanger, the shoes beneath it.

"I'm going out tonight," Yasmina informed him.

Her grandfather pinched his mouth as though about to spit.

"Whoring. That's what you're going to do."

Yasmina frowned.

"Whatever you say, Grandfather."

Abdul was particularly surly that afternoon.

"Whatever I say? Why are you talking to me like I'm an idiot? Do you think I need your condescension? The condescension of a whore who spreads her legs every time that old bastard Sture tells her to?"

"What is the matter with you today, Grandfather?"

"What's the matter with me? The whole neighborhood is talking about you, pointing at our family—pointing at me! 'There goes Abdul's granddaughter, the slut.'"

Yasmina thought of her father, on the sofa, unable to raise his head to face Grandfather's insults, collapsing like a castle in the air. He was like an abused dog, submissiveness is what killed him.

But she had no plans to submit.

"Isn't that what you turned me into? Am I not paying off a debt that isn't mine?"

Her grandfather's face went so tense it looked as if his skin would rip.

"You have no idea what you're talking about! You don't know a thing! Get out of my sight—go!"

The red dress with buttons down the back fit very nicely. The shoes too. Sture had her walk up and down the length of the restaurant, now closed to the public. Erick pretended not to pay attention as he washed glasses behind the bar. He was afraid Yasmina would see his eyes burning passionately.

"You look lovely," Sture declared. "There's just one thing." He walked over, asked her to turn around and fastened a beautiful necklace—an emerald set in antique silver—around her neck, and then kissed it softly. "There. Irresistible. I hope that asshole can see your true worth. Two of my men will take you to the hotel. They'll be on guard all night at the door. If there's any violence, if you get scared, they'll get you out of there."

Yasmina wasn't listening. She was petrified and knew that Sture's words were just an attempt to calm her down. No matter what happened in that hotel room, nobody would come to save her. She put a cigarette between her lips and searched for a match she couldn't find. Sture gave her a light while looking her over carefully.

"Are you having second thoughts?"

Yasmina shook her head.

"I'm fine, don't worry about it."

Sture stroked the hair falling over her right shoulder. He loved that it was so thick, yet still so soft and silky. It made him think of her mother at age twenty. He wondered why he'd never slept with Yasmina, as he had with Fatima when they were younger. Maybe it was true, after all; maybe he loved her like a daughter. Loved her in his own way, even if no one understood what that was.

"Good. Off you go then. I'll see you in the morning."

Yasmina headed for the door. Her shoes showed off her slender legs, and the dress accentuated her breathtaking hips.

"Yasmina, you look . . . very . . . beautiful."

Yasmina nodded toward the bar.

"Don't give me that look, Erick. Women don't go for puppy dog eyes."

The car dropped her off at the entrance to the Savoy. An elevator whisked her silently to the fourth floor, too quickly to process the transition.

Suddenly, Yasmina was in a luxuriously decorated room with lace curtains and a plasma-screen TV mounted to the wall. The first thing she noticed was a Hopper painting, *Morning Sun*, over the artificial fireplace. Yasmina examined it carefully.

In a way, the picture of the woman in a camisole, sitting facing an open window, reflected Yasmina herself. Her melancholy face expressed a jumble of thoughts, muddled concerns after a night the viewer knew nothing about; or maybe she had a secret, something she confessed only to the dawn. The use of color made the picture soft and appealing. The woman was ordinary, but Hopper had turned her into someone exceptional.

"Come over here."

Yasmina's eyes glanced from the canvas to the satin-covered sofa on the other side of the room. The *newcomer*, as Sture called him, sat there, reclining, arms spread across the sofa back, legs crossed over a low glass coffee table littered with walnut shells, ash, empty glasses and bottles, and traces of cocaine. He wore a white bathrobe with the hotel's insignia. The man had hairy toes with well-clipped nails, a mouth full of teeth covered in plaque. His face was deceptively friendly.

Could be worse, Yasmina thought as she walked across the soft carpet, her high heels sinking into it and making her ankles wobble.

"Sture, the old bastard. He sure surrounds himself with beautiful things."

This was the category she was relegated to, Yasmina thought. A decorative object, an exchangeable *thing*. The man stood and approached her. He stroked her hair, simply yet awkwardly, his virility barely repressed. Gövan had the same ungainly way of touching her, but she found the deputy chief's clumsiness sweet, and in this guy it revolted her.

"What should I call you?" he asked. His English was hard to understand. He moved his hands to the base of Yasmina's neck and she tensed.

"Who cares? I'm here. You don't have to call me anything."

The man gave her a cold look. His eyes were intelligent, betraying an ability to anticipate and predict. He was used to appearances not being what they seemed.

"I'm just trying to be nice, relax. I'm sure you've had worse assignments."

Yasmina fixed her gaze on the candle smoking by the bed, the gold ice bucket. At least he wanted to make it easy for her, be pleasant. As if it were a real date.

"Would you like a little champagne? Or even better, maybe a line?"

Yasmina chose the coke, though if she could have truly chosen what she wanted it would have been a magic wand to change everything and get her out of there.

"Sture says you sing, that you have a nice voice. I could help you. I've got contacts in my country, I know producers. Why don't you sing something for me?"

Yasmina looked down. It might have been taken as shyness but in fact she was simply hiding her ennui. After snorting her line, she threw her head back and let out a brief sigh.

"Listen, I'm here because I've got a job to do. No need for you to sugarcoat it."

The man feigned disappointment. But immediately a strange, vicious glint came into his eyes.

"That's how you want it? Fine by me."

He flipped Yasmina over and grabbed her from behind, shoving her to the bed. It hurt, but Yasmina didn't complain. She felt him press his hard cock against her buttocks, rubbing himself on that lovely red dress. Yanking brusquely, the man ripped it off, and buttons scattered across the rug like the beads of a broken bracelet. The bed was full of crumbs, its tangled sheets smelled of sweat and other women. He bit and squeezed her anxiously, then tried to put her on all fours.

"Not up the ass," she said sharply when she felt the tip of him circling her anus. She knew that if he really tried, she wouldn't be able to stop him. What Yasmina wanted made no difference whatsoever.

And yet he relented. Flipping her over again, the man lay on top of her.

It was quick and sickening, as was to be expected. From time to time, Yasmina tuned in to what was happening—hands on her inner thigh by her birthmark; heavy breathing in her ear—and then quickly escaped, focusing on the gladiolas in a vase, the fleur-de-lis wallpaper. More than the situation, what she focused on was the room. She couldn't escape the room.

She turned her face to the Hopper painting above the fireplace. The woman looked so beautiful now, it took her breath away. Her eyes reflected the open blue space, the absolute calm of a limbo where she was alone, where she was free, no other presence, no thoughts or voices, no one. In that moment, almost at breaking point, she found herself in a state of absolute purity. Yasmina at that precise instant felt profound love for the woman in the painting, the kind of love that can only be felt by those who understand. Because she too was alone. Because something was tearing her up. Was she unloved? Did she hate herself for things that others had done to her? Could her dreams save her?

Perhaps the woman in the painting, too, had a father who'd watched his hopes die from a balcony like the one in Rosengård, so unlike the rose garden it was named for. Perhaps her family, too, had handed her over to a drug trafficker when she was sixteen in order to settle their debts. And perhaps, despite all of that, the woman in the painting still didn't hate her father or her family. She just hated herself for having allowed it to happen.

The man came. Yasmina felt his semen trickle out of her vagina. She went to the bathroom and soaped and lathered every inch of her body, but the water could not cleanse her, despite her attempts to scrub off her skin.

When she emerged, fully dressed, she knelt on the carpet and began picking up the buttons from her dress, one by one. It wasn't hers, and she had to give it back. It would take hours to sew them back on. Lying on the bed, the man watched her indifferently. He said something about Sture, said he appreciated this little *gift* but it didn't change anything—business was business, it was a done deal. Yasmina wasn't listening. All she wanted to do was to get out of there. She counted the buttons. There was one missing. With a toe, the man pointed under the dresser.

"You forgot one."

Yasmina picked it up. Then she put on her shoes and headed for the door.

"Give my regards to your boss; tell him I'll see him soon. And I might request your services again before I go back to Ankara. I've got your card."

Yasmina walked out and asked Sture's men to take her home. Her insides ached, and she wanted to vomit but refused to let strangers see her weak.

t had been three days and something felt wrong. The newcomer had a nose for traps and sensed an ambush. He'd set them himself in Beirut, Berlin, all over the world. Maybe Sture wasn't as stupid as his bosses thought. Well, neither was he. If Sture thought his little gift was going to change anything or make him lower his guard, he was wrong.

The man felt in his pocket for his knife. At times like this, he wished he were less scrupulous when it came to firearms. A semiautomatic would have come in handy about now. But as a boy he'd been taught that killing from a distance wasn't real killing. He'd built his reputation on face-to-face combat and it was too late to do anything about that now.

A minute later, an SUV's headlights illuminated the narrow alley. The car crept along and then stopped a few meters from him. Sture got out with an affable smile. The man relaxed on seeing that he was alone, as they'd agreed, and looked carefree, like he had nothing to fear. Good, he thought, walking toward Sture, smiling in turn, fingering the knife in his pocket as he calculated the most direct route to Sture's liver. It wouldn't be easy to find under all that fat. Old Sture had gotten sloppy, not only in his business but in his appearance. Maybe it would be easier to slit his throat. Like a pig. Quick and clean. This was why he'd been sent to Malmö, and he had no intention of leaving his mission unaccomplished. A pro depended on his reputation, and his was unimpeachable. He never failed.

Suddenly, he stopped short. Sture's smile disappeared as he whipped out an extendable steel baton from his pocket. He now wielded it in his right hand.

"I've heard you don't like guns, that you believe in hand-to-hand combat. So I decided to fight fair. A duel, right?"

The man made no attempt to feign ignorance. Cards on the table, that was how he liked things. It saved him the small talk. He bit his lip and pulled out his blade, sharp and thin as a stiletto.

"It's nothing personal, Sture. I like you, and I appreciate your gift the other night. Quite a woman, and those different-colored eyes would drive any man wild. You're lucky you get to fuck her whenever you want. Who wouldn't love an open bar when that's what's on tap?"

"Don't talk about Yasmina. You know nothing about her."

"I'll tell you what I do know: that I'm going back to Ankara with your head under my arm so it can be impaled on a stake. And you have no idea how hard it is to get a man's head off."

Sture nodded.

"I knew why you were here the minute you set foot in my restaurant. And I get it, really I do. It's nothing personal for me either. Or maybe it is. Who the fuck am I trying to kid?"

Sture's approach was shockingly quick and agile for a man of his age and girth, and his opponent wasn't expecting that. Before the newcomer had time to react, Sture delivered a quick hard blow to the hand holding the knife. The sound of the man's wrist as it snapped rang out over his cry of pain. Without giving him time to recover, Sture delivered a series of blows with the baton's steel end to the man's mouth, nose, and right eye.

Within seconds, his rival's face was a mass of mangled flesh, broken teeth, and shattered bone.

He tried to counterattack, but Sture was ferocious, crashing the baton down on his skull sadistically, over and over, while holding the man's neck and trying to rip the Adam's apple from his throat.

In under two minutes it was all over. The man fell and Sture kicked him and slammed his foot onto his head until he heard the skull crack.

"Sorry for not crouching down to see how you're doing," he murmured, panting as he searched for his handkerchief to wipe the blood and brains from his face and neck. "I'm afraid my belly's too big for that. I tell Raquel not to pamper me so much, but she insists on feeding me all those meat-balls of hers, so what can I do? I'm crazy about the woman."

The poor wretch was dead. Raquel was right; business was business. But, man, did it feel good to get his hands dirty! He felt young again and thought of old times, back when he had no qualms about seeing to matters personally.

8

Málaga Psychiatric Hospital

The doctor assured Marqués he had nothing to worry about. The interview was merely "exploratory," he added, something they did with everyone admitted in order to assess their situation. It was a series of questions and exercises that he could, of course, choose not to respond to.

"And are you the one assessing me?"

The doctor nodded, and so Marqués undertook his own examination.

"How old are you, doctor? Over forty, I'd say. Your wedding ring tells me that you're married, but it's not scratched or worn, so it was either a recent wedding or you take it off frequently. Your casual yet trendy attire tells me you're self-assured—denim shirt under the requisite white coat; jeans tight enough to flaunt your bulge; no socks with your loafers; expensive watch and leather band. Your nails are manicured, chin meticulously shaved, and that carefully tousled Italian backsweep must cost you a fortune at the barber's each week. In short, you're one of those narcissists who looks in the mirror ten times before leaving the house, am I right? You probably work in a public clinic in the mornings and a private one in the afternoons, with a few under-the-table consultations thrown in. You must earn a good living. I'd guess your mortgage is about two hundred thousand, you have a hundred and eighty in your pension, a car that cost twenty and an average-risk investment plan with another sixty thousand. A man who feels pretty self-satisfied and has a comfortable safety cushion. I suppose anyone assessing you would deem you competent, maybe even feel a touch of unwholesome envy. But to me, you're one of those cookie-cutter assholes, like a Madelman doll. So. Does the shoe fit?"

The office had a window overlooking a small garden where the leaves had turned golden. A gardener was raking them into piles, which the wind kept scattering, and which he patiently raked together again. There was a sad feel to the day, and it seeped into the shadows on the walls, adorned with a few charmless landscapes and a couple of diplomas. The doctor sat at a small desk. Apparently, Marqués's diatribe was accurate. He must be used to it.

"We're not here to discuss me but you, although I appreciate your sincerity, but it was unnecessary given that I didn't ask your opinion. So, let's begin by going over your medical history."

He pretended to concentrate on Marqués's medical reports and reread a few lines, following along with the metal arm of his glasses. From time to time he nodded and gave a quiet murmur that made Marqués uneasy.

"Is this going to take long?"

The doctor raised his eyebrows and smiled condescendingly. This imbecile was trying to make Marqués impatient as payback for his insolence.

"I'm simply trying to get a sense of the evolution of your case."

"'The *evolution* of my case...' Euphemisms often sound worse than the unadorned truth. Look, I know what it says in there. I've lived half my life in physical pain."

"You have end-stage cirrhosis of the liver."

"If you play the lottery, eventually you win. Sure, I overdid it on the booze."

He knew what this was about. The idea of a liver transplant at his age, especially considering his pulmonary lesions, was absurd. They'd give it to someone else, someone who had time to *evolve* into a total ass.

"Think about this, doctor. You give someone a new liver or heart, happy to have saved the life of a young person with their whole future ahead of them. And years later that someone becomes a murderer, a rapist, a degenerate... How would you feel if you found out? What if that murderer broke into your house one night and took out your whole family, right in front of you?"

The doctor didn't fall for it. Every patient confronted the rage of anticipating death in their own way.

"So what do you suggest?"

Marqués was not sad or disheartened.

"It was going to happen regardless. I could pretend that my body and I are not the same thing, that we don't really know each other, as if the ills of one didn't affect the other. You, in turn, could leave me alone, sign off on my sanity, say I'm not a danger to anyone, and let me out of this place so I can enjoy whatever hours, days, or weeks I have left."

"And what would you do in that time?"

"Read books, take my last walks, have my final thoughts, maybe spend money I no longer have on a Ukrainian hooker, the kind that takes your breath away. Or maybe just lie down and go to bed without knowing if I'll ever wake up again. Don't pretend it's any of your business or that you care. I know you took an instant dislike to me the minute I walked in the door."

The doctor put his reports down and handed Marqués a pen and blank piece of paper.

"I'm going to propose a series of exercises. First, I want you to try to write the alphabet backward without stopping to think about it..."

Marqués did so with apparent ease. There followed a series of memory tests: three phone numbers, converting euros to pesetas, five European capitals, his passport number, alternate series of numbers and letters. Marqués completed them all with no trouble. After each one, the doctor made notes and continued to be friendly, but never seemed satisfied or dissatisfied with the results.

After half an hour, Marqués began to show signs of fatigue. That was when the doctor approached from an unexpected angle.

"Just one more thing: I'd like you to call to mind your earliest memory."

"What for?"

"Come on, give it a try."

Marqués closed his eyes and pressed his fingers to them as though attempting to push them into the dark and illuminate it.

"It's not always the same one; some days my memory is worse than others."

"Right now, I mean, the oldest memory you have right at this instant," the doctor explained, spreading his hands amicably and giving an encouraging smile.

Marqués looked out at the garden. How did that gardener have such infinite patience, raking the leaves toward himself over and over again only for the wind to blow them away? Didn't he see how pointless it was? He remained pensive.

"I think I'll choose not to let you ferret around in my head as if it was your lair. My memories and thoughts belong to me, and I don't feel like sharing them with a stranger. If you want to put me in a straitjacket, go ahead; if you don't, let me go already."

"Are you sure about that?"

"Absolutely sure."

The doctor made an annotation.

"There's something too forced about your carefree manner, Marqués. Your detachment is quite meticulous, don't you think? It comes off as..."

"A lie?" Marqués asked defensively.

The doctor set his fountain pen down on the paper carefully.

"No. More like a reconstruction. If you don't want help, I don't see how I can convince you to accept it. You're here by court order, not because it's my idea of a good time. I'm just doing my job."

"It's a despicable job, rummaging through other people's junk just so you can certify a conclusion you came to in advance."

The doctor pointed to Marqués with the tip of his pen.

"Director Roldán is right. You are truly unpleasant, you know that?" He leaned back against his chair and stroked the file folder on the table. "All sick people hope for a cure. Palliative treatment, at the very least. But not you."

"I don't need placebos. I don't need to live to be a thousand."

The doctor nodded thoughtfully and kept stroking the folder.

"I understand, but I can't help you. I'm not going to sign your release or write the kind of report you want; in fact, it will be the opposite. I'm going to recommend that you remain here, at least until you prove yourself to be a bit more cooperative. I think our meeting is over."

No chance, Marqués thought.

Two days later, the professor escaped from the hospital's psychiatric ward. No one could figure out how the ward door had been left open. They made a few inquiries, but when it came down to it, the place was a hospital, not a jail: staff came and went constantly, and although security measures there were a little stricter than in the rest of the hospital, there were no prisoners or detainees, just depressives, attempted suicides, men and women trapped in harmless fantasies, and addicts in rehab for a few days awaiting the results of an evaluation that would determine their final destination. The guards weren't overzealous, particularly toward the end of their long, twelve-hour shifts; the nurses had other things to worry about; and the cameras were basically decorative, given that they hadn't been functional for several months.

When the doctor assigned to Marqués's case heard of his escape, he wasn't particularly concerned and actually felt relieved not to have to do battle with the raging lunatic again. He advised reporting it to the police in case they felt like looking for him, which he doubted.

The avenue glimmered, as white as the modern conservatory itself. From the bus stop Marqués spent a good while watching students and professors come and go, lugging instruments in cases. He took out the pack of cigarettes he'd bought at a stall and smoked one after another until his wheezing lungs refused to let him inhale any more smoke. Marqués smiled on seeing the half dozen butts at his feet, and then took a long swallow from the bottle of gin and wiped his mouth on the back of his hand. He was quite drunk but still able to stand. Drinking and smoking. Nothing better for cirrhosis and emphysema.

At the bus shelter, a young woman was waiting with a small boy of about three who kept fussing. She shot Marqués disapproving looks but didn't seem to mind that her little boy was behaving like a loudmouthed beast.

"I'm dying," Marqués said by way of justification, his giant gnome head rocking forward and back.

The young woman looked away, visibly upset. She grabbed her little snot-nosed kid by the arm and pulled him to the other end of the bench, and the boy screamed and kicked her shins.

"Get a muzzle; you don't want him biting anyone," Marqués noted dryly. Then he belched, took one final sip, and set the bottle on the ground before crossing the street and heading for the conservatory entrance. He scratched his crotch and surmised that the stinging between his legs was not a good sign. The hooker he'd spent the night with looked clean enough, but you could never tell at those roadside brothels. Regardless, it was a hundred euros well spent, Viagra included. The girl—Moldovan—had found the professor's deformed body sweet and been kinder to him than her job and wages required. There were still good people in the world.

No one stopped him when he entered the conservatory. The lobby, modern and high-ceilinged, was abuzz with people, as was the rest of the building. Marqués checked the information panel on the wall to see if it said where the audition room was. The building no longer looked anything like the place he'd come to in 1940 as a boy, for his entrance exam. He thought resentfully of the shame and disappointment induced by a failure dictated by others, of the door that had been slammed on his future. He wondered if anyone would remember Don Gregorio Herreros, the piano teacher who'd rejected him. Probably not. That old black crow must have died decades ago.

I hope you're rotting in an off-key hell, he thought.

Marqués remembered that the audition room had been on the top floor, next to the library. Maybe it was still there. He took the elevator up and had to press himself to the wall in order to make room for a couple of teenagers pushing cellos in a wheeled cart. They didn't look like musicians, with their earrings and ripped jeans. They didn't sound like musicians either, chewing gum and tossing around insults every other word. Marqués bet they'd never in their life heard a Gaspar Cassadó concerto. These younger generations were something else—soulless performers of insufferable pastiche, like those Croatian cellists Hauser and Sulic.

"You should be ashamed."

The boys shot him a questioning look. Luckily for them, they got off at the next floor. Before the elevator door closed, once they were safe, one of them gave him the finger.

"Fuck you, old man."

Marqués walked down the long corridor, scanning the signs on every door until he came to the audition room. The door wasn't locked, so he pushed it open and walked into the empty space. It was a modern room, and he could hear the low hiss of central heating. Relegated to one corner were a piano, a bench, and a microphone on a tripod. Simple folding chairs were arranged in straight rows, like any old room. Recessed can lighting shone down from the ceiling, which was beechwood and matched the floors. Marqués felt disappointed. He'd been hoping to find musicians in taffeta gowns and suits with velvet lapels, a stage, cushioned theater seats arranged in a semicircle, as they would be for a small performance, and thick red curtains. A sort of cathedral for his final mass.

"I'll have to settle for this," he said, scornful of the cold functionality of his surroundings. He approached the piano—a lacquered upright Seiler that appeared to be in good condition. Marqués stroked the keys and heard the scales sound, no echo. He sat at the bench and rubbed his hands as though washing them at the sink, then held his fingers suspended over the keys and began to play the opening bars of Brahms's Concerto no. 1, his most intense, unrestrained piece. After that, Brahms never again let his emotions run wild.

Marqués hadn't played it since the day when, hardly more than a boy, he auditioned for that arrogant examiner who had asked him to stop after just a few bars, suggesting he choose another path: "Your ambition far outstrips your talent, kid. You don't have the hands for Brahms." Marqués hated himself for not having been able to overcome this initial devastating failure.

For ten minutes he dreamed he was back in time, making up for that defeat. It was exciting to feel the keys vibrate under his fingertips again after so long, to feel the hum of the notes climb from his fingers to his wrists, the touch of the pedals under his feet. But the excitement had a sour aftertaste, full of loss. His mind and his memory of the movements required were more agile than his fingers, and he lost the rhythm over and over. He would try again, and lose it again; it was all vanishing, like a bad joke. His hands shook. He stared at them for a time and imagined taking them off. They were no longer good for anything. The examiner had been right: you can love something to death and still have your love met with absolute indifference. His hands were made for pistons, cylinder heads, and grease; for rotating cams, or holding glasses and cigarettes. Grasping at air and catching nothing at all.

"Hey! What are you doing in here?"

Marqués stood. There was a young man at the door holding sheet music in one hand and a case in the other.

"Attempting the impossible."

Marqués headed for the exit, and as he passed the man in the doorway, gave him a speculative look. He examined his fingers, his narrow wrists. Maybe some people get to fulfill their dreams. Some people who want to be birds are born with wings.

He took the emergency stairs up to the roof. Metal fan blades revolved slowly, gleaming in the sun. It was a beautiful day. The sky went from an intense blue to an orangey swirl off in the distance. A gentle breeze blew, ruffling his hair. Marqués lit a cigarette and crunched across the gravel on the roof. When he'd finished his cigarette, he buttoned his jacket and smoothed a hand over his head, straightening his hair. He twisted his neck left and right, cleared his throat and walked to the edge without stopping.

Marqués didn't leap, simply took another step when there was no longer anything for his feet to step on. His tiny, deformed body crashed spectacularly onto the roof of a car many meters below, bounced up, and then landed facedown on the ground, his short legs skewed outlandishly, his head crushed and quickly turning crimson. For a second, his fingers kept scratching at the asphalt like a lizard who's had his tail cut.

PART THREE

April 2014

9

Málaga Municipal Mortuary

A wake is a performance of pain and departure, but if the deceased isn't visible it becomes a sort of dress rehearsal, a pantomime where those in attendance stare at a cedar or oak box and try to convince themselves that their beloved is inside. A ritual goodbye without which there is no closure.

Something of that hovered in the air in the sad viewing room where Marqués's coffin lay. The funeral home beauticians had employed all of their talents—which were considerable—in trying to give Marqués's body a lifelike appearance, or at least a peaceful one, but it had been impossible to reconstruct his shattered face and skull, so they'd opted for a closed casket. Anything else would have been too unpleasant, like those black-and-white images from family vigils long ago, where the deceased had handkerchiefs tied around their jaws, as though being forced not to divulge what they knew of death.

Helena, Director Roldán, and Miguel were the only ones in the room. It had proven impossible to locate any family. Nor was there any chance of recruiting residents at the home to make the ceremony less onerous. Director Roldán, who had been a bit softer of late and was acting more human, tried to excuse them: death, to those at the residence, was like leprosy: contagious. So, finding no one else to explain things to, the funeral home employees endeavored to make sure Helena knew that, despite the fact that Marqués's body was not on view, they'd done everything in their power to make his entry into the next world as presentable as possible: they'd combed not only his hair but also his eyebrows and dressed him in his best suit, although they could find no tie. The one he was wearing had been a gift from Miguel. Marqués wanted to go in style, that's what he'd written in a letter addressed to Helena: "Have them cut my hair, give me a shave, and clip my ear hairs. I want a blue suit, a white shirt, and a dark tie. And make sure to tell them to do a good job shining my shoes."

In his farewell letter, Marqués named Helena as his sole heir and confessed things she'd rather not have known. It seemed that those who'd always sworn Marqués was a fraud were right after all. In the letter, which the police had found in his pants pocket along with some spare change, Marqués ranted and berated himself, describing himself as a poor wretch, a deformed and self-conscious man whose wife and children had left him, who had earned his living as a mechanic, working on cars and motorcycles and in his free time earning extra cash as a piano tuner. "I like to be near pianos, to stroke their keys like a pipe dream, a life impossible." In the envelope, the police also found a small tuning fork that Helena showed Miguel.

"He tried to get into the conservatory but they turned him down for lack of talent. So instead of trying again, he spent his life harboring resentment and bitterness."

In the days prior to the funeral, Miguel accompanied Helena to the notary public. The fact that Marqués named her sole heir in his suicide note had occasioned a series of hassles. To begin with, dying turned out to be rather costly, and the funds Marqués had in his account were plainly insufficient to cover the cost of a funeral. Helena grew pale as the final expenses were tallied up. One truth uncovers another, not always happily, and Helena found herself forced to confess to Miguel that she too was broke. In fact, she had barely enough to pay her fees at the residence.

"Your grandparents didn't leave you anything?"

"A family name that did nothing but incur debt, and an old house that was sold long ago to pay off creditors, taxes, and Grandfather Whitman's failed business ventures."

"What about your husband?"

"Walter was never good at managing money, and despite what people think, a university professor's salary is nothing to write home about."

Miguel was in his element with taxes, fees, releases, and paperwork. He took care of it all, paying for the entire thing without acting remotely magnanimous. He didn't even mention it, except when Helena insisted that she would repay him every euro. He simply looked at her as though he had no idea what she was talking about.

"I don't want you to repay any of it."

"Why would you do this? You hardly knew Marqués; what's more, you didn't even like him."

To Miguel the answer was obvious.

"Because you're my friend and he mattered to you."

On Marqués's death certificate, the cause of death was listed as broken cervical vertebrae and crushed brain mass.

"But that doesn't convey what he really died of," Helena protested. "It doesn't say anything about loneliness, about losing the will to live."

Signing the papers was difficult. It was an administrative act that officially put an end to the existence that had proven too high a price for her friend to pay.

No one had written a single word in the condolence book, not a single memory or a farewell; meanwhile the next room over, which was full of people, had page after page of emotional paragraphs filling the book there. Perched on an uncomfortable chair beside Helena, Miguel wondered what happened to all those words written in a moment of grief, remembrance, or concealed relief. Maybe they were given to the deceased's family, or abandoned in some storeroom. Forgotten. Death was one of the great mysteries in a family's grammar.

Moved by an absurd sense of piety, he got up and approached the empty book. He took out his fountain pen and paused, pensive. Miguel wasn't very clever with words.

Words were Natalia's thing, she was always buried in a novel, reading something. She would have known what to write—something appropriate, a quote from some Romantic author. But she wasn't there to dictate to him, so he wrote the first thing that came into his head: *It's a shame to die alone.*

"We all die alone, Miguel. No matter how many people surround us."

Miguel turned. There he was again. His father. Amador.

"But we still have the consolation of God, heaven, the afterlife..."

"God doesn't exist, son. Or at least I haven't heard from him. Sorry to break the news."

Miguel pretended not to hear him. After all, his father wasn't even there; he was simply a figment of Miguel's diseased and weary imagination. And even if he was real, who was to say that the dead are infallible?

"Go, Father. Leave me alone."

Marqués's death and Amador's presence made him reflect on his mother's death. Miguel wished she had died at home. But that hadn't been possible—or at least he hadn't dared let it happen. When he finally gave in and had her admitted to the nursing home, she was already very sick; he did it to keep her from running away, and to prevent the self-harm she was prone to. Miguel went to visit every once in a while, but not weekly. It was like he wanted to have more important things to take care of, things that let him turn a new page and act like she was already dead before her time had actually come. He'd bring her magazines, and novels and history books on the Spanish Civil War, the Republic, and Francoism. His mother had been illiterate, but taught herself to read and write so she could understand the maze of ephemera, battles, political speeches, socioeconomic analyses, lives, lies, and inventions. By the end, she hardly recognized her own son but snatched the books from his hands and devoured them. She underlined and clipped out photos—which ended up in her trunk—scribbled notes in the margins, and smiled or seethed depending on whether she agreed or disagreed with what she was reading. The doctors monitoring her health regularly instructed Miguel not to keep supplying this kind of information: his mother was unhealthily obsessed, had trouble sleeping, and suffered anxious relapses. But Miguel paid no attention. His mother was an addict; she needed the drug that was killing her, and Miguel was her coldhearted dealer. If she wanted to go down for good, there was nothing for him to do but help her on her way. He wasn't too surprised when he got a call in the middle of the night to say that his mother had passed away. They didn't want to give him the details over the phone and asked him to come in to the clinic, so he dressed carefully so as not to wake Águeda. It was 1970; they'd been married just three years and still felt the need to be in physical contact when they slept—Miguel curled against her back, Águeda's hair brushing his face as he smelled her and breathed on her neck, one hand clasped to her chest. He got dressed in the hallway and then climbed into the Datsun, which he'd bought to celebrate his promotion to branch manager at the age of thirty-one, a brilliant career ahead of him. On the way to the clinic, driving along dark, deserted roads, he had time to reflect on the contradictory emotions that his mother's death occasioned. He refused to admit he actually felt relieved, that his mother had been a burden for too long, a pebble in his shoe that made him forever look down and kept him from enjoying his well-deserved happiness. But he was shocked to learn that his mother had choked on her own tongue. He grew pale on hearing that she'd bitten it off and swallowed it. Miguel exploded at the news—objecting, making threats, lamenting. It had been the staff's responsibility to keep watch on her! They knew she wouldn't give up until she'd taken her own life, and yet they'd allowed it to happen. His protestations stopped only when he realized that he'd tried to buy the attention that he, as her son, should have shown her. He'd neglected his duties, and unleashing his frustrations on a bunch of strangers who listened indifferently would do nothing to change that. Miguel demanded to see her room, and although they advised him not to, he insisted. He should have listened. He would never forget the shock of those bloodstained sheets, the pillow still molded to the shape of her head, the shattered water glass on the floor, her meds scattered on the nightstand, and the book she'd been reading—José María Gironella's epic *The Cypresses Believe in God*, with Amador's photo marking her page. His mother didn't want to be buried. She'd been terrified of what earth did to bodies: worms, insects, and beetles; larvae born in rotting flesh; soil getting into people's eyeballs and desiccating them; gums slowly receding and leaving teeth fully exposed; the white of bones sullied by dirt. But in 1970, getting a body cremated was no easy feat. Spain was still as Catholic as Águeda, and Miguel had to overcome opposition and anathema, use the newly acquired influence he had as a rising star at the bank, beg favors and promise to repay them. And once he had her ashes in his hands, he lacked the courage to fulfill his mother's wishes. Because the terrible thing about her death was that Miguel did not in fact feel relieved, as he'd hoped. He didn't feel free or at peace.

n the funeral home lobby, sitting in a chair and in full mourning, Director Roldán sighed and blew her nose into a tissue. Helena glared in silent rancor; she needed someone to blame and the director was there, in reach of her pointed finger.

"This is all your fault. Why are you even here?"

Roldán extended her neck like a heron and tried to maintain composure. They both knew Marqués's death was nobody's fault but his own and that sometimes grief is enough to excuse the things people say.

"It's my obligation," she replied simply.

The employees asked if they could remove the casket: they had to prepare the room for the next viewing. Helena looked at the box one last time. It was light oak, adorned with religious motifs, and had gold-plated brass handles and a small funeral wreath. Miguel had chosen it because she didn't feel up to the job. It befitted his style: somber and lacking in unnecessary decoration, yet tasteful and attractive. Helena nodded.

The cemetery, on top of a hill on the outskirts of the city, showed the ravages of time and neglect. The hearse drove through its rusty gates and down a narrow gravel path between mausoleums that belonged to prestigious old families who wanted to die among their own. There were ostentatious angels with broken wings and mossy faces, headstones with epitaphs from another era, bronze sculptures defiled by bird droppings, feeble-looking orange blossoms, graves dotted across an abandoned meadow, and funeral niches left open like a sinister premonition. The niches available for rent were tucked in an out-of-the-way corner, at the farthest point on a path dead-ending into the cemetery wall.

Two workers were waiting with the forklift and trowel beside the slab that would be used to seal Marqués's niche. Helena had had it engraved with his name, nothing more. No one had anything to say about the deceased. No memories, no anecdotes to tether him to this world for just a little longer. Helena placed Marqués's tuning fork on top of the casket.

"Perhaps he'll have more luck on the other side."

The whole thing went very fast. One of the workers smoked as he troweled on fresh mortar; the other whistled quietly until he realized how inappropriate his jollity was, and closing his eyes, apologized and fell silent. There wasn't even any rain to sober the mood, and on the other side of the cemetery wall they could hear kids playing soccer, shooting goals against it, insulting one another and laughing.

Miguel woke from a restless sleep in the middle of the night. Disoriented, he looked around. Sometimes he forgot that he now lived in a residence, that his daughter had abandoned him in this place, surrounded by objects that weren't his and people he didn't know. He let out a weary sigh and sat on the edge of his bed. The cold floor tiles brought a bit of relief. At least that was something to count on, the cold.

He tried to recall his dream. It was lingering there, hadn't entirely faded yet. He heard his mother's voice calling feebly for Amador. She said it over and over, in a muffled whimper.

This wasn't actually a dream. It was a memory, but one buried deep inside. Miguel had been very young, perhaps four or five, and had had his pillow over his head so as not to hear her, but his mother's lamentation had come through the pillow and bored into his brain . . . He would hear the animalistic moan countless times over the course of his life.

In his memory he was walking down a cobblestone street. Dirty snow that had hardened in the night was piled on either side of the road. He was holding his mother's hand, and he was cold despite being stuffed into a huge coat and wearing a scarf, hat, boots, and woolen socks. His mother's fingers were freezing too. She was pulling him along forcefully; he wanted to stop but she wouldn't let him. Little Miguel was crying. He could see his mother's old coat—which was missing all the buttons and had the collar raised—and a dark handkerchief tied around her throat; she'd scraped her graying hair back into a tight ponytail secured with bobby pins. He saw her red cheeks and the breath coming out of her freezing nose and parted lips. His mother was only twenty-five, but looked very old. War ages people. Sorrow does too. Miguel remembered her rough, wrinkled hands, her legs hidden under thick stockings like a widow, never looking anyone in the eye.

Why was he thinking about this? Why couldn't he stop? He knew where this memory led and had always tried to avoid it. A sad childhood full of hunger, the shame he felt when he saw her come home late with other men while he pretended to be asleep. Little Miguel heard her have sex with them on the other side of a curtain that acted as a partition between their rooms. He remembered the creaking mattress, the rhythmic sound of the headboard banging against the wall, the men's guttural cries. They would leave quickly, and his mother would be left there alone in bed, hugging the sheets. He was still tormented by the smell of those men stinking up the house, their presence tainting his mother's expression the following morning, when there was milk or fresh meat on the table, or perhaps some chicken.

Miguel inhaled and checked the time on his nightstand clock. A night of insomnia, and he couldn't even console himself with alcohol or a cigarette, like Helena, to kill time until the memories decided to go the same way they'd come. He got up, walked around the room a few times, looked out the window, and gazed at the sleeping city. He wondered if Helena was awake too, as disconcerted as he was. Days earlier, on Playa Bolonia, she'd mentioned her mother's suicide almost in passing, as though it were a trivial detail, and he'd been too cowardly to reciprocate with the story of his own mother. He'd never spoken about any of it—his childhood, adolescence, early adulthood—to anyone. Why did everything have to be death, shame, and the past? Was there nothing good to look back on?

Miguel moved away from the window and opened his desk drawer. There were Carmen's letters. He picked one up at random.

Barcelona, December 1986

The city turned on the Christmas lights today. It's two weeks from Christmas Eve. Some people hate the holidays and feel depressed by all the forced jollity. The lonely feel even more lonely, the unbelievers more vulnerable, and the melancholy are in their element. There might be a little of all of those things in me, but I love the holiday season. Fir trees decorated with garlands, the Santa Lucía fair with its nativity scenes . . . all those balls and ornaments remind me of my childhood, drinking hot chocolate on Calle Petritxol, the anise bottle my father would scrape with a fork to accompany the carols, and my mother making almond soup. I think of how cold it used to be at midnight, when we went to Christmas Eve mass. Did I ever tell you that I wanted to be a nun at one point? No, of course not. When would I have told you that? You know nothing about me, except what you saw in the few hours we spent together, which seems like a thousand years ago.

I'm not going to lie: I'm learning to forget you, and to do that I have to find a rationale to justify your silence.

I think of your wife, your daughter, your responsibilities. There must be a thousand reasons why you don't want to risk standing on this precipice; fear always finds a reason, but do I deserve your total silence? Not even a few lines, quickly scribbled in haste?

I no longer go down to check the mailbox every day to see if there might be a letter from you, but I still get chills when I see the mailman's scooter drive up the street, still pretend to be indifferent as I riffle through the day's post searching for your name. It's never there, and I know it never will be. My sorrow and disappointment fade a little more each day; they're almost gone now. Only rarely do I sense their deep echoes in the distance. Only rarely does nostalgia open the doors to the past, like this Christmas. Maybe that's why I decided to write again, without stopping to wonder whether you're going to read my letter or rip it up without even opening the envelope. I hope you don't mind. It isn't for you; it's for me. I need to tell you, need you to know. We can pretend you're an invisible friend, or that you're an ocean and from time to time I cast you a bottle with a message.

I try to laugh at your seriousness, your insistence on maintaining silence. Sometimes I think you have nothing inside, no desires. But then I start talking to the man I knew for a few hours lying in bed, I try to remember his vertebrae, the taste of his skin and his kisses, the expression in his eyes as he dared to dream, looking out the window. That's the man that belongs to me. This silent one I don't know. The other one is mine, at least in

private. Not even when I make love to other men, Miguel,
can I make you disappear entirely.

 You must find it absurd that someone could say she
loves you after just one weekend together. I don't mind
being absurd, and deep down I don't even mind whether
or not you believe me, or whether it makes you uneasy,
or fills you with hope. Life is not a movie, I know that.
It's not a novel or something out of a song. Life is not re-
membering in order to forget, or running away in order to
forget; I know that too. But tell me, Miguel: Who should I
explain my heart to? Is it you, maybe? The others? I feel
what I feel, and it's got nothing to do with what's appro-
priate or necessary, right or just, sensical or nonsensical.
I chose a man, my skin chose for me.

 You'll end up alone, Miguel. And that will be a
shame, but it will be your decision. One day you'll
understand that you only get one chance at life and it's
forever, and if you don't take it you die long before your
death.

           Carmen

"Are you crying, Son?"
Miguel wiped his eyes on the back of his hand.
"No."
The windowpanes shook and rattled in the easterly
wind, sadness howling through the cracks. Amador was

always near, like a dog at the door waiting for his dead master to return.

"You're crying."

"Why won't you leave me alone, Father?"

Miguel felt a kind of sorrow he'd never before experienced. It was as though suddenly he could see it all before him: the past, the present, the future. As though the signs of his life had shed their deceits. Perhaps he deserved to be alone, to die alone, like Marqués, because he'd never dared to give others more of himself. Something worth holding on to. When Natalia was born he thought he could do it, convinced himself that he could. He'd be a good father, take care of his daughter; he'd make sure she was never ashamed of him, would never see him lurking by her school to see who she was hanging around with. Natalia wouldn't act like other kids, who in time came to judge their parents with caustic indifference, just as he had his own mother. Now Miguel lamented the lies he'd told ("My mother is dead") when a new acquaintance asked about her. Perhaps Natalia did the same, said that he was dead, or maybe she soon would if there really was a cycle of justice, of reaping what you sowed.

Where had he gone wrong? He couldn't shake Natalia's dismayed expression at the restaurant where he'd shat in his pants, the feeling that if she could have she'd have left him there, pretended not to know him. Natalia had never been a saint or a martyr, despite Gustavo, that bastard, forcing her to wear a crown of thorns every damn day. At the age of seventeen she decided she didn't want to study economics, as he'd persuaded her to do, but literature. Shakespeare, Cervantes, Milton, Steinbeck, Woolf. She was in a goth phase, where everything was accursed. Black shirts, black military boots, black jeans, black eye shadow, too much mascara, wooden crucifixes around her neck, three piercings in each ear, skull and crossbones tattoos, butterfly specimens pinned on her bedroom wall. The smell of marijuana in the bathroom. Shouting, arguments. That was when he lost her, and maybe that was the way it had to be. Some things can't be avoided; people have to go through certain phases. Sometimes they have to go away in order to come back different. Natalia had left with Gustavo to get away from her father and all his stupid, strict rules. She slammed the door to escape the silence, the aseptic lack of emotion. Without intending to, without being able to avoid it, Miguel threw his daughter into that monster's hands.

The cell phone was still on his nightstand. Miguel glanced at it out of the corner of his eye.

None of it mattered anymore: the petty grievances and resentments. If he tried, he could find a barnful of good memories: her school parties; walks along the Guadalquivir; watching Natalia in a play during her first year at university, when she made a truly remarkable Antigone in Bertolt Brecht's rendition; afternoons she spent reading and doing homework at the kitchen table, when she was a schoolgirl and would still come ask him things; their private jokes about Águeda's piousness, which made them feel they had a united front against the religiosity she tried to impose. Watching her grow up and become an independent young woman.

All of that had been lost over one prideful gesture, his refusing to accept the possibility that his daughter could manage her own life and problems without coming to him. Miguel hated Gustavo with all his might but couldn't refuse her the right to love him, no matter how sick and dangerous that sort of love struck him. Natalia was going to be a mother, which meant he was going to be a grandfather, and there wasn't much time before he'd start to forget.

He picked up the phone, put it down. Picked it up again. It was three o'clock in the morning.

"Damn it," he said, reproaching himself.

He dialed Natalia's number. She probably wouldn't answer, Miguel hoped she wouldn't. He didn't know what he could say. But at least when she got up in the morning, she'd see that he had called. It was like leaving a little trail. She'd understand that he needed her, that he wanted to start over, if that was possible.

He waited three rings, and just as he was about to hang up, Miguel heard her voice on the other end of the line.

"Papá?"

Miguel pressed the phone to his ear. It took him a moment to reply, and when he did his voice sounded different, feeble. He cleared his throat and forced himself to adopt a serene tone.

"Hello, Daughter. I know it's late, but I needed to call you."

Natalia's voice sounded oddly bright.

"I'm awake. Is something the matter?"

Miguel guessed she was in the middle of copyediting something. He felt a wave of tenderness, picturing her fingers stained with red, her glasses with fingerprints on the lenses and tape on the arms to cover the spot where they hurt her ears.

"We buried one of the patients today. He committed suicide."

He heard a lighter click: Natalia was smoking.

"That's terrible, I'm so sorry. Was he a friend?"

"Not really . . . But he was a friend of a good friend. The thing is, it made me think about the past, which given the circumstances, doesn't seem very appropriate."

"What's going on, Papá? What are you trying to say?" She wasn't impatient, but she was concerned.

"I'd like you to come visit me this Sunday, if you can."

"Is this your way of apologizing?"

"It's my way of saying that I miss you, Natalia, and if you're happy with that man I can try to accept it."

"I'll settle for that."

"Thank you," Miguel said unexpectedly, as if he'd just finished a commercial transaction. Immediately he wanted to amend his tone, but it turned out not to be necessary.

"Sure, Papá. I love you too. See you this Sunday."

10

Tarifa

There was no celebration of Marqués's death at the residence, no toast to his passing, as might have been expected. No one, with the exception of Helena, appreciated the professor's honesty, which often surpassed the limits of politesse and was downright cruel. Pretty much everyone there had some unpleasant story about him: the obese platinum blonde who complained all day about being unable to lose weight and consoled herself by gobbling down cream buns; the former Don Juan who took his Peter Pan complex to grotesque extremes, harassing nurses forty years his junior; the pseudo-intellectual film buff who pretended to be Yugoslavian and whom Marqués embarrassed by proving he couldn't tell a Serb from a Croat; the organist; the priest; the security guards; and Director Roldán herself. All of them, at one point or another, had endured the professor's mockery and caustic humor. So discovering that they had all been right, that not only was he a liar and fantasist but had also proven himself a coward, should have given them occasion to celebrate, to take out their anger and exact postmortem revenge. But no one did.

Marqués had helped maintain equilibrium at the residence. He was the other end of the spectrum, the one who represented the absolute limit, and even those who hated him most understood this and granted him the role of border guard. They actually envied his wild freedom and less-than-sane outbursts. Without him, the emptiness was too big to paper over. Of course, everyone would keep going, continue doing the same things, but they would be a bit more reserved, more insecure, without the same unconscious optimism. Marqués's death had started a series, and sooner or later the rest would follow.

"No bones about it. Every one of us will kick the bucket," someone said in the flush of two glasses of wine, as though prior to the professor's death that possibility had not been patently obvious.

Those who overheard the comment pretended, awkwardly, that they hadn't. A sense of decency prevented them from speaking openly about certain things. Only Marqués had earned that privilege. Everybody wished that his backstory had been true. Even those who never believed it wished that at least one person had succeeded, had become what they'd wanted to, that one of them had triumphed over the odds. It would have allowed the others to preserve hope, if not for themselves then at least for their children and grandchildren: *You can be free, you can be anything you want, just look at Marqués.*

But if not even Marqués had managed, then who possibly could? The professor's defeat was all of theirs, particularly those who'd most hated him.

Helena was clearly the one who lamented his absence the most. Days went by, and still she was immersed in a disconcerting silence while everyone waited for her barbed comments to act as a balm, for her disdain to enable them to take death and suicide as a joke.

But Helena took refuge in melancholia, using it like salt and pepper to season her loneliness: eating alone, sleeping alone, gazing out alone. She spent hours on the veranda facing Isla de las Palomas. She liked the veranda; it was where residents gathered when the nice weather arrived. The flowerpots, now empty, would be filled with peonies and daffodils; breakfast would be served overlooking the sea, and in the evenings they'd hold dances with a live band. But June had not yet arrived, and the easterly winds still howled, dragging deck chairs across the grounds and furiously lashing the residence's awnings and Tarifa Castle's flags, out at the edge of the city; the sky was low and heavy, and maritime traffic through the straits shut down for the season.

Miguel often saw her there, leaning on the banister, still, divorced from her own body and from time, engrossed in Marqués's absence. He didn't know whether or not to leave her alone and give her space to recover, but it felt like a betrayal, like abandoning her to her sorrow. Sometimes he tried to talk to her, but Helena would give him a sharp look and he'd scurry off like a dog hoping to be petted that instead got hit with a stick. Miguel felt bad about the moments of joy he was experiencing now, having gotten his daughter back, and he feared Helena would see his recent optimism as an affront, so he tried not to talk about Natalia's visits or the things that made him and his daughter laugh in a newfound joy they treasured.

"You have to talk to her, get her to react," Director Roldán blurted out one morning. Miguel found this sudden concern for Helena surprising, coming from her. But it was also true that Marqués's death had softened Roldán. Miguel wondered if this gaunt-faced woman, who seemed to have aged even more, was torturing herself thinking that she'd been partially responsible for Marqués's suicide.

He decided to listen to her. Helena's descent into misery had to stop, or soon there would be nothing left of his friend.

Miguel found Helena on the veranda once more. She was sitting, wearing a cardigan, and hugging herself against the wind, to no avail. Unlike normal, she wore no makeup and had not done her hair, which the wind was blowing over her face. Miguel observed her before Helena realized he was there and for a moment got an inkling of her beauty. Startled at this sudden dawning, he cleared his throat awkwardly. Helena barely tilted her head. Miguel approached with a concerned air.

"You can't go on this way, Helena. You barely come to the dining room anymore, and I bet you're hardly sleeping at all. All you do is smoke and take swigs from that flask."

Helena arched her brow so high it looked like she was about to shoot an arrow. She may have had a snide reply on the tip of her tongue, but on seeing Miguel's hesitant, defenseless expression, she lowered her aim. She blinked, turning her face to the sun, which had not yet reached its apex. Her eyes sought refuge in a ferry just leaving the dock, headed for Tangier.

"When I was a girl, Tangier was the 'city of marvels,'" she whispered into the wind, as if thinking of her childhood made her realize how wonderful it had been. "I was a happy child. I've never been as happy as I was when I stared from the coast across the water at the twinkling lights of Spain without caring how ambitious my desires were. Ready to do everything, be everything, because everything seemed possible."

"You should go back and visit. It's right there, a stone's throw away," Miguel said in an attempt to encourage her.

Helena shook her head. There was no way for her to see the city now, to get lost in the sumptuousness of its streets, the amazing celebrations and festivities, the elegant dresses, luxury cars...

"The city I remember is gone. In fact, it never really existed. I don't think I could bear to see the evidence of that. But here on the veranda, staring out over the sea lets me hold on to the belief that at least one thing in my childhood was real and good."

"I always wanted to go to Morocco," Miguel said, in part because it was true, but mostly because Helena's silence was making him uncomfortable. It was as though he'd been banished from wherever she'd gone. He needed to feel her close, to share something.

For a second, her happiness seemed to return.

"It's a beautiful country. I remember a trip I took to Rif with my father and his Moroccan assistant, Abdul. It was a year before my mother died, and it was the adventure of my life. The day we left was quite the spectacle. My father was driving a convertible Citröen Mehari, packed to the gills. Beside him was young Abdul, and me in the back seat almost buried under all the suitcases and gifts that Abdul was taking his family. What I remember most is our joy: the car rattling along on unpaved roads; my father, laughing and singing; I could see Abdul's profile as he sat there with a dry twig between his teeth, in the gap between his top incisors. I can still see myself holding on to the canvas handles in the back seat to keep from flying out of the car on every pothole. I was radiant."

Mentioning Abdul made Helena close her eyes. When she opened them back up, her pupils were like two stones refracting light. Using her hands as a telescope, she gazed out in the distance, following an imaginary line from left to right, eyes sweeping the coast as though searching for something she knew was there and that only she could see.

"Abdul livened up the trip, regaling us with stories about the mountains where he'd grown up, legends, songs, and customs that captivated me. I was only ten, and he was almost thirty, but I was in love with his dark eyes and smile, like all the women and girls from the barracks. He was very affectionate with me and often made me toy animals from cloth, wire, and cork. He'd buy me sweets, teach me to speak his local dialect, and when I asked if he'd marry me one day, he would roll his eyes, smile wide showing all his teeth, and say that he already had a wife in the village but I would find a good man, inshallah. My mother was fascinated by Abdul too, in a different way. She often asked if he'd let her paint him, and he always turned her down with a shy, friendly smile. He said that to Muslims, trying to imitate the grandeur of God's creation was a sin."

Helena fell silent for a moment, thinking of the hours her mother spent not eating, not sleeping, locked in her studio, obsessing over Abdul's portrait.

"Was the trip worth it?" Miguel asked, attempting to bring her back.

Helena nodded with a little smile.

"I didn't even care that Abdul's village was a dump that had only one cistern, women with only their eyes and henna-tattooed hands showing, and a few half-starved goats. The inhabitants gathered around us, silent and distrustful except for the kids, who were laughing and rambunctious. There wasn't a single radio in the entire village, and obviously nobody had a record player; in fact, not many even had running water. So when Abdul turned up at his father's house with that box, and the turntable started to spin, everyone in town crowded around to hear the grainy sound of the lute and a song sung in Tamazight, one of the Berber languages. To my surprise, Abdul's father and mine threw their arms around each other and embraced. It seems they'd fought together in the war and had a lot to talk about."

Memories sprang to Miguel's mind, things his mother had told him about Franco's Moorish soldiers in the Spanish Civil War. She deemed them Amador's worst enemies, and he recalled all manner of adjectives and insults she reserved for them. Years later, when she was a raving old lady, she still spat and cursed when she came across a North African man on the street, which led to no end of mortifying situations. Miguel couldn't help but make a face.

"What's so amusing?"

He waved his hand vaguely, as though trying to give shape to his memory, make it solid.

"My mother used to tell me about atrocities committed by the African troops who came through her village. About the ancient hatreds that had been harbored for years, since the colonial wars; there was a black legend about them, and it got worse during the civil war. The descriptions of things they did were so grotesque as to be ridiculous. But they worked, manipulating children and their fragile minds."

Helena couldn't relate to this feeling. She'd grown up surrounded by African children, eating with them, playing on their patios, jumping rope in time to their legs. Walls were something erected by adults.

"While my father and Rachid were talking about old battles, Abdul took me to meet his young wife, whom he only saw a couple of times a year. She appeared like a ghost in the door of their hut, with thin dark arms and a body hardly more developed than mine. Her name was Bisava. I was surprised to see how young she was, and my jaw dropped when Abdul walked in almost without speaking to her and reemerged with a girl just a few months old in his arms. The baby had enormous eyes, and her name was Fatima. He let me hold her, and I felt grown-up for the first time. I liked her chubby little hands reaching for my face, and her tiny mouth and pink gums. In my arms I felt the warmth of a human life more fragile than my own, and that night I pestered my father with all sorts of transcendental questions: Could I be a mother too? Why didn't Abdul spend all his time in the village, so he could take care of his wife? Was he not a good father? The more I asked, the more my father's smile faded, and finally it turned into a troubled grimace. He looked up at the rocky outcrop where Abdul's family had built their modest home, the roof covered in brick and pieces of cloth that glimmered like tin in the merciless sun. There was no hint of a breeze, and the red dust got into your mouth, your clothes and hair. Abdul was sitting on a rock in the doorway, his daughter on his knees. He looked happy. Behind them we saw the girlish face of his wife appear for a moment in the window and say something, and Abdul took the baby inside. I'll never forget what my father said at that moment: 'People do what they have to in order to protect their own, even if they don't like it.'"

"A terrible admission, but very true," Miguel said respectfully.

Helena agreed.

"I got the feeling my father had just confessed some awful truth whose meaning I couldn't quite decipher. After dinner, the village men all gathered around a bonfire under the stars to smoke kef. I remember their striped robes, and I kept staring at their faces in search of something special; I wanted to ask what kinds of things they didn't like that they'd be willing to do, like Abdul, and—I imagined—my father. I kept watching as the hours passed well into the night; they talked in Arabic, peppered with French and Spanish expressions. Then I fell asleep, wrapped in a blanket by the fire as my father and Abdul smoked, lying on the ground and staring up at the stars. The last thing I remember before falling asleep was hearing men's muffled laughter and seeing an ant wandering between my toes, which were buried in the ground.

Helena contemplated the spiral of smoke rising from the cigarette she'd just lit. The east winds picked up, whipping the flags at Tarifa Castle ferociously, and it seemed the only thing the blustery gales couldn't budge at all was the sun. High above them, it would continue to shine even after the curtain went down on this production.

"I don't know why I'm remembering all this. Sometimes I think even at seventy there's still time for us to live new lives. The problem is that we still have the same backdrop, we have the same questions and the same lack of answers. In the end, we come back to the same thing, take comfort in the certainty of our memories. We've already endured their sorrows and learned to tame them, whereas anything new also guarantees new suffering. We lose courage."

Miguel didn't share her take on life, her view that the known world was somehow a form of death. Not everything had to be a roller coaster.

"Life puts things in their place. It's that simple. Maybe what we can't bear, what really infuriates us, is that things aren't as we wish. There's no point in shouting about it, no reason to carp and complain."

"Would you mind leaving me alone? I prefer silence to clichés."

Miguel felt hurt and tried to apologize.

"I wasn't trying to . . ."

"Honestly, right now I don't care what you were trying to do. Please leave."

Miguel nodded, distressed. And left her alone.

One way or another, Helena thought after a few minutes, she always ended up hurting those she loved, or else they ended up hurting her. Human emotion was shit. It bound you to people who ended up leaving you. And she didn't want to think about them: her mother and her father, Louise, Walter, Marqués . . . David.

What she needed to do was drink herself into a stupor. That was what her mother used to do when it all got to be too much. And it had worked fairly well, until not even that was enough. Helena locked herself in her room and gave it a good shot, first downing the gin she had in her flask and then turning to the reserve bottle she kept hidden in a drawer. But drinking without joy was hard work, an effort at oblivion that her whole body fought. Her mind knew she was trying to drown it out, sink it into some apathetic torpor, deceive it, and it refused to yield. Instead her mind forced her to remember. It wanted to remain lucid. Opening the drawer where she kept her father's postcards didn't help matters.

The postcards told an outdated tale of escape that had begun in 1955. A manhunt embarked upon by soldiers and

Spanish police who viewed a deserter as the worst kind of traitor. And Captain Enrique Pizarro was the worst of them all, a spoiled brat in the African army who'd been given an office by Generalísimo Francisco Franco himself, an officer of the "special police" in Tangier, the border guard who'd abandoned his post when he was most needed, the favorite son who—after having their trust, privileges, power, and authority bestowed on him—had bit the hand that fed him. A deserter is a godless swine, the greatest danger to those who profess faith in certain ideals, because his attitude could contaminate others, spread like the weeds that had taken over the English lawn at the Whitman estate. To the captain's superiors, finding that weed and yanking it up by the roots became top priority, to keep it from spreading and ruining all the work they'd done. They wanted to make an example of him, have an old-fashioned public execution by firing squad, strip him of his medals and ribbons. Because the captain of Tabor Company 4 Regular Forces in Tangier, Enrique Pizarro, the revered young hero of the Spanish Crusade, had not just deserted the army. He'd done it for what the military considered the most unpardonable sin.

Helena still recalled the sinister visit from that Spanish embassy official who had turned up at her grandparents' home. It was the winter of 1956, and rain was falling with calm familiarity, the comforting damp of London. The shoulders on the man's raincoat were dripping, and his wet shoes squelched across the carpet of Grandfather Whitman's library. He arrived with an affable smile but neglected to tell them whether he was police, military, or civilian. It was hard to tell them apart back then; they all wore the same shade of gray, the same Catholic-looking shirts and ties—modest yet impeccable—and had the same pale, bony faces that made them look like El Greco models. Sly and cunning in his attempt to win over the reservations of a little girl, who by then was no longer so little, the man asked Helena if her father had tried to contact her since fleeing Tangier. Helena looked to her grandfather, searching his face for help, and he encouraged her with a nod. "We're not going to hurt him; we just want to talk to him," the man insisted. Helena didn't believe a word. People like him were so used to giving orders and being obeyed that they'd lost the ability to lie convincingly. She responded that her father had not been in contact with her, which she believed to be true. She could have told the man about the postcards he'd sent from a half dozen European cities and shown them to him. But in 1956, Helena didn't know they existed, didn't know that they arrived each year on her birthday with a few words of affection and the promise that they'd see one another again one day. Her grandfather collected them all and hid them until he died in 1961.

News of her grandfather's death was somehow intangible, lacking in physical reality. It was simply a string of words spoken over the phone in Grandmother Alice's quiet voice. "Your grandfather died, Helena. You need to come home." Helena didn't feel the tragedy; it was as if it wasn't real. After hanging up the phone, what she felt most upset about was that she'd have to leave Louise sooner than planned. To Louise, Grandfather Whitman's death meant even less than it did to Helena; it came from the outside world, a place unrelated to them, a part of Helena she didn't need to know about and one she felt no sympathy for whatsoever.

"I thought you hated that old man. You don't have to go to his funeral. Our plans are more important."

Their plans had begun a month earlier, in the boarding school laundry room. Helena and Louise had kissed, aroused by the marijuana Louise had mysteriously procured—"Don't ask" was another of her phrases—and by the inevitable proximity of their mouths. It was as if nothing was simpler than bridging the gap between them by moving their heads slightly closer and joining tongues. It wasn't really a surprise to either of them, just the manifestation of something that had been building over the course of seven years. It could have not happened, but it did, and neither one pretended to feel uncomfortable about it, not even when Helena felt Louise's right hand stroke her breast over her shirt, as the fingers of her left made their way through layers of clothing to her vagina. She recognized the hardening of her nipples, the wetness between her legs; it felt familiar because in her mind, it had already happened many times before.

They both knew what their mutual crush meant, and wanted to explore it to the end. Grandfather Whitman's death and Helena's trip back to the estate meant delaying everything *sine die*. It would be twenty years before they saw one another again.

The return to her grandparents' house in 1961 was sad. Helena missed Louise, and the fierce wind lashing the pine trees and rippling the grass only depressed her, as the car Grandmother Alice had sent to pick her up approached the old mansion, mud flying as its wheels sank into sludgy tire tracks. She hated how melancholic the vineyard where she'd once played seemed in the rain, hated the sheep behind the wood-and-wire stockade, even hated Isis, her grandfather's favorite mare, grazing on the meadow, indifferent to her master's passing. Helena thought she'd die of sorrow, locked up in that mansion with old Grandmother Alice, engrossed in ancient books by a fireplace that took too much wood and gave off too little heat, surrounded by heavy curtains and dark silences, hearing the scampering of mice in the pantry and the low rumbling of the pipes every time the water ran. Missing the life she'd never have with Louise in sunny California.

Days after the funeral, Grandmother Alice brought Helena a cardboard box. Inside were all the postcards that her father had sent since the year he'd fled Tangier with Abdul.

"Your father never forgot about you. We should have told you, but your grandfather felt the need to protect you from him. And I couldn't go against him, Helena."

Discovering the postcards was a direct blow to the wall of certainties that Helena had erected. She'd grown up convinced that her father didn't care about her at all. After a time, she'd decided to kill him in her imagination, to simply pretend to herself that she didn't have a father, never had. She'd wrenched him from her heart. And now it turned out that he hadn't forgotten her at all, that at least once a year he thought of her. She stared at her grandmother in reproach.

"You let me go all this time thinking my father didn't care about me?"

Grandmother Alice couldn't look her in the face.

"Your grandfather wouldn't let me give them to you. He even ordered the mailman to stop delivering them, but I spoke to Mister Collins, who was in charge of the mail room and a good friend. He saved them and gave them to me without your grandfather's knowledge."

"Did Grandfather blame him for my mother's death?"

Grandmother Alice nodded. But there were other, less laudable and lucid reasons as well. Grandfather had never liked Enrique Pizarro. He considered Spaniards only a small step above the blacks, Indians, Muslims, aborigines, and Asians that Her Majesty's wars had massacred in Africa, Australia, and the Middle East. Cannon fodder. To Grandfather Whitman, the two-bit soldier his daughter Thelma had stupidly fallen in love with was as pathetic as General Franco, with his sissy voice, and as Spain itself, a country of superstitious Catholics who loved brass bands and parades, of peasants who wouldn't have been good enough to pick sugar beets in England. Grandfather Whitman—once a lieutenant—never set foot outside of what had been his territories, but ventured that Spain was a dry plain where they did nothing but plant orange and olive trees. Had it not been for their wolfram reserves, so necessary to the war effort, the country would never have existed in the eyes of the world. For Thelma, his only daughter, to tie her fate to that of someone so insignificant shamed him before his friends. Grandfather Whitman never took into consideration Enrique's vast culture, and found his refined nature and savoir faire suspect, bordering on femininity. Yes, his daughter's fiancé spoke perfect English, but was that not required of any civilized human? Thelma refused to heed his warnings, and he lamented having been so indulgent with her, having stood for her artistic whims. A rebellious girl, she married Enrique anyway, and off they went to Tangier, a putrid, chaotic city, a shameless Babel. The birth of his granddaughter Helena had reconciled them. But that Spanish braggart had run off with his daughter and then abandoned her, so Grandfather Whitman swore that for as long as he lived he would never allow Helena contact with her father, and that if it was in his power, he would most certainly hand him over to the Spanish authorities.

Helena listened sorrowfully to the revelations pouring from her grandmother's mouth. She'd spent days locked in her room reading her father's postcards for the first time, searching the letters for her father's voice, his essence, his presence:

> *Dear Daughter: Rome is an amazing city. Every day we stroll through the Coliseum, and Abdul has learned to ride a Vespa. We go to the market to buy fresh fruit. Never forget that I love you . . .*

> *Dear Daughter: I never thought Paris would be freezing. Abdul has a cold and shivers all the time. Sometimes he gets in a bad mood and says he misses his family and blames me. He knows it hurts me to hear this. Your father loves you . . .*

Postcard after postcard, in city after city, there was running and fear, a desire to return, reproaches and forgiveness, fighting and making up with Abdul: 1956, 1957, 1958, 1959 …

There was one other thing she still didn't know about, her grandmother confessed in this great revealing of secrets. The two of them went up to the attic. Grandmother walked ahead, very slowly, becoming fatigued; Helena followed behind, watchful lest her grandmother lose her balance. No one ever went up there except Grandmother Alice's most loyal servant, Mary, once a month to keep the rodents at bay, remove the pigeon's nests, and shake out the sheets over the furniture piled in one corner. The windows were left ajar to keep dust from settling. Grandmother Alice asked Helena to help her shift a French dresser waiting to be restored. She had trouble getting rid of things that had belonged to a once-magnificent family now on the road to ruin—something Helena knew nothing about.

"Grab that painting there, the big one. It's the last portrait your mother ever painted. We rescued it when we went to Tangier to get you. Take a good look at it, Helena. Never forget that face. That man is the cause of all of this family's suffering. And if God really does exist, one day he'll pay for it."

Helena recognized Abdul's face.

More than fifty years after that visit to the attic, she still didn't know if God existed, though she suspected not.

Helena kept her mother's canvas rolled up at the back of her chest of drawers and almost never looked at it. For the same reason that Thelma had never been able to destroy it, she too was unable to dispose of it. Abdul had personified more than Helena's childhood. More than that trip to Rif, the stories he told, and the cork and wire dolls he made. He was and would forever be an evil too deep to uproot, too complicated to understand, and impossible to cure. All she could do was hold on to the painting like a flame that kept the hate alive, to keep from forgetting, to remember that he was the one responsible for her father having abandoned her and her mother, that he was to blame for Thelma's pain, which made her lose her mind and try to kill Helena. He was solely responsible for Helena's loneliness. That's what she'd decided in order to make the pain bearable, and it mattered little whether it was true or not. She spread the canvas out on her bed and contemplated Abdul's face for a long time, her sad eyes asking him why, his portrait replying with indifferent silence. All these years, Helena had wondered what had become of him: Was he still alive? Did he even remember her on that trip to Rif with her father? Did he ever learn of Thelma's suicide? Did he feel responsible, or just carry on with his life, his conscience unburdened?

The last thing she knew about Abdul was what her father had written on his final postcard, in February of 1978. From Malmö, the same city where David and his perfect TV-commercial family lived. And that was no coincidence. Helena would never allow fate to choose for her. That postcard was the most laconic of all.

Dear Daughter: I found Abdul here, in this city. I also found my perdition and my salvation. My destiny. I hope you can forgive me one day for following its designs. Your father who loves you.

He'd forgotten to add one final sentence: Even if we never see each other again.

11

Malmö

No shortcuts and no running away. No excuses and no pretending, no whistling and turning the other way like he hadn't seen anything, because the body was right there, in full view, in the middle of a children's park. Sitting on a swing. The head severed from the neck, in the corpse's hands—which were crossed over its lap—staring out at the whole wide world with its eyes slightly rolled back. A real spectacle. And it was up to him to solve it quickly, tidily and efficiently. That's what his superiors were selling—that the police were infallible and could keep Malmö's good citizens far from the horror. His neck was on the line, and the public would rip him to shreds if he failed. The chief of police had made this very clear.

"You wanted a springboard? You got it. This is going to end in glory or in agony, Gövan." Chief of Police Helmut hated him. He would love watching the dogs rip Gövan to shreds if he botched this investigation.

Gövan was scared. "You'll do fine," his wife had said that morning, but he'd sensed a clear warning in her words: *Don't disappoint me. My father and I have big plans for you.* The rumors circulating about his intention to run for representative of Scania were true. He didn't want to disappoint his wife or his father-in-law, but the truth was he'd never wanted to be a cop and never dreamed of becoming a politician. Deputy Chief Gövan's best-kept secret was that he'd have liked to be a modestly ambitious farmer, like his father, grandfather, great-grandfather, and great-great-grandfather before him.

"Guy's been dead at least two weeks. He wasn't killed here. Someone brought the body here with the head already severed," said Inga, the chief inspector of forensics.

Gövan carefully inspected the body without touching it, aware that he was being observed by dozens of expectant faces. Watching him now, no one would have pictured him as the rustic type, but just a hundred years ago being a farmer in Sweden was a heroic act. Something akin to being one of the Europeans who settled the American West. Nothing like the huge landowners of today, of course. His family had never been of the gentleman class; they had no massive farms, no modern machinery, no teams of hired hands. Only small plots of land in the swampy bogs south of Vättern, just large enough to keep a few sheep and goats and a few hectares for their crops. He was born in the house that his great-great-grandfather had built with his own hands, as were the generations of Sjögrens who came after him. There was nothing but that old house for kilometers around, though over the years it expanded, came to include a barn, stables, and corrals.

Inspector Inga gazed spellbound at the scene before her.

"Decapitating a body this cleanly isn't easy. All that muscle to cut through, the vertebrae...You'd need a very sharp weapon and the know-how to deliver a blow as brutal and well-aimed as this was. A medieval executioner couldn't have done a better job."

"You're enjoying this, aren't you, Inga?"

The inspector blushed. She and Gövan had had an affair a thousand years back, in prehistoric times, when they were both patrol officers who didn't care about their respective professional careers. It only lasted a few months, until Gövan met the beautiful, rich heiress who was now his wife. But sometimes when they crossed glances in the hall at the station, Inga still felt something stir.

"Professional interest. Not something you see every day. This case certainly won't be boring."

Gövan nodded, though he couldn't take the matter as lightly as the inspector. Sometimes the deputy looked at his kids, who had all the modern comforts and every form of entertainment on hand and still managed to exist in a state of permanent dissatisfaction. He was never bored as a kid. On the farm where he was raised there were always other kids around—siblings and cousins. Everywhere there were men and women, kin who were looking out for one another. Protecting one another. They kept the fire lit twenty-four hours a day, and it was the little ones' job to feed it: tramp the forest in search of kindling, collect firewood and store it in the woodshed, make sure it stayed dry. The older kids took care of small domestic problems: fixing the plumbing, cleaning out the well, repairing any cracks in the walls, and fixing leaks in the roof. There was no such thing as old age or childhood, everyone had a job appropriate to their abilities. And everyone felt safe.

He glanced up and saw the lookie-loos behind the caution tape, recording the whole scene on their cell phones like it was a movie. Nothing was real to them. They were too removed from the carnage, the stench. Malmö was not a model city, just as Sweden was not the heaven on earth that politicians kept trying to peddle to the world, but this severed head was too much. Everyone thought they were safe from the horrors that they imagined only occurred far away, and suddenly it turned out that you could be face-to-face with bugged-out eyes and the pasty tongue of an actual head, left like carrion in a kiddies' park.

Gövan remembered his grandfather tilling the earth until he was eighty years old, and no one gave it a second thought. That was real. "Are you happy?" he sometimes asked his children, putting that excessive burden on them, forcing them to answer a question they couldn't possibly understand, a question that not even an adult could answer honestly. He had never stopped to wonder whether or not he was happy as a boy. Happiness, frustration—those were things he discovered far later, when he went to Malmö to study and another kind of ambition took hold: a desire for luxury, power, money, social capital.

"Why put on this show? A decapitated body holding its own head, sitting on a swing. It's sick."

"I'd stake my head on that."

"Very clever, Inga. But it's not funny." The body had been found by a boy, sitting there next to his favorite slide, in the same park where mothers took their little ones to play every morning as they sat reading books while their dogs ran around a special fenced-in area to do their business. If this could happen here, anything could.

As a boy, without even knowing it, Gövan was the happiest kid. But at the time there were no words for it. When he got sick, his mother would get the medicine she kept in a cabinet in the pantry where they kept important things: the good dishes for holidays, embroidery that his grandmother was making for Gövan's sisters' trousseaux, fancy knick-knacks brought back by a relative on a rare trip to the city. If anyone got truly sick, and aspirin, painkillers, or iodine were not enough, they tried some sort of poultice, something mysterious that the elders knew about. Roots, plants, flowers, or seeds. Then came commending oneself to the ancestral gods, and, only in the most extreme cases, when things were very grave indeed, would his father walk the twelve kilometers to the mail room, the only place around with a telephone. And he'd call for help. The doctor, if indeed he did come, took more than three hours to get there. Back then people saw intrusions from the modern world as proof that they couldn't handle things on their own, and so tried to avoid them. And horrors like this didn't exist.

"You think this is related to whoever slit the guy's throat at the port?"

Inga studied the wound on the corpse's throat. She didn't dare speculate without some test results.

"Sture? Anything's possible. If there's one person capable of something like this, it's the Turk."

The deputy chief looked up at the sky. It was going to rain. He thought about his new suit. It hadn't occurred to him to grab an umbrella when he left home. He loosened the knot of his tie. Despite the cold, his hands were sweating. He tilted his head and saw the investigators with their portable spotlights and the gray morgue van. Gövan's older son wanted to be a judge. He believed in justice. The younger one, though, wanted to be a cop; he admired his father, cut out all the newspaper articles that mentioned him, and stuck them carefully onto colored poster board to show his classmates. If his kids followed in his footsteps, they'd both see things like this, and their innocence would be destroyed forever.

"We all lose our innocence at some point, right? It's inevitable."

Inga recognized one of those looks Gövan sometimes got, she'd seen them on occasion when they had breakfast after a shift and then went to her small rental by the pier to have sex and then sleep, exhausted but energized.

"I suppose so. We all get to that point sometime."

For Gövan, it was when his older sister had died of appendicitis. The doctor couldn't do anything for her, said it was too late. If there had been a way to get her to the hospital immediately, she would have been saved. That was when Gövan knew he had to get out, move to the city, to *civilization*. Now he felt the tragedy of that belief, as if he were the victim of an ambition no one but he had ever felt. *Civilization* had created monstrosities like the one now before him.

"Do we know anything about the victim?"

The inspector handed him a slip of paper folded in two. She let their fingers touch a moment longer than necessary.

"Nothing. His wallet was emptied. I'll ask immigration— the guy looks Middle Eastern. We might get lucky with his prints, he must have a file in some country or other. This was all he had in his pockets."

Gövan looked at the paper and felt every hair stand on end. He glanced sidelong at Inga. Had she clocked his reaction? It didn't seem so; all she'd seen was a phone number, something to check out.

"I'll take care of this," he said, collecting himself. "You focus on the postmortem. District Attorney Fosen is very meticulous, and I don't want any procedural irregularities. There's a lot riding on this."

"Listen, deputy. I know this is important. I'm not going to make you look bad. For old times' sake."

Gövan frowned. He was still too young to think back on old times with any nostalgia. Sometimes he forgot that Inga was twelve years older than him, and that the older we get the more our memories act as a kind of balm. He needed her on his side.

"We should go have a beer sometime. When all this is over."

Inga furrowed her brow and pulled away.

"No need to buy me off with that crap, Gövan. I'll do my job properly, don't you worry."

Gövan sighed, exhausted. He didn't have time for any scenes.

He left the forensics crew to do their job in the tent they'd erected in the park, instructing them to contact him with any news. Then he left the park, avoiding journalists and the public, and lit a cigarette before climbing into his car. He wanted to be anyplace but here, wanted to be a better person. Different. But this was what he was, a phony who was sometimes authentic, who struggled to know when he was being which. No matter how much he triumphed, he would always be the farmer's son, the yokel who came to Malmö as a teenager who could barely recite his times tables. Back then, when all Gövan wanted was for his father to be proud of him, everything was easy. He had always had blind faith in his father, the man was his hero, represented order in a world where everything had a natural, fixed, permanent place. His father kept them safe, was the provider and the keeper of knowledge that his children would one day inherit. But when his sister died, Gövan watched him crumble and realized that the farm was no longer his place in the world. And he was still searching, trying to find out where that place was.

Gövan looked at his hands, still holding the slip of paper.

"Damn it," he whispered, tossing his cigarette to the ground. The journalists approached like a swarm of insects. The deputy chief had to do something about this phone number before Inga got too far in her investigation. He was all too aware of how efficient his ex-girlfriend was.

Abdul's favorite gem of the collection he kept in a leather case was the milky-white quartz. It had almost no impurities, and the cracks were so tiny they could only be seen under a very powerful magnifying glass. People said this particular kind of quartz had special qualities, could soothe the soul, bring good luck. But Abdul didn't believe in that kind of thing. The reason it was the one he most valued was because when he looked at it, as he did each morning, it reminded him of his youth and when he secretly got engaged to his dead wife, may Allah keep her in his glory. Abdul remembered the surprise on her face when he placed the little glass rock in the palm of her tiny hand. She was only thirteen, and her eyes—so hard to fill with joy—were deep and dark, a precipice he was afraid to approach. Maybe that was what had caught Abdul's attention: her melancholy air, so overwhelming in someone so young; she had an absent expression that complemented her long black hair, broad forehead, and wan mouth, her slender yet harsh body, so hard to conquer. Anyone else would have been put off by her premature bitterness and narrow hips, which prophesied difficult labors and few children. But Abdul looked past her

thirteen years and saw the woman she'd become: strong, re-
silient, willing to follow him anyplace. She was like a vicious
stray—loyal to the death to the one hand that strokes it.

How old was he when their marriage was arranged? He
didn't recall, but far older than her, that was for sure, so
much so that she was scared the first time she saw him. But
the quartz had smoothed the way. The marriage had been
arranged by their families, as was the custom. Her father
forced her to marry a *gadfly*: that was what he called him to
humiliate him in front of the whole village. It was his way of
saying: *You don't fool me. You're only half a man, so you deserve
no more than half a woman.* For some time, a rumor had been
going around the village that young Abdul did more than
clean Captain Pizarro's uniform to fulfill his duties as assistant. They'd heard that he'd taken to the good life in Tangier, riding around in cars, drinking European coffee, and
smoking American cigarettes. They also said he dressed
like a ridiculous hoodlum, wearing shirts and jackets that
Enrique handed down when he tired of them, that he slicked
his hair back and wore ludicrous sunglasses.

Everyone knew perfectly well who paid for all of that ex-
travagance. But what shamed his father Rachid the most was
not the gossip about his son's relationship with the captain—
in war, one learns to look at things differently. What Rachid
absolutely detested in his son was the boy's vanity. One must
never use another man's merits to pretend to be a man oneself. Abdul had never been to war, never eviscerated the
enemy with a bayonet, or engaged in hand-to-hand combat with unremitting Reds who never surrendered. His son

acted brave and manly but had no idea what it felt like to cut a man to pieces, slicing off an ear, a nose, a finger, his balls and penis to make him talk. He'd never looted or plundered or smashed a dead man's jaw with the butt of his rifle to take a gold tooth. He'd never rummaged through piles of corpses or fought others for a pair of boots or a bloodstained pack of cigarettes. He'd never parted a woman's—or man's— buttocks or gang-raped anyone, feeling nausea and desire at the same, ready to spill his seed. Nobody wanted to climax into a body that's been defiled by eight men, into a heap that's no longer even a hole but a grotesque whimpering pile of rags begging to be killed. But the sergeant orders you not to stop, to show no mercy, to bite the dying woman's breast, piss and shit on her, and no matter how sick you feel, you manage to get an erection and tell yourself that this is not a person, not anymore, that it's just a sack of bones, a cavity dripping blood and other men's semen, and that you have to do it because rape is the preferred tool of war for those who sow terror. It demoralizes the soldiers on the front and makes them want to return to the rearguard to protect their mothers, wives, and daughters.

Abdul knew nothing of that. All he did was go about the village putting on airs, acting like a conquistador, a two-bit hero with a record player and all the other baubles that colonial troops had once used to buy off the Kabyle chiefs. With Enrique Pizarro, his son thought he was better than his own father and every other man in the village. Rachid's onetime comrade had long forgotten the atrocities they were forced to commit together. Now Enrique Pizarro was on the Tabor

227

police, a man who cultivated friendships with politicians, hung around artists and important people. As if that could erase the other, eliminate the stench of the past. As if marrying an Englishwoman and turning up in the village with Abdul and his daughter—a girl who was Spanish, English, and Tangerine, three-thirds nothing—could ever hide what Enrique really was, what Rachid knew he was. And what he was turning his son into. His own whore. Rachid couldn't stop any of that, but he could force Abdul to honor his will and marry whomever he deemed appropriate.

Abdul never stopped to wonder what kind of husband he'd been; those were frivolous questions, the kind that belonged to another generation, one that questioned their lives and feelings ad nauseam. It all used to be easier somehow. After the wedding, his wife stayed in the village and he went back to Tangier. He'd go back and visit her from time to time, and on one of those visits, he got her pregnant, because that was what was expected of him. His wife never reproached him or asked for more than he gave. Abdul treated her well, as well as he knew how. She never asked where the money came from; she simply took it and administered it, obeying in silence. She was one of those who keep everything inside. Even the night in 1954 when Enrique and little Helena came to the village. Abdul was never proud of what he forced his wife to do that night but, truth be told, neither did he feel any tremendous regret. Besides, it wasn't his idea, it was Enrique's, and Abdul—half-drunk and afraid to displease his benefactor—either couldn't or wouldn't go against his wishes. And after all, ultimately, she was his wife and had to obey. After that night, whenever Abdul watched her doing chores, he got flashes of guilt, which he hid by yelling and hitting her for the most trivial of reasons.

"Remembering brings nothing good," he murmured, putting away the case of minerals. Memories were like termites, eating away at the present, boring holes in it and making it weak.

On TV they were talking about the head found in the park that morning.

"Savages!" Savages like Rachid the Spaniard, who delighted in gruesomeness as though it were a virtue, proof of manhood. Maybe what Abdul liked about Enrique at first was the fact that despite living through the same things as his father, he'd become a different kind of man. The other Enrique, the one who had survived the war with Rachid, only surfaced from time to time, like that night in the village. Occasionally, the captain had to get it out of his system, to snap and lash out before he could get back to sleep, tucked inside the other version, the father of the inquisitive little Helena, the refined husband of an English painter.

Thelma! How many nights had Abdul masturbated thinking of those huge eyes, which wanted nothing more than to paint his portrait, to trap him on canvas. Thelma drove him crazy with her offhanded benevolence: she let him wander around the house, play with Helena, sit with them in the afternoons drinking lemonade among the bougainvillea, join her in games of *mus*, and smoke her cigarettes. And yet she was indifferent to his innuendos. She made him think he was one of them, one of the family, part of the circle. But it was never true. Maybe that was why he stole what she cared about most from her, out of spite.

Seducing Enrique, or letting himself be seduced by him, was easy. Captain Pizarro was an open book if you knew how to read him. Moving from back alleys and dirty cots to infatuation and obsession wasn't hard. Abdul was aware of the urges he aroused in men and never felt ashamed of it. Sex with Enrique was something he didn't care about. He felt no real desire, but no disgust either. They started up a year after Abdul entered his service, when it seemed a necessary price to pay for the life Enrique offered him, as well as just revenge against Thelma. The captain was always gentle—sometimes too gentle for Abdul's taste—and never rushed, he didn't penetrate him until Abdul was ready. Enrique instructed his pupil well in the arts of sodomy and oral sex. Abdul had a greater repertoire and more stamina than Enrique; he knew how to exhaust the captain and drive him wild with desire, and lacked the captain's apprehensions. He knew Enrique liked him to be rough and penetrate him brutally, that he was turned on by dirty talk, by ridiculous things like "Come in my face" or "This is what I'm going to do to you." It was just a little show, and Abdul performed masterfully.

But not even by following him on his crazy adventure around the world could Abdul wrench Enrique's wife and daughter from him entirely. He never understood the stupid custom of sending Helena a postcard on her birthday.

"Why do you write to her?" he objected jealously. "You're like Tom Thumb, leaving a trail of crumbs that are easy to follow. Sometimes I think you feel guilty for having left them and actually want the army to catch you and punish you."

Enrique would respond jokingly, saying that the two of them weren't important enough—two outlaws on the run, and Abdul not even a soldier.

"Wake up, my dear friend," he'd tell Abdul. Sometimes Enrique distanced himself from Abdul in a way that was subtle yet hurtful. It was like he wanted to remind him that being on this adventure together didn't make them equals in any way. "Spain has more pressing things to deal with than a man who deserted four years ago. Don't you read the papers? Eisenhower declared Franco a loyal ally, the Valley of the Fallen has been inaugurated, Pope John XXIII formally condemned Communism, and that bearded lawyer Castro has taken power in Cuba. They've got enough on their hands with internal dissidents, chasing Communists to France, and trying to keep Western democracies from growing uneasy. Believe me, there's no reward on our heads, and nobody's wasting resources to find us. Sure, the generals would love to put me in front of a firing squad, but they won't do anything to find some captain they'd rather pretend doesn't exist."

Enrique's near-comic obliviousness bothered Abdul, the way he downplayed their life on the run. To Enrique there wasn't a ghost of a chance that anyone was looking for them, no threat of imminent danger at all. Once they'd successfully fled, gotten out, they no longer watched their backs to see if anyone was waiting treacherously to shoot them, no longer grew uneasy if a car slowed down as it passed them by. They were falling into routines ludicrously similar to those of any married couple. Sure, Abdul got to see a lot of the world, and at the time Enrique had sufficient funds for them to live the good life—fancy restaurants, nice clothes, traveling first class, and a few special treats like the watch he now wore—but he was beginning to realize that the world was the same all over. The faces changed, the smells and languages, the landscape, but basically it was the same everywhere: people coming and going; cities with public squares, fountains, buildings, and monuments that he had no interest in, even though Enrique insisted on describing their history; boring museums where Enrique spent hours contemplating the same painting; bookshops full of nothing but dust and old books and where Enrique wasted time chatting excitedly with some mousy-faced bookseller about *Amadís de Gaula*. Buses, trains, taxis, and ports wherever they went.

On the February morning in 1959 when Abdul betrayed Enrique, after four years on the lam, they were in Milan's bus station, about to board a bus that would take them to Rome. Enrique had promised with habitual enthusiasm that Abdul would love the Coliseum, St. Peter's Square, and the Vatican Museum. But Abdul wasn't listening. He was in a bad mood almost all the time; the smell of gas and oil from the buses depressed him; it was cold and rainy.

"I miss my family. Fatima is five years old, but the last time I saw her she couldn't even walk." Enrique had bought a postcard at a kiosk and was writing to his daughter, using the suitcase on his thighs as a table. "Are you listening to me? You get to write to your daughter but I can't see mine. It's not fair."

Enrique looked up. Four years of running had taken their toll: he'd lost some of the glimmer from his pretty green eyes. He'd grown older and thinner.

"I am your family now, Abdul. I take care of your daughter. Does your wife not receive a check each month? You could show a little more appreciation; after all, I'm doing all of this for you."

How many times had they had this argument? Hundreds, almost from the first day. And each time it ended the same way: Enrique, furious, would throw a few wrinkled bills at Abdul and tell him to go, leave forever. *Go back to your piece-of-shit village, with your goats and flies.* Abdul would ask forgiveness; Enrique would act offended until Abdul got down on his knees, pulled down his fly and sucked him off. Then Enrique would whimper and moan, weep and tell him that he loved him, that without Abdul he was nothing, that he'd thrown it all away—his life, his military career, his family—just to be with him. *If you leave me, I'll slit my wrists.* At first, these little numbers dissuaded Abdul. He really believed that Enrique was capable of taking his own life, and, in a way it flattered him, as did the captain's attentions; he was excited at first by all the things Enrique knew about the world that he himself did not. But he'd been fed up now for some time; Enrique disgusted him. The captain thought of himself as unimportant to the Franco regime, but Abdul wasn't so sure. If there were some kind of reward, no matter how small, if he could get some kind of bonus for giving Enrique up, he wouldn't have to go back to the village empty-handed and face the condemnation of his father and all the neighbors.

When they got to Rome, he managed to slip away for a few hours, and he used that time to take a taxi to the Spanish embassy.

Abdul didn't regret what he did. Not even when he thought of the look on Enrique's face as he stood there buck naked, shaving, when two embassy officials burst into their hotel room and threw him violently to the ground, twisting his arm as though he were a dangerous criminal. Enrique didn't take his eyes off Abdul for a second, staring at him not in hatred or in rage but in animal-like bewilderment, pain caused by something far deeper than the unnecessary blows the men delivered before dragging him to a car parked on the street. They didn't even let him put on his underpants.

"A man does what he has to do," Abdul said to himself now. He was watching the news, but in his mind's eye he was watching that car drive away from the hotel, seeing the tire marks it left on wet asphalt that morning in 1959, as he counted the thousand-peseta notes in the envelope they'd given him at the embassy, which also contained an Iberia plane ticket and a Spanish visa.

Abdul couldn't remember what he'd done with the money. He probably spent it on trinkets for his wife, father, and daughter, but that didn't matter. How much is a man's life worth? He didn't know. He'd have turned in Enrique for nothing at all, such was the scorn he'd accumulated over four years on the run. His ever-changing moods, arrogance—followed by obsequiousness—the sex, even his company, the smell of his cologne, and the sight of his clothes on a chair sickened him. Abdul felt deceived. When Enrique convinced him that they should run off together, he'd promised Abdul so many things that had never materialized. It was time to go home.

The old man turned down the volume and cocked his ear.

On the other side of the wall, he heard Yasmina humming. It was like another world. His granddaughter's voice sounded muffled and in its own way was like a gemstone trapped in a leather case. Yasmina was the punishment Allah had imposed on him for his sins. That was why he hated her so.

Yasmina was resting her elbows on the windowsill. Peter Bjorn and John's voices, singing "Young Folks," bored into her brain like a stiletto: "... it doesn't matter what we do, where we are going to, we can stick around and see this night through."

She was trying not to think about what Sture had told her a few minutes earlier. The phone was still in her hand, the conversation still buzzing in her ears.

"Things are going to get ugly, Yasmina. But I want you to stay calm, I'll take care of everything, like always. You just be strong."

He'd sounded like the same old Sture—good-natured, witty, and carefree. But Yasmina sensed fear beneath his words, like the distant rumble of an earthquake from far underground. Then she'd turned on the TV and seen Gövan giving a statement to a swarm of reporters in front of the playground. For a few seconds she didn't pay attention to what he was saying. "Chicken feed," she said to herself, using the deputy chief's word; that was what he said every time he talked to reporters. "They're like chickens, you just have to give them a little feed once in a while." What Yasmina was thinking was that Gövan's nice suit was going to get ruined in the rain, and that he looked handsome playing spokesperson. He conveyed confidence and resolve, like an honest man determined to do the right thing for the community. But the community he claimed to protect didn't know that their protector was also sleeping with her behind his wife's back, that he loved it when she licked his ass, or that he had varicose veins on his ankles—the result of years spent standing endlessly at roadblocks when he was a patrolman. The journalists shoving microphones in his face didn't know he had a smiling sun tattooed on his right butt cheek. So childlike it was more adorable than macho.

After a few seconds she started paying attention to the words he spoke at this impromptu press conference. A decapitated man sitting on a swing, a traumatized boy who had found the body while he was playing, indignant parents, low crime rates, some of the lowest in Europe, statistics, numbers to calm the plebes. Solemn promises to solve the case.

The phone rang again. This time it was Gövan's number. Alarmed, Yasmina let it ring without picking up. That was what Sture had told her to do, not answer the phone if the deputy chief called, not speak to him or see him until further instructions. She put out the cigarette she'd been smoking by crushing it into a pot of carnations and wondered for the umpteenth time, as she leaned out the window, why she couldn't make herself jump.

What a lovely sight that would be, smashing into the wet sidewalk below, to the astonishment of passersby. So why not do it, then? Seven stories, it was a sure bet. Her death wouldn't make any difference, nobody would care if she was gone. In fact, she was sure that plenty of people would breathe a sigh of relief. The constables would write up their reports and head off to bed; Sture would be free of the irksome burden of a witness; her grandfather would thank God; and her mother would gaze at her shattered body as though staring at a blank wall.

"Fuck all of you."

She got a WhatsApp notification. It was Gövan.

"I need you to call me. It's important; we have to talk."

Yasmina looked down, half her body still out the window.

Gövan. What would he feel if she jumped? Would he, at least, miss her?

12

Sevilla and Tarifa

When Natalia kept still it was worse. Weakness only upset him more. It was like beating a helpless puppy with a stick. Her darting eyes, her submission, her silence made Gustavo want to puke. It was easier when she fought back, kicked and scratched, insulted and spat. When she struggled with all her might until she ran out of steam. The struggle—fingernails on his face, biting his forearms—infuriated him, of course, but it gave him one more excuse, fuel for the fire of his rage. Now, the dull sound of his blows against her ribs as he kicked her was like taking anger out on a sandbag. Tedious.

Gustavo saw himself sitting on the chair in his T-shirt and underwear, still wearing his socks. Natalia was on the bed in front of him, turned to the wall, curled up and protecting herself with nothing but the sheet tangled between her legs and chest. Silent. Like she was dead.

"Say something," he muttered.

But she wouldn't. Gustavo was clenching and unclenching one fist. He was afraid that he might have hurt one of his fingers and thought about the concert; he needed his damn hand to play guitar. His knuckles were stinging. What had kicked it off this time? What did it matter? His rage was cooling, and regret surged up like a wave of bile.

"Natalia, I'm sorry. I . . . I don't know what comes over me."

Someone should open his skull with a hammer and chisel, poke around in his gray matter. Then they could tell him where the boiling lava came from, the rage that bubbled away beneath his normal exterior, making him think of Natalia as invisible until suddenly he became aware of her presence and felt a dull hatred for her, an almost uncontrollable desire to hurt her. Was it that he didn't love her? But if that was the case, why had he been unable to forget about her? Every day they were apart had been hell, but now that they were back together, now that they were going to be parents, Gustavo couldn't stop thinking that she was the reason he'd been locked up to begin with. He couldn't forget the days he spent in a cell, the humiliation of having to undress in front of the police, face accusing looks from the attorney, the prosecutor, and the judge—all female. And what had really hurt was listening to Miguel's insults, hearing the scorn in his voice. The old man had actually spit on him at the courthouse door, and Gustavo could still feel saliva sliding down his cheek.

"I'm crazy. That's the only explanation."

He looked at Natalia, but her lips weren't even moving. Gustavo's words seemed not to have the slightest effect on her. This wasn't scorn, it was far worse. Something he couldn't stand. Indifference.

If only he could blame his irrational violence on something, on someone. His father, for example. Didn't professionals say that an adult's warped behavior stemmed from childhood trauma? Gustavo had made up some bullshit about his father abusing him so the forensic psychologist on his case would leave him alone. A childhood filled with screaming and shouting, dark rooms, and sphincters unclenching in bed seemed like a good alibi. But it was all a lie. Maybe his father hadn't been the most loving man in the world, but he'd never raised his hand or even his voice to Gustavo. In fact, he was a softy. The man had no balls, and regardless of what his son did—even if he'd shat in the middle of the living room or lit the sofa on fire—he simply lowered his gaze and looked through Gustavo as if he didn't exist. No rage, no reproach, no emotion.

He touched Natalia's swollen eyelid. All she did was squeeze her eyes shut more tightly.

"You shouldn't go to work today," he advised.

He waited. She said nothing. One word would have been enough for him to feel okay again. She could straighten up the damn books that were all over the place, stop acting like a pregnant cow, be a little less sarcastic when he showed her the song lyrics he was writing. Change her expression so he didn't see Miguel in her eyes. The superiority, the haughtiness. It wasn't too much to ask, damn it! He felt rage lurking once more, creeping up like a form of solace. He clenched a fist. He hoped his hand wasn't messed up. How would the group find another guitarist at such short notice?

Exasperated, he left Natalia's side and started concentrating on the lyrics he'd been writing before this had all kicked off, before she interrupted him with one of those stupid arguments about Miguel's disease, about going to see him in Tarifa. Stupid old man, that son of a bitch. Even without being there, his presence somehow poisoned everything. He found his song in the mess of other papers on the floor, under an overturned chair. In tiny cramped letters—the writing of a conscientious, introverted boy—was the chorus he'd been trying to compose. Every word chosen with care. But it wasn't working, it was a piece of shit. It sounded like a childish refrain. A fucking Christmas carol, that was what the guys in the band would say, laughing at him derisively. Gustavo had lost his touch, that was the simple fucking truth. He used to have it, the talent, the touch, that special something that made people shiver. But now he was all washed-up.

He wadded up the paper and turned back to the bed. Misery was written all over Natalia's face.

"For fuck's sake, enough with the song and dance. It wasn't that big a deal!"

He grabbed the chair off the floor and hurled it against the wall to let off some steam. Crows began fluttering in his eyes, their feathers jet black. He had to get out of there. He wasn't about to let her see him cry. Gustavo grabbed his jacket and stormed out of the apartment, slamming the door behind him.

One after another, hours dripped and then fell from the clock, but it wasn't until darkness began to overtake the cloistered garden and the last visitors were saying goodbye to their relatives that Miguel accepted that Natalia wasn't going to show.

He walked back up the gravel path to the main entrance, still hoping in vain that he'd see her rush up in that harried, out-of-breath way she had, jabbering excuses, smiling and overheated: *Traffic was terrible* or *I took the wrong exit.* But there was no one there. He looked at his cell phone again. He'd called a dozen times, and each time it had gone to voicemail—the slightly irreverent recorded message, his daughter's voice saying, "Clearly, I can't get to you right now. If it's urgent, keep trying." What if something had happened on her way from Sevilla? She shouldn't even be driving in her state. Natalia would have laughed at that idea: *Papá, I'm not dying, I'm pregnant.*

Miguel wondered if he'd written down the day she was coming wrong. He could no longer trust his memory entirely; he forgot simple things, like where he'd put his glasses, whether or not he'd brushed his teeth, or how far he'd gotten in whatever he was reading. But there was no way he could have gotten this wrong. Natalia had promised she would come today, and even said it would be without Gustavo. She'd seemed so happy about seeing him again!

Something had happened. This terrible feeling had grown stronger with each passing hour. *You always imagine the worst, a professional pessimist*, his wife used to joke. It was true, at least as far as his daughter was concerned. If Natalia was late coming home from school, Miguel agonized, thinking she'd been hit by a car or kidnapped; if she had the slightest fever, he imagined some devastating virus was attacking her. And it only got worse when her body started to develop, when she began dressing differently, wearing makeup, going out with friends, and staying out late in discos. He had lain awake, listening for her to return in the wee hours of the night, watching her drunkenly take off her shoes and drag her feet to bed, and wondering if she might be on drugs. He listened to her getting into the shower and agonized over whether she might be having unsafe sex, whether someone might be abusing her. He had never dared to show these fears openly, but the thought that anything bad could happen to his daughter didn't stop tormenting him, ironically, until she married that bastard Gustavo.

"She must have forgotten," Helena said at dinner, hours later, absorbed in her own thoughts. Miguel felt disenchanted by his friend's offhandedness.

"My daughter would never do something so cruel."

Helena shot him a frosty look.

"Children are capable of the worst sort of cruelty."

Miguel stood up, offended.

"And you think we're not partially to blame for that?"

He spent all night clicking his cell phone on and off. The screen would light up his face in the darkness for a second and then go dim, with no news from Natalia. He'd called the Sevilla hospital: his daughter wasn't there, which was good. The Civil Guard Traffic Department had no record of any serious accidents on the road between Sevilla and Tarifa that night: another relief. He'd even called the local police. They had sent a car to Natalia's apartment, but no one answered when they rang the bell.

There was still an endlessly monotonous stretch of hours before dawn, and all he could do was keep spinning his wheels back and forth without getting anywhere. That and wait. Up and down, back and forth, Miguel's thoughts danced and swirled from one minute to the next. He was going to drive himself nuts. It was like when he used to spend the night waiting for a call from the police or some hospital to tell him that they'd found his mother wandering the streets naked, bruised, and disoriented, showing signs of having been the victim of some form of violence that she had no memory of. Once they had asked him over the phone to describe any scars or birthmarks his mother had on her body, because they'd found an indigent woman totally drugged-out in an abandoned car, after being brutally raped. Miguel swallowed. He'd never seen his mother naked. In the end, he went in person to identify her. It had turned out not to be his mother, but Miguel had broken down and sobbed and had to be given a tranquilizer.

He sat by the window gazing out at the moon; it was low, orange, and liquid, like an egg yolk. Everything seemed so easy out there, so calm and in harmony, in its place, all connected by invisible threads. Suddenly, Miguel sensed

Amador's presence in the room. His father was lying in wait, crouching in the shadows, but Miguel could hear his breathing—like a hidden tiger, waiting for . . . something. The dead breathe. When Natalia was a baby, Miguel would wake up, startled, and put a finger to his daughter's tiny nose to feel the warm air going in and out, making its way through the mucus. That was the only thing that calmed him. Breath is life.

Closure, he thought suddenly. That was what his father was waiting for. For something to happen. In Águeda's puritanical view, his father would be a *heraldic angel*, a messenger on a mission whose meaning would only be revealed at the end. But Miguel didn't believe in that.

"A half-wit, that's what you are. A bump on a log in the forest of other people's sorrows."

His father made no reply, nor did he step out of the shadows. He kept breathing in the dark, watching over Miguel's insomnia.

At nine o'clock the next morning, Natalia finally picked up the phone. Miguel's exhaustion after a night spent tossing and turning magically vanished.

"Daughter. Are you okay?"

"Hi, Papá." Natalia's voice was distant, impersonal. Like the voice on an answering machine. It sounded deep, as though she'd just woken up—or had taken a sedative. Her words were slightly slurred.

Miguel could hardly contain his concern.

"Are you okay? Good God, Natalia, you have no idea what a night I had. Imagining the thousands of terrible things that could have happened to you."

Her voice became more distant, almost evasive. Miguel pictured her speaking with the receiver pressed close to her mouth, hiding in the bathroom or bedroom.

"Nothing bad, Papá. I'm so sorry I couldn't let you know I wasn't coming. Something came up."

There were plenty of things Miguel didn't know about his daughter, but he could tell when she was nervous or impatient, and it made the lies she gave as excuses flimsy. A wave of fear mixed with growing rage crept up his spinal column and took hold at the back of his neck, like a metal claw.

"It happened again, didn't it?"

Natalia's voice broke, turning hesitant.

"I don't know what you're talking about. I'm fine."

"Did you and Gustavo have an argument? Did he lay a hand on you?"

She feigned indignance, shock. But her breath became shallow and she had a sudden pressing urge to end the call. Miguel could hear Gustavo's voice in the background.

"I've got to go, Papá. I'll call you. I'll come see you next week, I promise. We'll talk."

"Listen to me, Natalia. Tell me what's happening. I'm here for you . . . Natalia?"

He heard shouting, arguing. Gustavo had snatched the phone away. He was drunk, the kind of drunk that becomes obvious precisely by concentrating so hard on feigning sobriety. When people are so careful pronouncing words and moving limbs, they become robotic.

"You can't help it, can you, old man? You can't stop meddling in your daughter's life and accept the fact that she's not a little girl anymore. Listen to me, Miguel. Why don't you just stay there in that fucking home and die? Don't call Natalia again. She's not going to answer the phone and she won't be seeing you. Do you hear me?"

Before Miguel had time to react, Gustavo hung up.

Call the cops. That was the first thing he thought. But he discarded the idea, knowing what would happen. The officers would undertake a routine inspection, maybe see something strange—the apartment in disarray, Natalia's head bowed, a scratch on her arm or a red blotch by her lip. They'd ask questions, insist, offer to take her to the hospital, file a complaint. But she would refuse, and when they left, Gustavo would be furious and make her pay for Miguel's decision. Still, he couldn't just sit there with his arms crossed. He'd done that once, as did everyone they knew: friends, neighbors. Their complicit, exculpatory silence is what had nearly cost Natalia her life. Miguel wasn't about to let that happen again.

"It's painful to know those you love are suffering and not be able to stop it."

His father was there at the window, where dust-specked daylight streamed in, making him look real. Miguel felt self-loathing radiate from every pore. What kind of father had he been to Natalia? An impatient one. His anger passed quickly and he didn't harbor grudges, true, but it soured his character and earned him unnecessary enemies. Perhaps his daughter had ended up hating his tics, the way he talked, the things he did—and those he didn't do. But he was her father; she was his daughter. And when you love someone, you never abandon them, ever.

"Let me tell you something, Father: you're a sham, so don't you dare try to tell me what it means to love someone."

Helena looked pensive. It was a distance of three thousand kilometers, drawn in a straight red marker line on the map. On paper it was a clear shot, no corners, no detours, no hesitation or mistakes. That was how Louise liked things, the straight line being the shortest distance between two points. "Look," she'd said excitedly, a cigarette between her teeth, unfolding a map of the United States, "this is the route Kerouac describes in his novel. This is how I'll get to Los Angeles—to Hollywood. The Walk of Fame awaits! Easy, right?" Easy. Everything was easy for Louise.

But LA was not Malmö. And Helena was not Louise. In Malmö, at that time of day, under a layer of fresh snow that would harden on roofs and form thick icicles on gutters, people slept all toasty and warm with the central heating blasting, though David had told her that houses there were all energy-efficient. Helena had no idea what that meant. It must have been beautiful, a port city with orderly streets, low houses, everything so clean, all green and blue. The wooden homes with their windows painted white, a tram gliding silently through the snow. That was more or less how she pictured them: a Nordic TV-commercial family, charming and modern, with their DIY furniture in their energy-efficient home, a family car with snow tires, a 40-inch plasma-screen TV and a wrought-iron fireplace, two well-behaved and slightly timid kids whose bicycles were parked by the door, and a dog that didn't leave slobber or hair all over the carpet. Though she was afraid things weren't so nice. The truth was, she didn't even know if it was snowing in Malmö. Maybe it was unbearably hot right now, the streets filthy, and it smelled like rotten fish. Maybe David's house was impersonal and lacked the warmth of a real home.

Days earlier, her decision to go to Malmö had seemed like a great idea. But as the hours ticked by, she felt increasingly wracked by doubts.

What would she say to them? She was going to show up unannounced, because David kept postponing and making excuses, and play granny, a suitcase in her hands. She'd be the inconvenient guest, met at the door with a nervous smile and insincere graciousness. The kids had never even met her, Marta couldn't stand her, and David hardly knew anything about her—what music she listened to, what books she read, what she liked to eat. Over the past three years their contact had been limited to short weekly Skype calls where they made small talk, joked a little, and avoided awkward silence. His family would welcome her stiffly, she'd be invading their privacy, wouldn't find anywhere to sit on the toy-strewn sofa, and the live-in housekeeper would eye her with hostility. They wouldn't know where to put her—maybe in a small guest room or the library, which would have a pull-out sofa bed. They'd have to find a set of sheets and towels, give her a cursory explanation of how the heating and TV worked, show her where the fridge was, where the bread was kept. The dog and the children would follow her around the house, staring as if she were a Martian, asking impertinent questions. Or, worse yet, they'd ignore her, too intent on killing enemies on their video consoles. She might last a few days before tension erupted in the form of nighttime whispers from David's room. Without wanting to, Helena would overhear Marta's voice: *She's got to go; we need to take back our lives. The kids have school, you and I work. We can't be responsible for her. Why did she even come?* And the worst thing would be hearing no reply. David's silent acquiescence.

Any way she looked at it, it was madness. She chided herself for the purchases she'd made that morning in the supermarket downtown, gifts to take them: olive oil, almonds from Alicante, white anchovies, a leg of Jabugo cured ham. She saw herself traipsing up and down aisles, poring over shelves crammed with products, wondering what David and the kids might like, acting like one of those German tourists in flip-flops and a floral-print bathing suit who ask the clerks where to find the "authentic" products, the ones from the famous Mediterranean diet. It was ridiculous. Did she think she could buy their affection? Were there no supermarkets in Sweden; did they not know olive oil or cured ham? Was she planning to pack all that stuff and take it with her, only to have it confiscated so a pack of savvy customs officials could have a toast in her honor?

"You're thinking like an old lady at a wedding who stuffs her purse with leftover bread rolls," she quipped aloud in self-reproach.

She couldn't keep lying to herself. This trip had had nothing to do with David and his family from the start, so she couldn't pretend to be the mother who lived too far from her son, the grandma who missed her grandchildren. The real reason she'd planned the trip was because she was afraid, more afraid than she'd ever been. Not even in the years of silence she endured with Walter had she felt the imminence of her failure so intensely. It was all Marqués's fault, that bastard had left her alone with the bare, naked evidence: *This awaits you too, lady. Loneliness, self-deceit, and a death that, no matter how tragically it plays out, won't change a thing.* Helena wanted to escape this fate, didn't want time to have the final word. She wanted to decide for herself how and where to live out her final days rather than languish, trapped in her memories like the resigned-looking old biddies she saw every morning. And she owed no one an explanation.

What about me? Don't you owe me an explanation? Walter came out with that every time they got into an argument— on account of Helena's independence—over whether she should take the job at that export business that wanted to hire her for her Spanish skills. "What do you know about Spain? You've never set foot in the country." That was true, but it was also true that when Grandfather Whitman died, and Grandmother Alice two years later, Helena discovered that she was poor, that she depended on Walter's salary as a professor, and she couldn't stand it. She'd feel bitter thinking of Louise—off in the US, conquering the world—while she was supposed to settle for being someone's side-kick, bringing children into the world, keeping house, and reading Jane Austen novels while Hubby brought home the bacon. She felt the need to prove herself, and Walter tried to accept her diatribes with poise, managing not to voice ironclad opposition but also expressing his bewilderment. He saw marriage as a sum of possibilities rather than a competition between individuals. And when he said as much, Helena would deride him. *What if it were the other way around? What if you were the rich kid who discovered he actually had nothing, instead of the prestigious professor who brought home his wages? What if you were the one who was supposed to cook, iron, and contemplate how to decorate the baby's room? Would you accept it with the same grace, or would your male ego feel humiliated?* Walter, in turn, would resort to disdain: to him it made no sense to entertain hypotheses that were impossible a priori.

No, Walter, not even you. I don't owe you anything; I control my own life.

Did she still actually believe that? Or was she just trying to pretend? These past few years had been difficult indeed, but what about those to come? Did she have to sit there just staring at Abdul's portrait, reading her father's postcards over and over? Did she have to act like she didn't know who she was or what she needed to do? Spend her days filling her lungs with smoke, stroking Louise's flask—and with it her unfulfilled dreams—staring at the sea, and wondering each morning if she'd ever dare to put her feet in the water? Did she have to wait for the girl she'd once been to leave the shore behind once and for all?

She couldn't do it; she'd thought she could be like the rest of them, accept the inevitable, but Marqués's death had awoken in her a desire to live, one last time.

She had to get out of there. And not come back.

Two days later, Miguel found Helena in the cloistered garden. She was sitting on one of the stone benches in her nicest clothes, as though headed off to a wedding, looking pensive.

"Isn't it sad how neglected this garden always looks?" she asked lightly, not weighing her words; it was a fleeting thought, trapped for an instant, something she really hadn't considered.

Helena blinked, emerging from her daydream. She smiled sincerely on seeing her friend, but it was only a second before her mouth returned to a flat line.

"It wouldn't have to be that way if the gardener did his job."

Miguel glanced back and forth from the garden to the old man in leather dungarees, raking leaves at the farthest part of the garden.

"Yes, I suppose things would run better if everyone did their jobs properly."

Her attention was caught by a flowerpot of withered tulips. It occurred to her that they were a sign of nature trying to breathe life into the stones, and that it wouldn't take long for them to die of the gardener's inattention. Things always die, inexorably, from the moment they're born.

"Director Roldán told me you're leaving."

"News travels fast. I'm sure no one will cry over my departure."

Miguel sat down beside her. Helena's perfume smelled lovely, inviting.

"Were you even going to tell me? I thought friendship bestowed certain privileges."

"I haven't been very good company lately, I think you'll agree." The ironic flash had disappeared from Helena's eye. There was no reason to lie or pretend. Miguel gave a slight nod. In the background he could hear the trickling of the fountain and, beyond the cloister, the residents' voices.

"Malmö is pretty far away."

Helena gave an unenthusiastic nod.

"Far enough."

Miguel remained pensive. He stood up and walked over to the fountain in the middle of the garden; it was almost impossible to see his own reflection in the murky green depths. *Life isn't worth much if you haven't lived it.* That thought had been boring into his self-assurance for days now.

"If you accept me as a travel partner, I'll go with you partway. We could make a few stops first, and then go to Barcelona. And from there, you'd be on your own."

Helena looked at her friend in concern.

"You're not serious. You and spontaneity aren't exactly best friends."

"I've never been more serious. And you'd be surprised how adaptable I am."

Helena approached Miguel and forced him to look into her face.

"What makes you want to come with me?"

Miguel looked away.

"I have my reasons. And my conditions."

"Conditions?"

"Yes. And they're nonnegotiable. I won't travel by plane; you know I'm scared to death of flying."

Helena eyed her friend at length.

"Some travel partners we'll make. You don't fly and I don't swim."

"There are trains, buses." Miguel gazed at her, so sphinxlike.

Helena smiled. For the first time in weeks, it was a liberating smile.

"What about the reasons? You suddenly caught the travel bug?"

Miguel shook his head. In a few months, maybe a year, he wouldn't even remember the names of things. He'd be stuck in the home, and nothing and no one would be able to do a thing about it. So why sit there waiting for the end rather than venture out in search of it?

"My reasons are my own."

Helena scrutinized her friend's face and found nothing but determination. She hadn't imagined things going this way, but wasn't afraid of a little improvisation.

"Well if we're going to be pilgrims, we'd better get walking," she joked.

The following morning, they left an hour later than planned. They'd been just about ready to go when Miguel suddenly contorted, grew pale, and said he needed to use the bathroom. He locked himself in there for over half an hour, and when he came out didn't look like he felt much better.

Nosey residents clustered at the windows as Miguel helped the taxi driver load their baggage into the trunk. A few gazed on the scene with wistfulness in their eyes; others stated flatly that this was insanity. And a few were happy to see them go, whether because borrowed dreams and hopes went with them or because they'd no longer have to mask their hostility; these were the same ones who had bristled impatiently at Professor Marqués's whims.

Helena raised her hand, waving to goad them on:

"You stay here with your noses to the glass and watch life pass you by."

The taxi driver started the engine and drove slowly between the pine trees, down the winding gravel path to the gate. Helena realized she'd never actually paid attention to the high wall with vines spilling over them. She felt no sense of loss on her way out of a place she knew she'd never return to.

"Well! Where to now?"

Miguel didn't hesitate.

"First, Sevilla. I have to take care of something."

Helena was tempted to ask what he had to do there, but something in Miguel's resolve made her desist. She leaned back against the seat and nodded. After all, nothing and no one was waiting for her. Nothing but the trip.

"Sevilla it is."

PART FOUR

May 2014

13

Sevilla

hrist, what happened to you? You look like shit."

Ivan jumped out of bed, pulled on his underwear, and examined his body in the mirror on the back of the door.

"War wounds."

He was proud of his muscles, the way they conveyed strength and determination. Given what he did for a living, Ivan couldn't afford not to be in shape. He wasn't like Ramiro and the Gypsy, his constant companions. Ivan never spent the day in bed jacking off and watching soccer, sniffing and smoking anything he could get his hands on. He spent two hours a day at the gym and practiced martial arts and extreme boxing with crazy Guillermo. People said Guillermo had broken a guy's trachea in a disco, which sent his career down the pan before he had a chance to go pro. Ten years in jail had put an end to it all. Now he fixed dogfights and trained a bunch of losers at the local sports complex.

But Ivan was no loser. "You've got what it takes, you're disciplined," Guillermo told him. That was why Guillermo was harder on him than the others, why he hit him harder and made him bust a gut in every fight, at every training session. Ivan saw him as the older brother he wished he'd had. His real brother, the one he'd left back in Ukraine, hit him like Guillermo did too, but that was different. His blood brother hit him just to vent, taking out his rage and frustration on him. Guillermo, on the other hand, hit him because he knew Ivan could take the blows, the black eyes and broken ribs. He did it to harden him, to school him. To help him.

Ivan massaged his jaw in the mirror and noticed it felt slack, like its spring had sprung. Feeling around with his tongue, he noticed a couple of loose teeth. It had been a good fight at the Coop last night, he thought smugly. It was hard to get a fight at the Coop, and only the toughest survived. Normally, the abandoned basement was used for dogfights, but from time to time, if the bets were high enough, Guillermo arranged bouts between good fighters. According to Guillermo, dogs and Ivan were pretty much the same thing: "They walk on four legs and you walk on two, but your bite is just as vicious. The only difference is dogs feel no hatred for their rivals. They fight because I teach them to, tell them to. You fight out of rage, though you're scared shitless. In case you didn't know, fear is what fuels hatred." Ivan wasn't so sure that was why he took to fighting. He didn't hate his rivals—they were just an obstacle to overcome—just as he didn't take any particular pleasure when Guillermo put him in contact with some third party wanting to get someone beat up, teach them a lesson, or have them spend a few days in the hospital. All for a fee. Ivan saw himself as a man with talent in a certain professional arena—hurting others—which he sold to earn a living, as anyone would: eight hundred euros to go up against two North Africans up to their eyeballs in coke, no spikes, chains, or clubs. Those were the wages of a modern-day gladiator. And the glory that came with victory is what earned him the right to sleep with girls like Zona.

Zona was for winners only, and Ivan was a winner. Guillermo had told him after the fight last night that he'd never met a nineteen-year-old with such a big reputation. "You fight like an Iraq War vet, kid. Those are some balls you got." And they were. Huge balls; he felt them in his underwear. He'd waxed for Zona. He liked her to lick them when they were full, liked her to watch him come. He waxed his ass too. It drove him wild when she played with it with her fingers and tongue, and occasionally the vibrator he kept in a drawer. Zona was solid, she wasn't about to tell anyone.

Ivan saw the reflection of Zona's perfect body in the mirror and thought of his brother, Pieter. He'd never have been able to handle a woman like Zona; he wouldn't have known what to do with her. Ivan smiled bitterly, thinking of the things Pieter had done to him in Ukraine back when he couldn't defend himself. Things were different now; Ivan was a warrior, and thumped his chest like a gorilla to remind himself he wasn't afraid of anyone or anything, even if he did wake up screaming, scaring Zona as she slept beside him. She'd ask grumpily what the hell was the matter, and Ivan would tell her to go back to sleep. He couldn't say he'd had a nightmare about his brother's rat face crawling into the room with flashing eyes, big and pointy gray rodent teeth, and a repulsive tongue that covered his face in slobber.

It was better to show off his scars. The marks of a true warrior.

"This gash here I got in the Kiev correctional facility when I was twelve. This one was in Madrid last year—two Colombians. And this one here, on my kidney, was last year at the local derby. Those Sevilla fuckers cornered me, but they got what they had coming."

Don't fuck with Ivan, that guy's a badass. He stuck out his chest, flexed his abs, and thought about something kinky to get hard again. He knew Zona would tell the other girls how it had gone in the bedroom as soon as they came downstairs. *Jesus, the Russian fucks like a madman. He wore me out.*

The Russian, those cretins called him Russian. They didn't even know where Ukraine was. But Ivan didn't bother to set them straight. How could he explain the difference between a fucking Russian piece of shit and a Kiev Ukrainian? Perestroika, glasnost, Yeltsin, Putin—it was all Greek to them. They knew nothing about the war of the oligarchs, Chechnya, or the Orange Revolution. His friends cared about nothing but soccer and getting off their faces. Their expressions glazed over if anyone talked about geostrategic interests, politics, international conflict. They were suspicious of anyone who talked stuff like that, so Ivan played dumb to earn their respect. Scratching his balls, belching, occasionally hitting a guy for no reason at all, those were his calling cards. But not long ago, Ramiro had caught him reading the poet Ivan Bunin—his father had named him after him—and been mystified, staring at the book as if he had no idea what it was for.

"Why are you reading that?"

"It's a book. And inside it is something called poetry."

"What's the point of that shit? What use is it?"

"This *shit* is beautiful. And it's not *used* for anything, which is why it's good for everything."

"Warm and heavy was the day / but now the night draws near / erasing all sorrow on its way / and whispering a lullaby," Ivan read, trying to imitate his father's declamatory style as he read "Evening Calm," his favorite poem. Like Ivan, his father had spent his life pretending to be a hard guy, a fierce soldier, almost apologetic for loving Bunin's poetry. When the military helicopter he was piloting over the mountains of Sinjar crashed in northeastern Iraq, they found a copy of this collection among his charred remains. Ivan remembered when his dad used to come home on leave, during a months-long mission, walk in with his rucksack over one shoulder, his Tartar-style mustache, and big open laugh. "I'm expecting great things from you, Ivan. You're going to be a real man, with a capital M." His father would be disappointed to see what his favorite son had become.

He turned to Zona, who was smoking in bed, legs crossed. Her crotch was waxed bare, and when she saw that

Ivan wanted her, she spread her legs like butterfly wings, opening to welcome him in again.

"The glory of victory," he repeated, like a mantra. Happy to play his part.

Opening the door to his old house, Miguel felt like he was walking into an unknown place. Though it had only been a few months, absence had taken hold, definitively set in. There was no impatience in the air, no life in the light filtering in through a curtain. The furniture was all in the same place, the paintings were on the same walls, but even if they weren't, if that were all different, it still would have been the same.

"It's not very cheery," Helena pronounced.

Miguel agreed. He'd put the house up for sale, and maybe the new owners would be lucky enough to turn it into something resembling a home.

"Don't get comfortable. We're not staying long."

Helena saw a framed photo of a much younger Miguel with no gray in his sparse mustache, no glasses on his face, more hair on his head. She thought he looked handsome now, he had a different glow. A woman and child posed, on his right.

"Your wife?"

Miguel glanced at the photo unemotionally.

"Águeda."

"She looks very serious," Helena added.

She had her reasons, he thought. The morning that photo had been taken, he'd just returned from Barcelona and still had Carmen's smell on his skin. Águeda had suspected something between them had definitively broken. That same night, Natalia had vomited after eating too much cotton candy and other sweets, things Miguel had used in an attempt to absolve his conscience. He and Águeda had fought bitterly about it, but the candy was just a pretext.

"Águeda wasn't very expressive."

Helena felt an instinctive dislike for the woman, whose appearance implied she'd fallen victim to the apathy that sets in with a comfortable marriage. She wore an expression of contained cynicism, unopen to any possibility of surprise or serendipity. She must have bored the pants off people.

"And that's your daughter?"

Miguel nodded proudly.

"She was eight or nine, that was back when she still had faith in me."

It looked like they got along, understood one another. The girl had one arm around her father's neck and smiled timidly at the camera, still bearing traces of a benevolent naivete.

Helena thought of herself at that age, back when she still thought her father was God and obsessed over obtaining his approval.

"My son, David, never looked at me the way your daughter's looking at you in that picture. He saw me as weak—too distracted and absent, off in my own world. We could have been a happy family, but instead we settled for not being too unhappy a family. And in the end, I suppose we didn't even manage that."

"How did he and his father get along?"

"Walter was too intellectual; he claimed to dislike sentimentality, said it was verbal pornography—sugarcoated words, the family grammar of diminutives, kissy faces, and exaggerated gestures—and that it poisoned reality and turned kids soft. He wasn't hard on David, but he was often distant, almost cold, and he really only felt at home surrounded by books and garnering his students' admiration."

Helena glanced around. It felt a bit like the family home she'd so carefully constructed that had ended up shattering, crashing to pieces and leaving behind the same desolation she saw here.

"Is something wrong?" Miguel asked. "You look pale."

Helena gazed at Águeda's bitter face and was shocked to realize that there was a time that she, too, had worn the same expression. The same silent accumulation of bile and resentment, the same reproachful look that not even a screaming match or an argument would relieve. Not an accusation, a recrimination, or a slammed door would help. There was only silence, a terrible silence that became a prison.

"All memories gather the same dust."

"I'm not sure what you mean."

Helena forced a smile.

"No matter."

Luckily, Miguel raised a hand and jangled his key ring.

"I want to show you my greatest treasure."

They went down to the building's parking garage. Miguel walked ahead and pulled off the canvas covering an old car. Hundreds of specks of dust floated in the air.

"Beautiful, isn't it?"

Helena shook her head.

"You're expecting me to get into *that*?"

"*That* is a Datsun 280Z coupe: 170 horsepower, leather interior, the best two-seater ever built."

Helena glanced at the vehicle dubiously and frowned.

"There isn't even enough room for my legs. If I cram myself in there, they'll need a crane to get me out."

Miguel didn't bother to reply. He opened the passenger door, and with a nod invited her to climb in.

"Let's go for a drive; it's a beautiful afternoon."

It was, in fact, a beautiful time of day. Slowly, the sky was darkening, and small pink cloud formations suggested a coming storm in the distance, still far away, announced only by a lovely cool breeze. The trees flanking the river swayed lazily, their green reflection dancing in the light and dark of the water. Miguel put the top down and slipped a cassette into the player: Sibelius's Concerto for Violin in E Minor, opus 47. Helena found it a little sad, but Miguel was enjoying himself. The music and car he clearly loved so much showed her a different side of the man she actually hardly knew. They could have been driving through the streets of Vienna, Leipzig, or Prague in a horse-drawn carriage; Miguel could have been some tasteful nineteenth-century gentleman in his riding boots, gloves, hat, and cane, gazing out at the road on his way to the opera. An imperial squire who had accidently been deposited in a time when he didn't belong. There was very little traffic, and Helena was amused by Miguel's meticulous driving, the cautious way he changed lanes, accelerated, shifted gears. More than driving the car he seemed to be caressing it, slow dancing with it. Helena lit a cigarette. She saw the clear displeasure on Miguel's face but chose to ignore it, assuring him that she had no intention of burning his precious upholstery.

"I just hope that wherever we're going, we arrive before the next ice age. Where did you get your driver's license?"

Miguel didn't bat an eye. Instead he chose to ignore the comment, since in actual fact he didn't have one and wasn't supposed to be doing this, driving around listening to music. He'd had that privilege taken away: he was too old, his reflexes were not fast enough, he was a danger to other drivers. That was one way they made old people feel useless, by taking away the few realms in which they could still have any autonomy, continuously reminding them that they were unnecessary, unproductive, had nothing left to offer. In the digital world of constant electric consumption, a six-year-old child could drive better than him, could easily negotiate an airport's info panels, could update the apps on his phone. Young people had mastered a jargon he couldn't comprehend, drove cars with no stick shift or gasoline, cars that parked themselves. Old people were given brightly colored free or reduced-cost public transit passes so everyone would know they were no longer contributing members of society; the city built them pigeon-filled parks and occasionally other places to kill time, entertain themselves, stare off into space. The lights at pedestrian crossings changed quickly, without taking into consideration their ailing feet, and drivers maneuvered impatiently around them as if they were boulders in the road.

But he still had things to say, and didn't need anyone patronizing him, telling him he could do what he had a right to do. Forty years of driving experience didn't disappear overnight just because some bureaucrat who hadn't even been born when Miguel got his driver's license in the military service said so. People nowadays drove all kinds of cars that went 125 mph, even women. What was the point, if the cops were always lying in wait, ready to dole out speeding tickets? Everyone today was expected to have résumés that proved they had foreign language skills, master's degrees, computer literacy—and even that wasn't enough. When he was young, a driver's license went a long way toward getting a job, just like accounting skills, or typing. Now there were loans, installment plans for people to pay off enormous gas-guzzling cars, and everyone wanted leather upholstery, GPS, ABS; and airbags, power windows, and all those other terms that made them think they were safer, that they could drive without driving. But back when he had bought his Datsun, you still had to decide if you wanted metallic paint or not, a cassette player (which would increase the cost significantly), or the ultimate luxury: power steering. Having a car like his, being able to afford it, to drive it, was the closest thing to freedom Miguel had known. Even Águeda, so austere and forever worried about finances, didn't say a word when she saw him behind the wheel the day he brought it home. And not saying no, for his wife, meant yes. He wasn't about to let a simple piece of paper take away that privilege.

"Are you all right?" Helena wanted to know. "You sound like you're muttering under your breath."

"I'm just dandy. Never felt better."

Helena narrowed her eyes.

"I'm happy for you. But do you mind telling me where we're going? I feel like we've been down this street already."

Miguel had been too lost in thought to realize that, indeed, he was driving up the street he'd just driven down.

"I want you to meet my daughter. She works near here."

"Near this roundabout. I see."

He tried to remember how to get to the publishing house where Natalia worked. It was in one of those office parks on the outskirts of town, but after crossing the Barqueta Bridge he'd gotten distracted and now he felt unsure. Shouldn't he have crossed Alamillo Bridge, or driven by the Pasarela? He didn't remember that tall building on the right, or recognize those landscaped parks and the buildings to the left. This was his city, but he felt as if he was seeing it for the first time.

"Is everything okay, Miguel?"

Miguel cleared his throat, troubled. So this was how it was going to go. Blackouts, fugue states, time elapsing without his knowledge, like he'd been beamed from one universe to the next with no chance to assimilate. It was like the starship *Enterprise* crew on *Star Trek*. This was a crash landing. He thought of William Shatner playing Captain Kirk. Natalia's bedroom walls had been plastered with his image. And she'd had a phase when she wanted to be Captain Janeway, convinced she was going to be an intergalactic astronaut.

"We're almost there. I just have to find the freeway on-ramp."

It was humiliating, but an hour later Miguel had to admit that he was lost and disoriented.

Somehow, they'd ended up in eerie, unfamiliar territory, as though Captain Kirk had selected the wrong coordinates before takeoff. Over their heads was a bridge, whizzing with traffic that made the entire concrete structure rumble. Far off, at what seemed an incredible distance, lay Sevilla's old quarter, the city lights just starting to turn on. The sun was going down, and its dim bleak rays shone weakly, almost horizontally, elongating shadows. The storm that had sent a comforting breeze through earlier was now announcing its arrival less amicably, with thunder. They seemed to be in some sort of industrial graveyard, with abandoned prefab warehouses, scrap, and a junkyard. In a nearby vacant lot lay a huge pyramid of trash and rubble. The asphalt was torn up and led to dead-end streets, as if the building craze had lost its steam before the projects were finished. Everywhere were oily puddles that seemed to gurgle up from the cracks in the road like wounds on the land's skin, revealing the squalid nature of whatever circulated beneath.

To the right stood a row of a dozen or so half-built terraced homes, next to a promotional billboard picturing the idyllic image of an intensely green lawn, a swimming pool, and an SUV in the garage. A large stockade fence, carefully concealed by climbing vines and soundproofing panels, should have been installed around the development to protect residents from the sight of the abandoned industrial park and the noise of freeway traffic. As though living in forts in Comanche territory, the future inhabitants of those homes could have been out washing their cars with a hose, walking their dogs through common areas, and playing with kids on swings without having to see anything beyond the tips of their noses once the lush, fast-growing trees were trucked in from a nursery. The demo house would have smelled of fresh-cut grass, orange blossom, and night-blooming jasmine, a mix of aromas enabling agents to camouflage the smells of filth, bearing grease, burnt rubber, and diesel. But it had all gone down the pan through the work and grace of unscrupulous developers and city planners who—for a tidy sum—rezoned industrial land overnight, turning it into developable land. They convinced the happy buyers by using fraudulent blueprints that had been fraudulently approved by fraudulent city architects, leaving defaulted mortgages, disgrace, broken families, suicides, and depression in their wake. Goodbye to planned communities—an absurd middle-class invention, created for those who could afford to live neither in the center of town nor on the beach, and yet refused to give up their little dream. The whole country was filled with these profane altars—ghastly developments languishing in homage to past avarice and lunacy. Someone should write a guidebook for this landscape of disaster, one aimed at tourists who wanted to see the result of collective failure up close and personal. Miguel could suggest it to Natalia, he could give her the information firsthand. He'd played a role in this ruin himself: questionable mortgages approved with a handshake in the knowledge that, after a time, the buyers would be unable to pay the note and the bank would show no mercy, swooping in to execute its claim on appraisals well above their true worth, loans to developers with no solvency, plunderers, climbers, everyday mobsters. He couldn't let himself off the hook, claiming he was only the messenger, as he had been when he started at the bank and simply delivered envelopes from one office to another. As a manager, he'd played a role in all this: it was part of his legacy, his work, and there was a time when Natalia hated him for it. Not a night went by without a dinnertime argument over the environment, the destruction of the coastline, the artificial property-value inflation in poor neighborhoods that priced longtime residents out and brought new ones in to colonize land bought at luxury prices by wealthy Asians.

This was all before Natalia left with Gustavo, a period when she used fiery rhetoric, wore kaffiyehs around her neck, and smelled of marijuana. Her revolutionary twaddle made Miguel smile, because it reminded him of the same sermons he'd heard as a kid—Marx and Engels, class struggle, productivity, production, added value—except that in Natalia's day there were other, poorly absorbed concepts like global warming and agrarian utopias that she took to mean the environment and wearing grass-soled sandals and peasant blouses and going braless. The flowers in developments like these smelled of tar, and scoundrels like him cloaked themselves in respectability, but they'd robbed their children of a decent future. *You're stealing the hope of future generations!*

It was curious. Now he missed Natalia's irate rebellion, her eyes flashing, the confrontational phase that parents and children go through and which sometimes passes and sometimes remains an open wound forever. He preferred her back then, with her boyish haircut, the Hindu-style teardrop on her forehead, the macramé bracelets, a pack of Ducados—working-class cigarettes for the new Spanish democracy—on the table by her lighter, which she left on display like a loaded weapon, a challenge. *Don't even think about smoking at the table. We're having dinner.* And she'd light up and stare at him defiantly, blowing smoke at the ceiling, at the clouds. *I'm screwing a guy at college, Mamá, but don't worry, we're using condoms.* She loved scandalizing Águeda, practically giving her a heart attack to see what Miguel would do, see if he had blood in his veins, had the nerve to slam a fist on the table or tell her to leave and not come back.

But Miguel survived those months, her first year at university and the poorly absorbed readings, the heated debates with the cafeteria conspirators she hung out with, her air of intellectual and moral superiority. He put up with his daughter's onslaughts because he understood her, and deep down he envied her and was secretly amused when her digs at God and religion made Águeda grimace melodramatically and cry churchy tears. He'd never had a chance to be like that, an undefined project, a bundle of desires with no clear path, a simmering rebel; he couldn't afford it, had neither the resources nor the energy, and was too busy trying to get by to worry about the meaning of life. Secretly, he was happy that Natalia had been able to escape the bleakness of a childhood and adolescence like Miguel's. That had been another Spain, and, yes, the one his daughter inhabited also had fissures, filth, and traumas, but at least in this one she could travel, study, fritter away her time discussing incomprehensibly pretentious books, smoking, and drinking beer with her little friends. Despite the armchair pessimism she wore like an ill-fitting suit, Natalia argued because her generation was optimistic and didn't feel indebted to the war or the dictatorship, to the past. The future was Europe, she said. As if one future was different from another, as if the future truly mattered. And Miguel had given her all of that, and if in order to do so he'd had to look the other way, swallow a bitter pill, pretend to be thick or act corrupt, he did it with no regrets. Everyone wanted what he and others like him were peddling. Dreams, cheap and affordable. He wasn't going to change the world. But his daughter could have. She had the chance to go beyond theories and could have done something better, far better, with the fire in her heart before it turned to stone, a lump of coal. Natalia should have been happy, it was her obligation, it should have been her commitment to the humankind she spoke of. But she hadn't managed.

Miguel, you have no earthly idea where we are, do you? In case you hadn't noticed, it's almost dark and there's a storm coming. It's time to do something—unless you think we should camp out here. Not that I mind, it's just not a very inspiring panorama."

Miguel finally reacted. At the end of one street, between two industrial warehouses, he saw three young men playing soccer, using a couple of oil drums as goalposts.

"I'll go ask."

It turned out not to be necessary. The young men had clocked his presence and were slowly approaching; they fanned out, taking up the whole street, and didn't look very friendly.

Miguel glanced at Helena out of the corner of his eye.

"This doesn't bode well."

He'd read in the paper about gangs of juvenile delinquents roving the suburbs, seen atrocities in the media—robberies, rapes, assaults. Miguel felt frightened. Should he put the car in gear and speed off? He had never been brave, disliked conflict, wasn't used to it.

As it turned out, there was no time to decide. His heart started pounding when the young man who looked to be the ringleader walked over and kicked a hubcap. He looked both the car and its inhabitants over carefully, wearing an expression that said he was having a bad day. Then he sat on the hood as though taking possession of his throne and lit a cigarette.

"Nice car," he said, rubbing one hand over his shaved head. On his neck was a deep gash; it looked like a hunk of flesh had been ripped out. His hands were tattooed, and he and his friends were all dressed in jeans, khaki puffer jackets, and military boots. His scarred face was covered in signs of battles long past as well as recent. The kid had an accent, foreign but hard to place. Miguel guessed he was Eastern European. He couldn't have been more than twenty, and was the oldest of the three surrounding the car, prowling like wolves, cautiously weighing their plan of attack.

"We're lost," Miguel stuttered.

The young man smiled maliciously.

"Sometimes it's good to get lost. You end up someplace unexpected and find the gates of paradise. Other times, a mistake is a terrible thing. You take one false step, stray a meter from your path, and you're fucked. Someone tosses a coin, and you never know how it's going to land: heads or tails."

The guy took out a ruble and showed it to him.

"Tell me, old man. Do you believe in chance?"

14

Sevilla

Pieter loved the little coin toss game: *Heads or tails, little brother, pick one.* If it was heads, it was bad for Ivan. And if it was tails, it was worse. But he had to obey his big brother and toss the coin. It was perverse and, in a way, ridiculous—like all rituals of evil—but Ivan couldn't escape the bizarre interplay of fate and chance. Maybe because he'd never understood the rules they obeyed. His mother always said that there were people who fell on their feet and others who fell on their faces, people born lucky and those born luckless. She was also convinced that Ivan belonged to the former, while Pieter was one of the latter, as though her older son had been afflicted by some evil cosmic force, while Ivan had been chosen by the gods. According to his mother's theory, Ivan shouldn't hate Pieter but pity him. Things could have been the other way around, the reasoning went: Pieter could have been Ivan, Ivan could have been Pieter. It was a question of luck, a coin toss.

But Ivan's mother never wanted to admit that those marked by tragedy, like Pieter, were only happy when they destroyed the thing they envied, the thing that they themselves could never be. She was too kindhearted, and blinded by the love she felt for the monster born of her loins. She thought she could protect him from himself, behind her wall of affection, yet all it did was give him an excuse to unleash his cruelty. Ivan never blamed her for being deaf, blind, and dumb to what went on between him and his brother under her roof. Or perhaps she pretended not to know because she had too much faith in Ivan's strength of character, in the invulnerability that the gods had bestowed upon him so he could endure Pieter's dirty tricks. Regardless, it didn't make her responsible for Ivan's tortured childhood. After all, it wasn't her who came home drunk and slipped into Ivan's bed, wasn't her who squeezed his testicles under the sheets. His mother wasn't the one who put his mouth to Ivan's ear, circling a sickening viscous tongue around his earlobe and whispering filth. It was Pieter who beat him half to death, just because he wanted to, because he could, to show his superiority; Pieter was the one who kicked him in the gut and hurled him against the wall like a rag doll. *If you tell Mama, I'll come see you tonight.*

And even though it no longer mattered, sometimes Ivan wondered if the violence coursing through his veins was venom that his brother had injected him with on those endless nights. Why did Pieter hate him so much? It wasn't Ivan's fault the gods had chosen him. Their parents had equipped them both with the same tools, and the boys had chosen what to build with them. Pieter chose scorn and self-pity, gratuitous violence, giving in to his instinct to fight, unable to control his perverse inclinations. Pieter detested his father for recognizing what his mother refused to see. He didn't acknowledge Pieter's acts but did see his true nature. And yet he couldn't help his son, because the boy didn't want help, only pity. One night Pieter announced, drunk, that he'd enlisted as a volunteer and was off to fight the war in Chechnya, and their father—a career military officer—far from congratulating him, actually told Pieter that if what he wanted was to give free rein to his base instincts, he'd do better getting a job at the local slaughterhouse, where he could cover his hands in blood and guts without putting himself in danger.

Ivan never knew what happened to his brother in Grozny, but Pieter came back not a different person but more himself, only now completely unmasked. A big brother is supposed to tell his little brother stories at night to help him fall asleep, but the atrocities Pieter recounted were nightmares, tales that made Ivan wake up screaming, feeling for his limbs to make sure they hadn't been chopped off by a machete. Oh, the evil that lies in the human heart! And Pieter brought it all back from the war with him, came home with his pockets overflowing. It was impossible for Ivan to fight that darkness with Bunin's poetry or his mother's sad, blind love. Pieter had all the power, and his last mission, the final task he'd been assigned, was to destroy Ivan, steal the light from his soul, and then crush and annihilate it. Pieter did a good job. He deserved a medal.

Maybe that was why Pieter turned up years later in Sevilla. He wanted to see and enjoy the fruits of his labor. Ivan's bed, his house, his money, his food. Wanted to take possession of his brother by right of conquest. It didn't even occur to him that Ivan might rebel when Pieter tossed the coin with a defiant air and caught it in his right fist. *Heads or tails, little brother. Pick one.* Ivan turned without responding, aware now that fate was not the only path.

He wasn't brave enough to do it himself—Pieter's power over him was still too great—so he asked Ramiro and the Gypsy to take care of him. Ivan didn't want to watch, but he told them to make it slow and painful, make him suffer, and use a hammer, just as Pieter had done to the children in Chechnya that he told Ivan about at night. *I'd make them kneel and look me in the eye, their parents tied up and watching, screaming and begging. Then I'd take a swing and bash them right here*, and he'd tap Ivan's forehead, right between his eyebrows, with his index finger.

That had been two years ago, and Ivan still didn't know what Ramiro and the Gypsy had done with the body, what river bend it was decomposing in, or how many rats had gnawed at Pieter's entrails. He felt nothing, when he stopped to think about it. Hate is like love: without action, it's merely an aesthetic exercise. Something people theorize but never really feel.

The only one of Pieter's things that Ivan had kept was the ruble, which he was now showing the two old farts who'd fallen into his hands. The same coin that had been tossed for so many others, bringing them the same luck it had brought him: none at all.

"Come on, old man. You have to pick. Heads or tails."

Miguel stared at the coin in terror.

"I don't like games of chance."

Ivan smiled.

"Well then, maybe *you* do," he said, turning to the old woman, who looked far calmer. In some deep part of what people called the soul, a thing Ivan swore he did not have, he thought of his mother. "What do you say? Dare to try your hand with Lady Luck?"

Helena stared at the boy—because that was what she saw behind his whole urban warrior getup, a boy who might have been like David at his age.

"What's your name, son?"

Ivan exchanged an amused look with his friends and slid off the car hood slowly, convinced of his power. His left brow was split and had a small scar. He came much closer to Helena and looked her up and down.

"What do you care what my name is? And don't call me 'son' or you'll swallow this coin, lady."

Helena was not about to be intimidated.

"My name is Helena, and this is my friend, Miguel."

"Did I ask what your name was? Does it look like I care? Nice necklace, by the way. Are those real pearls?"

Instinctively, Helena touched her neck. They were—a gift from Walter, to celebrate David's birth.

"So. You like pearl necklaces and classic cars. You've got good taste, a kid who's got his priorities straight."

Ivan looked at her more carefully, surprised. The woman had balls, not like the dipshit she was with, who didn't know which way to look. Ivan gazed up at the sky pensively. It would start raining soon, and Guillermo was expecting him at the Coop, to train. He had a fight with a black guy in a few days, one of the Sudanese immigrants who'd traveled half-way across the world just to end up selling tourists a bunch of knockoff purses on the sidewalk outside the cathedral. By all accounts, the guy was tough. People said he'd eaten dead bodies on the boat, but Ivan didn't want to believe that. Fighting a cannibal wasn't something that appealed to him.

"I don't have time to make friends. You got money on you, Helena?" She shook her head slowly and the boy got impatient. "Are you going to make me disrespect you with a body search?"

Helena thought of David. What he'd have been like at this kid's age. Perhaps not so very different, the same cocky posturing—broadening his shoulders, wearing a practiced hard-guy expression. It was like a casting call for a bad movie, or the tough guys in *Grease*. David used to spend hours practicing expressions in the mirror like De Niro in *Taxi Driver*, hoping to look convincing on the playground; he stuffed his boots in an attempt to look taller and liked puffy jackets because they made him seem more muscular. Once, in the bathroom, Helena had seen him stuff a wad of toilet paper into his underwear and quietly closed the door so as not to humiliate him. David could never really be tough: he was too handsome and had a kind face that not even the horrendous punk haircuts he got could hide. When he was thirteen he started stealing from the piggy bank in the kitchen and from Walter's office. Just loose change at first. "It's for cigarettes," he confessed, the day Helena caught him with a pack in his socks. "If you want to smoke, ask me, don't steal," she told him. And then she lit a cigarette and they smoked it together. When she told Walter about it, he hit the roof. She would probably be reviled by every mother on the planet today. But those were other times, and the fact was she was learning to be a mother on the fly.

"I'm sure there are plenty of other ways to get money. I bet you can think of lots."

Ivan let out a dry cackle, a failed attempt at arrogance that faltered into a question at the end.

"Are you trying to mess with me, grandma?"

"I told you my name is Helena—though I certainly could be your grandmother, or in this day and age even your mother."

It wasn't that David came into her life too early, it's just that she hadn't been expecting him. The whole obsession with having children was Walter's, and though she wanted them, she kept putting it off. "Let's wait a few months, a year, however long it takes me to adjust to my job, my schedule." The truth was, having a child scared her, because she didn't want to defer her other life, the one she pictured when she occasionally spoke to Louise on brief transatlantic phone calls. She was still expecting something of herself, and saw motherhood as a door that closed off all other options. At the time she didn't know she could be a mother without giving up on being herself, didn't realize there could be more than one Helena. But there came a time when it was impossible to delay any longer. The first thing she felt when seeing David as a newborn was that her life was now on a certain course, that she'd spend the rest of it traveling an assigned track, like a drawer sliding in and out. She'd never be like Louise, party hopping, taking Hollywood by storm. She had to accept it.

"What if you play nice and give me that necklace, and your little mustache friend gets out of the car? You can go, walk away, and thank me for not beating you and leaving you under a bridge. Sound like a good deal, Helena?"

It hadn't been a good pregnancy; she'd felt deformed, weird, a stranger to herself. Her mind traveled back, and she thought of the moment Walter spilled his seed inside her and imagined closing her legs, getting him out. But slowly she got used to being that other woman, began to see herself in a new light, something separate from her parents, from Thelma and Enrique, even felt a stab of pride on realizing that she now had something Louise spurned: motherhood.

"You didn't toss the coin," she said.

"Excuse me?"

"You don't know whether it's heads or tails. You still don't know. And I don't believe in chance. I believe in the theory of red strings. Do you know what that is?"

Walter had gotten mad at her, because when she was more than four months pregnant she insisted on painting

David's room herself. "The ladder is dangerous, you could fall. And factory paint emits gasses that are terrible for you, especially in your state. If you inhale them, you'll put the baby at risk." But by that time, she already knew that the baby would hold on until the moment came, and that even when he finally decided come out, to leave the sea of darkness and calm behind and enter the world, in a way he'd still be inside her forever. They'd be joined by an invisible red string, wherever they were, no matter how far apart. Everyone told her that the gift of life was marvelous, and Helena smiled without telling them that it was David who'd given *her* the gift of a new life, given her life meaning and put an end to her anxieties. The boy had healed wounds she didn't even know she had, and did it before he was even born.

Ivan was toying with the ruble between his fingers.

"I can break the rule. What's stopping me? It's just a coin."

Helena nodded.

"Rules are made to be broken. Nothing stays the same forever."

The morning the school principal called to say that David hadn't been to class for days was one of the worst Helena could remember. He was thirteen at the time. Helena waited for him for hours and watched him walk into the house with his books and backpack like nothing was wrong. She asked about math, geography, history, how classes were going, and he replied absently. "Fine, they're all fine." The following morning, Helena followed him from a distance and saw him turn off the route to school on the last street, meeting up with a group of boys who were older than him, tattooed, and wearing knockoff leather jackets, imitations of the ones they didn't have the money to buy. Together they headed to Blackfriars Bridge, throwing beer cans and scaring people. David walked with them, pretending to be one of them, but he wasn't. Helena knew how he walked when he felt forced into something, the way he dragged his feet and slumped his shoulders, with his hands in his jeans' pockets. She was horrified to see what they did at the bridge: hang over the Thames. Throwing caution to the wind, not caring about the shame David would be subjected to, the laughter and scorn his new friends would shower upon him from then on, she made a scene and dragged him home. Hours later, back at the house, when she'd managed to calm down and ask him why he would do such a thing, his response chilled her to the bone: "Because I know I might fall." That was when Helena realized that David, in his own way, was crying out for help, and she didn't know what the matter was. "Well, could you try to find another way to test your limits, one that doesn't put me through the wringer? I'd appreciate it." David said yes, but didn't keep his word. He found a way to punish her and make her hear his cry for help.

Thunder boomed over their heads and the wind gusted in. Darkness was starting to fall. Ivan's friends tried to hurry him, but the kid took his time. It was clear that Helena disconcerted and charmed him in equal measure. He dropped the ruble. Bending down to pick it up, he saw the scar on Helena's leg and quickly looked away.

"Providence protects children and idiots. I know because I have tested it," he said, focusing his gaze on the coin.

"Impressive—a man who can quote Mark Twain."

Ivan put the coin in his jacket pocket. Suddenly, his face softened.

"'Luck doesn't always have the face we expect it to.' That's Mark Twain too. And you're in luck because you have eyes like my mother's, the same expression, hiding your pain. And I'm feeling generous today. Now get out of here, and take your little deaf-mute friend with you."

Helena shook her head. They should have jumped at the chance, rushed off while they could, or backed away with a smile, not taking their eyes off these punks, who were still muttering, undecided. But it wouldn't have been Helena's style. She couldn't leave David there, hanging from the bridge.

"It's funny you should say that, because your expression reminds me of my son." The eyes that had learned to cut like a knife but which, from up close, were young and tender, needy and insecure. "You know what? You should throw away that damn coin, not let chance decide your actions. It's not like a compass, you know; it won't get you anywhere."

Ivan set his jaw. It was starting to rain and he pulled up the hoodie he wore under his jacket.

"And you should button your lip, Helena. Maybe next time you'll bump into someone whose mother's eyes were brown and not green. You know, the kind of kid who takes the wrong path in life because he's only got one coin, and it's tails on both sides. Now, get out of here before I change my mind or one of my friends decides they don't like the 'kindly granny meets converted hooligan' routine."

When they finally left, Miguel was pale, livid.

"Have you lost your mind entirely? Do you know what they could have done to us? You shouldn't have spoken to him that way, like you wanted to egg him on."

Helena calmly narrowed her eyes.

"They're just kids, Miguel. Kids parading as men who need somebody to see beneath their armor."

"Well, those 'kids,' as you call them, are perfectly capable of smashing someone's head in for a pair of running shoes, or just for the fun of it, to prove they can do it, to see someone bleed. Those 'kids' deal drugs, earn a living beating people up and stealing. They're criminals, not house pets. You had no right to endanger yourself or me that way."

Helena's reply was eloquent.

"We both know what the alternative would have been had we tried to run away. You're not exactly Niki Lauda behind the wheel now, are you? Didn't you see their motorcycles parked there? How long do you think it would have taken them to catch up to us?"

Miguel was driving back to the city. It was almost completely dark, and car headlights twinkled like party lights. The rain was torrential, gusty wind blew sheets of water across the windshield, and the wipers couldn't move fast enough to clear it. The dotted lines in the road were blurry, and Miguel gripped the wheel so tightly his knuckles were white. He felt rage creeping up from his guts and burning his esophagus like a sour, bilious ulcer he couldn't control.

"It's all a game to you, isn't it?" he spat angrily.

"Do you mind telling me what's the matter with you? It's not that big a deal. Sometimes you perplex me, Miguel. I don't understand your mood swings. You seem happy, and then a minute later you look like you want to flatten the earth. You act like a spoiled child."

Suddenly Miguel jerked the wheel and stopped short on the shoulder, making cars behind them flash their lights and honk their horns in angry protest.

"Are you insane?" Helena shouted. "You could have caused an accident!"

Miguel stared at the metal barrier separating the road from the countryside. The rain had brought out the smell of something decomposing, it could have been a dead dog or rotting leaves. A vision rose before him, that of a filthy world covered in maggots and larvae, parasites wriggling on the ground. Lately he'd been unable to concentrate on the positive and saw only ugliness, as though his mind were being warped into something else, turning him into a different person, one at times irascible and unpleasant. He couldn't stifle the urge to hurt Helena, to force her to look and see the same putrefaction he saw.

"Your nonchalance drives me crazy, in case you hadn't noticed. The lighthearted, trivial way you talk, smoke, drink—it's totally selfish, I see that now. You pretend to be curious, pretend you empathize with people, but actually you don't care about anything but yourself."

"Where is this coming from, Miguel?"

He wasn't listening to her. All he could hear was the sound of the worms getting closer, wriggling through a bed of rotting twigs and leaves. His good manners and social graces could not repress the unexpected outburst. Miguel was abandoning prudence. And finally, now, unmasked, came fear.

"You've never once asked me about my condition, what led me to move into the home. Do you know what dementia is? Have you ever been afraid you'll forget who you are, who you were, afraid you won't recognize the people around you, that you'll be a stranger in a world you once knew? No, of course not. Always so sharp-tongued, so lucid, with that cynical attitude that hides the past, since all that matters is the present."

Helena was starting to take offense.

"You have no idea what you're talking about. I don't know what's gotten into you, but I think we need to go back to Sevilla and end this conversation. It would be in the best interest for both of us."

"Best interest? What exactly is this 'best interest'? The ridiculous trip you're taking? Showing up at David's house unannounced because if you tell him you're coming the family might say they don't want to see you? What kind of mother are you, if your own son doesn't want to see you?"

Helena searched in her bag for a cigarette. Her hand was trembling and she couldn't find her lighter. Exasperated, she threw the cigarette against the dashboard.

"Don't you dare talk about David! You know nothing about him, about me, or our relationship. What gives you the right to judge me? The fact that you're sick? Well I'm sorry, but that's not my fault! Hating me, and lashing out like a child against everyone around you won't change that." Helena seemed about to say something else, but instead she pressed her lips together, forcing her mouth into a pained grimace. Slowly, she moved her hand and massaged her shin beneath her skirt.

Without trying to, Miguel saw the enormous scar on Helena's marble-white leg. It was an ugly one, shaped like a jagged thistle. The story of wounds, why some hurt and others don't, is personal, and Helena's whimper went beyond physical pain. Touching her leg that way, her face took on a forlorn expression, a look that was both very human and very private.

"Are you okay?"

She didn't respond immediately. Slowly, her pallor waned. She inhaled deeply, searched for another cigarette as a crutch, and averted her gaze, looking out the window through the rain at cars and asphalt. The stabbing pain in her leg subsided, yielding to the familiar tingling that would last a few hours and force her to limp more noticeably for a couple of days.

"I was in a car accident, in 1982, and surgery back then was less advanced. The doctors managed to reconstruct the bones fairly well, though I had to spend months in rehab with this orthopedic contraption made of steel and screws, and have a series of operations, do painful exercises and physical therapy for the muscles to recover. I was able to walk again, but some of the nerve endings died permanently."

"I'm sorry."

"You're sorry about an accident that took place in 1982 but not about the words you spoke ten minutes ago."

The following morning, Miguel gave a taxi driver the address of the publisher where Natalia worked. He didn't want to risk getting lost again.

The building glimmered like a huge metallic phallus surrounded by landscaped gardens. It was so pretentious: part nightmare, part waste of steel and dark glass. A sort of Tower of Babel filled with hundreds of offices, companies, consortia, law firms. The whole city wanted an office in this monstrosity, which pointed to the sky like a symbol of modernity that nobody understood. What did it symbolize, what did it leave behind?

The circular lobby with a gray tile floor was buzzing with people and display panels. Half a dozen elevators zoomed up and down in constant motion, like the pistons of a motor going full blast. Miguel felt intimidated. He didn't like crowds or the feeling of pointless open space. He preferred his office in the bank—unassuming, everything close at hand, cozy and small-scale; wall partitions painted white, the clickety-clack of typewriters, voices he recognized whenever the phone rang. He liked knowing the first and last names of all the employees, the birthdays of his clients, whether they had diseases or children at difficult ages, where they were going on summer vacation and what soccer team they supported. It was inconceivable to him that his daughter could enjoy being in this building, where no one seemed to know anyone or have any interest in doing so.

The elevator took him to the top floor. Fifteen endless flights accompanied by soporific background music. Reception was manned by a Sancho Panza–like figure sprawled in a chair, who barely glanced at Miguel when he asked for Sepulcro Publishing, where Natalia worked as a copy editor. The man's apathy bothered Miguel as much as his questionable hygiene. Did no one tell this idiot not to wear a wrinkled jacket with two buttons missing to work? Did no one dare insinuate that he ought to shave off the black bristles poking out of his ears? The receptionist, if you could call him that, glanced in annoyance at his registry, dialed a switchboard number, and spoke Natalia's name as though spitting up, then nodded and hung up as though the whole process had required too much energy on his part. Like a victim undeserving of such torture, he raised a nail-bitten index finger and pointed to the right.

"Your daughter is on a half-hour lunch break. At the cafeteria lookout point."

The cafeteria did, in fact, have a lookout. And it was undoubtedly the best thing about the whole building. The views over Sevilla were incredible. Glorious sunlight shone joyously through the huge bay windows, showering the tables on the terrace—full of palm trees and plants more befitting the tropics—in sparkling blue light. There weren't many people at that time of day, just a few small groups on either side of the bar and executives drinking coffee, focused on the business section of some newspaper or other. You could only just hear the murmur of conversations and the sound of steam from the espresso machine.

Natalia was at one of the tables farthest from the entrance. Alone. That was exactly the impression she gave, her head bent over a manuscript, hair kissing the pages and partially covering her face. From time to time, she tucked a lock of hair mechanically behind one ear. She blinked as she turned a page and jiggled a pencil back and forth in her right hand. *She looks lovely*, Miguel thought, noticing that her belly had grown. She'd gained weight, but her bright dress fit well.

"Hello, Daughter."

Natalia blinked as though blinded by a sudden intense light, and the pencil in her hand stopped moving.

"Papá. What are you doing here?"

Miguel's smile froze as he pored over every bit of his daughter's withered face, the faded blue around her left eye, which she partially covered in shame. On her cheek he could still see traces of a scratch running from her bruised cheekbone to her lip, and despite the thick layer of makeup, she'd been unable to hide the swelling. A silent scream rose from his gut, blocking his throat and drying his mouth.

"My God . . ." was all Miguel managed to whisper as his fingers reached out to try to touch her face. She pulled away just in time, glancing around. Frightened little mouse eyes.

"You shouldn't have come unannounced."

Miguel's fingers hung in the air for a moment, trembling, and then clenched into a fist he held up, not knowing how to vent his rage as he searched for something to say, something that wasn't a string of insults, accusations, regrets, and curses. But he couldn't come up with any light-hearted quips, any banal comments. Miguel was unable to look away from Natalia's shattered face. He'd never felt so incompetent and useless.

"Did he do this to you?" What was she going to say? An accident, she'd slipped, the door.

But Natalia made no effort to deny the obvious. She simply looked down at the text she was editing. It was covered in red—things underlined, crossed out, notes in the margins. A conscientious job, that was just like her. So intelligent, so intuitive, and yet trapped in this inconceivable situation.

"I've got a lot of work to do . . ."

"Leave him, Natalia. You don't even have to go back to the apartment. We'll send someone for your things. Come with me. We can go anyplace you want."

Natalia looked at her father, and it was as though her eyes had become smooth stones on a deserted beach, worn away by time and the elements. Unable to make any kind of decision, unable to be anything but stones. Gustavo was erasing her, making her invisible, isolating her from the world and pulling her to him, convincing her that hell was the only possible existence. There was almost nothing left, just a faint glow, the weak beat of a dying heart.

"I don't want to talk to you about this, Papá."

"If not me, then who?"

Disconcerted, as though in search of help, Miguel glanced around. Could nobody see what was going on? Did no one care? Someone should have said something: her workmates, her friends. Somebody must have suspected that so many accidents couldn't be a coincidence, must have sensed what was happening. Someone had to know. They probably looked at his daughter in well-meaning sympathy, sent her noncommittal compassion, felt no obligations. Nobody wanted to meddle, do anything more than gossip at the coffee maker and fall silent when she approached. And if anyone had actually been willing to listen, take a single step, give advice, or hold her hand, they'd no doubt have been met with Natalia's icy stare, her distant, inscrutable look. *I'm fine, mind your own business.*

"I'll go to the police. I know you can't do it, but I will. I'm not going to let Gustavo destroy you."

Natalia stiffened.

"You will do nothing of the kind. It's my life, and I can manage by myself."

"You need help, Natalia. Think of the baby."

As though someone were trying to snatch the child from her loins, instinctively she covered her belly with one forearm as she stood.

"If you want to help me, keep out of it." Her hard voice broke for just a second, imploring and insecure. "Please. Don't make things any more complicated."

Natalia grabbed the manuscript and put on her sunglasses.

"I have to get back to work." She kissed her father's head and Miguel felt as if she'd deposited something cold and foreign on his skull. He couldn't make her stay, couldn't even reply. Miguel stood awkwardly, tripped over the chair and watched her walk off like a stranger, as if he was no different from the other people in the cafeteria, as if there was nothing he could do to help a woman who didn't want help. Blind and indifferent, just like them. But this woman was his daughter. The only thing he cared about. At that moment, if he'd had two hearts, both of them would have stopped beating.

On the dresser sat the bottle Helena had ordered that night after finishing off what was left in the minibar. She felt among the rumpled bedsheets for her cigarettes and lighter and then sat down to smoke, gazing vacantly at the white wall. Helena couldn't remember the last time she'd drank or smoked so much—or maybe she could but preferred not to. There was something liberating about getting drunk alone, feeling petty and deceitful, and wallowing like a pig in her own muck without having the burden of pity or compassion. About accepting that she had not been a good wife or mother, and certainly not the friend that Louise deserved. Their triangle had confined her, and she'd always felt trapped by its tight angles. Unable to move, to break its geometry. She'd focused on other people's faults so as not to think of her own. And she'd spent half her life playing redeemer, taking care of Walter for the whole of his endless pitiful agony, offering her friendship to Marqués. Even pushing Miguel to be something else had a redemptive mission to it. And why? Was she in any way a better person than they were?

She was just an old lady who smelled like an old lady despite covering the stench with perfume and nice dresses. A selfish one, scared and lonely, exhausting herself with all that phony passion, a smiling mummy with no faith in anything or anyone, someone who delivered cheap shots, emotional fluff, clichés, and quips. But the truth was she didn't care about them, not at all. She just used them so she could keep hiding, wasting time philosophizing, fooling herself into believing that old age was really wisdom, that all was said and done.

What a stupid way to die, waiting for enlightenment.

Someone knocked at the door. Helena opened it and there was Miguel, looking like he'd walked straight out of a Pasolini film, gaunt, drawn, hollow-eyed, his soul flagging. His expression reflected a new kind of fear.

"Can I come in?"

Helena quietly let him in and then sat on the edge of the bed, folded her hands between her legs, and waited. Miguel's hands worked as if he was kneading the air, trying to give solid form to an as-yet-amorphous idea.

"Why don't you tell me what happened? You look like you've seen the bottom of the abyss."

Miguel had to force himself to enter the terrain of emotion, let himself go, surrender himself, and disclose everything: his quiet marriage, Natalia's childhood, the existence of Gustavo, the hell his daughter was going through, his incompetence as a father, the total lack of logic, order, or sense in Natalia putting up with it, how guilty he felt, the dark conviction that he'd failed as a father but couldn't figure out how or when. How desperate he was.

It took a titanic effort, one entirely out of his comfort zone: sincerity, the heartbreak of the evidence, accepting helplessness, and chaos. And he broke down and cried, and was afraid of his own tears, of the door he'd just opened. There he was, balled in a corner, hiding his face between his trembling legs, like a figure made of sand, exposed to the pitying eyes of a stranger, a woman he hardly knew, begging her for help. Help understanding, help figuring out what to do.

"She's my daughter, Helena. My little girl. The only thing I care about in life, and I'm losing her. She's being ripped to shreds before my eyes and there's nothing I can do about it. Absolutely nothing."

Helena didn't respond with words. She went to Miguel and placed her lovely hand, with painted nails and jeweled rings, on his cheek. She did it gently, as though to keep his face from crumbling. Helena, too, knew how it felt when a child falls apart in your hands. She hugged him tight to let him know that he wasn't alone. But also to feel that she wasn't entirely dead yet.

15

Malmö

here was a knock at her door. It couldn't be Grandfather, he never knocked. It was his house, and he'd
walk in or out of any room whenever he liked with no regard for Yasmina's privacy, as he reminded her constantly:
You're here on loan.

It couldn't be her mother, either; this wasn't her day off
from the house where she worked as a live-in maid, plus it
would have been the first time in years she deigned to enter
Yasmina's bedroom.

She knew who it was. Knew the same way birds know
when it's going to rain.

"Hello there, little one."

Sture looked her up and down as though appraising an
object that he'd forgotten he owned, an object that brought

back a sense of pleasure now, as he rediscovered it. Yasmina recoiled, feeling his gaze upon her. She was still in her pajamas, and they were too skimpy.

"What are you doing here?"

"Better get dressed. We're going for a little drive."

Sture watched as she put on a pair of jeans and a sweatshirt that said "University of Stockholm," which she'd never attend. The girl stirred contradictory feelings in him: she reminded him too much of Fatima, and that was worrisome. Now more than ever he needed a clear head.

"Honestly, I prefer you in pajamas," he said walking over to stroke her cheek.

Yasmina flinched away just in time.

"What about my grandfather? I can't go out and leave him here alone."

Sture clenched a fist, lingering in the scent of Yasmina's perfume. He nodded in resignation. Raquel was right. He had to be harder on this girl, much harder, or things would get complicated.

"He's in the living room with one of my men, don't worry. He was quite friendly, even offered to make me a coffee." Sture's irony was alarming, like a dog growling, ready to bite.

He hadn't made coffee. Abdul was huddled in the armchair in the living room like a frightened animal, keeping a close eye on Sture's goon.

"How's death coming along, Abdul, old friend? Almost here, or are you holding out?"

The old man shot Sture a fierce look and then aimed another at his granddaughter. His disgust trumped his fear.

"God knows it will come for us all at some point."

Sture nodded, then made a point of looking dramatically at his watch.

"Well, yours is running late. Or maybe your God has forgotten about you."

The old man didn't reply. He turned his face to the chair, and Sture gave him a scornful look.

"You didn't use to be so proud, Abdul. I still remember the day I saw you walk in the door of Old Sweden. January 1977, it was. I remember because we had heavy snowstorms that month, even for us."

"That was a long time ago."

"Not so long, at least not for me. I look at you now and see the same miserable wretch, shivering in a flimsy coat and mittens with his fingers almost frozen, stamping his feet to try to get warm, dejected and ashamed, that beaten-dog look, asking if you and your daughter and that scumbag of a son-in-law could take shelter. They were just frightened kids. Fatima was the same age Yasmina is now. Seven or eight months pregnant and looked like she was going to collapse on the spot, give birth on the dirty, wet floor. But all you cared about was getting warm, taking care of yourself. You wouldn't let her sit, wouldn't let her eat or dry her feet, until you and that dumbshit husband of hers had been served. Gave her your scraps, like a dog. Isn't that right?"

Yasmina furrowed her brow. Her mother had been pregnant before? Before she'd had her?

Sture picked up on her surprise.

"He never told you about that, did he? You never even knew about your brother, the one who died a few months after being born. Ask your grandfather who paid for the medicine while the baby was sick, who covered the hospital bills. Who took care of his burial and made sure your mother had everything she needed while her husband went from bar to bar drowning his sorrows and your grandfather turned all religious, becoming a holy man who went to the mosque every day. Our beloved old Abdul decided he'd rather put his forehead to the ground and pray to God than hold his head up high and take care of his family. After all, he had me and my family for that. Back then what I did for a living didn't matter to him at all."

Abdul bared his teeth like a rat that wanted to bite but didn't dare. He wasn't strong, never had been; all his life he'd been overshadowed by men stronger than him. First his father, Rachid the Spaniard; then Enrique Pizarro; and later, Sture. He'd never been able to rebel against them directly. He could betray them, sure, and detest them, but never confront them openly. He was always lying in ambush, awaiting his chance. That was why he'd chosen that idiot as a son-in-law for Fatima, a callow lowlife hick who couldn't look him in the eyes. That way Abdul could crush him, know what it felt like to put his foot on someone else's head.

"It was Allah's decision to take my wife with Spanish flu first, and his will to take my grandson next. There's nothing one can do to fight God's will."

Sture spat on the floor.

"Look at this scumbag, Yasmina. Still doing the same thing all these years later. Hiding. So, Abdul, why don't you tell your granddaughter about the debt you incurred with me?"

Abdul entrenched himself in murky silence.

"Cat got your tongue, Mister Pious? Nothing to say? Of course, talking's not your style. You let others get their hands dirty for you. Sometimes I think I should have killed you the minute I laid eyes on you. People like you make me sick. If it hadn't been for your daughter Fatima, I can assure you I'd have saved your God the trouble. Anyway, I'm taking your granddaughter out for a bit. Don't worry, though. I'll have her back in time to wipe the shit from your ass and get your dinner on the table."

Sture rarely drove, and venturing out of Rosengård without his Praetorian Guard was almost unheard of, but he told his men to go home and got behind the wheel himself this time. They took the beltway toward the Malmö suburbs, heading east. Sture slipped a CD into the player and relaxed.

"Have I ever told you how much I love Plácido Domingo?"

"I don't know who that is."

"Come on, Yasmina. And you think of yourself as an aspiring singer? Nobody does 'Nessun Dorma' like Plácido Domingo. People will try to tell you Pavarotti is the maestro, but don't listen to them. I remember seeing him years ago, in Barcelona. I've never forgotten that concert, it was one of the happiest moments of my life. Listen: the subtlety and inflections in his voice are astonishing." He turned up the volume and seemed quite moved, as if the tenor were somehow capable of bringing out whatever good there might be in humanity. At that moment Sture felt more human than ever.

Yasmina was still fixated on the revelation that she had a brother she'd never met or even heard of. She couldn't process the information.

"Did he have a name?"

"What does it matter? If he did, it meant nothing."

"It means something to me."

"You didn't even know he existed until a few minutes ago."

"What else don't I know?"

Sture thought about his long winter afternoons in bed with Fatima. In the beginning, she hardly spoke. She'd take off her clothes shyly and lie down in bed, covering herself with the sheet, fulfilling her duty unresponsively, mechanically. But as the months and then years went by, before Raquel entered Sture's life, Fatima came to feel something for him, he was sure of it. He wasn't naive enough to think it was love, or even passion, but she did open her heart to him a little. She told him about where she came from, talked about her mother, and the day Abdul returned to the village with a huge pile of money and a suitcase full of European suits and American cigarettes. That was in 1959. People said he'd betrayed his benefactor, the Spanish captain, by turning him in to the authorities. Fatima hadn't even remembered Abdul, and when he picked her up, she burst into tears, struggling to break free and return to her mother's arms.

He became furious and beat his wife in front of the other women, accusing her of turning his own daughter against him.

"I don't know much about my family. No one talked much about the past at home, and my grandmother was never mentioned."

"Your mother told me that she was a pretty girl, but her beauty faded early. Abdul has always been cruel to anyone he could, and subservient to anyone he couldn't. He made her life miserable. The women in the community tried to help, take care of her when Abdul went off, sometimes for weeks at a time, without saying where he was going. She'd come back to life when he was away, but he'd always return, and then it would start up all over again. Nobody wanted any trouble. She withered, got sick, grew weak, and died a few years later."

Yasmina gave Sture a pained look.

"Why you? Why would my mother tell you all those things when she never told me any of it?"

Sture's calm vanished like a wisp of smoke when he glanced at the traffic headed out of town. "Nessun Dorma" was still playing, but he was no longer in a state of awe. Not a vestige of sanctity remained in his expression.

"Your mother learned to trust me."

Yasmina shook her head.

"I find that hard to believe."

"Don't make the mistake of thinking you know me, Yasmina. Your mother was more important to me than you can possibly imagine."

"I do know you. I've known you since I was born."

A deep notch formed in Sture's brow as he shot Yasmina a cold look, and she felt like nothing.

"Well, you thought you knew your mother and father too, right? And your grandfather? You never thought they'd do what they did to you. They sold you to me, Yasmina. It's their fault that I own you. And you still think you owe them something, you go around taking care of an old man who hates you and keep begging for the slightest sign of affection from your mother."

Yasmina turned away, settling her gaze on the traffic. She'd tried to hate them, of course she had. She'd imagined all the ways she could do it. But her hatred fell apart like a flimsy rag.

"I can't just choose to hate them. Just like I can't choose to hate you, despite trying with all my might. To my regret, you're all family, and you're all I know."

Sture snorted in exasperation.

"A fucking saint, is that what you are? Fine, we're going to put your sainthood to the test."

Sture parked in front of a cluster of two-story houses with wood facades and gray slate roofs. He fixed his gaze on the one in front of them. It was basically the same as the others, perhaps slightly bigger, the yard perhaps a bit more looked after, the grass cut, the food bowl in front of the doghouse clean and empty.

"Look at these houses. A regular fairy tale, right? Sustainable architecture, renewable energy, young families, parents with liberal professions, two kids, a boy and a girl.

All right out of a Botticelli painting. And underneath it all, it's people like you and me, like your mother, propping up their lie, bearing the weight on our backs."

"Who's playing martyr now?"

Sture was about to respond, but suddenly he looked up. Someone was coming out of the house.

"There she is. Get a good look."

Yasmina's heart skipped a beat. Through a gate in the low wall in front of the house came her mother, holding two small children, a boy and a girl, by the hand. She looked very tired, her eyes dead. She lumbered like a bear, as though forcing herself on through sheer willpower, through necessity.

Sture lit a cigarette and then, rapping his lighter on the steering wheel, watched Fatima walk off.

"Now that we're revealing things, there's something else you should know about your past. The truth is, you weren't supposed to have one. When your mother got pregnant with you, your grandfather was furious. He tried to force her to have an abortion, beat her to see if he could induce a miscarriage. But your mother came to me for help. That's why you're here now. Because I wanted it that way. I wanted you to be born with those different-colored eyes, wanted you to have a life and hopes and dreams. I wanted you to live."

Yasmina felt sick in the pit of her stomach upon seeing her reflection in Sture's glassy eyes. It sickened her, the way he could see inside her head, see her thoughts; she felt violated, like she had no way to protect herself.

"Why are you telling me all this now?"

"Ask her," he replied, pointing to Fatima.

Yasmina shook her head. Her mother was the keeper of silence, the one who locked it inside, and with a single look made Yasmina seal her lips when she was a girl, too. Her mother was the one who wordlessly endured her father's melancholic fits of rage, the one who kissed her grandfather's feet when, after beating her with a belt, he asked forgiveness through his tears. And her soft silence turned into a hard wall, into dog-like obedience, into the ability all of the women in the family had to turn to pillars of salt when the men of the house spoke. And there were always men: fathers, uncles, brothers, husbands. That's how Yasmina remembered her childhood: men on one side, women not even on the other since they were on the very periphery of existence, rendered invisible until they were called, and then appearing half-heartedly. Her mother bit her fingernails—it was the one act of rebellion Yasmina could recall. Fatima's nail-bitten fingers covering Yasmina's mouth when she, a girl who didn't understand and didn't want to, dared to raise her voice against Grandfather's decisions. Yasmina hated her for a long time, far more than she hated her grandfather and father.

"I'm asking you, Sture. What reason could my grandfather possibly have for not wanting me to be born?"

Sture didn't speak again until the children had gotten on the bus. Fatima waved goodbye from the sidewalk.

"Getting old without a single victory to your credit is fucking tough. You should have seen her when she first got to Rosengård. She was like hot lava, setting everything and everyone on fire with a glance. And look at her now."

Yasmina's eyes began to sting. Yes, she should hate her mother. Hate her because she loved her. Because she'd needed to feel her mother's arms around her and never had, because she'd searched for an ally in her and found only the same intransigence and finger-pointing she'd found in her grandfather. The wordless accusation, the shame that weighed on her each time Sture dropped her off at home. And despite it all, she couldn't stop loving her, relishing the few comforting memories of some sign of affection shown almost by accident: a word of consolation, a smile, or the tiny gift of a handkerchief held out, an orange peeled for her, a fresh cup of coffee, a few minutes spent detangling her hair after a bath. And once, just once, many years ago, the time her mother told her that as a girl she'd dreamed of being a magician, traveling from town to town like a Berber peddler, inventing magic tricks, making things disappear and then reappear in unexpected places. She wanted to learn to turn men into pigs, deserts into oceans.

Yasmina watched her mother walk back in through the gate. Then she saw her briefly through a window where the shutter was open. She was holding the curtain, staring out at some distant point. If only Yasmina could forgive her. And she would, if her mother said one thing: "I'm sorry, Daughter. I should never have let the men in this family destroy you the way they destroyed me, and my mother, and my grandmother..." Yes, Yasmina would rush to embrace her. She'd forgive her, kiss her eyelids, sing her happy songs, buy her clothes that weren't all dark and somber, force her to dye what little hair she had left. She'd take her to Europe, to a different Europe. To France, or Spain, to the sun she missed so much. They'd travel together, Yasmina would take care of her and smile at her and they'd have experiences that brought her back to life, lifted her sickly spirit. All Yasmina needed was to feel her mother's hands on her cheeks, the whisper of a kiss on her forehead, a loving look free of blame.

Sture had rolled down the window. Slumped against the seat, he looked as if his willpower had disappeared entirely. He was watching the house.

"I'd like to be done with all this. I'm tired. Raquel and I have thought about moving to Portugal, where the weather's nice. Who knows, maybe that useless stepson of mine would actually thaw out."

Yasmina didn't believe a word of it. She'd heard the same song and dance many times, but she had to give Sture credit for his acting skills. This joker could persuade anyone of anything if he wanted to.

"So why don't you do it?"

It was all part of an act he'd carefully rehearsed.

"I would, if I could tie up a few loose ends. I don't want to spend the rest of my life watching my back. That whole business at the port, the decapitated guy in the park...there's too much noise, too much attention, it's no good. Did you know the police raided two of my clubs? They're identifying girls, scaring the clientele, confiscating drugs. I can feel them, Yasmina. They're close, very close."

"What does any of this have to do with me? Or my mother?"

Sture stared at her for a moment, until her foundations began to crumble. At first it was only a small tremor, but then came the earthquake, and finally the collapse. And that was when he went in for the kill.

"You once asked what kind of debt your grandfather incurred with me. I could tell you. What's more, I could free you of it, you and your mother both, forever. Free, nothing to pay back. Goodbye Malmö, hello Paris. You wanted to move to Paris, didn't you? All it would take is one mutual favor. I need you to go back and see your boyfriend Gövan."

Yasmina's eyes bored through Sture.

"He's not my boyfriend."

Sture didn't bat an eye.

"You speak to the deputy chief and ask him to withdraw the evidence, make a procedural error, render it inadmissible, break the chain of custody, or fuck the judge presiding the case. I don't give a shit what you do, but this can't go to trial. Threaten him, tell him you'll destroy his marriage, ruin his career, tell everyone he was off sleeping with you while his beautiful, influential little wifey was home looking after the kids. And when everyone has turned against him, when nobody will lift a finger for him, then tell him I'll be waiting with a sledgehammer and a pair of pliers, to settle scores."

"What if he won't listen to reason?"

Sture put his right hand on Yasmina's thigh. When she tried to move her leg away, he clamped his fingers like a vise. Raquel was never wrong. His wife was smarter than him, she could see things he missed and knew him better than he knew himself. There was no point denying it. He'd tried to be a father to Yasmina, or at least something resembling one. Everyone knew she was his favorite, just as her mother had been, for a time. Yasmina wouldn't betray him for money, or out of fear, cowardice, or disloyalty. But he had to make sure she'd do what he expected of her and needed her to realize what disobeying would mean.

But there was something else too. Raquel had said, "I know you cheat on me, I know you sleep with your hookers. But you've never touched her. Why?" Yes, Raquel was right: Yasmina had made him soft. He'd given her too many privileges, made too many concessions. And now it was time to make matters clear.

"Please, Sture. You're hurting me."

Sture removed his hand and regarded his fingers like they belonged to someone else. He opened the glove compartment and placed a semiautomatic in his lap.

"If Gövan won't listen, you'll have to shoot him in the head."

Yasmina stared at the pistol in horror, as though a dead rat had just been dropped onto her lap.

"I can't do that! I'm not like you, I can't shoot a person."

Suddenly Sture pounced, squeezing her neck with one hand as the other darted under her sweatshirt and twisted her nipple.

"Enough bullshit! You're going to do it, of course you are. Because you're nothing but a little slut who thought she was a princess. And if you don't, I'll shoot you myself. But first I'll force your mother to watch my men rape you and make you watch them rape her. And then you can both take a little trip together to the bottom of the port. Got it?"

Yasmina felt the pressure on her neck and the intense pain of his fingers squeezing her nipple like a pair of pliers. Finally, the wolf was showing his true face, panting and anxious; the mask had come off.

"Why are you doing this to me?"

Sture hesitated. He let her go and inhaled deeply, glancing in the rearview mirror.

"I do what I do, that's what matters. Now get out of my car."

Sture didn't even give her time to get all the way out before screeching off. Yasmina fell out and then rolled on the asphalt. Stumbling, she tried to stand. One of her right toes hurt, and that was the one thing she let herself think about as she tried to reach the sidewalk. She'd lost a shoe. Someone called out and a hand appeared, trying to help her. Then more voices.

"I saw what happened. What did they do to you? I'll call the police."

Yasmina turned to look at the Good Samaritan. A large man with a carefully trimmed beard and kind face; the sort that lived in this paradise.

Someone called from the gate.

"David, what's going on?"

"I think this girl's been attacked. Call the police."

Yasmina let go of his hand. And then she saw her.

Her mother, one of the people gathered on the sidewalk, unwilling to give up the role of curious onlooker, standing in the distance. She saw her though all the heads, through all the whispering: "What happened?" Her mother, staring right at her as if she didn't know her.

"No, don't call the police. It's nothing, I'm fine."

Nothing that hadn't happened many times before: having her sense of self stolen, feeling robbed of everything she was. Not everything she had, but everything she *was*. Being torn apart, piece by piece. It had happened since she was a girl: her grandfather in his armchair, her mother with her silence, her father and his cowardice.

16

Sevilla

The police officer was kind and very young, nothing like the ones Miguel remembered from his youth who went around on foot or horseback, stopping at the olive orchards in Almendralejo when he was a boy, the ones who made him come pick up his mother at stations in Badajoz, or Sevilla, or Madrid, every time she ran away. And yet despite his friendly demeanor and upbeat attitude, the young man couldn't help him. Even though the victim wasn't required to file a report in person, the officer needed more than Miguel's statement to actually intervene.

"But those bruises—didn't you see her face? He did that to her."

"I did see them, yes, and I suggested your daughter accompany us to the hospital to the doctors to determine how they were caused. But she refused and said she fell off her bike."

"Her bike?" Natalia didn't ride a bicycle. When she was little she'd even been afraid to ride a tricycle.

The young man folded his hands on the desk. He probably wasn't even thirty years old but already had that tired look that takes hold of people who spend too long fighting the inertia of the system.

"I believe you, Miguel. But based on what we have, the only thing we can do is file a report with the courts, asking for protective measures to be taken. In the meantime, we'll keep an eye on things. I'll ask for a patrol car to go by your daughter's place regularly. It's not much, but it's all I can do for now."

"But what about him—Gustavo? Aren't you going to arrest him? He's got a record, you could at least scare him."

"We don't go around scaring people; that's not our job. And his record doesn't give him a life sentence. In this country, we abide by the presumption of innocence."

"What if he kills her? Or seriously injures her? How can you have that on your conscience?"

The officer set his jaw, and his expression hardened.

"I think we're done here, Miguel. If there are any further developments, we'll let you know."

Waiting for Miguel in the police station foyer, Helena toyed with the wedding band in the palm of her hand. She recalled the words that had rung out in the crypt of Saint

Matthew's one rainy October morning a million years ago. "God took Eve by the hand and led her to Adam and said: 'It is not good for man to be alone.'" The priest had spoken solemnly, then looked in turn at the bride and groom and added the archetypal holy words: "What God has brought together, let no man separate." Gazing through the waiting-room window, she recalled the weak light filtering in through the crypt's high stained-glass windows on her wedding day, remembered that throughout the ceremony she'd felt as if she was watching herself, as if she was being dragged into something beyond her control. Picturing herself in her wedding dress—kneeling beside Walter at the altar, swearing to him before God and all men that she'd love him for all eternity, in sickness and in health—was like staring at a blank wall with a dark shadow being cast on it. Did she love him back then? She wanted to think so, to think that despite everything that happened in the years to come, they really had loved each other. Perhaps not in the way God and the guests expected, not in the way a young lady from a good family was supposed to, not even in the way Walter himself would have wanted. But she'd been a loyal, faithful companion, attentive to her husband's desires in the way a good friend would be; she'd dedicated herself to her marriage with reserved passion. There was no excess and no drama, but nor did she fail him when he needed her to be there.

"Why did you marry me, Helena?" he asked, only once. At the time he'd already had one operation, for the throat cancer that would kill him a few years later; he now spent all day in maroon pajamas, sitting on the sofa, hardly taking visitors, and he almost never went outside. In fact, he almost never left his office. They'd already stopped sleeping together, but the distance between them grew even larger when Walter bought a folding cot and asked to have it set up next to the fireplace, in the library. Though he'd never been a big man, Walter had lost weight in just a few months: his cheekbones jutted out and his lips lost their fullness, making it look like his teeth were too big. His hair, which had always been coarse and dark, turned completely gray, and silky to the touch. He drank water mixed with a teaspoon of sugar, taking tiny sips from a blue glass, and despite the doctor's orders sometimes he still smoked Royal cigarettes, filling the office with a sickly odor. Helena couldn't recall the last time they'd spoken of anything that wasn't strictly practical or functional. The bitterness of their first few years after the accident in Spain, and the mutual hatred expressed in barbed silences, morphed into a new kind of loneliness, one in which each of them saw the other as the perimeter wall of their personal prison.

"What crazy things we do when we think we're sane," Helena mused with a sheepish little smile, observing the people in the waiting room.

Miguel was taking a long time; perhaps that was a good sign. She hoped things with his daughter would work out. Hoped that everyone who needed help would receive it. We all need hope, need to believe that strangers will save us simply because it's their job. Save us and protect us. We all want to be understood, want others to see our sorrow and desperation, want them to make our problems their own.

In order to kill time, Helena examined the missing persons poster: children, adults, old people. People with histories, a past, their families living lives of anguish since their disappearance. "If you have seen any of these people, contact the following number." How could anyone identify a face from that sea of thumbnail-sized photos? We care about tragedy only when it touches us personally, she thought.

In the past, Helena had often agonized when David was late coming home at night, fearing something terrible had happened. Walter had a different disposition; he was more laid-back. He thought David needed to experiment and find his own limits, that he needed his freedom. But she spent those nights on the sofa—watching for headlights, her ear trained to any sounds outside—until she heard his key in the door. David would walk in sweaty, euphoric, a little tipsy, and she'd be angry seeing him in that state.

Miguel walked out, escorted by a police officer. He dragged his feet, a piece of paper in his hand. Helena didn't have to ask: she could tell by his expression that the angels in uniform were not going to help him.

They took the bus back to Miguel's apartment in silence, and he went straight to Natalia's old room and closed the door.

Almost no sign of Natalia's presence remained. Just some marks on the wall left by old posters of Barry Gibb dancing to "How Deep Is Your Love?" and bookcases that had once been nailed up, their shelves once lined with dolls and then slowly replaced by hardbacks and Russian novels, and later by university reading packets full of brainy postmodern literary theory, surrealist poetry, and the odd guilty pleasure in the form of Jane Austen. It was clear that Natalia had left this life behind long ago and had no plans of returning to it.

Miguel paced back and forth in the hope that his thoughts would settle of their own accord. But he couldn't get his daughter's injured face out of his head. After a few minutes, Helena knocked and came in.

"Are you okay?"

Miguel shook his head and sat down on Natalia's single bed.

"Why would she stand for it? I don't understand."

Helena couldn't soothe him, though she understood his feelings of impotence.

"She thinks she deserves it. Gustavo has convinced her of that. She's punishing herself."

"But he beats her, he hurts her. How can she think she deserves to be abused?"

Walter had never laid a hand on Helena—she'd never have stood for it—and yet she'd despised herself, felt sick whenever she looked in a mirror, whenever she saw that a man was looking at her in desire; she was revolted with herself each time she felt hope, or desire, or wanted something, no matter how small. It got to the point where, in the final years of her marriage, she forbade herself any sign of joy, even a smile, or humming a song. It was like her happiness was a crime against her bedridden husband. Why did she do that? How did she let herself be buried alive?

"The labyrinth of a wounded soul is impenetrable to anyone who tries to find their way through with logic and reason."

Suddenly the intercom buzzed repeatedly.

"I'll go," said Helena.

She walked to the entry hall and picked up the phone. Before she had time to ask who it was, a strident voice began shouting.

"I know he's in there, I know that son of a bitch is in there. Open the door!"

"Who is this?"

"Gustavo. Who the fuck is this? The slut that old man is fucking? Open the damn door."

"I'm going to hang up. If you bother us again I'll call the police."

She heard a nervous laugh and someone panting heavily, like a galloping buffalo.

"The police? Those assholes have already come by to bother me. I told Miguel to leave us alone. I warned him but he wouldn't listen. Tell that coward he won't be seeing his daughter again, you hear me? Tell him he'll never see her again. If he comes anywhere near us, I swear to God I'll kill him."

Helena hung up. Turning, she saw Miguel, standing frozen in the middle of the hall, staring at her.

"That was him, wasn't it? Gustavo."

elena was unable to sleep that night and lay there worrying, listening to Miguel pace the house. His footsteps were like a mouse scampering around on the other side of the door. Finally, she got up in the wee hours and found him in the kitchen, meticulously drying the sink with a dish towel. Judging by the half dozen origami birds on the Formica table, he must have been up for hours.

"They help me think," he said by way of excuse. Miguel cut a lemon in half, squeezed the juice into a glass of warm water and held it out to Helena.

"It's a good antioxidant."

In other circumstances, she would have mocked his attempts to stay healthy, but the open bottles of Aricept and Razadyne on the counter stopped her.

"Miguel, are you okay?"

Miguel had gone very still. His mouth hung open and his gaze was fixed on some point between them and the doorway.

"He's going to hurt her again. He's going to hurt my little girl and no one is willing to stop him."

You could just close your eyes and accept the fact that Natalia is old enough to make her own mistakes, she thought. But he wouldn't: parents never follow the dictates of logic when it comes to their own children.

Miguel kept staring vacantly into space.

"When I was a boy and had to take care of my mother, I felt the same sense of impotence. I didn't know how to read her moods or needs, I dreamed of having a super-power that would tell me what to do and say, how to react in every situation. One would always rather do things right, succeed the first time, keep from messing up. But we don't know how."

Helena bridged the distance between them, taking his hand. It was a sinewy hand, covered in age spots. Cold.

"People often accept things and act unthinkingly, by instinct."

"I can't resign myself to this. I've been tossing and turning all night. I don't know what to do. It's maddening."

Helena wanted to prove to her friend that he wasn't alone. But even more than that she wanted to help him out of the fog enveloping him.

"I spent all night thinking, too, and I only see one solution."

She described her plan to Miguel, and when she was done they looked at one another without speaking. There was no need for words.

After several minutes, Miguel nodded slowly.

"There's no other way, right?"

"Right. And then go and don't look back."

He shook his head.

"Running away is not an option."

"But there will be consequences, and you might not like them."

He nodded again.

"I'll accept the consequences."

He'd just aged ten years. The decision was made, and there was no turning back.

The best way to bust a kneecap was a forceful blow, coming straight down. You had to make sure the bat hit the entire surface of the bone. It generally made a loud crack as it broke. No better way to fuck up a guy's legs. But it was a whole process; you had to warm up a little, make him understand what you expected from him. The limp would serve as a reminder, in case he started to think about reneging on what he agreed to, going back to his old ways.

Ivan had acquired this knowledge through experience, and everyone knew it, which is why he and his two buddies were never short of work. But this time the job had not come through Guillermo, the usual channel.

"I need you to know exactly what's going to happen if you go through with this."

"I don't need you to tell me any of that."

Ivan drank straight from his bottle of beer and sucked his teeth.

"I have to, Helena. Putting someone in the hospital is no joke, it's a crime. And it's not cheap, I can tell you that."

Helena set a plastic bag on the table.

"Will this be enough?"

Ivan opened the bag. Inside were the keys to Miguel's Datsun and her pearl necklace. The young man gave a low whistle.

"Damn, you must really hate this guy. Is your little four-eyed friend with the mustache down with this plan? Do the two of you know what you're getting into? I like you, Helena. I could just hand this bag back, you buy me another beer, and we'll call it even, forget about this little conversation."

"I want you to do it."

"You and your friend could both end up in jail. And it's not a nice place."

Helena lit a cigarette with Ivan's lighter.

"I saw what prison did to my father."

"Your father was in jail?"

"For longer than you've been alive."

Helena narrowed her eyes. It had been a Sunday in February, her thirty-fourth birthday. It wasn't raining in London that day. The sky was unusually clear and bright, and people rushed eagerly to the park to lie in the sun and enjoy themselves. Helena was alone in the house they'd just bought in Southfields. Walter had taken David to the local pub to watch the Arsenal-Everton match. Their living room didn't even have curtains yet, and they still hadn't bought much furniture.

"There was a knock on the door and there he was," she told Ivan. "It had been over twenty years, so at first I didn't recognize him. He was wearing secondhand clothes, including a brown jacket with frayed cuffs that was too big and missing all the buttons. He was almost bald, and his head was bony and covered in scars. His green eyes looked muddy, his lips were dry and the skin on his cheeks was all tight. He'd done a bad job shaving. I almost closed the door on him, but then he spoke and I recognized his voice. It was the same one I'd heard in my bedroom when I was a little girl, the one that used to wish me good night before he gave me a kiss on the head. 'Hello, Daughter. It's been a long time.' Those were his first words."

"Why did they lock him up?"

"For trying to be himself at a time when it was forbidden."

Helena remembered she'd let her father in but didn't know what to say. All she could think to do was make coffee and put out some cookies. Then she sat facing him, on the edge of an armchair, with her back very straight and her knuckles white from clenching her hands so tightly. She felt like a robot, unable to ask him anything or even to think. Her father drank his coffee and gazed at the wallpaper as if there hadn't been a quarter century of silence.

"It was only when he made some banal comment about the cookies, told me they were good but he preferred butter cookies, that I started to cry. Then my father stopped talking and stared at me idiotically, visibly uncomfortable. He made an effort to try to hug me, but I flinched and told him not to touch me."

"Why? What had he done?"

"He left me when I was too young to understand." Helena recalled his coward's eyes and lukewarm protest. And then she voiced what she'd been holding inside since that trip to Rif with Abdul in 1954.

She'd seen them that night in the village. It was a strange sight for a ten-year-old girl. Like a dream that made no sense. Helena had been asleep. The temperature had plummeted, and her father had covered her with his sheepskin jacket. She loved sleeping in that jacket because the wool lining smelled like him. But then she heard a strange sound, like two animals growling at each other, fighting over the same piece of meat. It worked its way into her dream and made her open her eyes. She saw the fire, and the play of light and shadows. Abdul was on his knees, naked, thrusting his hips back and forth and holding onto a man's head. The man was flat on the ground like a felled animal, making a noise like crying and laughing at the same time. He turned his head, his face contorted. And then she recognized him in the shadows: it was her father.

They weren't alone. Beside them, on the ground, was Abdul's wife. She was trying to look away, but they made her watch. Helena would never forget the woman's sad eyes, overwhelmed by something far greater than she could fathom. When Abdul finished mounting Enrique, he pounced on her, ripped her blouse, spread her legs, and penetrated her. And all the while, Enrique watched with a crazed, drunken smile on his face. When Helena told him all this, her father stammered. He didn't know how to defend himself.

"I would have accepted any excuse, even a lie about him always having loved me and being sorry he left me. All I needed was for him to say something, anything, and I'd have forgiven him. I needed to grant that forgiveness so much more than he needed to receive it."

But her father hadn't said a word. Just sniffled and snorted loudly, sucking his snot, then searched his jacket pocket for a cigarette, got up, and turned to examine the living room.

Ivan twirled his beer bottle pensively.

"I still don't understand what he went to jail for. So he was a faggot. What difference does that make?"

Helena laughed bitterly.

"You don't understand. You think you know everything, but you don't know a thing. You're just a kid who's mad at the world. My father loved that man, loved him more than my mother, more than me, more than his own life. He left it all behind for him. And that man betrayed him. They brought my father back to Spain, tied up like a dog, and locked him up with a bunch of animals. He spent fifteen years waiting for his death sentence, but they just kept transferring him. At night he was beaten, raped, and the guards just looked the other way."

Ivan clenched the bottle as if to strangle it.

"I'd have hunted down that Abdul guy and ripped him to shreds with my bare hands."

Helena half closed her eyes. A shadow of exhaustion crossed her face, multiple layers of accumulated sadness.

"Most people, like you, would want vengeance. Or at least want to forget about him. But my father still loved him. He told me that the only way he'd managed to survive all those years in prison was by keeping Abdul's memory alive. And as soon as he got out, he set out to find him. My father went back to Tangier, looked up old acquaintances who had tips on how to find him, and traveled to Abdul's village in Rif. That was where he found out Abdul had gone off to Sweden. My father was planning to go after him. But he wanted something from me first. He didn't know how to ask; he wanted the painting. He wanted me to give him the portrait of Abdul that my mother had painted all those years ago."

Helena could still feel the burning sensation she'd gotten in her throat when she heard her father beg. She wanted to hurl the set of glasses and cocktail shaker from the side table, wanted to scream until the walls tumbled down, wanted to scratch the air until it bled. But instead she inhaled sharply and turned to face her father. What was the matter with him? Was he so blind he couldn't see the extent of the damage he'd done? And at that moment, Helena realized that the man who had been her father no longer existed, that he'd probably died in jail a long time ago. The old wreck of a man staring at her, stiff as a board, was scarred by humiliation, derision, and disillusionment. He had suffered and was still suffering.

"Seeing him like that later helped me understand the nature of sorrow, the kind that comes from loving someone who doesn't love you back, someone who uses you while you do nothing to keep from being destroyed. My father destroyed his life for Abdul—his career, his family, he lost it all. But there was no way for him to turn back, and he chose to forge ahead instead, despite knowing that he was living a lie. His lie, his choice. He'd never get that portrait; he'd never get me or my love or understanding. And I knew he'd never get Abdul either. My father was already dead but didn't know it. I could have helped him, could have done something for him, opened his eyes to the truth, freed him from the burden of that monster who destroyed him. But I didn't. I felt deceived and hurt, I kicked him out, and he never contacted me again. Three months later I found out he'd died in a brawl at the port in Malmö. I didn't want to see his body, didn't even go to the funeral. I erased him from my life. But he's still here; he's always been here."

Ivan had finished his beer some time ago. He was staring at Helena in curiosity, and respect. She stood.

"Sometimes we have to make decisions for those who can't make them themselves, even if they hate us for it. I should have freed my father from his burden but I couldn't do it. I won't let my friend go through the same thing with his daughter. If you won't do it, I'll find someone who will."

She turned, ready to walk out, but Ivan reached out and grabbed her wrist.

"Wait. I'll do it."

van had never had anyone remotely famous in his clutches. From up close, though, bleeding like a pig and whimpering like a sissy, the singer and guitarist of Los Cuatreros was quite a letdown.

"You are never to go anywhere near Natalia again—ever. You will disappear from her life without a trace. Nod if you understand me."

Gustavo's head flopped forward like a broken marionette. He spat blood and felt around his mouth with his tongue. They'd knocked out two of his teeth, and he ended up swallowing them. His nose felt like it was on fire; he was sure these animals had broken it with the first punch. He could barely piece together what had happened. He'd left a club in Tablada pretty wasted, and suddenly these skinheads in bomber jackets had surrounded him. At first, he thought it was a holdup, just bad luck, an unfortunate co-incidence. But now he got it. Had Natalia paid these thugs? No, she'd never have done that, she didn't have it in her. She loved him, forgave him, needed him. Gustavo was a like god to her—omnipotent and untouchable. This could only have been Miguel, it had to have been that meddling old man. Just thinking about him made Gustavo furious. As soon as these assholes let him go, he was going to find him and make him pay for what he'd done. He'd kill him.

Ivan grabbed Gustavo's chin. The idiot wasn't taking it seriously, he was planning revenge; Ivan could see it in his shifty look.

"You're not too bright, are you?" he asked, brandishing the baseball bat like he was about to hit a home run. He took one step back, calculated the distance, and delivered a quick hard blow that struck Gustavo's entire right kneecap. Gustavo let out a horrific cry and collapsed like a building whose foundations have given way.

"You will do exactly what I tell you and nothing else. To-morrow you will go to Plaza de Armas and take a bus. You will disappear forever, never call her again, never even attempt to contact her or anyone who knows her. If you do, I'll find you, and it won't just be your kneecap I bust." Ivan crouched down and pulled Gustavo's hair, yanking him up until the man's red face came to his lips. "What I do will leave you in a wheelchair, but first I'll take a pair of scissors and cut off your balls."

Ivan stood, shot his buddies a look, and then nodded. At his sign, they started kicking Gustavo like kids playing ball on the street. And while they were letting loose, venting all their rage on a sack of flesh who didn't have enough hands to defend himself from the blows, Ivan calmly sauntered off down the alley. He lit a cigarette and slipped the lighter back into the pocket of his bomber jacket, where his fingers touched the pearl necklace. Ivan smiled. It would look so good on Zona. And though that made him happy, what he was really excited about was at the end of the alley. Parked under a streetlight, the Datsun glimmered like the dream of a new life within reach. And it was his. A good deal, indeed.

Macarena University Hospital was abuzz with activity. The air-conditioning had gone out and people were coping with the heat as best they could, with fans and newspapers—and resignation. Lots of resignation. Hospitals are full of the stuff: tense waits, loved ones imagining the worst, commending themselves to various saints. Natalia stood in the waiting room, sweating buckets and holding her stomach. Although several people had offered her chairs, she chose to stand. She couldn't stop fidgeting. When the nurse finally appeared and called for the family of Gustavo Oriza, she felt the baby kick.

"Two minutes," the nurse warned, accompanying Natalia to one of the ER examination cubicles, separated from one another by blue curtains.

The hallway was full of wheelchairs, cots, patients, and healthcare professionals. Despite the signs on the wall requesting silence, the place was as loud as flea-market day at Charco de la Pava. When the curtain opened, Natalia could hardly contain her horror, clasping both hands over her mouth. The figure lying on the cot looked nothing like Gustavo. He was a mass of deformed flesh that went from yellow to blue to black; someplace there were eyes and a nose. His right leg was in a cast from the ankle to above the knee, and his head and both arms were bandaged.

"Dear God. What happened?" Natalia tried to take his hand but he pulled away, giving her a cold hard look full of hatred.

"Forget about me. I don't exist to you. It's over between us," he said with a devastating, deadly calm that left no room for questions. Natalia began to tremble violently and stumbled backward as though she'd been hit in the face.

"Why would you say that?" Natalia didn't understand. She tried to get near to Gustavo but he turned his head away.

"I said we're though. Now go."

Natalia returned to the hospital for ten days in a row, and Gustavo reacted the same each time: with a cutting silence that hurt her and that he seemed to enjoy. On the last day, when she begged him, sobbing, to speak to her, he gave a gaptoothed smile and said, "Give my regards to your father."

The next day, when Natalia arrived at the hospital, Gustavo's bed was empty. He'd been released and had left, just like that. Forever.

t was you! I dare you to deny it."

Natalia's hands flapped wildly in her father's face. She was livid, shouting, crying. She scratched at the air and would gladly have scratched his face, as he stood there unable to say a word. Pale, remorseful, Miguel watched his daughter's explosion of hatred in devastation.

"I could go to the police, I could report you. I should do it!"

Miguel blinked. Ironically, they were standing next to the foot of the cathedral staircase, at the Gate of Forgiveness. Tourists came and went incessantly, wearing baseball caps or hats, holding bottles of water. A horse in the line of carriages stamped anxiously. Someone laughed, gypsies with branches of rosemary eyed up the tourists, a shirtless boy took pictures of his friends posing at the church's facade. Miguel saw everything going on around him, but nothing reached him. He felt removed from it all.

"Go ahead," he said submissively. "You should. But don't expect me to be sorry. You're my daughter and I love you."

Natalia closed her eyes, feeling nauseated, and silenced him with an imperious look. She backed up and pointed at him like a pariah.

"I'm not your daughter anymore, and you're not my father. Mamá was right. You're a hypocrite. Love me? You've never understood love in your life. Always reading your damn letters in secret, living a hollow life, never really present. You didn't have the guts to love that woman, just like you didn't love Mamá. You were even ashamed of Grandmother, of your own mother. You know nothing about love, all you ever did was pretend, go to work, meet obligations, duties, spend your time with orders, numbers, logic. And wear that self-righteous expression, like you were being put through hell on earth. You arrange the world by your own narrow vision, make everything adhere to what you can accept."

"That's enough, Natalia."

"It is *not* enough!" she cried, her eyes burning with thick tears. "You have fucked up my life ever since I was a little girl, forced me to be what you expected me to be, just like you did with Mamá. You oppressed her all the way to the grave, betrayed her just like you're betraying me now. I never want to see you again. Ever! You're dead to me."

Miguel looked at his daughter imploringly, but Natalia stormed off, her words ringing out like a wake-up call. "You're dead to me." There was no worse punishment for a parent than those words spoken by a child.

He returned home distraught. Helena was waiting for him in the living room. Seeing his dejection, his slumped shoulders, and the way he looked around without actually seeing anything, she realized what had happened.

"I guess it didn't go as you'd hoped. Still, what could you have expected?"

Miguel collapsed onto the sofa. He shook his head in disbelief.

"She hates me. My daughter hates me. She will never forgive me."

"Yes, she will. Maybe not today. Or tomorrow. But sooner or later she'll realize that she left you no choice. Love flattens anything that gets in its path. Give her time, Miguel. She'll come around."

Miguel felt a bitter prick.

"Time is the one thing I don't have, Helena. I don't want my last memory of my daughter to be the words she spoke to me today."

Maybe Natalia was right and what he called love was nothing but selfishness. Maybe he couldn't stand the idea of being somehow responsible for her having so little self-esteem that she let Gustavo destroy her.

"I did something wrong, terribly wrong. But I don't know what it is. I never asked her what she was feeling, what she needed. I took for granted that it was enough for her to know I was there for her, taking care of her expenses, her financial well-being. But I never really tried or managed to get inside her head, her heart."

Helena went to him and stroked his shoulder.

"We can't let our last days be wasted picking up the crumbs of our failures, Miguel. We have to keep going."

"Keep going? Going where?"

"Forward, Miguel. While we still can."

PART FIVE

June 2014

17

Madrid

The sound of the Valentine typewriter rang out from behind the study door. The clacking keys and ding of the carriage return were a good sign. They meant that old Simón had gotten out of bed today, and that he was in a good mood and felt like working. His children agreed not to disturb him: these moments were becoming ever scarcer, and they didn't want to steal them away from him. At lunchtime, someone would take him in a bowl of soup with chunks of bread floating in it, the way he liked, and a glass of soda. As he wrote, Simón thought back—no longer with any pain now—on his time as a prison guard at Valley of the Fallen, and the bleak office where his superior, the Archangel, worked. It was a small room, not very comfortable, and resembled a booth. It was annexed to the "special prisoners" barracks, which were almost entirely full of Communists, and you had to climb up three wooden steps to get to it. A huge map of Europe hung on the wall behind his desk. Spain was bigger than the rest of the continent, and across the coast of North Africa it said, "MCMXXXIX: Year of Victory." Every time he walked into the office, Simón was transfixed by that map. Other walls had blueprints of the future basilica and the roads leading to the Valley's esplanade. On a sawhorse table were models made to scale, showing what it would all look like when the monument to fallen soldiers was completed. They were two years behind schedule. The final gallery, where the crypt would be, had yet to be finished, and the pressure to make progress was intense.

Nearly every time Simón entered the barracks, some song by Imperio Argentino was playing on an old French record player, and the Archangel was behind his desk in shirtsleeves and suspenders. On the table were often bottles of Scotch and ashtrays full of cigarette butts. They called him the Archangel—one of the few things that prisoners and guards agreed on—because he kept an image of Michael, the leader of God's Army, in the pocket of his combat jacket, and when anyone questioned him, he repeated the archangel's maxim: *Quis ut Deus?* He wasn't fueled by hatred. A well-bred and well-educated officer, he was incapable of hating the men in his charge because he didn't know them. They'd done nothing to him—there was no offense, no death to blame them for, no resentment to deal with—but he felt no regard for them either.

"I'm a professional," he'd say. "I've been given a mission, and I have a duty to it." As though being a career officer made him immune to the desire for revenge and to age-old hatreds. The Archangel didn't feel guilty. He'd never killed anyone, hadn't fired a shot during the war, hadn't given a single order leading to dead or wounded men that might trouble his conscience. And yet having nothing to weigh on his conscience seemed to exasperate him.

"You, at least, have blood on your hands, Simón. You can be accused or absolved."

Simón's long nights often began with this insidious claim. The ritual never varied: the Archangel would invite him to sit and smoke, pretending they could behave cordially, as if rank was somehow suspended in the room's wooden walls, under its leaky roof, as if they were not officer and subaltern.

"Have a seat, Simón. Come on, relax, man. You're among friends."

And Simón would pretend to relax but never get too comfortable, just in case. His superior's mood swings were notorious. The Archangel would pour him a Scotch, and as they drank he'd tried to make sense of something that was basically senseless: Reds, fascists, Franco, the Republic, order, country, God, chaos...

Those were the words Simón was now typing on his Valentine typewriter, as though in the years gone by, they'd somehow acquired meaning. But they were still words—theoretical constructs that could potentially hold water—and not real reasons. It mattered little whether they came from the Archangel's mouth or Simón's fingertips. All Simón knew was that war held humanity at bay.

Occasionally he had tried to explain this to his grandson Raúl, who was doing a doctorate at the university and sometimes interviewed him as part of his dissertation on collective memory: *The first thing you have to understand is that wars just start. Five minutes after the first explosion, nothing else matters. Suddenly, civilized people who've lived together in peace start to tear each other to pieces, steal, murder, set things on fire, rape. In war we are capable of biting, destroying, surpassing all limits, and it's all justified by the existence of an enemy. The only condition imposed is that we run back to the cage when our master whistles, signaling that the whole affair is over. Then we have to bandage things over, look for justifications and excuses for our atrocities, rebuild what was destroyed, put out the fires, return the dead to their catacombs, and forget—or pretend to.*

"You, for example, Simón," the Archangel would say to him on those long guard shifts, "look what war has done to you." And Simón, slightly intoxicated because he rarely drank, would look down at his flak jacket as if it were dirty or coming unstitched. "You can explain to me what it feels like to kill face-to-face. But I didn't do any of that. I missed the chance to put myself to the test, and now here I am, a loyal administrator of victory, devoted to the catechism that must lead people back to the fold or get them out of the way."

Once, Simón's grandson asked him if he'd ever killed anyone. Simón tried to explain that he was never a murderer: *We were the heroes. Officers like the Archangel brainwashed us, told us that it was the other side, the enemy, who were*

346

the murderers; they told us that they came down from the hills at night to carry off children as they slept in their beds. That they were boogeymen. They convinced us killing them was necessary, said God was on our side and that ours was the just cause. They forced us to attend mass, gave us communion and sent us off to kill, absolved of sin. But his grandson would insist: *My father told me you killed two men in the war.* And then Simón had to rummage through his drawer of old excuses. *It's true, I killed two men in the war, near Don Benito; they were so young, and as scared as I was... small-town kids who could barely take the bolts off their rifles. We came face-to-face by chance on an abandoned farm; we were lost, all of us far from our respective lines, in no-man's-land. We could have just turned around and gone our separate ways, no one was going to execute us or call us traitors since there were no witnesses. But fear and mistrust got the best of us, our hearts and minds were full of hatred, slogans, and lies. Their fear paralyzed them, but mine made me attack, like a cornered animal. I jumped on the first one and speared him with my knife. Then I chased the second one through a field as he fled. It didn't take long to catch up to him. I knocked him down and stabbed him in the back until he stopped moving. I could have let him go but I was overcome by panic, utter panic at the idea of being found alone, at the idea of him telling his side about me. I stared at his body, knife still in my hand, and listened to him die; and I felt sorry for him, just like he would have felt sorry for me. He died like so many others. Blameless, no idea what the hell he'd done to deserve it.*

Simón's son had told him not to speak so bluntly to his grandson, said kids today were highly impressionable and quick to judge about things they didn't understand. So Simón had decided to go back to writing, to tell his side, reconstruct his fragmented memory and weave together some kind of cohesive narrative. But it was painful: sometimes his hands hurt, and he could no longer work for hours on end without a break. He missed smoking, missed the way cigarettes made the air so thick with smoke it was almost unbreathable. But he wasn't allowed to smoke anymore.

Simón was embarrassed to admit that he almost couldn't remember the faces of the boys he'd killed despite remembering every feature of the Archangel's face, which he had come to despise. When the war ended he'd been refused a furlough and forced to transfer to a detachment sent to oversee construction at Cuelgamuros Valley, guarding the prisoners who were building the monument. He felt sorry for them. The war was over, and everyone had to get on with life. The Nationalists had gotten what they wanted, victory was theirs. Why keep drubbing the defeated so mercilessly? Did they want to wipe them from the face of the earth? If they got rid of all of the Republicans, who could they lord their victory over? Who would they pour scorn upon? Victory is like inebriation. Two years after winning, the victors were still drunk on it: glory, hymns, brief moments that had granted them immortality. They wanted to drag it out as long as possible, seize their piece of history. It was what people like the Archangel lived for.

"Think about it, Simón, don't look at it as punishment; this is an opportunity. One day, historians will talk about you and me, what we did here. Erecting a monument to the fallen for the glory of Spain. Every one of those stones being blasted night and day will bear our names."

Simón knew all of this hogwash was simply a prelude to something worse, and as he listened he was unable to conceal his disquiet. And then one night, the Archangel laid his cards on the table:

"I've seen you talking to that prisoner from Badajoz, Amador Gandía. You like him, don't you?"

Simón knew which prisoner his superior was talking about. Everyone knew Amador, everyone had seen his young wife and son come from far away in the hopes of being able to visit him, seen them stay out there in the elements because the Archangel refused to let them see him.

"You think I'm cruel to him, don't you? All the guards do. But all you see, Simón, is a husband and father, kept from his loved ones. I see a recalcitrant Red who can barely contain his pride. Look at his steely expression; it's full of hatred. I see a man who is a piece of human waste and refuses to renounce what he was. And it's my job—and yours, Simón—to make him forget, do you understand? It's not about this basilica, this monument to victory we're building. Anyone could do that, there's certainly more than enough manpower in this ravaged country. Our job here consists of bringing each and every Amador Gandía left to his knees, forcing them to accept that their past no longer exists, that never again will they be the men they thought they were. It's called submission, acceptance. Obscurity. Victory is worth nothing if you don't crush the vanquished. Who can say that Amador Gandía won't steal more dynamite, try to provoke another prisoners' revolt? Don't give me that look, Simón; I'm not accusing you of neglecting your duties as a guard. I know you act in good faith, but do you really think I can't see what you're doing? It's grave misconduct, I could have you court-martialed."

After the Archangel had hurled that threat, Simón remembered him going very still, contemplating the color of his whisky. He smiled sadly, his rage trapped in his gums, his flushed cheeks, the pale fingers clenching the glass. Then he took his pistol from the drawer and laid it on the table.

"Believe me, Simón, I'm tired of martyrs too. I want to go home as well, but that's not possible. So tell me, how are you going to rectify your misconduct, soldier? How are you planning to prove to me that you're loyal to your superior and your country?" He got up, circled behind Simón, placed his hands on his shoulders, leaned over, and then whispered in his ear: "I know of only one way, soldier." And Simón could smell his whisky-fueled breath.

Someone knocked on the door. He heard the voice of his grandson, the oldest one. Simón stopped typing and wiped his tears. It hurt to remember, and it was such old pain. His great-grandchildren came in to say goodbye. Simón never thought he'd live this long, never thought he'd live to see his wife and two of his children die. See his grandchildren grow up and get married, watch as they had their own kids, who looked at him in childlike bewilderment as if he was a mummy in a wheelchair, with a strange smell coming from the wet spots between his legs, feet bandaged because of his wounds. He hardly spoke since he had nothing to say. It had been a struggle to listen to his grandson's questions; why talk about things that no longer exist? *So they will continue to exist, Grandfather.* Young people put too much stock in the power of memory, had too much faith in words. But it was thanks to his grandson that he was now typing on the Valentine, all these years later.

Now he was alone again, and like fog that won't lift, his memories flooded back into the room. He could hear the Archangel's laughter, his jokes.

"Don't give me your answer now, Simón. Go do your shift, think it over, and then tell me. I trust you."

Simón would never forget the road that dead-ended at a huge esplanade, right at the entrance to the tunnel being dug, stone by stone, into the mountain. In the moonlight, the road looked like a river of milk. At night you couldn't hear the blasting, and the mountain was still. Thousands of cubic meters of rock and dirt were being piled on either side of the road, after having been transported by masses of men who came and went like an army of dejected ants. Excavation dust mixed with the fog rolling in from the hills and drifted into the pines and elms on the hillside.

He still went up to Cuelgamuros from time to time, so he could explain the terrain to his grandson, make him see things that couldn't be expressed in words: the prisoners' footsteps in the muddy rain, the sound of droplets bouncing off the guards' helmets and improvised tents, the little rivers that formed in the ruts worn into the ground by the trudging of prisoners and beasts of burden, the trucks' wheels stuck in muddy tracks and potholes. At the door to the barracks, the night shift was full of boredom and dread, listening to prisoners drag themselves to their bunks and collapse against the wall. Simón watched them in the dark and they pretended not to hear him, see him, know he was there. Their faces and hushed voices, the expressions they wore as they hid in the darkness between tongue-and-groove wallboards, under a zinc roof, stretched out in their cots like corpses. All dead.

In the end, he won, Simón wrote. *The Archangel beat me. He erased me, turned me into nothing.*

"Where are we?"

Helena had opened her eyes when the bus jolted as it drove over a speed bump. It was still dark out, but a warm glow was starting to come from behind the hilltops. Miguel gazed at the Castilian sky, specked with increasingly distant stars.

"We've still got a while before Madrid. Go back to sleep."

Helena curled lazily in her seat, covering her shoulders with a cardigan. She saw the letter Miguel was holding, but didn't ask and instead closed her eyes once more, thinking about how badly she wanted a cigarette and a strong coffee.

Miguel stared through the window at the restless landscape, fingering the letter in his hands. The lights of Madrid twinkled in the distance, a luminous mass that would slowly fade as the day dawned.

He turned back to the letter. On the back of the envelope was a return address in Madrid:

Madrid, August 1944

I want you to know your husband was a good
person. He thought about you and your son all the time.
He died without God's grace since he refused Commu-
nion, but he had the respect of the man sending you this.
Sometimes the heart can see what the eyes cannot.

Simón Andújar

Maybe he still lived there, the man who'd struggled to
write those words, his scrunched handwriting on the coarse
paper clearly betraying a lack of education. A man who could
easily be dead, who didn't know what impact those few
poorly scribbled lines had had on his life. It was disheart-
eningly simple. *Your husband was a good person.* For years
his mother had kept that letter with the other things in the
trunk. She must have run a finger over that sentence daily,
clinging to the small consolation written by a stranger. *He
thought about you and your son all the time.*

"Is that true, Father?"

But his father didn't come when called. In return, Miguel could only say that he hadn't thought about his father
when he was a boy. It was hard enough just trying to fight
for his own place in the world. When he was five years old,
he hated being challenged to do something, because failure was his greatest fear in the world. And though he knew
he was inferior to other boys at everything, he didn't avoid

353

fights or challenges; he threw himself into them body and soul as if his life depended on it, literally. He recalled one cold winter day at the Montijo Reservoir, where the steely waters of Guadiana River were contained. Miguel had no reason to accept the challenge: he was the smallest of the four boys and there were no witnesses to shame him if he backed out. But he didn't. Shivering with cold and fear, he slowly undressed and took two steps forward to the edge of the plank. He was scared of heights but didn't want the others to know, so he forced himself to keep his eyes open and look down. It was raining, and drops of water fell onto the reservoir like pellets. It was impossible to see the bottom. Miguel inhaled deeply and looked back. The others were waiting expectantly, somewhat incredulous. They knew Miguel was afraid of heights and could hardly swim. They'd just wanted him to admit he was scared. They wanted to make fun of the scrawny, quiet boy with the hot temper. They didn't think he'd really do it.

But he did.

Their cries of surprise blended with Miguel's scream of terror. It was a violent leap, and he knew his body wouldn't stay close to the surface, that he'd be trapped deep underwater and not be able to hold his breath long enough to make it up to the top. But the second he touched bottom, his body sprang up with momentum, and he paddled up until he could see the ripples of the raindrops on the water's surface. As he moved through the dark turbulent waters, Miguel knew he wasn't going to die and was flooded with the pleasure that came of realizing that the limits he could surpass exceeded his fear. Once at the surface he dog-paddled to the shore, swept along by the other boys' cries of admiration. Miguel felt the tremendous confidence of having finally found his true identity. He pushed himself out of the water and felt rain on his bare skin, little rivulets of mud running down his legs. His lips were purple and his teeth chattered, his chest scratched by the branches at the bottom of the reservoir, but he didn't care. He was euphoric.

The glow of having just experienced the best moment of his life lasted all the way home. His friends surrounded him wordlessly, in reverence. Miguel was thinking about the rain soaking his clothes and the perfect, muted sound it made as it fell. He had a brief moment of doubt, wondering what he'd say to his mother, but then was overcome by optimism once more. He wished she could have seen his act of valor. She'd be proud. And that was what Miguel needed most, his mother's approval.

When he got back it was almost dark and he had to grope his way along. He walked into the small living room, where a charcoal brazier sat under the table, and found his mother sitting there, the tablecloth over her knees to keep in the heat. Miguel sensed something indescribable, as if the air were full of tiny particles he'd never seen until that moment. And suddenly, all his self-confidence came crashing down. Hunched over the table, his mother stared into space, eyes vacant, as her fingernails scratched the tablecloth mindlessly. A few centimeters from her hand was a letter folded in half and a wad of bills. Miguel touched her forearm.

"Mother?"

She startled, looking up at Miguel with wide eyes.

"Where were you?" Miguel tried to explain. He needed his mother's praise and would have lapped up any sign of affection like a dog. Or perhaps he was a sparrow, a few crumbs enough to keep him fed. But his mother listened with a twinge of resentment, and Miguel slowly felt himself shrinking, his voice trailing off, and finally he fell silent. Her expression was rock-solid, showing not one crack of kindness or understanding. And then suddenly she, his mother, the person whose job it was protect him, the one person Miguel loved above all others, did it again. She pounced, claws out, and sank her fingernails viciously into his face.

Miguel knew how it would end, knew it was best not to put up a fight, not to cry or ask questions. All he could do was wait for it to pass. She dragged him by the hair, whipped his head back and forth as though trying to wrench it off, slammed him into the wall while hurling insults, and he didn't even put up his arms. Miguel let himself be tossed around like a rag doll. Sooner or later it would end; it always did. Suddenly, his mother went still, her fingernails still in his face as Miguel cried silent tears. Her expression morphed into a different kind of madness, a sort of disgusted shock, and she let him go.

"Go to bed," she whispered, lips trembling. She didn't dare look at her son.

Miguel picked up his pieces: the shredded T-shirt, the tennis shoe that had flown off. He knew he mustn't look at her now, mustn't sympathize with her or try to hug her. He mustn't say that he loved her but was afraid of her. If he did, it would start all over again. The only thing he could do was curl up in bed, pull the sheet over himself, scrunch his eyes shut and cry so softly that she couldn't hear. And try to sleep cherishing the realization that he'd had at the reservoir: he had a place in the world. At some point in the night he felt the familiar weight of his mother's body lie down beside him in the narrow bed, felt her breath on his neck, her hair against his ear, and heard her whispered voice asking forgiveness, calling herself terrible names, telling him how much she loved him. Miguel didn't respond. In his own way he'd already come to realize that his mother wasn't actually talking to him but to herself. He was her mirror, something that was there but didn't exist.

The next morning, he found his mother sitting on the wet grass. The previous day's rain had washed the sky clean, and it looked like a freshly ironed sheet. A brightly colored bird sat on the branch of a fig tree, singing. It was a pretty song, the best song this bird, so tiny it would fit in the palm of his hand, could sing. His mother looked up, and he saw deep dark bags under her sunken eyes. She blew her nose on a crumpled handkerchief and then wrinkled it up and patted the ground next to her.

"Come sit beside me." It wasn't an order; she was begging. Miguel obeyed but sat warily at a distance. His mother smiled in sorrow and pulled him gently to her, their bodies touching. She didn't say she was sorry. She never did when she knew he could hear. Instead she asked him to tell her about the reservoir again. Miguel didn't yet fully understand it, but he was starting to sense how grueling it was to love someone. He told her, recounting all the details of his plunge, but felt no enthusiasm now. His mother nodded and kissed his head, and Miguel's body shuddered in fear and gratitude.

"There are few people in the world who are brave enough to change it, Son. But you're different. Extraordinary in many ways." She didn't say what ways. She didn't say anything else for some time. Then she pulled the letter and wad of bills Miguel had seen the night before from the pocket of her robe. Her eyes trembled.

"I want you to study, Miguel. Something worthwhile. You have to get an education, learn to control the world so no one can hurt you anymore. You need to be far away from me."

Miguel felt a flush: he was flooded by something far more powerful than what he'd felt with his friends. He curled up between his mother's legs and felt her hesitate before resting a hand on his head to stroke his hair. A drop fell onto his cheek, by his ear. And he let his mother's tear burn his skin like an invisible, painful tattoo that he could never remove.

"Your father died. We're alone now."

Helena was still asleep on his shoulder. Her breath was as calm as the sea, her smoker's lungs whistling rhythmically as her eyelids darted through a dream.

Miguel tucked back a lock of hair that had fallen over her eyes. His friend had managed to take standing up the punishment he'd callously inflicted on them both. Blame, regret over what they'd done, accusations, and a much more wicked and difficult truth that he didn't dare voice: What if he hadn't done it for Natalia's sake but for that of his own pride? Helena and that kid, Ivan, were now inconvenient witnesses to his weakness, knew his fear and fragility. Helena had seen him cry, Ivan had seen his lack of empathy. Miguel was no longer an infallible god who made or broke his loved ones' futures at will; he couldn't control the chaos or senselessness of things as he had all his life, and in his weakness he'd implicated Helena. He was afraid she too would tire of his mood swings, his constant carping, the newly discovered feeling of having lost his way, of being unable to look to the future or reconcile the past but instead be trapped in a no-man's-land, wasting away, lashing out against shadows. *We have to get out of here*, she'd told him, exhausted, tired of Miguel being constantly glued to his phone, leaving pitiful messages on Natalia's voicemail. She was tired of following him every day as he absurdly stalked his daughter's office and apartment. *She doesn't want to see you, Miguel. You have to accept it. We do things, and those things have consequences that we can't escape.* Miguel thought now that maybe he should never have left the old people's home, should have stayed there hopelessly, like an encapsulated insect. Pretending to be blind and deaf and mute. Maybe he should just forget, try to find some consolation in the act of forgetting. But instead, when Helena packed her bags and told him she needed to carry on with her journey (*Are you coming or not?*), he grabbed the newspaper clippings his mother had saved in an old shoebox and saw the letter he'd read all those years ago in along with them. He read it again, and suddenly it all made sense: he'd created a necessary order to keep from losing his mind, a mission borne of the need to keep going and not sit still. That was what mattered. He put his mother's ashes in the suitcase, along with the shoebox and the letter, went to his friend and said: *Let's go to Madrid.*

Helena nodded with a cynical smile. "My trip is turning into your trip. I don't know if you're coming with me or I'm the one who's going with you."

The lights in the bus went on, and the driver pulled off into a dirt parking lot, announcing a thirty-minute rest stop. Sleepy passengers stretched and yawned, and Helena opened her bloodshot eyes. She started on seeing that she'd been asleep on Miguel's shoulder.

"You need to eat more; you make a hard, uncomfortable pillow."

Miguel smiled. He was starting to get used to his friend's quips. The cafeteria turned out to be one of those places where hunters gathered in their khaki shirts, camouflage trousers, and many-pocketed vests to drink coffee spiked with brandy, eat olives, and spit out the pits while their dogs barked from cages in the trailers outside. It was soulless and filthy, and years' worth of dust had collected on the desiccated animal heads hanging on the walls: a bull with dark glass eyes, a deer with antlers like a rickety tree, and a boar whose tongue stuck out as though he'd been teasing his executioners. A few lone truck drivers in faded jeans and wrinkled shirts stood, leaning their elbows on the bar and one foot on the wooden footrest; other people read out-of-date papers in an attempt to avoid conversation, or watched the muted TV tuned to the 24-hour news station, pretending they could read the newscaster's lips.

The passengers' arrival changed the atmosphere of the place. Some swarmed the bar, others sat at tables, and a few stood in line for the bathroom, each making their own kind of noise. Helena ordered a double espresso, poured part of a sugar packet into it and slowly stirred. From a distance, anyone would wonder what she was doing there. Sometimes, people don't fit in with their environment, seem out of place even in their place, as though life had played a trick. With no makeup, her clothes all wrinkled, and her hair a mess, she still emanated a light that made her shine and distanced her from her surroundings and the people near her. She was a presence, nothing superfluous.

"Do you mind telling me why you're staring at me like that?" she asked, noting Miguel's speculative look. He didn't turn away. On the contrary, he continued to gaze intently for a moment, as though testing what could be said with the eyes, detaching meaning from words.

"Sometimes the heart can see what the eyes don't."

"What's that supposed to mean?"

"Just something I read once. Someone wrote that about my father."

Helena nodded. To Miguel's surprise, she simply took his right hand, turned it palm up, and looked at the lines there.

"There are two kinds of people in this world: those who rise up and those who bend over. That's what Ivan told me."

"Only two? Why not three, or five, or a hundred?" Miguel asked, visibly upset at thinking of what they'd left behind. Helena traced his life line with her finger.

"Your hand tells me you're the kind who rises up."

Miguel didn't believe in that sort of nonsense. All he saw in his hand were memories of a man who'd had and lost many things. A cracked vessel, which he closed into a fist as Helena slowly wriggled her finger out.

"What does that mean, to rise up or bend over?"

"I'm not in the mood for one of our arguments. First, I have to go to the bathroom. I'm not turning up in Madrid looking like the walking dead," she said, taking out a purse where she kept a small makeup kit. She walked off like a painting with no frame, rebelling against the filthy backdrop that the café imposed on her. *I'm not of this world*, the swish of her hips seemed to imply.

"Strange woman," someone said with the kind of scorn Miguel found pitiful.

"Why strange and not extraordinary?" he murmured.

By the time Helena emerged from the bathroom, the passengers were heading back to the bus. But not Miguel. He was staring in horror at the TV news.

"What's going on?"

Miguel pointed to the television. There had been a terrible accident on the outskirts of Sevilla. Three young men had driven the wrong way on the freeway in what seemed to be not an intentional act but a drug-and-alcohol-induced tragedy. Their pictures were on screen: known delinquents. The vehicle, a 1970 Datsun convertible, had been driving at high speed for over two kilometers before crashing head-on into an eighteen-wheeler with Belgian plates. All three occupants of the Datsun had died instantly. The truck driver was in serious condition. The television showed images of the Datsun crushed beneath the wheels of the truck, surrounded by firemen, police, and paramedics. The camera zoomed in on a hand sticking out of the mangled metal. It had a tattoo on its wrist and clutched a broken necklace in its fingers. The impact had scattered pearls throughout the car.

18

Malmö

The bars and restaurants in Lilla Torg had their lights on already, the atmosphere lively at 6:30 p.m. Yasmina found it strange that Gövan had asked to meet her someplace so central. Normally they went to discreet places on the outskirts of town. Meeting on a Saturday was unusual too, but the deputy chief had been adamant.

They'd arranged to meet at Harry's Pub in the little plaza at 4:30 p.m. Yasmina checked the clock on the wall and took stock of how many beers she'd had. Maybe Gövan's euphoria had dissolved, just as her girlish excitement was now fading, giving way to sadness and disappointment that increased with each passing minute. She was tired of glancing at her phone and guessing what kind of excuse he'd offer for being late when he finally arrived—if he even showed up. Furious with herself, she downed the last of her beer and prepared to go. She was paying her tab when a hand touched her shoulder and his voice whispered in her ear.

"Were you going to stand me up?"

Yasmina's anger vanished with astonishing ease.

"Apparently our watches aren't synchronized," she replied.

He forced her to turn and look at him. The deputy chief looked younger and leaner in his jean jacket. Gövan's red hair was messy and his cheeks sagged; he had tired-looking blue eyes and razor stubble on his neck. The dusky light coming in through the pub's door silhouetted him, giving him a different air, less real but more intimate than the image he normally projected in his senior officer suits and ties.

"I'm sorry. I had work."

"I'm not your plaything," Yasmina said, attempting to defend herself. On the one hand she was disgusted at how the mere presence of Gövan dissolved her rage, on the other it showed her how viscerally she needed him. "The decapitated guy? I saw it on the news."

Gövan nodded.

"Come on, let's get out of here," he said, taking her hand.

Yasmina allowed herself to be led to the parking lot. In a darkened doorway, Gövan stopped and kissed her, briefly but passionately, erasing any remaining resistance Yasmina might have felt.

"What on earth?" she asked once she'd recovered, her cheeks flushed.

"My wife and kids have gone to Gothenburg, to my in-laws'. They won't be back till tomorrow night. I have a little house on Lake Vättern. We could go . . . right now."

Yasmina wrenched free of his hands.

"Are you crazy? I can't go away for a weekend just like that. I have to take care of my grandfather."

"You can call the neighbor, ask her to take care of him; she's done it before. You're the one who complains he doesn't even notice you, that you're invisible to him."

"What about your job? Aren't you supposed to be catching a murderer?"

Gövan gazed at her more intensely than usual, with a new kind of glimmer in his eyes. It was as though he had a secret, something that no one else knew, and it had transformed him.

"I want to get out of Malmö," he begged, as if what he really wanted was the chance to escape from himself. Yasmina's eyes slowly scanned Gövan's remorseful face as he struggled to remain composed. She said yes and felt a surge of joy mixed with tenderness in spite of herself.

They took the road to Jököping, heading for the southern shore of the enormous Lake Vättern. Night fell faster than they could drive, darkness spreading from the northeast. The old Škoda's engine clanked relentlessly, sounding louder in the silence that had fallen once they left Malmö. It was an uncomfortable old car, but Gövan refused to get rid of it and buy a new one.

"It reminds me where I came from, so I don't forget who I am," he said as they drove up a steep slope, the engine sounding like it was on its last legs.

Yasmina examined the deputy chief's profile. His boxer's nose gave him the irascible look of a big angry bear. The dashboard lights played shadows across his face.

"Who are you really, Deputy Chief Sjögren?"

Gövan buttoned the top button on his jacket. It was really starting to get cold; once they turned inland from the coast, the barren landscape was dotted with increasingly dense forests.

"Right now, I'm someone who'd rather be something else."

Yasmina realized she knew almost nothing about Gövan's life. Suddenly he was no longer the man married to a wealthy heiress, the father of two children, the cowardly adulterer, the ambitious cop determined to reach the highest echelons of power. Sture's enemy. It wasn't hard to see the boy he'd once been, and that made it easier to understand his lack of sophistication, the way he struggled to hold subtle conversations or lower his voice. It was easier to love him. She put a hand on his thigh and left it there.

The landscape on both sides of the road was almost completely dark. All they could see was the road ahead, illuminated by the car's headlights. The outlines of huge trees flew past. They'd come to a lookout point at a curve in the road, and from there you could just barely make out the valley below and, off in the distance, Lake Vättern. The metallic gray of the moonlit lake was like one enormous shadow that overshadowed all others. Thousands of stars dotted the sky. Yasmina had never seen a sky like that.

"It's so beautiful," she murmured, rapt. She had the urge to cry but held it in. She wouldn't have known how to explain that joy is sometimes so like sadness. Like when you find something, only to learn you're about to lose it. Everything around her was so lovely, so perfect, that it made her feel utterly alone.

"What's the matter? You seem sad all of the sudden."

She shook her head silently.

"I was just thinking that everything disappears when you stop looking at it."

He stroked her head, his tenderness more paternal than carnal.

"What makes you say that?"

Yasmina shivered. Somewhere inside herself she felt disgust at the role she was playing.

"What are we, Gövan? An immigrant from Rosengård and an unfaithful deputy chief pretending to live out some romantic fantasy."

He gazed at her intently. Her eyes were strangely glassy and fragile, her expression about to crumble.

"I'm not pretending anything, Yasmina."

She held his gaze. *Of course you are*, she thought: *you're pretending not to know what you know, you're pretending you're strong enough to take me out of my world and bring me to this other one, and I'm pretending that it exists. And we both accept the lie because it hurts less than the truth.*

"Are you pretending with me?" he asked.

Yasmina didn't respond. Instead she hugged herself, leaned the seat back and closed her eyes.

They drove down to the southern shore of Lake Vättern. A gentle breeze blew, rippling the lake's surface. All you could hear was the water lapping gently at the shore and the wind in the trees. Speaking, or anything else that might break that calm, would have been a crime.

Gövan's cabin was actually a small stone-roofed bungalow. Yasmina got out of the car and followed him down a gravel path. They stopped at a porch with two wicker chairs and a wooden table. Seasonal flowers that Yasmina couldn't identify in the dark gave off a lovely, fresh scent. Gövan retrieved a key from the mailbox and opened the door. The place looked small but comfortable. It had pine walls, and the floor was covered in plush rugs. In the center of the room was a large oak table and chairs with colorful cushions. Records and a few books lined a shelf over the fireplace.

"Well, what do you think? Was it worth the drive?" he asked, dropping his overnight bag onto the carpeted floor and turning to her. The country boy could be simple and sophisticated at the same time. All he wanted was for her to appreciate it.

The question was, could Yasmina stop being—at least for a few hours—Sture's whore; could she accept the ambience created just for her without questioning things, forget that she was just a visitor to Gövan's world, that she shouldn't get used to things she'd never have. She wondered how many times Gövan had arranged a night like this for his wife, or other women, but managed to squash that lucid insight. She was there, now, with him. She went and kissed him on the mouth.

I'm going to leave you, she said to herself as she felt his lips and breath on her skin, making the hair on her neck stand on end.

I am, she repeated to herself as he opened her blouse and covered her breasts with his hands.

You mean nothing to me, she insisted silently as she moaned on feeling his penis draw circles between her legs.

But Yasmina stopped thinking anything when, wrapping her legs around his waist, she let him pick her up and carry her gently to the rug.

They entered into a sort of dance, a fight that she lost in order to win. Gövan, like a totally different person from the one she knew, made no attempt to prove his dexterity or engage in wild acrobatics, nor did she resort to the pornographic routines that normally got him off. There was no dirty talk, no chest or bicep flexing, no mental count of how many times he thrusted before changing position. He didn't want to be macho; he just wanted to be her lover. The tender way he kissed her, stroked her vagina, licked between her legs, was all poison to Yasmina. She didn't want to see his sweet face or let herself give in to the sharp urge to cry and laugh. She didn't want the words rising in her throat to come out of her mouth: *I love you, I need you to hold me, I want to you tell me that you need me too*. The only way to combat it was to whisper dirty things into his ear, straddle him and clench him tightly inside her, offer him her ass and beg in a fake voice for him to take her from behind. But Gövan wasn't taking the bait: he refused to react to her expressions and gestures. It was as if he was trying to calm her and offer her something sincere, something true. Love. *Fuck*, thought Yasmina. *Love!*

Their dance had taken them from the floor to the sofa, the sofa to the table—who cared about dinner?—and the table to the bed. A trail of clothes lay in their wake.

Gövan was asleep, naked, faceup. Yasmina lay on her side, watching him. She put one hand under his nose to feel the kiss of his even breath, and with the other stroked his flaccid testicles. She whispered to him in Arabic, telling him she was in love with him, that this had nothing to do with her debt to Sture. That this was insane, suicidal. But she couldn't help it. She knew he couldn't hear her, or that if he heard, he couldn't understand what she was saying.

She closed her eyes and tried to sleep, but half an hour later Yasmina was still awake. She felt thirsty and wanted a smoke. She also wanted to get Gövan excited again, to make love to him—this time she wouldn't play games—until dawn. She opted for the first of her desires, put on her panties and Gövan's jean jacket, grabbed the bottle of Spanish wine they hadn't touched, and went out to the porch.

Dawn lorded over the lake with a silence more absolute than the one a few hours earlier. The moon had moved east, and the sky looked more intense, more alive. Yasmina sat in the armchair. She hadn't showered and could smell dried semen mixed with the scent of cologne on Gövan's jacket. She poured herself a glass of wine and lit a cigarette. Sometimes, she thought, happiness was absolute; you didn't have to think about it.

Yasmina thought about walking down to the shore and diving into the lake. She'd never gone skinny-dipping before. But she discarded the idea, blushing absurdly. Besides, it was too cold.

She thought of her mother. Fatima would be asleep right now, in a tiny servant's room at the rich family's house she worked at in the Malmö suburbs. No doubt her knees and elbows hurt, her joints ached, and she fell asleep in a sad little single bed after counting and recounting the wages she kept hidden in her clothes in the armoire. It made Yasmina sad, to think of her mother's fate. Her mother, who would never visit a place like this or know the pleasure of making love to a tender man, or even wonder if she'd ever been in love. Her life was glued to the floor, literally. She was condemned to a life of cleaning floors on her hands and knees and taking care of her father as she'd once taken care of a husband, a man too cowardly to be a *real* man. Yasmina wished she could tell her mother what she felt at that moment, share it with her, wished she could hear words of love and encouragement come from her mouth. But that would never happen. Ever. To her mother she was nothing but a whore, a permanent reminder of public shame.

Yasmina raised her glass in a toast.

"To you, Mother."

After a while she got cold and decided to go back to bed.

Coming back inside, she saw Gövan's bag in the living room, open, his laptop inside it. Easy. Within reach. She hesitated a moment, shook her head, took two steps but then stopped.

Dreams were all well and good, but she had to live in the real world. There was a debt to pay, the promise of a life far from Rosengård. She had to do it. She took a few steps back and looked into the bedroom where Gövan was sleeping— and then grabbed the laptop and sat down at the table.

Yasmina was nervous, frightened. But also determined. Better to get it over with as soon as possible. The screen lit up, a Christmas photo on the desktop: a full-length shot of Gövan and his family standing at a tree decorated with lights and garlands and colored bells and cherubs. Gövan and his beautiful wife were dressed for an elegant dinner. It stung, to see the kind of bliss that looked so fake on him. There were several icons, folders, on the right of the screen. One was called "Background-Sture."

Law enforcement wasn't very original when it came to naming cases. Yasmina tried to open it, but the file was password protected. She thought for a few seconds and had an absurd idea. She typed in her own name: *Yasmina*. The folder opened. A wave of guilt filled her throat like a lump of sorrow.

There were photos of Sture and his associates, phone numbers, addresses, jobs. They knew everything: his relationship to the container at the port, the dead guy who'd been found floating in the water, the decapitated man in the park. They were going to nail him this time. Yasmina's eyes darted back and forth, searching for anything that might implicate her, searching for her own name on a line, in a paragraph. She didn't see anything, and though that should have calmed her, she actually felt more nervous. The whole thing was about to blow up.

Every few seconds she turned to the half-open bedroom door to check on Gövan. He was still sleeping the sleep of the righteous. Yasmina was sweating. She closed the computer and slipped it back into his bag.

Yasmina awoke to the sound of an outboard motor. Light was streaming through the window. She was alone in bed. Gövan's side was cold. Checking the time, she saw it was nearly eleven. She could hear his voice coming from the porch. Gövan was on the phone, sounding serious. Yasmina heard him raise his voice, argue, then make a couple of quick, blunt remarks. She got out of bed to shower.

On her way past the living room, Yasmina froze. Gövan's laptop was on the table, open. *Take it easy. That doesn't mean anything*, she said to herself. He'd probably gotten up early and been working for a little while. She tried to convince herself of this as she showered.

When Yasmina emerged from the bathroom, he was sitting at the table. He'd disassembled his service pistol and was using a set of rags and ramrods, oiling the parts with loving care.

"Do you have to do that here?"

Gövan's eyes barely flitted up to acknowledge her. Gone was the previous night's tenderness.

"It's a habit. I'm sorry if it makes you uncomfortable. Besides, a weapon is harmless; it's the will of whoever's holding it that matters. A weapon has no mind, it simply obeys. It doesn't question whether its action is right or wrong, doesn't have morals or scruples. It abides by its owner's wishes." With precise gestures, he inserted the barrel into the slide and pulled back the hammer. It made a sharp crack.

The sound made Yasmina flinch.

"Do you mind telling me what's the matter?"

Gövan slid the gun into his holster, leaned back in his chair and looked out the open door. Part of the lake, the trees lining the rocky shore, was visible. Day had dawned hazily.

"My father used to bring me out here to go fishing, and now sometimes I bring my own kids. Maybe one day they'll bring theirs, if there's anything left to fish. In my day, we fished for pike. I wasn't very good. I'd watch my father select his bait and lures and imitate him, but he always caught huge fish and I never caught anything. Until he told me that each pike is different, they each respond to different lures. To catch them, you have to choose the time and place carefully, and it's not always the same time or place. Even more important than that, you have to be patient. If you're impatient, your hand trembles, the quivering travels through the rod, and it creates vibrations in the water that scare off the fish. I didn't learn to fish until I learned to be patient. I discovered which bait worked best, how deep to look, and I learned to pay attention to changes in the light shadows that might mean a tree trunk on the bottom. And now I know when it's pointless to try to catch a big one, when I have to let it go because it's simply too clever or too wily for me, or I picked the wrong target. I'm pretty good now. I never go home empty-handed, always catch something."

Gövan was no longer being evasive but staring at Yasmina ominously, his eyes boring into her, his gaze joyless and solemn. He went to his laptop and turned the screen to her. Sture's file was open, dozens of photos on-screen. Photos of the bodies from the port and the park, and others Yasmina knew nothing about. Their faces were waxy or green; they had algae in their mouths, eyes rolled back or empty sockets; wire marks on their wrists, their ankles, their necks. There were broken bones, dismembered bodies half-eaten by rats or forest creatures, shots to the head.

"Is this what you were looking for last night? What did it feel like, Yasmina? Or was relief the only thing you felt, thinking you were safe when you didn't see your name in the reports? Sture's number one whore. Don't you dare look away! I want you to know who you work for. Not that you don't already know, of course you do. You're not blind, not dumb. But seeing it up close, having the evidence right in front of you, doesn't let you bury your head in the sand, does it? Tell me how you feel, go on. I'm curious."

It hurt. Seeing Yasmina's terrified face, seeing her breathtaking beauty come crashing down, disappear, her eyes darting in search of escape and finding none. It hurt. And his own naivete hurt too, the realization that he'd fallen for the oldest trick in the book, the honeypot, intoxicated by a siren who promised to take him away only to sink him to the bottom of the sea and drown him. To be so stupid, so drunk on his own ego, on himself. Good for Sture, the old bastard; he'd trapped him in his own vanity. How could Gövan resist the fierce carefree beauty of a girl twenty years younger and with a throbbing pussy, her desire wide open to him?

She was silent now, staring intently at her hands spread on the table as though expecting some light punishment, a ruler rapped on the very hands that had held his dick, his balls, his heart, his soul—and devoured them all. Gövan almost preferred it this way—her silent, not saying a word, not trying to deny it. And to think he'd almost believed her, even the night before, when he set the bait, left it within reach. *If she doesn't do it, if she doesn't try, I'll believe her*, he'd thought. I'll believe anything she tells me. Because for those few hours he'd felt that some part of it was true, that it wasn't just a job or pretending. He still couldn't accept that her shuddering as he embraced her was just an act, no one was that good, not even her. If only she'd told him, if Yasmina had asked for help, he would have believed her, would have been willing to leave it all behind, his career, his family. All he needed was a sign. And now he had it, though it wasn't the one he'd been hoping for.

"The decapitated guy in the park was a heroin trafficker. His name was Omar Trezk . . . Ring a bell?"

"Why would it?"

Gövan slowly turned to her, his eyes a mix of rage, accusation, and sadness. He took a folded-up slip of paper from his pocket and threw it onto the table.

"Because he had your phone number in his pocket. The guys who killed him were thorough—took his wallet, rings, chains, phone. But they left this slip of paper. Or maybe they planted it there. Can you think why? Come on, Yasmina, you're a sly fox, a woman of the world. I'm sure you can come up with a reason. Your friend, your boss, your pimp, Sture . . . He wanted to incriminate you."

Yasmina bolted up in her chair. She felt an army of spiders crawling up her legs, encircling her, trapping her, pumping all the blood in her body to her heart and making it pound.

"Are you going to arrest me?"

Gövan clucked his tongue and looked around as though searching for a place to spit out something distasteful.

"You'd better get dressed. This place is drafty."

Yasmina took a cigarette from the pack on the table. She didn't usually smoke this early, but what did it matter. She was overcome by the unreal feeling she sometimes got, a state between wakefulness and dreaming. Maybe if she just opened her eyes wide, she'd see that this was all her imagination. Nothing had changed, nothing was going to change. She could believe that Gövan had made bacon and eggs and good coffee, and that after breakfast they'd go for a walk on the lakeshore, sit under a tree, and gaze out in silence at the water's glassy surface. She'd curl up in his lap and he'd stroke her hair, trying to be gentle and keep the trembling from his fingers. At some point, they'd both say *I love you* to each other. And it would be true.

She thought of the first time she saw him. Sture had pointed him out from afar. She thought he was handsome, maybe a bit ungainly, as is often the case with big men, but handsome in his dark overcoat and wet hair, lighting a cigarette on the police station steps. Sture knew everything about him, knew the bar by the port he went to when he got off work on Thursday nights to play piano over a pint of beer. He played piano—not very well, true. But those clumsy fingers of his could dance across the keys and play simple arrangements, nice improvisations. Sture also knew that he was married, that he had kids and a future that was tied to his father-in-law and that, secretly, he smoked marijuana and occasionally went home with girls from the bar. Not hookers, just strangers who helped him to forget. They were all the same type: dark, young, with a sad air about them. It had been easy to walk over to him, sit beside him on the piano bench and take a sip of his beer without asking. She'd stared at him with her different-colored eyes, told him that it was a genetic mutation, something that had made her feel weird as a girl but that men liked now. She also told him she wanted to be a singer and move to Paris, or London, or New York. And she wasn't lying, four beers later, when she told him that she'd like to fuck him.

"It's not that easy, Gövan. You can't free yourself from Sture just by putting me in handcuffs."

He wasn't planning to. He wasn't that stupid.

"Arrest you? Why would I ruin my career and my life? I know how Sture thinks. We've been chasing each other for years in this game of cat and mouse. He sent you to grab me by the balls; that's his style. He does it with other people, police, judges, politicians, lawyers. Like a good communist: "From each according to his ability, to each according to his needs." He knows what men need—drugs, money, sex, power, influence. And he offers it in exchange for permits, information, looking the other way. If I arrest you and you're connected to him, things will surface: home videos, photos, conversations. Am I right? This is the moment, the bastard will think. Now that I'm in the spotlight, close to having that pig's head. That's when he plays you as the ace up his sleeve to get his way. I've thought about it, Yasmina. I've been thinking about it all morning. Throw away all the years I've spent, lose custody of my kids? Get kicked off the force or put in jail, be subjected to everyone's ridicule? Or worse, spend the rest of my life watching my back, waiting for Sture to send a thug to bump me off in some alley? I know what you want, I know what he told you to say, to do. Bribe me, threaten me. Turn me into one of his whores, like you. Save it, Yasmina. Come on, get dressed. We have to get back."

There was a place near the lake that Gövan and his sister used to go. To get there you took a partially concealed dirt road through the underbrush. It led to an abandoned fishing cabin. The only people who ever went were random hikers who'd gotten lost and stumbled across the path and the crumbling cabin by chance. He and his sister never did anything bad there, just kid stuff: smoke cigarettes, light bonfires and roast potatoes over the flames, drink warm beer and talk. They always had things to talk about, stories to tell, secrets, dreams. Normally, what they dreamed of was growing up, and growing up meant very different things to each them. To his sister, it meant developing breasts. She'd show him her boobs, make him touch them—two little bumps that transmitted no warmth. Sometimes she'd bring a bra that she'd stolen from their mother and try it on for him, cat-walking up and down through the rubble like a high-fashion model. She'd lift her skirt and show him her panties. He'd laugh when she said she knew how to tongue kiss, that she'd seen their parents and aunts and uncles do it. And to prove it, she stuck her tongue in his mouth and he pulled away, wiping his lips on the back of his hand. His sister's saliva was thick and tasted of beets. To him, growing up meant being able to drive their father's Škoda, going to the city to buy whatever they needed, strolling around with a girl on his arm, and teaching her to smoke. And being together, all of them in the same house: siblings, grandkids, parents, and grandparents. Lighting a fire, sitting around a table drinking blackberry liqueur, carving meat. Watching winter pass.

"Why did you turn off?"

He never wanted his sister to die, but she did. Her appendix ruptured, and they never went back to the cabin. He never wanted to be a cop either, or a politician, or to marry a rich woman. He never wanted any of it, but this was what he had. This was all he had.

They were almost there. It hadn't changed much over the years, if anything the underbrush was even more overgrown and the path more concealed. The Škoda advanced slowly, bumping along through the ruts, branches dragging across the windshield and scratching the car. It had rained a few days ago, so the car would leave tire tracks. He'd have to keep that in mind. And remember to empty the ashtray of Yasmina's cigarette butts.

Once, he saw a deer emerge from the thicket. His sister was ahead of him and hadn't seen it cross the path. She didn't believe him when he described it to her. A huge gray deer with enormous antlers: a dominant male with glassy eyes. He wondered how long a deer lived and if it was possible he'd see it again now, walking in front of the car. Maybe it would be a sign, a signal that he should turn back, change destiny. Escape the inevitable.

He considered telling Yasmina about the deer. But he didn't. No one even believed there were any deer left in these woods anymore.

He was glad to see that the cabin was still there, though very little of it was still standing—all that was left were crumbling walls and part of an A-frame roof that miraculously hadn't lost the few tiles it once had. The weeds had grown waist-high, and a tree he remembered being a sapling was now large, full grown, casting the shadow of a branch that dangled perilously over the cabin. Birds were singing. Behind the cabin, the woodshed lay in ruins. That was where he and his sister used to hide their treasures: clothes she stole from their mother, matches they used to light their cigarettes, a supply of potatoes, and a few canned goods. He liked to take off his shirt and chop wood to prove that he was strong, that she could feel safe. He used an old ax with a rusty blade and broken handle that they'd found by chance, which made it much harder, tore up his hands, and made him sweat. Soon he'd switch to smaller branches, but his sister still smiled and clapped just the same.

He parked close to the shed.

"Get out, I want to show you something."

Yasmina followed a few feet behind. He didn't worry about her running away. Why should he? Some animals have a mortal fear that prevents them from fleeing, drives them inexorably to their end. They sense it, as she did, cock their heads nervously, smell the inevitable, stop, and take a step back. But once given an order, or a simple glance, once it's all been decided, they obey and come meekly forward.

"Wait here." He went into the shed. It was dark and damp. The old smells were gone. No sign of the past—except the ax. It was still there, more unserviceable than ever, broken and rusty. When he emerged, his hair and beard were covered in cobwebs. On his neck was a six-legged insect that crawled onto his shoulder and then fell.

Yasmina did react, after all. Gövan was happy for her. He didn't want to think of her as a deer in the headlights or a lamb led to the slaughter without batting an eye. Yasmina saw the ax in Gövan's hand, turned, and began to walk off. She didn't run, knowing she wouldn't make it, but wasn't about to stand there and wait for him.

Gövan followed, observing her silhouette, which kept disappearing in the high weeds and then emerging again a few steps farther on.

And then finally, in full understanding, Yasmina stopped.

"Sture will kill my whole family," she said without turning.

Gövan inched forward until his fingers brushed her black hair. He was glad not to see her different-colored eyes, not to see the genetic mutation that made her strange and extraordinary. Gövan gripped the back of the ax blade, raised it above his shoulders and brought it crashing down onto Yasmina's head. He was forced to repeat the operation several times, dislodging the ax from her skull, raising it back up and plunging it down again, until he heard it fracture and felt the blade sink into gelatinous brain matter.

When he'd finished burying her, he dried his sweat on his jacket, now stained with blood and bone shards. Gövan was panting, struggling to breathe, like when he used to chop wood. He turned to the cabin and thought he saw his sister there, gazing at him in sadness.

19

Madrid

The address took Miguel to an old four-story building surrounded by a yard with tall chestnut trees, their crowns as high as the tallest balconies. The building stood at the end of a steep, one-way street where the sounds of the city could be heard in the distance, blending with those of children playing on the playground at the German school across the street. The trees cast shadows over the sickly reddish vines and dusty creepers covering the building's dark stone facade like veins, which gave the place a somber appearance. Miguel walked through the tall gate with spearhead rails, climbed a crumbling set of marble stairs carpeted in dead leaves, and approached the iron door. The intercom, a modern touch, seemed to take from the overall majesty of the place.

He pressed the buzzer for apartment 3 without much hope. Simón Andújar was probably dead. And Miguel would have almost preferred it that way, so he could leave with the sense that he'd done everything in his power to find the man who knew his father, without having to confront questions he wasn't sure he wanted the answers to.

Against all odds, a woman's voice answered the intercom. She not only confirmed that, indeed, Simón did live there but even invited him to come up.

Simón shifted uncomfortably in his wheelchair, despite the cushioned seat. Sometimes his buttocks got sores and he was forced to accept his eldest daughter's help, looking the other way as she applied antiseptic cream.

He was supposed to try to get up—the doctors had said he could do it with the help of his walker—take a few steps back and forth, go look out the window where he could see the children at the German school playing whatever children played when they knew they were being supervised. But that morning he didn't feel up to it, and didn't feel like reading or writing either.

All he wanted to do was sit there staring at the calendar on the wall and thinking that the world was still stunningly empty, that it never changed. The same mornings, same sounds, same smells, same aches and pains, and the same voices on the other side of the door. The years on the calendar kept changing, but the days were all the same.

He heard his eldest daughter's grandchildren's footsteps. They used to come in and say hello when she forced them to; they were good kids and pretended to love him, to listen to and learn from him—though the little girl had a hard time hiding her urge to go play on the game console. She wasn't from the world of oral traditions, the way Simón was. Reality, at this point in her life, was of little interest. The younger one, Mario, was different. Simón managed to hold his interest for longer, draw his attention by dangling a carrot: the uniform from his days as a soldier, which he kept in protective plastic in the wardrobe. *When I die, you can sell it wherever people sell stuff that's just taking up space.* The boy liked the leather straps, the cartridge belt with clip holders, the boots and gaiters. It was like the video games where he got to murder people in cold blood. They looked like people, but they weren't, just as the explosions, the shouting, and the bloodstains too, were fake.

Maybe that was why it had occurred to him to show his grandson his best-kept secret: the pistol he kept hidden, wrapped in a cloth with its ramrods, under a stack of newspapers and magazines in the back of a drawer. He'd even let the boy hold it once he unloaded it. His daughter would have thrown a fit if she'd seen: *Are you crazy? That's insane, showing that to a boy!* But as far as Simón was concerned, what was insane was making an eleven-year-old boy believe he could massacre an innocent village, throw grenades, and laugh every time someone got disemboweled just because he was doing it from a sofa. Simón found that sort of virtual pornography sickening. Holding a real gun, feeling its heft, hearing its mechanisms—the firing pin, the hammer, the trigger, the slide—that was real. Evil, but real.

At any rate, he and his grandson had a gentleman's agreement, a pact of silence to keep it between the two of them. At least from now on, the boy would no longer be afraid of him or get disgusted when he kissed Simón's bony cheeks, or wipe the saliva from his face when he thought no one was looking.

"Are you awake?"

Of course he was awake, and had been forever and a day. Sleep was a luxury he could no longer afford.

"There's someone here to see you."

The door opened and Simón saw a stranger's face, concealed behind glasses and a mustache.

"Who are you?"

"My name is Miguel Gandía. I'm Amador Gandía's son."

Simón knit his bushy white brows so tightly they met in the middle.

Miguel assumed that his father's name didn't mean anything to the brusque, shriveled-up old man whose skin resembled jerky. He looked desiccated from the inside out. It had been so long, and there was no reason for him to remember the letter he'd written; perhaps it was one of many he wrote at the time, notifying the next of kin of a prisoner's demise.

But Simón tilted his head, observed him pointedly, turned to the table piled with his manuscript and a type-writer, and sighed in relief.

"What took you so long? I'd almost run out of energy waiting."

"You were waiting for me?"

Simón spun his wheelchair, turning his back to Miguel.

"Come, have a seat in that armchair. We have a lot to talk about."

Simón's daughter was still there, attentive, as though hoping she'd be asked to take part in something she sensed was going to be revelatory, but Simón sent her off with a friendly yet unwavering smile.

"Don't forget to bring the kids back next week. They keep me company." His daughter, visibly disappointed, gave him a quick kiss goodbye, shot a fleeting glance at Miguel, and closed the door.

Simón and Miguel gazed at one another for a full minute, long enough to accept the other's existence, something they'd imagined so often it had turned into mere speculation.

"I came because of this letter. If I'm not mistaken, you wrote it," Miguel said finally, holding out the envelope.

Simón barely even glanced at it.

"I was almost illiterate back then—even more than now, I mean. I had a friend on the Aragon front who tried to teach me to read and write, but he gave up on me. I would have liked to study, make the effort, but in war the only thing there's time to learn about is death. Life is a deadly distraction. Later, I read and wrote plenty, but I don't feel much wiser than I was then. Writing those few words took heaven and earth for me."

"It seems you knew my father. I'd like to ask what made you write to my mother by hand, in such a personal tone. Normally, a death notice like this would be typewritten, a brief official document in impersonal language."

Simón looked up at the ceiling. Someday soon, the house would come crashing down, taking everything inside with it. He lowered his eyes slowly, finally depositing his gaze on Miguel.

"I remember you, a scared, malnourished little boy. I never imagined what kind of man you'd turn out to be. And now here you are almost as old as I am."

"You remember me?"

"Of course I do. Little slip of a thing, scrawny, all eyes and mouth, almost mute, hiding in your mother's skirts. What I'd like to know is whether it's the boy or the old man who's come here now."

"Does it really matter?"

"It certainly does. Because each has different motives. The old man is in search of peace; the young man is looking for vengeance or justification; but the little boy just wants to understand."

Miguel remembered those trips to Madrid, the cold windows of the train, the smell of its wooden carriages, and the passengers going out into the hall to smoke. Sometimes the landscape outside flew by and other times seemed not to move. Like his mother's expression, glued to the small woven bag that held a little food—homemade sausage and candies for her husband. Fear rose to her face every time a police officer asked for her documentation. She would count the money they had left, pitifully anxious. Sometimes they'd end up spending days and days in Madrid, scraping by in some pension his mother paid for by exchanging favors in an alley while he waited on the corner. And if permission was granted to visit Amador, she'd spend hours fixing herself up at the bathroom mirror, buy some decent clothes, a little makeup, and arm herself with her best smile. He remembered the excavating too, the material extracted from the mountain where he'd wait for hours in the rain or the beating sun with his mother, not knowing if they'd actually be allowed to see his father or not. Remembered the terror he felt at the dynamite explosions echoing throughout the valley, at the guards' uniforms and the dusty air. The families of prisoners sentenced to forced labor for things that were only crimes because they were on the losing side. Miguel used to secretly hope that permission would be denied, that they wouldn't be allowed to visit; he preferred spending his time wandering among the pines, oaks, and elms in the mountains, eating the food his mother had brought for his father himself. Surrounded by the smells of wild thyme and rockrose, hungry and selfish, all he could think of were the meatballs that he wanted to devour.

"I suppose the boy and the old man decided to sign a sort of armistice in search of the truth."

Simón pushed his wheelchair over to the wardrobe where he kept his uniform, opened the door and showed it to Miguel.

"If it's truth you're looking for, this isn't the way to find it. I was just a guard, a soldier like so many others. That's the whole point of uniforms, they make the faces disappear so all that's left is a threatening presence. Someone with no thoughts of his own."

"But you wrote to my mother, you sent her money."

"I remember you and your mother behind the wire fence at the camp's entrance, hoping the gate would open and your father's name would be on the list of visits that day, hoping that the Archangel, standing there with his hands on his hips and his legs spread like a toy general, would be in a good mood and let you through. I used to get embarrassed when I heard him say all of you were lucky, having your families serve out their sentence at Cuelgamuros. We didn't see it that way, and the prisoners—your father among them—certainly didn't either. He told me that when Franco signed the decree to have the Valley built, he was counting the days to his firing squad execution. And then news spread and lots of men like him requested a pardon to work there. At that point he couldn't have cared less about ideals and convictions. All he wanted was to survive, no matter the cost, no matter what it took. Your father told me that in order to get sent to the Valley he had to humiliate himself, write a pathetic letter where he repented of his 'crimes.' But even if he beat his chest and cried mea culpa till he was blue in the face, it wouldn't have been enough without your mother's help. He told me that too."

Miguel knew what Simón was talking about. His mother didn't hesitate to sleep with any man who wanted her—and there were many—if it could possibly open a door for her husband. She didn't hesitate for a second, went to bed with them all, humiliated herself, gave everything she had, got down on her knees and begged, endured whatever she had to. She was a fierce young woman whom everyone wanted, but she never belonged to anyone but Amador. Rosa, who wouldn't beg even a crust of bread for her son, never broke down during the civil guard's harshest interrogations while Amador was off playing at being a guerrilla in the hills, thinking he could change fate. She achieved her goal but never recovered from it, was never the same in the eyes of those who knew her, who pointed and laughed, or spit. Nor was she the same in the eyes of her son. And she lost her mind.

"Your father knew what your mother had to do to save him from execution, and he never forgave himself for that."

Miguel hadn't forgiven him, either. His mother had forsaken her life for Amador. Not just her body, soul, and dreams; she'd given everything, lost her mind. Anyone who went through even half of what she did would have. Miguel never forgot the sorrow on his mother's face as they returned home on the bus at dusk. She would weep into a wrinkled handkerchief, stifling her sobs, while the passengers on their way back from a Sunday in the mountains looked on curiously. Observing the boy and his mother carefully, they could tell that they were the family of a prisoner doing forced labor at Cuelgamuros. Some took pity and touched Miguel's head, *Poor boy*, while others—not many—shot spiteful looks.

His father couldn't have known that, because he wasn't there. He was too busy. First changing the world, and then becoming a martyr. And yet, despite having hated his father and expelling him from his memory, here Miguel was, letter in hand, seeking out the man who wrote it, trying to convince himself he'd been wrong.

"What was my father like?"

Simón remained pensive, his shoulders hunched forward. Something in his expression, his sad face as he turned the window, was not right.

"Remembering is an old man's job, but how do we separate the wheat from the chaff, the truth from the tale?"

What did he remember about that prisoner, so different from the others he dealt with over his years as a guard at Valley of the Fallen?

"Your father had a heart of gold, all he wanted was to be happy and make those around him happy. I know it pained him to kill as well as to die. He was tormented by the thought that the insanity of war had made him someone unrecognizable, that if one day he was able to go home, you'd be afraid of him, or his wife would feel there was a stranger in her bed. Amador was a beautiful human being, even at his weakest. Not even the Archangel, who detested him, could keep from admiring your father's nature. In another life, it might have been what he wanted for himself. Did you know your father wrote? He kept a secret notebook, red Moroccan leather. I knew about it but pretended not to. At night, after the tattoo, he'd write, sitting on his knees, using a pencil nub barely long enough to go through his fingers that he kept in his corduroy jacket. He never took that jacket off, no matter how cold or hot it was. And he never let go of that notebook. One day I asked him what he was pouring his heart and soul into. He showed me the swollen pages, filled with neat minuscule handwriting, quite unusual for a man his size. 'War, the war still being waged in this deathly peace,' he told me. I asked him what the point was, writing about the horror and ugliness that we all knew so well. He looked at me like the ignorant, arrogant boy I was. 'One day, as incredible as it sounds, we'll forget what we did and what others did to us. We'll look for excuses and find them, and we'll forget the truth. Forget it in order to keep going.' When he wrote in that little notebook, your father was transformed. Plenty of men made fun of his historical ambitions, but not me. At night, he'd read me a few paragraphs by candlelight, in a storyteller's voice that could frighten and amaze at the same time. Your father had a gift for words, knew how to use them to fire up the other prisoners and even guards like me."

"And what did he talk about?"

"Simple things, important things. I've never had any time for show-offs and people like the Archangel who are full of hot air, but your father was different. He was fighting for a more basic understanding of freedom: to be able to go where you wanted, earn a living with dignity, not be afraid. He thought that by resisting, even being held prisoner, he was building a future for you. Plenty of people were willing to follow him in that dream."

Simón wavered for a moment, ordering the kinks in his memory. His face, half-hidden in the darkness of the room, looked like the chipped mask of some forgotten monument. But ultimately the flesh of memory is flaccid, and when it's stretched too far, the bruises and scrapes of the soul become visible.

"That's why the Archangel feared and detested him. Because your father was free. And that's why he used me to destroy him. Because I had the soul of a slave."

"What do you mean?"

Simón recalled dented stockpots crackling in the fire, men huddled around with dirty ladles to drink soup with a few crumbs of bread. A wolf howled, or perhaps it was just a runaway dog that had fled to the mountains, fearing the cruelty of men. Amador was among them, smoking leisurely, his eyes half closed.

"It was two nights before he died. There was no way that anyone knew, though anything was possible, and death was more likely than life. And yet everyone knew, the way people sense things they don't think about, don't dare say. Amador was humming a song, and the sky was so full of stars that it was beautiful enough to get lost in. You had to fill your eyes with the universe, things that were distant, immortal. Looking up at the stars makes it seem like maggots aren't so bad. He was singing to your mother, a romantic song, very nostalgic. He told me he was convinced that, wherever she was, she could hear him. He clung to the hope that one day, he'd make his way out of the sea of pain and still know how to laugh, to feel love and happiness. I don't know how he managed to think like that, have such perspective, when all around everything was sadness."

"I never imagined him like that."

"One morning there was an accident in one of the galleries, and a prisoner from Burgos, a friend of your father's, was killed. I remember because it happened on my watch. The man's name was Fermín. He'd been a slinger in the war, specialized in launching grenades with a slingshot. He had a strong arm. That was why they chose him for the blasting crew. He was the one who helped your father steal the drills for the mass escape."

"My father organized an escape from Valley of the Fallen?"

"They were stealthy about it, but there's no way to hide anything when you live in a chicken coop, and the officer in charge got suspicious that something was up. The Archangel could have arrested your father and his friend, ordered them transferred out of there, sent them back to prison. But that seemed too easy; the Archangel wanted to teach a lesson, earn the respect of the veteran guards like me as well as the most hardened prisoners. So he sent Fermín out to blast with a bunch of defective cartridges. Fermín knew what that meant, but he was undaunted. He lit a cartridge and it blew him to bits. It was impossible to recover his remains, they were strewn over a one-kilometer radius. Everyone got the message—except your father. Amador knew he'd be next, knew the Archangel had a hunch they were planning something. He could have pulled out, but he didn't. He kept calm, moved the stolen dynamite, hid their store of food and maps, gave the prisoners their instructions, and prepared to wait with the kind of tranquility that comes at the very end, the kind that elevates victims over their executioners. Existing without really existing, dying without really dying.

"He knew he was doomed but refused to accept defeat."

Simón nodded.

"I knew what he was doing, we all did, but his indifference in the face of death was disconcerting. His silent challenge to the Archangel. No one doubted his commitment or bravery, he had nothing to prove, but he was as willful as free verse. Didn't flinch the night the Archangel turned up with two guards, smiling like a lunatic, and threw your father's notebook at him. Amador stood up, looked at him calmly for a moment. The Archangel mocked Fermín's death, said he knew about the stolen dynamite and the meetings Amador held at night."

"And what did my father do?"

"He just smiled and told him he reeked of cheap gin. Then the Archangel took a step back and gave the order. I watched them beat him with the butts of their guns, but your father didn't resist, didn't even raise his voice, and that made the Archangel even madder, so he leaned over your father's bloody face and told him what he was going to do: give him a summary trial and have him executed by firing squad in the Zaragoza prison yard. Without batting an eye, your father told him that even if the Nationalists had won the war, men like him had already lost. History would devour them, sweep them away without a trace, and even the monument being erected would be nothing but a calcified tribute to insanity. The Archangel was spluttering, spitting as he spoke, ready to have a heart attack. Red with rage, he shoved his gun in Amador's face. I think that he'd have shot him right there had it not been for the witnesses. Even the Archangel respected bureaucracy and the protocol for execution. He straightened up and kicked your father in the mouth before ordering us to lock him in the punishment barrack. I still remember the sound of his teeth cracking. Your father had such beautiful teeth..."

Miguel looked away, uncomfortable. He felt like he was witnessing something he had no right to see. He set his gaze on a bookshelf with a picture of oleander and an open book.

"'Late Ripeness,' by the poet Czeslaw Milosz," Simón said.

Not soon, as late as the approach of my ninetieth year,
I felt a door opening in me and I entered
the clarity of early morning.
One after another my former lives were departing,
like ships, together with their sorrow.

"Over the years I've spent learning to read and write, I've found myself venturing into parts of myself I'd never have dared to go. Places I didn't even know existed. I thought that telling my story would do some good, but as the pages pile up I realize that remembering becomes as exhausting and pointless as weeding the jungle. You hack your way through with a machete only to find that the further you get, the more overgrown it gets. And still, you attempt to keep going, despite knowing that you'll never get anywhere, never escape the impenetrable trap that you yourself made."

Simón gave Miguel a meaningful look before continuing.

"I want you to understand that I'm not telling you this because I feel indebted to you. I don't owe you anything, and I won't accept your judgment; it hardly even matters to me."

"I don't understand what you're trying to say."

"I was terrified of the Archangel, and it was different than the terror I'd experienced in the war, because it was cold and calculated, it slowly paralyzed me like a poison he injected with his eyes. He made all resistance impossible, that was his power. The man moved silently, used polite gestures to camouflage his own terror, his fear of turning out to be the nobody his father had predicted. His tactic never varied: he looked down to mask his satisfaction at having me under his thumb, drank and lit a cigarette calmly, made friendly threats: 'Soon you'll graduate, Simón, and be able to do what befits a man your age—live, have a wife, a family, build a future. And I'm going to let you go with my blessing, but now you have to return the favor, tonight.' The reason I was terrified was because he wasn't stark raving mad. He was simply deranged by jealousy, obsessed with your father. He thought about him constantly, suspiciously, anxiously, in a way that subverted the natural order of things. He had power but lacked charisma, had strength but no soul, and your father's existence was like a mirror that reflected his failure. An unexpectedly fragile rock, he was. He had no intention of having your father sent to the wall, letting him walk fearlessly out to the firing squad so he could be admired by executioners and prisoners alike. There was to be no justice. Amador was never to leave the miasma that was the Archangel's kingdom. But he wasn't stupid and had no intention of getting his hands dirty, risking his military career. Amador was to disappear. No one would ask questions. And everyone, though silent, would know the truth."

Simón rounded the table, opened a drawer, and there was the cloth where he kept the pistol the Archangel had put in his hands that night. The same one he'd shown his grandson that very morning.

"Do people really need to know everything? Isn't it better for some things to remain forever in the limbo of the unknown? It's better to leave old bitterness crumpled in the back of our souls, hidden behind the many other experiences we've lived."

"I didn't come this far to be afraid of the truth."

Simón shook his head slowly.

"There wasn't one single truth that night. When I went to see your father in the cell that was his purgatory, he was awake. Amador was leaning against the wall gazing at the patch of night coming in through a high window. He greeted me with a smile as I walked in, but he wasn't fooled. He stood up and looked at the pistol in my right hand. He could have tried to take it off me, he was much stronger than me. That was the Archangel's idea, to give the appearance of a struggle and an escape attempt; I'd be congratulated for having fired before he could grab the gun. But he just stood there in silence, then straightened his shoulders, broad as a bear, opened his corduroy jacket, and told me to take aim."

Simón recalled that when he'd left—the smoking gun still in his hand, his clothes stained with blood—it was raining. The door was open and Amador was inside, his body bent at a grotesque angle. Simón tried not to look, but then he heard him. Amador wasn't dead yet; gravely wounded, Amador moaned and took his dying breaths, calling for his mother.

"Do you know why men call for their mothers in the throes of fear, of that last, ultimate fear? Because that's where their sense of being comes from—their mother's bellies. It's an attempt to return to the womb, the placenta, the warm tranquil magma of unconsciousness. The first kindness."

Simón could have walked away, forgotten about it, and left him there until the moaning came to an end. But he didn't, he went back in. Delivered a single shot, behind the ear, with the barrel of the gun pressed to his head just to be sure.

"I can still hear that night breathe a sigh of relief when Amador finally fell silent, his head jerking forward with the impact of the bullet. And I can see the young despondent soldier that was me, somber, lost in thought, gun in hand, with that incessant rain pounding down onto the wet ground and the creaking of a wooden wagon."

"It was you... You killed him."

"I told myself a thousand times that there was nothing else I could have done. I got married, had children and grandchildren. Every day I get up and tell myself that the world exists, that I'm a different man, and that if I held out my hand I could reach through the clouds and the storm and touch him, embrace him. Feel the warmth of the sun, see the blue of the sky, and know that the evil is in the past. But I still remember that boy in the rain who wanted to go home, toss the gun, tear off his bloodstained clothes, and run. Run and run, until the rain couldn't catch him."

Simón turned to Miguel. He never cried anymore, his tears had solidified, like glass in his eyes.

"And that's what I have to say about your father."

Miguel left, went outside, and the bright sun forced him to squint. He was glad to be out of that place so he could breathe. He felt as if, in the hours he'd spent with Simón, his lungs had refused to do their job and he was about to suffocate. Leaning his elbows on the fence, looking back at the building's facade, he didn't know how to explain death. Maybe death was sitting in a room with a typewriter, like Simón, submerged in total darkness with nothing solid to cling to, nothing to distract you from overwhelming, unending loneliness. And yet he got the feeling there was a distant glimmer in his conscience, like a remote star that died long ago but whose light still shines. His father had lived. He was important to people, heroic even. And he cared about his wife and son, about his own dignity as a free man. But that too would slowly be forgotten when Simón died and his manuscript was left in the bottom of a drawer, no one wanting to read it. That's when real death would come: silence, darker than darkness. And living on in others' memory would be all that could be hoped for.

20

He asked one of the Benedictines in charge of the basilica where to find the common grave. The young monk looked friendly and spirited, as though trying to contradict his habit—the tunic and scapulary both covered by the obligatory black-hooded cape. The man seemed unsurprised at his question.

"The columbaria are in the five chapels of the central nave, though there are also funeral chambers in the underground crypts. The truth is, the whole basilica is a necropolis, to a large extent. In the abbey's archives we have records of over twenty-two thousand people buried here. Unfortunately, there are many more, perhaps twice that number, whom we have no record of."

"I've consulted the archives. My father is not listed in them. But I know he's buried here."

The monk tried to be delicate.

"You know, or you think?"

"I know. He died here, during the construction, in 1944."

The monk frowned and gestured with his delicate hands. Miguel guessed he was one of the instructors at the abbey's famous Santa Cruz choir school for boys. Miguel realized that he himself might have been one of the boys taken in by the school. It made him smile to think how different his life would have been with a single administrative decision, had they accepted his mother's request to live in the Valley. He had never had an ear for music, anyway.

"I'm afraid that's impossible," the monk apologized. "The first columbarium didn't arrive at the basilica until construction was finished, in 1959. And the last one is from 1983. Before that no bodies were buried here."

Miguel nodded impatiently.

"I've seen the books, I know what they say. My father shouldn't be here, with the same men who took everything from him before taking his life. It's a travesty, a crime. But I know this is where he's buried."

"I assume your father was one of the prisoners serving his time in the Valley."

Miguel clucked his tongue.

"A prisoner is a person who serves a sentence for committing a crime. The regime that sentenced him legitimated themselves by virtue of their military victory, enacted laws, and then condemned him by virtue of those laws. He never recognized the laws, that's the only reason he was a prisoner."

"I see. I'm not trying to argue politics with you." The monk glanced around. There weren't many visitors: a few tourists, a couple of newlyweds taking selfies beneath the juniper cross, a group of schoolkids and their teachers. Still, he lowered his voice considerably and bent his head. "But believe me, he's not here."

"Yes, he is."

The monk furrowed his brow but then immediately regained the jovial demeanor of a man at peace with himself and the world. He took a more careful look at the old man carrying a small backpack over his right shoulder and saw that he kept looking off to the right, as if he wasn't alone. He thought of his own grandfather, buried there too, beneath the tomb of José Antonio Primo de Rivera, founder of the Falange. His grandfather had been a committed Falangist to the end, a war veteran who for years had bought special lottery tickets that were sold each May to help defray the cost of the Valley. After Franco died, he dressed in blue every November 20 and took his grandson on the bus to commemorate the generalísimo as part of the demonstrations held on the forecourt.

"Do you smoke?"

Miguel shook his head in bewilderment. The monk smiled by way of excuse. "I do, and this is my cigarette break. Do you mind accompanying me outside? There's something I think you might be interested to hear."

The moment they got to the staircase, the monk took out a pack of cigarettes and lit one, turning to face the imposing cross that crowned the bluff. He shook his head nostalgically, recalling boyhood mischief from his days at the choral school, long before he'd even dreamed of becoming a novice. They used to climb up to the base of the cross and clamber around the four evangelists, each eighteen meters tall. *I could've cracked my skull*, he thought, blowing smoke up at the sky to the shock and disbelief of the two old ladies on their way to twelve o'clock mass. The monk acknowledged them with a quick and somewhat ironic nod of his head.

"Matthew is my favorite," he said, pointing to the base of the cross. "The winged man. He's actually an angel. And there's the symbol of Christ himself, the man turned son of God, descendent of David, of Abraham; the Messiah. The man attaining freedom, the freedom from all that oppresses him on earth and in his conscience."

Miguel listened in curiosity, thinking that this was one strange monk. He'd have chosen Matthew as well.

"Those are unusual ideas coming from a Benedictine. Most Benedictines would have chosen Luke, or even John or Mark."

The monk smiled. Maybe he should have followed his instincts and been ordained as a Jesuit. He crushed his cigarette under the tip of his shoe and slipped the butt into his pocket.

"There are things you may not know. Things you should take into consideration if you're thinking of trying to find your father. There are dozens and dozens of boxes full of remains here. My grandfather was one of the employees who moved them into storage. Officially, there are thirty-three thousand bodies, but he swore there were many more. Trucks full of exhumed remains were arriving every day."

Miguel knew this part of the story. His mother had told him about it. The minister of the interior at the time, Blas Pérez, had insisted that the remains of fallen Nationalist soldiers be transferred to the basilica if their families so requested, to give meaning to this enormous mausoleum, which was intended to glorify those who rose up in 1936.

"To the minister's surprise, very few families requested exhumation and transfer."

Miguel nodded.

"Nobody wants their dead to glorify others; they'd rather keep them near, to mourn them and feel their absence up close."

The monk looked at Miguel in curiosity.

"You're right. At any rate, construction was nearing completion, and they started looking for dead on either side buried in mass graves all over the country."

"There are plenty of people under there buried against their family's will. Victims and executioners, irreconcilable enemies, and now their bones are forever jumbled together. Doesn't it strike you as too cruel an irony? Someone needs to put an end to this nonsense."

The monk inhaled. It pained him to talk about it; he felt responsible. After all, he at least knew where his grandfather was.

"Memory is costly; it's much more expensive than oblivion. In addition to administrative costs, there are requests, certificates, delays; leaking crypts have rotted many of the columbaria, dumping their contents and mixing the bones. You speak of enemies, victims, and executioners. But what I see is oblivion, neglect, shame, denial, and abandonment."

"Couldn't they even leave the dead in peace after they killed them?"

"I can only comment on the madness of the present, not the past. When the columbaria were created, those buried in church cemeteries, individual graves, or mass graves were taken along with those in trenches, ditches, or the middle of a field. They only asked families' consent to move the bodies for those on Franco's side, but since there weren't enough, they exhumed the others without permission, without even notifying the families. At first there might have been an attempt to undertake orderly burials, but many of the dead on the Republican side could only be identified by the location of the grave. And some of those graves had over three hundred bodies in them. Given their haste, and the politicians' demands, things got out of control, and they stopped differentiating between one side and the other, filling the columbaria with up to fifteen decomposing bodies, regardless of where they came from. Believe me, families of all ideologies come here looking for their dead without even knowing if they're here. They're trying to get things back on track, but the Valley is in such a state of neglect that identifying bodies and delivering them to their families is simply unviable. Even if your father were here—which, as I said, is extremely unlikely—given the current state of chaos and disorder, it would be almost impossible to find him. You don't have to believe me, of course, you can begin the administrative process, but it's long and sad, and you'll no doubt end up in a San Lorenzo court awaiting a resolution that will take years. Forensic proof, documentary evidence, DNA analysis . . . I hate to say it, but it won't get anywhere."

They were both silent. In the harsh sun, wind swept through the cypress trees lining the way to the forecourt, making them whistle. The monk straightened his shoulders. At least his face reflected sincere compassion and not standard Christian resignation. The difference between the two lay in perceiving an injustice, which led the monk to shake his head in restrained frustration.

"I have to go give mass. This is, after all, still a place of worship."

Miguel watched the young monk bound up the black staircase energetically. He waited a minute, watching people go in and out of the basilica. For years, the place had attracted his mother like a magnet, it was the center of her life. And now that he was here, he felt nothing but despondence, exhaustion, and an emptiness bordering on nausea.

He shifted the backpack on his shoulder and started on his way.

t was a steep incline. Miguel stopped and leaned against a pine sapling to get his breath back. He took off the small backpack and set it on the ground, which was blanketed in pine needles. He took off his glasses and used the hem of his shirt to wipe his sweat from the lenses, then put them back on and looked up.

Miguel took in the landscape at a glance: a few meters of rocks and tree roots to the top of the hill, and beyond that, the top of the Stauros—the concrete cross on the rocky Risco de la Nava crag. That cross didn't exist when he was a boy, and neither did the Benedictine abbey, the inn, or the basilica. He seemed to recall that not far from there, halfway to San Lorenzo del Escorial, were the workers' villages. He watched blackbirds flit about, singing from one pine tree to the next. At the top of the hill, a light breeze ruffled the wild rosemary bushes. Down below was the basilica's forecourt, built beneath the rocky pedestal of the monumental cross—a hundred and fifty meters high and visible from forty kilometers away.

He hadn't been back since his father died, and now he got the feeling that he was returning to a place that no longer existed. The Valley of the Fallen had grown up, lived, and died without him. This near-senile calm betrayed his memories, the present usurping the past just as barbaric emperors once did, ordering their predecessor's chroniclers killed so as to erase their stories and reinvent history. There was something missing; something that had nothing to do with space or objects, something not included in the guidebook in the pocket of his backpack, something that could not be read about in any of the books he'd consulted or heard in the accounts of sensible historians he'd listened to, all colored by their own rationale and reasoning. Where were the

411

men? Where were Amador, Simón, the Archangel, Fermín? Where were the traces of his mother, or even of himself, and so many other families who'd camped out on the outskirts, sometimes for days on end, for the chance to glimpse their loved ones from behind the fence, even for a minute?

And yet despite that, he couldn't be disappointed. After all, there was more than one way to die, and the Valley was at death's door, agonizing in a precarious balance between apathy and the inevitable recognition of its presence: a somber granite place, grandiose spaces, architecture from another time intended to exalt a country that no longer existed, the dead no one wanted to remember. Everywhere, the perhaps irreversible decline into which the Valley was destined to sink was visible: in the nets placed at the base of the cross to catch falling rocks, the shored-up arch that led to the cavern, the funicular that was no longer in service, the chinks in the staircase to the basilica, the water leaks.

"Do you recognize any of this, Father?"

Amador blended into the torrid day, bright and uncontestable. His presence no longer unnerved Miguel. He'd accepted his father the way you accept your shadow, which sometimes walks ahead of you and sometimes behind. But in this landscape, which belonged more to his father, Miguel was the shadow. Seeing him here, sitting on a rock and looking at what his and so many other thousands of hands had built, it was easier for Miguel to understand the man he must once have been, the stories his mother sometimes made him listen to, the things he'd read in the newspaper clippings, and the books she stored in the trunk. *He didn't leave us, Miguel. They took him from us; you and I were the ground his roots grew in.*

He could picture his father hiding out in the mountains, or in the valleys of Badajoz and Cáceres, missing his family, alone in the countryside, wanting to be with them every minute. He imagined Amador spending long nights with nothing to drink or eat, gazing at the houses of Almendralejo in the distance and knowing he couldn't let himself be seen, running from one hamlet to the next, stealing food from farms, running from traps like a cornered rat. In the end, his father stopped caring about any of it. He wanted to come home, to feel like a person again and not a wild dog, to shave and take a bath with hot water, to have dry socks. That's why he came down that night, disobeying his superiors' orders and the advice of his friends. *If our side finds you, you'll be shot for desertion; if theirs does, you'll be shot as an enemy.* But he had to see Rosa and his son. The streets of his town had become hostile territory for Amador. The war was over, and it was as though it had never happened, as though everyone had signed a pact of forgetting. They'd rebuilt their burned-out houses, plastered over the cracks in the church, painted the cemetery walls to erase any vestiges of the firing squad executions. Out on the streets, rifle in his belt, people must have seen his father as the reminder of a period of insanity that no one wanted to remember. Doors and windows were closed on him, old friends—now deaf or mute—turned him away, breathing the sickly air of those who sleep in fear, those whose guilty consciences are further afflicted. He could sense the fear embedded in the whitewashed facades of homes, in the telltale echo of cobblestone streets, in the dogs barking crazily. There were signs of it everywhere. His wife, Rosa, said nothing when she saw him jump through the window into what had once been their bedroom. She pulled him to her in the penumbra, took him to the bathroom, heated water, and poured it into the tub. She took off his clothes very slowly, as though afraid of hurting him by removing rags that had become a second skin. She led him to the tub like a little boy and used a cloth to clean him for hours, slowly washing every inch of his body so as to engrave the memory of it in her hands forever. She shaved him, cut his hair. And only once she'd finished, when he looked in the mirror and was able to recognize himself, did she burst into tears. They both knew what that night meant. She held him to her belly, and it was like being home again, like stopping the passage of time, altering it, going back to the beginning, when there was no war and no defeat. Just the two of them in the old tin-frame bed that creaked each time they made love. At dawn, the guards surrounded the house. It made little difference who had betrayed him, whether his side or the other. That difference no longer existed. There was only him, his wife, and his son—and everyone else.

Miguel dropped onto his side at the base of a pine tree sticky with resin. He was tired, but at the same time felt profoundly liberated. He watched a bird of prey circling the sky over Cuelgamuros. The ghost of Amador looked up at the sky as well, but in a different way, as though he could see through the mirage of the blue cupola. The dead have memories, too, it turns out. And regrets.

"You're here, aren't you, Father? Buried somewhere. Mother said she could feel you, your presence, every time she came, said she could touch you or reach through you with her fingers, see you wandering like a shadow by the cross with the four evangelists behind, climbing the limestone rock, in the wispy clouds and blue sky, weeping in the silent darkness of space and dying stars. It was your presence that brought her here again and again. She heard your anguish, said you called out and asked her not to leave you."

Miguel unzipped his backpack. Inside was the urn with his mother's ashes. He took it out and placed it between his knees. He watched an ant that had climbed from his boot to his sock. It marched in circles among the folds of fabric as if trapped and searching desperately for a way out. Miguel took pity and offered a finger, helping it escape through the pine needles. He could have crushed it between his fingers without a second thought, and nothing would have changed. One less ant, that's all.

"Do you know what the worst thing is, Father? Not that you washed your hands of me, never came back to see if I was dead or alive. The worst thing was that I chose the easiest lie to live with. I saw the person I loved lose her mind, suffered her punishments for years, and even grew to hate her, to despise her. I wanted to punish her for all the pain she caused me. I learned to shield myself head to toe in order to endure the neighbors' stern faces. Even after moving to the city I still always had the feeling I was being watched, stared at with disrespect. Shame is like poison—you imagine people smirking and offering phony compassion when it's not true. *Poor boy, look at all he's gone through, a Red for a father and a mother who's not only crazy but a whore. He barely managed to turn out okay, with that little mustache he grows to look older and more respectable.* I was ashamed of my mother and I can't fix what happened. But I can give her what she wanted."

He caressed the urn holding his mother's ashes just as she'd caressed him the morning she told him that his father was dead. Miguel didn't even mind his father's silence, his shadow, his ghost, or his insanity. Didn't care if he existed or not. Miguel struggled to his feet and walked to the edge of the promontory, where he could see the basilica's forecourt off to the west. It was getting late and he had to get back to Madrid, back to Helena. The air smelled of rockrose and cypress, and in the distance, on the horizon, were the peaks of Mount Abantos.

"This is as good a place as any."

He opened the urn and stood upwind. The dark ash was like sand from a volcanic beach awaiting its fate. His father was there, in the stone, a buzzing insect, an ant, a bush, in everything and nothing, like the thousands and thousands of dead who were buried in the Valley. What did it matter if they had died there or someplace else, if some had died sooner and others later? The same war had killed everyone and everything: the legitimacy of memory, law, justice, truth. No one wanted to champion the old stories anymore, stories peopled with ghosts, angels with swords, gigantic evangelists armed with false magnificence. With a little luck the valley would continue on as the kingdom of deer, stone marten, and wild boar. No men, no footsteps, no monuments except the spruces, elms, linden, and birch.

Miguel let a fistful of ashes fall through his fingers, then another, and another. He didn't want to dump his mother out all at once, preferring for her remains to be swept up in the breeze, to merge with it, fly far away rather than fall at his feet without the spirit to disappear.

Within a few minutes, Rosa, his mother, had gone forever.

Miguel climbed slowly back down the path, holding onto rocks and tree trunks for support. He struggled to keep his breath but at the same time felt strangely light. A single gesture and he was free from the exhaustion of a lifetime.

He turned just once, for proof of what he already knew—that his father no longer followed him. Amador had stayed up there on the promontory, where he could contemplate the horizon that was now filled with his wife.

Miguel had decided to grow a mustache when he was sixteen, to show the world that just because he had a boy's face didn't mean he was one, that he was ready to take his place in the adult world. The mustache grew, year after year, turning into the bushy caterpillar that had kept him company most of his life. Águeda hated it, said it made him look like Bismarck, that all he needed was the Prussian helmet. She thought that it made him look dour. But Miguel paid no attention. The mustache was a distinctive mark, and as such it gave him personality. A bank director needed that image, he told himself every day standing before the mirror, trimming rebel hairs while listening to the radio and smoothing down his well-groomed declaration of intent, which gradually turned gray.

Now he'd decided to shave it off. He was curious to see if the sixteen-year-old boy who wanted to grow up still lurked there. What he discovered was a thin, not-very-distinct upper lip that made him look like he was in a constant state of distress, like he had a painful canker sore. He found it curious how easy it was to take off certain masks. All that was required was a pair of scissors, a razor, and a little shaving cream. He was no longer a young man in need of his elders' respect, hiding behind his mustache and his suit, longing to escape his past as the son of Crazy Rosa and Amador the Priest-Killer. Nor did he still need to go against Águeda's wishes to prove he still had a degree of independence. What remained was a vaguely dried-out-looking face that bore a slight resemblance to Don Quixote, a protruding Adam's apple, a still-considerable shock of hair now whiter than it was gray, and eyes that no longer sparkled.

That night he treated Helena to dinner in a fancy restaurant. She gave his new face an admiring glance.

"You look like a new man. You almost are one. Whatever happened in the mountains today helped free you of the cross you were bearing."

Miguel smiled. Something was different about both of them, definitively different.

Helena was wearing faded low-cut jeans, leather sandals, and a white tank top with a yellow blouse over it. She'd gone to the hairdresser's that afternoon, gotten her hair cut and had it dyed auburn with dark lowlights at the temples.

"And you look just lovely," Miguel said admiringly, forcing himself not to stare at her nipples, which he could see beneath her tank top. The effort at nonchalance made his desire to look all the more obvious, and Helena chided him in amusement.

"Relax, you can stare all you want. They're nipples, not radioactive warheads. Your corneas won't fall out."

Miguel became flustered.

"You love calling me out, don't you?"

Helena burst out laughing.

"What I really love, Miguel, is the way you turn the most natural things into some sort of moral catastrophe. It must be exhausting, denying reality over and over: I've got tits, I'm a woman, and I'm not wearing a bra. Feeling attraction doesn't make you a rapist or a freak."

"I didn't say I was attracted," Miguel replied quickly, flushing.

"Because I'm an old lady and you picture my tits all shriveled and saggy? You'd be surprised, darling. Want to touch?"

"Don't say things like that."

"You see? You're blushing. I'm just teasing; come on, relax. It's me, your friend."

"Can we change the subject?"

So they did. They chatted animatedly until late into the night, drinking a bottle of 2004 Reserve Viña Tondonia. By the time dessert rolled around, Miguel had forgotten all about Helena's breasts; he took off his jacket and didn't even care that the knot in his tie was crooked.

"It's funny," he said shaking his head, "I haven't thought about Natalia for quite some time. Does that make me a bad father? Having fun while my daughter is miserable and thinks I'm to blame for it?"

"Maybe," Helena joked. Raising her umpteenth glass of wine, she observed its contents in the candlelight. "Yes, a terrible father who betrayed his daughter; then again, it's pretty common for children to blame their parents for their emotional turmoil. Having a bad mother or father is the universal excuse children use to justify their failures."

"Does David consider you a bad mother too?"

Helena arched an eyebrow. She downed her wine and kept holding the glass up for a moment.

"We're having a nice time. Why ruin it?"

By the time they left the restaurant, it was late, and it took some time to find a taxi. The driver was a young Goth-looking woman who smelled of marijuana.

"Did you know that marijuana is a psychotropic derived from hemp?" Helena asked Miguel. "*Cannabis sativa*. The Romans used to get high by smelling its smoke, and the Egyptians used it as a hallucinogen for medical purposes."

Miguel leaned back against the seat.

"Very interesting. I'm betting you know this from experience."

"Don't be so dismissive. At seventy-five, you run no risk of getting addicted. You could let yourself go for once, be corrupted by this crazy old dame with no morals or ethics."

"We're too old for stuff like that, Helena. In fact, I was always too old for it. I hate drugs." He was tipsy since he rarely drank, but not drunk. In fact, he felt lulled by a pleasantly meditative state.

Helena smiled and leaned her forehead against the taxi's window. The driver was nodding her head in time to a Juan Luis Guerra song. Helena rolled the window down and felt the warm Madrid air. The city lights looked like fireflies twinkling, its wrinkles and imperfections invisible. Reality seemed distant enough that they could make it whatever they wanted it to be. Helena's friend Marqués used to say it made no sense to keep pretending to be someone you never wanted to be to begin with. No matter how seriously you took your life, it hadn't been chosen freely but built on a series of mirages. And mirages could disappear with the wave of a hand. To find meaning in life was your only sacred responsibility, and once you did, you should never let it go.

She looked at the driver in the rearview mirror.

"Excuse me—would you mind sharing the spliff you put out before you picked us up?"

PART SIX

July 2014

21

Barcelona

Carmen felt the familiar touch of Jan's hand on her back, his finger grazing her bra clasp through the silk camisole.

"So this time it's for real. They just published it in the company bulletin: you're retiring."

Carmen hugged herself a bit tighter and declined the drink Jan held out. She only permitted this sort of intimacy when they were alone.

"In two weeks, as soon as I close on the transfer with the Chinese and collect my commission."

Jan situated himself to her right and gazed down with her from the twelfth-floor window: Avenida Diagonal at rush hour, the mountain, Calatrava tower in the distance, modern office buildings all identical to hers, tennis courts at the club, outdoor cafés, and a swimming pool.

"I can't believe you want to give up this view," he said, holding the whisky to his nose before tasting it. He smacked his lips in satisfaction and turned, taking in Carmen's office with his gaze, "that you'd say goodbye to all this."

Carmen half closed her eyes and did not turn with him. Why was everyone finding it so hard to accept her decision?

"It's just an office, Jan. Things that never belonged to me; I knew I was only passing through, so I never got too comfortable."

Jan let out a whistle.

"You made it higher than anyone in this company, the twelfth floor. And it took twenty years, so I wouldn't call that passing through. But now that you have it, you're throwing it away. And don't tell me it's your age: look at the Koplowitz sisters. Still giving it their all, they haven't lost a shred of their business sense. Plus, Óscar told me that the board asked you to stay one more year and you turned them down."

There was a hint of irritation in Jan's tone that Carmen had learned to recognize. When she left, he'd be losing his biggest supporter, just when the greatest privileges of making it to the top were within reach: first-class travel, a limo and driver, dinners at the tennis club, official receptions, influence. Carmen had never fooled herself about Jan, he was as ambitious as he was good-looking. He'd get over it, because in addition to a pretty face, he was refined, efficient, pragmatic, intelligent, and knew how to swim with the sharks. And it was his pragmatic intelligence that made him realize maybe he was showing too much of his hand.

"I'm sorry. You know I'm the talkative one on the team. It's just that I can't stand to lose you ... as a boss." He tried to give her a kiss, but Carmen held up her hand between them.

"I have a few matters to take care of. And I'm sure you've got things to do as well. Very important things, like earning lots of money for someone."

He gave her a slightly dubious look.

"Isn't that what we do for a living?"

"Of course, forgive my sarcasm."

Jan set his glass on the drinks cabinet and stood for a moment gazing at the Miró on the wall, perhaps imagining what it would be like to see it from the armchair that was Carmen's for a short time longer.

"Will I see you tonight? There's a new restaurant I found on Calle de Calvet that has a fantastic wine list."

Carmen forced a tired smile. Sometimes when she looked at Jan, she became more aware of what she'd sacrificed to make it to this office. And when he shot her a theoretically seductive look or flashed the smile of a gym rat turned gentleman, she wondered if the friends who so envied her for sleeping with a man thirty years her junior could ever know how lonely she was.

"Yes, I'll see you tonight."

The truth was she'd already decided to break up with him. She was going to leave *the man you can talk to because he knows how to listen*, as he described himself, though in fact he listened only to the Narcissus inside. Carmen thought she'd earned the right to live without faking it and without placebos in the form of supposed white knights.

That evening, Jan found his cardboard box at the door. In it were his toothbrush, a change of underwear, a pair of Chicago Bulls pajamas, and a bottle of hair-loss prevention shampoo. That was the sum total of personal space that Carmen had allowed him to invade over the course of a two-year relationship. Less than his predecessors: with each successive lover, the box got smaller. In a way, the size expressed how much of herself she was willing to give up. A detachable relationship, weekends only. No longer even Wednesday nights, when her favorite show was on. She used to like having someone on the sofa to stroke her shoulder, but no more. Every Monday she would gather Jan's things, place them in the box, and put it under her bed; then, before he returned on Fridays, she'd put them back in their place. But even this kind of à la carte relationship had grown tiresome. She would rather be alone at the house she'd bought in Sitges, sitting on the balcony with a glass of wine and a Günter Grass novel, Freddy Mercury playing in the background. Or just the sound of the waves and gazing at the moon. Maybe she'd sail to Formentera and lie in the sand surrounded by Italians, rent a scooter and buy a loaf of bread and the paper, go out dancing at night to Blue Bar, where she'd pick up the occasional lover when she felt like it. And it would all be with her habitual aplomb: she'd pick a dress, buy some shoes, try on earrings or a bracelet, have a couple of mojitos, and hold a trivial and supposedly flirty conversation with some stranger as if she was happy, as if she wanted nothing more.

At her house, which was only half-furnished and had too much open space, there were no wedding photos or family snapshots. Just steel, glass, stone, and wood. Elegance that was cold and distant, like her wardrobe, like her. Not a cat, dog, fish, or bird. Shiny gray floors and high white walls disguised what was essentially a prison. Why had she never committed, never gotten serious with anyone? She was attractive, conscientious, successful, and predictable; every night she went to bed with the following day planned out, a woman with no surprises. Outwardly she was quite a catch, as her younger sister said every time she saw her. "It's not too late, Carmen." All of the women in her family had done what was expected of them; her mother, her aunts, and sisters had all settled down and had families; they now had children and grandchildren. They claimed to be satisfied and fulfilled, and Carmen had no reason to doubt them. But she was different; even as a girl she hated the titanic effort her parents made to stay together till death. She hated the bickering, the friction of cohabitation that infected everything in the end: angry Sunday strolls with the girls, visiting friends that they bad-mouthed and backstabbed the moment the left their houses, the tears and pretending every time her father took a trip. *Love is a battle won through hard work. Nothing comes easy in this life, least of all love*, her mother once told her, an old lady by then. But Carmen had never agreed. Love couldn't come at the cost of tears and grievances, couldn't be the fruit of effort. It should be pleasurable and easy, frictionless, two people fitting together, people who knew the moment they met that they were the ones without having searched for one another. Her younger sister, an old woman at forty, tied down with a husband and two kids, teased her. *You read too much nineteenth-century German poetry, Carmen. You want it all to be like one of those romantic comedies you watch while munching on popcorn, a ninety-minute roller coaster that always ends the same: the couple running toward each other on a Manhattan street at dawn, Brooklyn Bridge in the background. Well, sorry to tell you, Sis, but if you want something that's worth it, you've got to roll up your sleeves and deal with reality: hair in the bathroom, bad breath in the morning, doubts, sometimes jealousy, exhaustion, awkward questions you ask yourself at night after making love, resentment that builds up, little things that needle and irritate you. Things you don't find out about in poems and movies.* Carmen knew her sister was right. She knew when she saw the way she touched her husband's butt or caught the way her sister sometimes looked at him when he wasn't paying attention, the complicity, the way they whispered in each other's ears at family get-togethers, the genuine laughs they had with their kids, the way they sat on the sofa with their fingers entwined without even being conscious of it.

And yet, she'd chosen to leave it all to luck and fate. Carmen saw love as a dogmatic faith, one she believed in too intensely, perhaps, expected everything from, but one way or another, it ended up letting her down. Her lovers never lived up to her expectations. She'd tried again and again but always with the brakes on, reluctant, anticipating failure, almost willing it so as to confirm the idea that perfect love exists only in fantasyland. She was in love with something unattainable because behind the pretense lay something darker and more desolate: her inability to truly let go, her need to start over time and again, never getting anywhere, because that was what kept her on her toes, alert, alive. How sweet the bitterness of hiding behind spite and disappointment, saying goodbye with a smug, wounded expression before anyone ever left her. Taken one by one, each lover could have been the right man had she not been obsessed with the nuance of each feeling, the precision of each detail, constantly splitting hairs. On the other hand, taken as a set, the men who had passed through her life were a messy picture of where the true problem lay. It was her, she was always the source of the breakups, the cause of hostilities, the one who was unfaithful. Jan was simply the final step in an inevitable downfall that left Carmen increasingly self-absorbed, entrenched in her unattainable utopia, more given to self-pity. She no longer let anyone get close enough to see the real her because she was afraid of herself, had voluntarily banished herself to a place somewhere between reality and fantasy to keep from confronting the evidence that she had to *not* love someone to be sure he loved her.

Once she thought she got close to breaking through the wall, jumping over it, daring to live outside her books. She had still been young and didn't know enough to recognize the traps she had set for herself. She remembered that weekend in 1980, albeit with a grimace, feeling a bit ridiculous. She had no idea why she'd kept writing to that man for a decade. A decade spent reminiscing about twenty-four hours! She could never make sense of her insistence on an illusion, one that became almost a caricature for how often she invoked it. There had been other weekends both before and after, far better ones, in more beautiful places, with lovers who were more skillful, or more handsome, or more interesting. And yet she kept thinking of the man's mustache tickling her belly, his small eyes darting without his glasses.

"So stupid!" she reproached herself. Jan was right; she'd triumphed, achieved what none of the friends who'd chosen to go out Friday nights rather than stay home studying had done or ever would do. She was alone because that was how she wanted it; it was her choice, end of story.

Retirement wasn't so bad. Having time and the ability to use it however she saw fit. She'd started running on the beach in the early mornings, before the sunbathers arrived. She liked being in shape without resorting to surgery—a boob job or tummy tuck; injections in her forehead, cheeks, or lips; tensor threads in the neck—or dressing like a twenty-year-old. She had even taken up smoking again, a vice she'd given up twenty years earlier. It was nice to indulge in whatever she wanted and still feel men, both young and old, look at her when she sat down in a café to relax and read the paper. And she hardly missed Jan, who'd only tried to see her a couple of times before turning a new page and moving on to other conquests.

She'd even thought about getting a pet, maybe adopting one of those little dogs that fit in your purse and hardly needed to be walked.

That's what she was thinking when she got home, sweaty, her legs aching after an hour-long run. While opening the mailbox, she glanced at her running watch to check her mileage, pace, calories, and heartbeat. Carmen almost never paid attention to the mail anymore; it was always just bank notices, ads, or bills.

She deposited the mail and her keys on the table and took a long invigorating shower. Then she made a fruit smoothie, grabbed the mail from the table and went out to the balcony. It was a beautiful morning, the sun wasn't too hot, and the sea was calm. While drinking her smoothie, she shuffled through the envelopes, not even bothering to open them, until one caught her attention.

Seeing her name and address written out by hand was what made her stop. She turned the envelope over but there was no return address. Setting her smoothie on the side table, she opened the envelope with one finger. It contained a single sheet of white paper with two paragraphs neatly written in blue ink. Carmen skimmed the text and opened her eyes wide as she read, stunned.

Her hand began to tremble, and the letter fluttered gently to the floor. Kneeling to retrieve it, she sat there, without getting up, to read it once more in disbelief.

Two weeks earlier, in Madrid, Miguel and Helena had spent a morning at the Prado. They skipped the most crowded rooms, hardly even stopping at the museum's most emblematic pieces. Helena was intent on showing Miguel one particular painting.

"Here it is . . . What do you think?"

She'd led Miguel to the room with Hieronymus Bosch's *The Garden of Earthly Delights*. There was a bench in front of the triptych, occupied by two visitors who sat gazing at the panels, searching for hidden meanings expressed by the painter. One was consulting details in the Hans Belting guide and then pointing out the most striking motifs to his companion. Miguel observed the visitors, two brainy-looking boys, indifferently.

"I'm no art expert," he said defensively.

"*In the end, one must paint just the way one is*. My mother used to quote that. Juan Gris. She was self-taught, learned it all on her own. She was no expert either, but she did understand that just as painters can only paint what they are, observers can only see from their own perspective. What I want to know is what *you* see. We all see different things—those kids sitting there, you, me . . . I want *your* opinion."

Miguel stepped back a bit to get a more complete picture of the three panels and let his gaze take in the infinite images, explosions of color and darkness.

"It's dizzying."

"That's it?"

Miguel inhaled and looked more carefully, following the triptych's logical order: paradise, earthly life, hell. None of it was normal, not the mythological animals, the nightmar-ish futuristic scenes that looked ephemeral and unreal, the city ablaze, or the devil-bird devouring men and excreting them. It was disturbing. Like some insane labyrinth that kept returning to the starting point, with no way out.

"I find it distressing . . . What do you see?"

Helena gazed at the painting; she looked as though she was being inhabited by a ghost. The images were reflected in her pupils. Like the painting, her expression, too, contained a mysterious secret language, impossible to decipher.

"No one can know the uncharted territory of the individual, not even the individual in question. Because what's beneath the surface is terrifying, it's disconcerting."

"I'm not sure I understand what you mean."

"The day I buried Walter, I returned home alone and walked into his office. All of his papers were there, his empty appointment book and pencil case, the ashtray and empty whisky glass. It was strange, being there without him, in the silent presence of his things. They said nothing to me, observed me like a stranger. And there was the print of *The Garden of Earthly Delights*, hanging on the wall, ready to be studied, offering insignificant details that went unnoticed on first glance. The more I looked at it, the angrier I got. I took a heavy paperweight from the table and smashed the glass of the frame. I felt like ripping it to shreds with my bare hands, but I didn't. We have no right to profane a world that doesn't belong to us."

"Why were you so angry that your husband had this painting in his office?"

Helena remained pensive.

"He chose it to hide from me. Rather than actually speak to me about his pain, suffering, and incomprehension, he decided to let hallucinogenic images do it for him."

Miguel felt disconcerted. He gazed back and forth between Helena and the painting, searching for some connection between the two.

"What was this terrible pain he felt?"

She pursed her lips as though unsure herself what it was. But Miguel recognized the evasive gesture.

"I thought I loved my family, thought I was ready to be a good mother, a good wife. I tried as hard as I could, but it wasn't enough. Maybe we all inherit a self-destructive gene. Call it the disaster gene, or the gene that makes you fuck up the lives of those you love. I was unfaithful to Walter with another woman. My best friend. And my son caught us, just as I caught my father with another man when I was a girl. What a ludicrous, tragic parallel. Walter never forgave me."

Miguel remained silent. Hearing that Helena had had a lesbian relationship didn't strike him as any worse than being unfaithful, or the turmoil that its discovery must have caused her son. But he had no right to question Helena's intentions or feelings. All he could do was be a vessel for her secrets. Listen and try not to judge.

"If you want to see, you have to train your eye," Helena continued. "That's not my line, it's something Louise used to say. David saw me with her and drew his own conclusions, just as I did when I saw my father under Abdul. Hasty conclusions, no doubt. We look but we don't see. Sometime later, my son asked me if I preferred women. I didn't know what to say. When I was a teenager and Louise and I used to kiss in the bathroom at Mayfield, I was afraid I'd inherited a kind of sickness, a disease transmitted through my father's genes. So, when Walter came into my life and I had David, I thought I'd been cured of some kind of malignant virus. I told myself that my questioning had been a phase, part of being a teenager. It was the need to explore sex, confusing friendship with desire—nothing could be more natural, if the world would accept what's natural. But years later, in 1982, Louise came back into my life and we started our relationship back up again. That's when I realized that I was never like my father. I loved my son, and I'd never give him up for anyone, not even Louise. But I also loved her and didn't want to choose between my two loves. I thought I wouldn't have to."

Helena still recalled the morning Louise turned up at her door, on January 12, 1982. Her hair was in a high bun that made her look much taller, and she was wearing earrings and tons of bracelets and a Greenpeace vest and leather sandals despite the London cold; she had a backpack on. She'd come straight from the airport and was just in from New York. There she stood, as if no time had passed, with a mischievous smile that seemed to suggest she'd gotten sidetracked on her way back and taken slightly longer than anticipated. They spent the day on the sofa, smoking and drinking, chatting, laughing, and making confessions.

Louise blew into Helena's life like the storm that she was—wild and dangerous and delicious; no half measures and no holding back. She hadn't returned from the United

States with her dreams fulfilled; she'd gotten only small roles with no-name theater companies. Yet despite that, she didn't feel like a failure. *I know who I am, I know what I feel. That's more than some people can say*, she'd said in a tone that bothered Helena, staring into her eyes through spirals of smoke that hung in the air. Was her friend looking down on her, did she perhaps feel superior? Helena showed her a photo of Walter and David as an act of self-defense. Louise replied, disguising her cruelty as sincerity, saying Walter looked like a "good man." In translation, this meant she found him bland, boring. David, however, she was immediately enthralled by. She wanted to meet this boy who had an unnervingly grave, focused look.

"Walter and Louise took an instant dislike to each other. He saw her as a threat, felt excluded from our laughter, left out of our secrets and private jokes. David, on the other hand, was taken with her from the start. He was thrilled to let himself be spoiled by *mother's friend*, who took on the role of the indulgent, exotic, slightly foul-mouthed auntie. She was more American than English and exasperated his father with her outlook—a blend of Eastern teachings, a little Nietzsche, and rock lyrics—that David found so amusing. Young men always ended up falling for Louise, and David was no exception."

One afternoon when they were alone, Helena confessed to Louise something that she'd never believed she would confess to anyone, even herself: she didn't love Walter, not the way she was supposed to.

"Louise didn't even let me finish. She gave me a kiss that, if I'm honest, deep down I'd been wanting from the moment she returned. We were no longer boarding school friends, there was no more Miss Clark, and we couldn't pretend it was just curiosity or a form of rebellion. On the same sofa where Walter read his model airplane magazines, we made love—only now we did it like adults, slowly, without rationalizing, our desire expressed through patience. It made me realize how much I had inside, how much I was capable of feeling, and of giving to someone else, to Louise, who was experienced and knew how to give and receive, to submit—though never entirely. It gave me the kind of pleasure you get from sharing a secret that you're the only one who knows."

Had Louise had other women? Helena chose not to find out; she didn't need to. As for herself, what did she feel? Hours later, taking a shower, her mind filled with images and colors, she told herself it was just something that had to happen, unfinished business. But when she began touching herself under the water's spray and became excited, she knew that she'd do it as many times as Louise wanted to. And that thought made her happy.

"We became lovers. We took advantage of every minute we were alone, found out-of-the-way places where we could pretend we were a normal couple; we went to the theater, the movies, concerts, and when the lights went down we'd behave as if we'd just fallen in love. I felt like I was high, in a state of unconscious joy that I never wanted to end. And then at night, when I got into bed with Walter and he'd say I was distant, when he'd make plans for David's future at university, I would nod along, but deep down it all felt foreign to me. This went on for several months of peace and delirium, tortuous arguments and passionate reconciliations, moments of silent complicity—our legs entwined—doubts that were kissed away, and insane plans. Until that summer in 1982, when I was stroking Louise's hair, both of us naked after having made love, and I looked up, and there in the bedroom door stood David."

Helena stopped, unable to continue. Her lips were trembling, tears welled up in her eyes, and Miguel did something unusual for him. He put a hand on her shoulder, by her ear, and with his knuckle brushed the dangling earring she'd put on that morning. The air-conditioning wasn't working well, and suddenly he felt stifled by his jacket, tie, and cufflinks, by the shoes pinching his feet. He needed to strip down. That was what he needed.

"Let's get out of here. Come on, let's go see the Velázquez paintings, or the Goyas, or the Dutch painters."

Helena nodded mechanically, still engrossed in the painting. She kept seeing her son in the doorway, his army jacket soaked from the rain, water dripping from his nose, brows, and lips as he glared at her in hatred.

That night, Helena got on Skype. She needed to speak to David, feel his presence, distant yet comforting. But it was Marta, his partner, who appeared on-screen.

"Helena, what a surprise," she said cordially but noncommittally. Marta must have been the most efficient person in Malmö, perhaps in all of Sweden. Not a minute to waste, she exerted minimal effort for maximum efficacy.

She dressed with an unshakable sense of confidence—a loose-knit sweater, no bra, jeans that were well-worn but high-end, and sandals; her hair was pinned up with a wooden chopstick. Marta was breathtakingly beautiful, a fact that must have seemed to her like the most natural thing in the world. But Helena rejoiced in thinking that one day she'd no longer have such an amazing ass or such taut skin or such a defiant look. David would no longer come running at the slightest provocation to make love to her on the kitchen floor or on top of the desk. The kids would grow up and find their way, and she'd be sidelined, limited to the role of guardian of family memories, a venerable figure on the altar of expendable objects.

Marta inhaled in displeasure and gestured to the space behind her.

"Forgive the mess. Our cleaning lady has been away for a few days because of a family issue."

Helena raised one eyebrow. From what she could see on the screen, the office was what anyone would consider the picture of tidiness. At one edge of the screen smoke or steam wafted up. Maybe herbal tea, or perhaps Marta enjoyed the luxury of a cigarette when she was home alone, when David and the kids weren't around. No doubt she could easily control her urge, taking it and leaving it when she pleased, no struggle.

"I wondered if David was there."

"No, I'm sorry. Did you want me to give him a message?"

Helena took herself to be a patient woman, generally happy and well disposed toward others. But she couldn't quite manage it with Marta; there was something profoundly dislikable about the woman, something she couldn't put her finger on. David always raved about the life he led, his kids, his house, his job, and his dog. Marta, too, seemed more than satisfied with life, but Helena thought that people like Marta could never truly be happy; happiness, to her, was probably crossing the last task off a to-do list.

"I just felt like chatting, that's all."

Marta's face took on a rigid, marblelike quality.

"I guess the two of you need to stick to the schedule," she said in a slightly apologetic tone, though she seemed really to be saying, *All things have an order, and you can't simply change the rules.*

"I understand. I didn't mean to bother you."

Marta seemed relieved. For a second her eyes darted sideways, glancing at something beyond what the camera showed. Helena frowned and got a bad feeling. Was David actually there, hiding off-screen? Was he refusing to speak to her? The possibility horrified her, spreading like the dark crater left by a bomb. She felt pathetic, picturing him gesturing and shaking his head out of the webcam's frame.

"You're not bothering me. You're welcome here."

"It's nothing important. Give David my regards, I'll try to talk to him another time. Goodbye." Shutting down the computer, she felt a profound sense of emptiness, an inner silence that must have been like the weeks she spent in a coma after the car accident that terrible summer thirty-two years ago. She remembered the innumerable sensations that bombarded her upon waking from the coma:

penetrating light, tubes connecting her body to a respirator, Walter's unreadable expression, the rumblings of fear and sadness, the certainty that something awful and irreparable had happened. Something that was all her fault.

Helena put on her jacket and went into the hallway to find Miguel's room. She didn't want to be alone with those memories.

He opened the door in his pajamas. He was about to go to bed.

"Are you okay?"

Helena didn't have the strength to fire off one of her sarcastic comebacks.

"What I told you today in the museum...I hope I didn't come off as pathetic."

Miguel shook his head.

"I know plenty of pathetic people, and you don't fit the profile. Do you want to come in?"

Miguel's room was identical to hers, even the hunting scene picture on the wall was the same. Miguel had the TV on with the volume muted. Judging by the desk light that was on and the chair now askew, he'd been writing when Helena knocked on the door.

"I don't want to interrupt you," she said, glancing at the half-written letter, pen abandoned on the paper.

Miguel sat down beside her on the edge of the bed.

"I was finished. It's a letter to Carmen, the woman I told you about. What you said today made me think about the things we thought we did right, the things we renounced in the name of common sense and propriety, cop-outs that were really just cowardice. I told myself maybe it's not too late to pick up a few loose threads, give them a tug, and see where they go."

Helena feigned applause.

"Finally, he makes a decision. So, what do you say to someone you've left hanging in the balance for ten years?

"I asked her to go out with me in Barcelona."

"And you expect her to say yes? You've got some balls, Miguel. Well, good for you. Don't forget to take her flowers."

"Flowers?"

"Yes. The oldest trick in the book still works. Flowers soften a woman's heart, make it tender. I remember the first bouquet Walter ever gave me: lilies of the valley. He looked sadly comical holding a tinfoil-wrapped bouquet so tight it was like he was strangling the flowers rather than offering them to me. But it was a lovely gesture."

Miguel smiled sadly. Helena's voice sounded phony, she was trying her hardest to show him that this was merely a courtesy visit.

"I guess our journey together has come to an end. My train to Barcelona leaves first thing. What about you? Did you and David agree on a date so he can pick you up at the airport? You said you were speaking to him today."

Helena avoided her reflection in the wardrobe mirror. She was squeezing her hands so hard it was as if she wanted to pull them off at the wrist.

"I was wondering if you'd mind my coming with you to Barcelona. I've never been, so while you're off winning

444

back your true love, I could be a tourist: Gaudí, Picasso, Las Ramblas—the usual tourist things."

Miguel hesitated.

"But, what about your trip to Malmö?"

Helena shrugged.

"Malmö can wait a few days. I'm still not sure it's safe to leave you on your own, even if you did shave off your mustache. Someone's going to have to pick up the pieces if Lady Love gives you the brush-off."

Helena's nervous giggle disconcerted Miguel as much as the insecurity in her voice. She was begging him not to leave her alone right now.

"That's not how we planned it."

Helena pouted.

"What's wrong with a little improvisation? I just feel like being with you for a little longer, that's all."

"Okay, no problem," Miguel replied, not understanding what lay behind Helena's sigh of relief.

22

Malmö

The woman looked up at the storm clouds and cursed. She'd never come this far before. She realized just how far she was on catching sight of Lake Vättern's western shore in the distance, the colors of the landscape reflected in its glassy surface: blues, reds, and the ocher tones of the trees. She was unfamiliar with these less-traveled trails, and the recent rains had rendered them almost impassable.

She shouted for her dog, increasingly upset. He'd strayed from view on a trail with fallen branches that was almost hidden by the brush. Leash in hand, she made her way along carefully, stepping slowly for fear of cutting herself on a rusty can or broken bottle hidden in the high grass. With each step she had to pull branches back so as not to scratch her face and arms, and sidestep big dead roots and large rocks. From time to time, her sandals sank into sludgy fresh mud.

"I swear to God, this time you're going back to the pound," she mumbled as she yanked aside a branch brushing her cheek.

The woman struggled through the brush until the path—long since abandoned, overrun by tall weeds and thistle, no trace of humans—suddenly opened onto a clearing. She could see a tumbledown sort of shack at the end of it, and beyond that, a lush forest.

Suddenly, she crinkled her nose at an intense, unpleasant stench. Insects buzzed and, somewhere, she heard a growl.

"Byron, is that you?" As she approached, the smell got stronger, more concentrated, almost stifling—the smell of rotting flesh. She had to cover her mouth and nose with one hand.

Finally, she saw her dog struggling furiously with something.

"What on earth are you doing, dumb dog?"

The dog stepped back with his hind legs for leverage, his head whipping quickly back and forth with something between his teeth that he was frantic to unearth.

The woman fell silent as her eyes processed what they were seeing. A hand, sticking out of the soft earth that her dog had dug up. One finger was in his mouth, the others jutted out like hooks, pointing to the sky as if desperate for fresh air.

Her eyes wide in horror, the woman backed up, stumbled and fell to the ground but kept backing up on elbows and heels. Finally, she stood and ran for the path, no longer caring about the branches scraping her cheeks and limbs, arms windmilling to clear a path through the foliage.

The dog grew still, slobbering, with a piece of flesh between his jaws; he looked around with yellowy eyes until, hearing the first clap of thunder, he started, raised his head to the sky—now like a solid-gray block of concrete—and abandoned his treasure, running off after his owner.

Raquel felt like a little girl throwing pebbles against a wall. A pointless gesture, something done out of tedium rather than having any concrete objective.

She'd been told that this fortune-teller was the best, the heiress of ancient arcana, the offspring of wise old witches skilled in forbidden religions and deeds. Maybe so, but Raquel disliked the woman's smile, which displayed a set of gums with no teeth except two nicotine-stained incisors. As though embracing stereotype, the diviner wore excessive makeup in a crazy combination of colors: dark eye shadow and blue eyeliner, very red lipstick and pale blush; she even had a fake mole. Her hair was in a high bun, and she wore an Egyptian-style necklace, huge gold earrings, and a mauve dress that clung to her generous proportions. It was hard to guess how old she was under the getup; she could have been thirty or a thousand.

The room the fortune-teller called her *consultation office* was lit by a single candle placed in the center of the table, its flickering flame projecting shadows of crosses, rosaries, pagan images, and angels on the wall. Sture would have found the over-the-top atmosphere comical, but Raquel found it bleak and formidable.

"The stone that was blocking your path is now gone," the fortune-teller said, opening her eyes, which until that moment had been closed, flitting nervously as if in a trance, during which she'd pronounced some sort of incomprehensible mantra.

"What does that mean, exactly?" She may have been the best fortune-teller in all of Malmö—at fifty euros per thirty-minute session, not including "requests"—but clarity was not her strong suit. It was as though her only job was to say things, and the responsibility of making sense of them fell to others.

"It means what you want it to mean," she responded, placing her hands on the tablecloth. She had rings on every finger, with different colored stones set in old silver.

Raquel looked up and saw a cabinet full of elixirs, ointments, and potions—part of the props. Undoubtedly the bottles were all full of water, but that's as good a placebo as any when a gullible client wants to believe.

"So, what I asked you to do is done?"

"Your enemy is no longer an obstacle," the woman replied with a conniving look and a nod.

Raquel sighed in relief. Yasmina wouldn't be interfering in her plans anymore, the whore. But the fortune-teller took no time in quashing Raquel's optimism.

"But now another danger lurks, a much greater one that will require all my efforts and energy."

Sture would have burst out laughing. Swindlers are always hiding an ace up their sleeve. They manufacture needs and then offer to meet them, for a price. That kind of thing tried Raquel's patience.

"I thought that slut was the only thing in my way."

The fortune-teller gave her words a sinister tinge to generate fresh insecurities:

"There are two sides to every truth. And without them both, the truth does not exist."

Raquel was starting to lose her cool.

"I'm not paying you to speak in riddles."

The woman gazed at her like a hunk of flesh with eyes that saw nothing.

"You paid me to invoke forces and remove the girl from your path. I have done it, so you have nothing to reproach me with. But the greater dangers are those we don't see, the ones hiding right beside us. Is it not those closest to us who have the power to do us the most harm? Those we trust wholeheartedly, to whom we are endlessly devoted. They are the cause of our greatest pain."

"Are you talking about my husband, Sture?"

The woman shook her head slowly.

"You've built your castle on dangerous ground, Raquel. At the confluence of two rivers with equally strong currents: love and ambition. And one of the two is going to burst its banks."

Raquel's face darkened. She'd gone to the fortune-teller in search of good news but now things were taking on a more ominous bent.

"If not Sture, then who?"

"It's not your husband you give your real love to. He is not the one who wields that power," the woman said mildly, her words light and fluffy, floating through the room. Raquel felt a sudden chill and got goosebumps. It was as if someone had opened a window in the middle of a snowstorm.

"My son?"

"You spoke those words, not I."

Suddenly Raquel no longer believed this impostor. She now saw her as a ridiculous, toothless caricature with a hoard of phony paraphernalia. The more she looked at her, the sharper her fury.

"You're crazy. Erick would never turn against me. Everything I do, I do for him, and he knows that."

The woman didn't bat an eye.

"There are two sides to love, and one doesn't always match the other. Your faith in your son is unshakable, but perhaps the same cannot be said of his faith in you."

Raquel slammed a hand on the table so hard the candle trembled, making the shadows on the wall flitter.

"Enough! You're insane, and I'm doubly so for having believed you."

The fortune-teller placed her hands in her lap and then stood solemnly, like a nun after prayers. But in the back of her eyes the glint of scorn twinkled.

"That's not what you thought when you came looking for me to curse an innocent. You cannot choose the part you like and simply cast off the rest. It is what it is, like it or not. I only tell you what I see. Do with it as you will."

The woman glanced at the door and pressed her lips together before speaking again, this time in a lighter tone.

"I have another client waiting. That's fifty euros, please."

Returning to Old Sweden, Raquel found Erick behind the bar, as he was every day at that time. When there were no customers, he used the time to do his homework.

"What are you reading?"

With a bored expression, her son held up his history book.

"The French Revolution—gripping," he said sarcastically.

Raquel banished the fortune-teller's words from her mind. She went to her son and kissed his head, not minding that he flinched.

"Did I ever tell you about when you were born? Such a difficult birth. It took you almost ten hours to finally come out. You wanted to stay where you were, but I rescued you, brought you into the world. You and I both almost died in the process, but we stuck together, did what we had to do."

Erick nodded wearily. He'd heard this story hundreds of times: how his mother had to go against her parents, who wanted her to have an abortion because she was so young; how she got sick after giving birth, but in spite of that, exhausted and feverish, fled from the hospital with her child in arms after finding out that her parents had given permission for the nuns who ran the maternity clinic to put him up for adoption. It was the same old story: the hard life, the adversities, the effort she'd made to always feed him first, make sure his needs were met at all costs, and try to find them a new family and a better future. Together. Always together.

"Do you mind, Mother?" he said, pointing at his history book with a pen. "The sansculottes are about to guillotine a bunch of aristocrats, and I don't want to miss it."

Raquel nodded.

"Where's your father?"

"Dead, the last I heard. Or at least that's what you've always told me."

"Don't get smart with me. I can still smack you, you know. Sture, I mean."

Erick pointed his pen scornfully over his shoulder to the storeroom.

"The great man is at rest."

Sture was sitting on the sofa. In one hand an open beer, in the other the remote control. He was preoccupied by whatever was on the screen and hardly reacted when Raquel came over and gave him a kiss on the right corner of his mouth.

"What are you watching?" She looked at the TV.

A legion of police officers were swarming over a section of scrubland near Lake Vättern as a helicopter buzzed overhead, circling one particular spot repeatedly. The officers had cordoned off the area with crime-scene tape and were stopping the lookie-loos and the press from getting too close. Though they'd tried to keep the scene private by erecting a cloth partition, cameras had managed to capture the moment the forensic team lifted a mud-covered body and carefully deposited it onto a metal stretcher.

"It's her," Sture murmured sadly, suddenly forlorn.

Raquel flinched. She clenched her jaw and got closer to the TV to make sure her eyes weren't deceiving her.

"How do you know?"

Sture turned his head to the side, as though he wanted to look away but couldn't. He rubbed his hands over his face brusquely, but his expression was unreadable.

"They had her prints; Yasmina was on their radar. And it won't take the police long to link her to me."

Raquel sat down beside him and stroked his shoulder cautiously. She gazed steadily at Sture, her own expression equally difficult to read. He looked at her ringed fingers, her perfect nails, knuckles strong and knotty. This was a hand that knew what it wanted and was prepared to grab it.

"They can't do anything to you. She's no longer a threat. We can move on with our lives now."

Sture flipped the channel absently. The weather in Lapland: Who needed eighteen hours of sun a day? All that would do is drive a person mad. The weatherman informed them that in parts of the north, temperatures would drop below zero and there would be snowfall, while in Stockholm temperatures would reach 17 degrees Celsius. He clicked to another channel: political disagreements in Parliament. Sture frowned. Sometimes he hated his country. Especially when he couldn't recognize it. The Social Democrats put him in a bad mood. Where were the good old patriots? Sweden needed men like Åkesson, leader of the Swedish Democrats, to take the country back for the Swedes.

"Why the fuck should we be the ones to take in the outcasts of the world?"

Suddenly, from the kitchen, came the aroma of the roast *falukorv* that Raquel had prepared that morning; no one in all of Sweden could take a simple sausage dish and turn it into a delicacy the way she did. He had to concentrate on the familiar aroma, and on the same old arguments, pretend that life went on, that a death changed nothing. Keep pretending to be a modest restaurateur, an honorable citizen concerned about nuclear disarmament, saving the whales, European values, all the crap normal people were supposed to care about when in fact they didn't give a shit.

Raquel stroked his cheek.

"This is all connected somehow. The world has its logic, you know? For her to disappear now, of all times, that's a sign."

He gave her a weary look.

"Logical for who?"

"For you, for me. For our son."

There were no secrets between them, never had been—at least not the kind that might ruin a marriage. Raquel knew what Sture did and didn't care about that. She didn't want to know the details and wasn't worried about the future as long as they were together. The one condition was that his activities not put Erick in danger.

"Our son?"

Sture would have liked to have a son with *his* blood coursing through his veins. Erick was timid and wimpy; the only reason Sture took him in and gave him his last name was that Raquel would never have married him if he hadn't. She had big plans for Erick, wanted him to study economics at the University of Stockholm, saw him as a future entrepreneur who'd turn Old Sweden into a chain and expand it like IKEA or Volvo. No whores, no drugs, no underhanded dealings with two-bit traffickers. Nothing that might distract the boy from his promising future. And yet the more Erick attempted to get close to Sture, the more he was spurned: like an abused dog, the kid offered his affection to a man who didn't deserve it.

"Yes, your son," Raquel responded categorically. "We're a family, Sture. We protect each other at all costs."

Sture felt his wife's persistent stare. He knew she was fixing her gaze on the drops of sweat in the fleshy folds of his neck and his worn collar. Sometimes when she was really turned on, she licked the sweat from his groin and chest. Raquel wiped his sweat with the palm of her hand.

"I have to ask, Sture. Was it you?"

She knew the history between Sture and Fatima from years ago. It was a difficult period full of jealousy and sleepless nights, violent arguments and threats of leaving. It all came to a swift end the day Raquel showed up at Fatima's wretched apartment, grabbed her by the hair right in front of Abdul, and dragged her down the stairs with a ham knife to her throat. Raquel gashed one of Fatima's breasts and then left her on the street, bleeding like a stuck pig, as a warning.

"Me?"

"Were you the one who had Yasmina killed?"

She suspected that the story was repeating itself with Yasmina. The women in Abdul's family exerted a strange, destructive power over men. But as far as Yasmina went, Raquel was totally off base. His wife would never understand. Otherwise she'd never have asked him if he'd had her killed. His own daughter. Sture smiled wryly. He wondered what Raquel would think of what he'd done to the girl weeks ago, the vicious way he'd punished and threatened her, pushing her to this tragic end. Obviously, he'd been that hard on her in order to send Deputy Chief Gövan a strong message. But had that been the only reason? No, of course not. Love is a weakness if it's not reciprocated equally; it gives one lover control over the other. In the depths of his murky heart, Sture had discovered his weakness, a deeply buried love that gave Yasmina power over him—as years ago it had with her mother—and she'd begun to exercise her authority, dragging him into the dangerous terrain of emotions.

By forcing her to confront Gövan, to pick a side, Sture had intended to kill that feeling, to prove to himself—and to her—that he was still the same, that nothing had changed. Had he succeeded? He told himself repeatedly that he had, but the fact was that now, seeing Yasmina's open eyes, staring blankly at the overcast sky, covered in mud, carried by strange hands from one place to another, he pictured her body being explored by cold eyes, looking only for signs: the temperature of her organs, her state of decomposition, whether there were abrasions in her anus or vagina. Those strangers might make sick jokes as they examined her at close proximity, opening her chest with an autopsy saw, breaking her sternum while sweat fell from their faces onto Yasmina's dead heart.

"Is that what you want? You want me tell you I was the one who had Yasmina killed?"

Raquel didn't reply, and Sture realized that she'd never have any compassion. That she'd never forgive him if she knew the truth. She would never have accepted a threat to her son's future, any kind of competition. Suddenly, a muffled sound made them turn in unison to the storeroom door. Erick was watching, furious. The history book had fallen from his hands and he hadn't even realized.

ight tended to soften death. Covered with a white sheet that was folded primly under her chin, Yasmina looked like she was having a sad dream, vaguely absent but on the verge of waking up. The humming of the cold storage seemed to invite contemplation and hushed tones, as if the morgue were a chapel.

"It seems a fleeting death, somehow not final," said Inga, chief inspector of forensics.

Gövan didn't respond to his colleague's poetic attempt. The last thing he needed right now was poetry. People just die, and death is definitive. His hands unclenched and he slipped them into his jacket pockets.

"Any indications?"

The inspector pointed to Yasmina's shaved head. Fat stitches covered a good part of her skull.

"At least four blows, probably with an ax or some fairly blunt instrument. It must have been rusty, and whoever did it had to use a lot of force. But there's not a single print."

Gövan looked grim and didn't turn away from Yasmina's face. He was trying to find any sign of guilt within himself, a trace of regret, but he couldn't, and that was what scared him. He didn't see himself as a murderer or a sicko with no capacity for empathy; he'd slept with her, had been inside her—his semen, his saliva—had shared things about his past with her that not even his wife knew. He'd even, at some point, been convinced that he loved her. But now all he felt was relief. That body on the stretcher was foreign to him, it was like there was no link between them, or between what he'd done and the result that now lay before him on the slab. He wished she hadn't been found this quickly, so that he had had some time to erase the images of the lake and the way he'd beaten her from his mind. But there was nothing to be done about that. Now all he could do was feign determination.

"She's one of Sture's whores."

The inspector confirmed it:

"That bastard turns up every time we investigate a murder: the junkie at the port, the decapitated guy in the park, and now this girl. It's like he's out of control. He feels cornered and he's lashing out. We've got to stop him once and for all."

It's an ill wind that blows no good, Gövan thought. All he had to do was take advantage of circumstances. Plus, in a way, it was true that Sture had killed Yasmina—sending her to spy on him, to blackmail him like that. Did the man really think he was going to just stand there and watch as his future went down the drain? If so, he had no idea who he was dealing with.

Gövan didn't see himself like other officers, or even like the politicians, only in it for their own gain. His aims were greater than personal ambition; he had plans, big plans, to change the country. First, he'd become a member of Parliament and then, thanks to his wife's influence and money, who knew? There were no limits on his horizon. He could be truly important, do something good, put an end to the Stures of Sweden once and for all. Yasmina was just collateral damage, a sad but inevitable loss. Maybe in time Gövan would manage to bury her permanently, kill her off forever. As if none of it had ever happened.

"It's still early. We need conclusive proof, or his lawyers will get him off yet again. We'll keep tabs, watch him, let him know the circle is tightening. Maybe he'll get nervous and make a false move." In fact, Gövan was already hatching a different plan in his head, one in which he was the hero his country needed.

The inspector remained pensive.

"What about that phone number we found in the decapitated guy's pocket? Did you get anything on that?"

The mention of Yasmina's phone number made Gövan's stomach clench. There's always a loose end that needs tying up, one that could ruin everything. He'd have to pore over all the details with a fine-tooth comb. How many people could have seen Yasmina in his car, taking her to the lake cabin? The thought made his palms sweat.

"Dead end. But I'm still on it."

The inspector thought she detected a falsely exasperated tone. Maybe she was imagining things. The deputy chief was under a lot of pressure. Sometimes she thought back on the brief affair they'd had, about how idealistic Gövan had been back when they were just starting at the academy. She felt the urge to stroke his cheek to show him that he wasn't alone, but refrained. They weren't the same people anymore.

"One more thing. The girl's mother is here. We called her in to ID the body. You want me to take care of it?"

Gövan shook his head. He'd rather do it himself, he owed Yasmina that much at least—being the one to notify the mother, watching her reaction when she saw the smashed-in skull of the daughter she'd always spurned.

"Send her in."

Fatima walked in with her eyes downcast, as if searching for a place to fix her gaze. Then she saw her daughter's body, now immune from the chaos of the world, free of attachments past and present, and the woman's sphinx-like expression shattered and became one of pain. Her eyes glimmered, but more than tears, it was like they were chunks of ice, melting. She felt an intense emptiness in her stomach, fraught with ghosts, as she walked slowly toward the metal gurney in the middle of the room. Fatima stopped a few centimeters away, unable to move any closer. Her lower lip began to quiver slowly, as if she was reciting a mantra under her breath. She raised her right hand to Yasmina's waxy face but left it suspended in the air, as though an invisible partition kept her from moving farther.

"Can I touch her?" she asked in a voice that seemed to come from the depths of a cavern. Gövan and the inspector glanced at one another. It seemed odd that a mother should ask a couple of strangers for permission to touch her daughter.

"She's cold," the inspector alerted her.

Gövan said nothing, simply watched the woman he'd pictured so differently from Yasmina's stories. He didn't expect her to be this young, or this calm. There was a wounded pride to her manner, as there had been to Yasmina's—a sorrowful aura, a sense that the world owed her a debt that could never be paid but that she refused to write off. He glanced at her fingers as they touched Yasmina's cheek gently, as if the inspector's warning made her fear getting burned. Cold always burns more than heat. She ran her hands over her daughter's forehead, perhaps searching for the curls that the medical examiner had shaved off. These were the hands of someone who'd lost all her dreams.

"We need a positive ID."

Fatima gave a nod, though in fact she didn't feel that this was her daughter or even had been before she died. Her daughter, the real one, had only been hers at the very beginning, a newborn with black fuzz on her head, tiny hands clenched into fists as though already defending herself from what was to come. Back then she had no smell, nothing to say, all she did was sleep on Fatima's chest.

"I didn't want her to be born."

She was talking to herself, eyes sliding over the face that had been smashed in, reduced to nothing. Berating herself for so many lost things it was too late to recover, for the blame she heaped on her daughter before she'd even been born, when she was still in her womb. She remembered the time she threw herself down the stairs, trying to induce a miscarriage, the nights of rage when she'd pound her swollen belly in fury. The hatred dumped on her daughter, the harsh words. Yasmina was born against everyone's will, like a shattered bone sticking through the skin and causing pain, a fracture that leaves permanent scars, a reminder of what Sture had done to Fatima that night on a table in Old Sweden. Every time she saw Yasmina scampering through the house with her different-colored eyes—her blood and Sture's, mixed by force and violence—Fatima was reminded of that night, the intense pain, humiliation, and vileness. She'd been unable to protect her daughter from that, to keep her from the shame and silent recriminating looks everyone had given her from the moment she was born. They'd stolen her childhood, all of them, stolen the joy that should have belonged to her inherently. Yasmina never understood their scorn, never knew why no one put up a fight when Sture came to claim her and turn her into what he did. Fatima tried to rid herself of the vision of her daughter's imploring eyes, her husband's face turned away so as not to see it, the infinite scorn on Abdul's face. She'd bitten it off violently, wrenched it from her heart, amputated a part of herself, and then gangrene had set in and done its job, bringing on a slow death. And now it was too late to do anything. Even if she

463

now told her things she'd never said before, her daughter couldn't hear. She'd come into this world alone, and alone she had gone out. Though blameless, she'd been hurt a thousand times, and when she asked for help was met only with silence.

"She looks so alone," Fatima said. "What did they do to her head? Where is her hair? She had such lovely hair." *In the trash.* That's what Gövan would have liked to say. As incredible as it seemed, he was disgusted by the sudden pity expressed by a mother who'd let all this happen. *You should have protected her. You should have been with her.* He felt the urge to spit in her face.

Inspector Inga touched Fatima's arm gently.

"You're going to need to go now." *Why not look a little longer?* Gövan asked silently. *You don't dare, even now that she can't meet your gaze.*

"Did you know your daughter was a prostitute? She worked for a pimp named Sture," he said with calculated cruelty that brought a look of reproach from the inspector and one of shock from Fatima. *Yes, of course you knew. And you didn't care.*

Fatima pressed her lips to keep them from trembling and lifted her chin, challenging the deputy chief.

"Was it him? Did Sture kill her?"

"We're looking into it."

Fatima shot him a furious look.

"Then rather than judge and try to hurt me, why don't you do your job and arrest that animal?"

23

---

t was the longest letter Carmen wrote him. The last one.

Barcelona, November 1990

Dear Miguel,

Sometimes I stand naked and stroke my belly in the mirror. I did it today, just before sitting down to write to you. I try to picture what my body would be like if I were pregnant—taut skin on my stomach, a heaviness in my lower back, swollen breasts. I shouldn't be thinking about things like this; I can't have kids. Nature gave me a raw deal on that one.

I don't know why I'm telling you this. Maybe because you have a daughter, or I want to tell you something about myself that I'd never tell anyone. Sterility is frowned upon, like a defect, and I don't need people giving me strange looks. I confess I've never felt the draw of motherhood. No doubt if people knew that I don't care about my ovaries shriveling up they'd think I was some kind of monster. People are happy to pity me as long as they think I'm a useless piece of furniture, but not an aberration. My father once told me that a woman who can't have kids is an unnecessary luxury. He's really old now and thinks that gives him the right to hurt my feelings with impunity. I pretend that I feel incomplete around him, as if I were missing a leg or arm. But when I see a pregnant woman or a mother walking by with a stroller, I honestly don't feel much of anything. Slightly curious, maybe dubious, but no resentment.

You might wonder, that being the case, why I started this letter—which I know you'll never answer but hope you'll at least read—by telling you about something impossible and then saying it doesn't matter. My mother died. Her funeral was today. She was seventy-nine years old, and I'm sure some people think she had a long life, but the lives of our loved ones are never long enough. Even if they're sick or in pain; we're selfish, we don't want them to go and leave us alone, locked up with their photos, smelling their clothes, evoking their memories, missing them.

My mother was no longer my mother; in the past few years she only resembled her: bone cancer had reduced her to a slip of a thing who complained of terrible pain, and that pain soured her character. But sometimes, when there was a lull in the agony and she could get out of bed, we'd go for a walk on the beach, just the two of us, and I'd light cigarettes that she smoked, one after the other. She liked to walk barefoot on the shore, and would point to little polished stones and ask me to put them into glass jars that she lined up on a kitchen shelf. She said even the most solid objects got worn down and perished. My mother found existential metaphors in everything. I don't know what I'm going to do with all these jars of stones now. Maybe give them back to the sea so they can finally die in peace.

Today I thought of the last time my mother and I sat by the beach to watch the sunset. It was last winter; it had been raining all day and the air and sand both felt sticky. I felt privileged to have her to myself, to be able to hold her swollen hand, her fingers lightly stained with nicotine. And for the first time, even though I knew she wouldn't approve, I told her about you.

I don't know exactly what I told her, I mean, what could I say? I hardly know you, and I've never heard from you in all these years, so I'm sure whatever I told her was an illusion, some idea I'd fallen in love with after a few hours in an apartment that I turned into some fictional-ized version of my happiness. I ended up crying, despite realizing how crazy it is to miss something that probably never existed outside of my own head.

My mother listened warmly, neither nodding her head nor shaking it; she did, though, offer the certainty of her presence and the infinite love of her gaze. After I calmed down, there was a long silence, and she just stroked my hand across the table without looking at me, gazing at the horizon as it began to turn red. She seemed at peace with herself. And then she told me I should love somebody who deserved my love. That the miracle of a heart open to anything shouldn't be given to someone who doesn't understand the power of that magic. "Love is an adventure for the brave, Carmen. Only for those who dare to go all the way." I asked her if that's how it had been with my father, and she just smiled like a mischievous girl and asked me to light her another cigarette. Now I know that I didn't need her to answer the question for me to know, because the answer was always right in front of me.

I'm sitting here writing to you with my father in the living room, so tall and thin and lost, in his dark suit, as somber as his confusion. He sees my mother everywhere, can't figure out how to prevent the vast loneliness he feels without her. And I don't know how to console him. There's nothing I can do. I know he wants to give up, climb into the bed they shared for so long, and close his eyes. He's stopped telling me to find myself a good man— someone like him, he always seemed to imply. A man for whom happiness was sitting on the sofa with his wife, holding hands as they watched TV, and falling asleep, exhausted. A man who finds it impossible to lie or be fake, who never gets mad at those he loves. A man who, deep down, always thought he fell short of the woman he worshipped.

No one believes in that kind of love anymore. My colleagues, casual boyfriends, they all talk about equality, the importance of being yourself, not being dependent on anyone—personal choice above partnership. The kind of honorable man my mother loved is like a moth-eaten suit—passé, embarrassing. Nobody wants to believe things last forever anymore. Live a little, they say when a man gives me the eye in a club; no complications, no commitments. Carpe diem.

And yet despite all that, despite being witness to the vast pain of losing your rudder, despite realizing the tremendous danger of hanging your happiness on someone else and then ending up alone, I'd like to be like my mother.

You, Miguel, were never that person. At least not for me. I'm not blaming you or reproaching you for anything; nor am I berating myself for having nurtured an unrealistic desire. We all make our choices, and we live with them, but we also have a right to change course. I won't be writing to you anymore. I hope there's someone in your heart who can make you smile the way I saw my mother smile that afternoon on the beach.

I think it's only fair that I give those jars of shells to my father; he'll know what to do with them.

Take care,
Carmen

Miguel shouldn't have reread the last letter. Not before seeing Carmen. It was painful, and true. Without realizing it, the life had gone out of him, and now more than thirty years later here he was, sitting on a bench across the street from the restaurant where they'd arranged to meet so he could monitor the entrance. Miguel didn't expect Carmen to respond to his invitation. But when he heard her voice on the phone—he'd timidly scribbled his phone number in a P.S. by way of suggestion—it was as familiar as if he'd continued to hear her through her letters all those years.

Their first conversation had been short, awkward and bumbling, neither of them having much to say. Not painful, but all very formal. The moment they hung up, after making this date, Miguel got the feeling it had been a bad idea to try to force the past into the present. Now, watching people walk in and out of the restaurant, seeing little groups of elegant men and women clustered around the entrance to smoke, catching a glimpse of the interior—comfortably luxurious—whenever the amber-colored glass door opened, that feeling intensified. To the point that in the last ten minutes, he'd almost left twice. The only reason he didn't was because standing Carmen up seemed as despicable as the stubborn silence with which he'd met each of her letters.

Miguel passed the time inspecting his attire for the hundredth time. He was as nervous as a schoolboy and regretted having taken Helena's advice that he dress informally. As soon as they got to Barcelona, Helena had insisted on taking him shopping around Portal del Ángel. *You don't want your girlfriend turning up to meet a camphor-smelling ghost.* She insisted on calling Carmen his *girlfriend*, which Miguel found as grating as the mocking tone she used to say it. Ever since Helena had found out that Miguel was going to meet Carmen, she'd been behaving strangely, sometimes encouraging him and saying they should live what was left of their lives fearlessly, other times being reticent and sarcastic. Regardless, she was the one who'd selected the jeans Miguel now had on—which made him feel like a totally different person—the blue loafers he was wearing without socks, the pale shirt and summer jacket. Before he left her hotel room, Helena had inspected him and helped adjust the knot of his—overly loud—tie, as Águeda used to do. Then she'd given Miguel the thumbs-up, as though sending him to battle and being unsure he'd be coming back.

"If you need a rescue force, I'll be here reading."

Now the tie seemed more like a noose and he felt overly constrained by his jeans. Miguel sensed that people were giving him looks and he felt ridiculous in young-man's clothes that said nothing about him and were simply a deception. It was all so childish. What was he trying to prove? He'd do better to turn around and go back to the hotel, watch a movie or listen to music, and forget once and for all about the letters, Carmen, and things that didn't exist.

He considered hailing one of the many taxis on Vía Layetana, but then he saw her on the other side of the street, in front of the restaurant. She was smiling warmly. It was her: Carmen. Despite the years gone by, Miguel had done a good job conjuring her up in his imagination. She looked just as he'd pictured her.

And then the thing that had happened to him before happened again, though in a different way. The world disappeared again—or actually maybe the world went silent, leaving him in a hazy dreamlike setting. He couldn't hear the heavy traffic, the honking horns, the pedestrians' footsteps. The whole city disappeared, and there was only a direct path from him to Carmen, or maybe the other way around.

That impression lasted only a few seconds, but it shook him to the core. He looked to the right and saw his father not far off, a few meters away, leaning against one of the lampposts that had gone on, despite the summertime light lingering in the sky. He was smiling. Amador was smiling, encouraging him to cross this river and make it to the other side. *Go on, Son*, he seemed to say. Miguel hadn't seen him since the day he left him in the Valley of the Fallen, surrounded by his mother's ashes. He wanted to talk to him, but his figure departed from the present and vanished into the passersby.

Armed with a self-assurance he didn't actually feel, Miguel crossed the street gazing straight at Carmen's face as she watched him, analyzing each gesture—his stride, the breadth of his shoulders, the passage of time on his face. If she was disappointed, she did a good job hiding it with a warm expression and a relaxed, open greeting. Miguel hesitated, and she took the initiative, giving him a warm kiss on the cheek that left a lipstick mark and the lingering scent of lovely perfume. She told him that he looked good, that without his mustache he looked like a slightly different person, but she could tell by his expression that he was still the same man. She didn't stumble over her words or seem at all fake, just slightly expectant. Miguel wasn't the kind of man to lavish detailed praise but did manage to say that she looked absolutely beautiful. And she really did. He hadn't remembered that she was slightly taller than him, and in the elegant heels she wore that night she was even more so. She wore a black dress with an appreciable yet modest neckline and a wide-buckled belt that accentuated her waist. Her bare arms were toned, and he could see by her legs that Carmen exercised daily. He, in contrast, felt stodgy and flaccid.

It seemed as if their conversation was going to die before it even got started. Then Carmen came to the rescue, taking his arm and steering him to the entrance of the restaurant, which at that hour was crowded enough they didn't feel self-conscious but not so raucous as to prevent intimacy. The maître d' greeted her affectionately; clearly, they knew each other. Carmen was a regular, and when she introduced Miguel as an old friend, he flushed and felt vaguely guilty.

As the maître d' led them to a reserved table in an out-of-the-way spot, Miguel wondered how many men he'd seen Carmen with and what exactly it meant to be an *old friend*.

He intended to start with an apology, but Carmen quickly stopped him with a smile that allowed no dissent. *That's life, what's done is done*, she seemed to say, raising a glass of Bordeaux that had been waiting for them on the table.

"A toast to the here and now."

They toasted, but Miguel barely touched the wine to his lips. Carmen was like a specialist in bridging silences and kept the conversation from faltering; she asked questions and listened actively. She wanted to know about Miguel's life, and although he found it unremarkable, she appeared truly interested, was attentive, nodded and shook her head and made opportune comments, asked follow-up questions. She barely talked about herself, though. Somehow, without their realizing it, time passed, and toward the middle of dinner, Miguel had relaxed enough to be honest and say some of what he'd been practicing with Helena in the hotel.

"I don't really know why I didn't reply to your letters. I think I was afraid of what I might feel. I was scared of emotions."

Carmen tilted her head for a moment and fixed her gaze on a brick wall that gave the dining room a rustic look. Then she slid her glance across the other tables and diners and back to her wine glass, intentionally avoiding Miguel's eyes. Circling the rim of her glass with a polished fingernail, she sighed.

"You know? I told myself I wouldn't talk about the past tonight. Your note surprised me, and made me happy, and I can tell you I've been nervous as a schoolgirl the past few days. You should see the state of my bedroom! I emptied the whole closet trying on clothes. But seeing you now, even if I want to deny it, I can't help thinking about it. Because the past is what brought us here tonight, isn't it? Two people trying to find out if we still are what we once were. So saying that it doesn't matter is pointless, because it does. I was hurt by your silence all those years, every time I wrote to you, of course I was. It's irrational, unbefitting people like you and me who operate on logic, to think that something could happen, to cling to the few hours we spent together and daydream that it could be like that for a lifetime. Maybe it's a sign that my life was too empty if it could be filled by so little."

Her confession had a bitter undertone, but Carmen covered by taking a sip of wine and fixing an impenetrable smile on the table.

"But I don't want to hear any more about the people we used to be, Miguel. I'm here to find out who we are now, at this moment. I shouldn't have written you those letters."

"And maybe I shouldn't have held on to them."

"Then let's burn them tonight. A toast, to the doors we close."

They both gave slightly fake laughs, full of goodwill but not passion. After dinner, they ordered another bottle of wine, and when they looked around and saw that they were almost the only ones in the restaurant, began opening up. Miguel realized, raising a wineglass to his lips, that he was telling Carmen about Natalia and her awful relationship with Gustavo.

"Give her time; she'll come around."

He shook his head with a slightly faraway look in his eyes.

"Strange, that's what Helena says." Carmen straightened up and pouted.

"Helena?"

"A friend."

"Tell me about this friend."

"She's just a friend, nothing more. We're taking a trip together—well, part of it."

Carmen insisted, so Miguel gave her a few details about how they'd met and why they'd decided to start a journey together: his ended here, while Helena was going on to Sweden. Though he didn't realize it, when he described Helena, his enthusiasm made Carmen give a sad smile.

"It seems she's more than a friend, at least to you."

Miguel leaned back in his chair, not comprehending Carmen's stunned look. He waved his hand dismissively.

"No, no, nothing like that. We're like night and day," he said quickly.

Carmen narrowed her gaze.

"Isn't that precisely what attracts people to one another?"

Miguel felt slightly flustered by what her look seemed to imply. He wasn't sure why but he didn't feel comfortable talking to Carmen about Helena.

"Goodness, it's so late," he said, looking at the last table, where people were now standing.

"Thirty years late, apparently," Carmen said, only half-joking.

They walked out onto the street far calmer than they had been hours earlier. The city was silent and looked different under the light of the streetlamps. They decided to walk for a bit, up to the taxi stand by the cathedral plaza. Carmen lit a cigarette and slowed her pace to match Miguel's.

"You know what I liked most about you, Miguel? Your fear of making one false move. It made you timid and tender at the same time. You were a man with a boy's expression, a man who felt out of place among all those bankers even though you knew more than any of them. I have a feeling that deep down you're still like that. You have the same passion when you talk about your daughter, the same contained gestures, the same way you hide behind your glasses so no one can read your expression. You're even uncomfortable having me this close, aren't you?"

"It's just that I don't want to be an inconvenience, that's all," he apologized stiffly, uneasy at Carmen leaning her body against his as she took his forearm.

She laughed, recovering her earlier relaxed joviality. She took a long drag on her cigarette before stopping, her arm forcing Miguel to do the same. Then she looked into his eyes, up close.

"You didn't tell me why you wanted to see me. What are we doing here tonight, Miguel?"

Miguel diverted his glance to the small park by the Roman wall, where a young homeless couple slept, hidden among piles of backpacks and street dogs.

"Miguel, look at me, stop running away. Tell me: What, exactly, were you hoping for tonight?"

He forced himself to turn to her, hesitation in his eyes.

"I honestly don't know. I felt that I needed to come to terms with it all. That I owed you an apology."

"That's all? No unfinished business? Because I'll tell you why I'm here—to close a circle between us."

She was the one to make a move and kiss him. And though Miguel had wanted it for so long, he would never have dared to take that step. Helena would have laughed at him, at what she called his near-pathetic caution. Still, when their lips touched, Miguel felt that it was all too much effort, that none of it flowed naturally, and that kissing Carmen was like kissing the aura of something that no longer existed, maybe never had existed anywhere but his imagination. Her letters were real, and so were the fantasies he harbored all those years and the woman he'd spent a few unforgettable hours with in 1980. He'd been hoping to find her exactly the same, immutable—the woman in the letters, her familiar voice. But the beautiful woman now pressed to his lips was just a reflection of that memory, and no matter what tricks or self-deception he employed, no matter how hard he tried, that wasn't going to change. They could keep it up, venture a little further, get into a taxi and then lock themselves in a room, press their bodies together, but not truly become one. That was impossible now, and afterward what was left would be far worse than the memories they'd cherished and nourished. Before their lips even parted, they both realized as much.

"It's not working, is it? Our train left the station."

Miguel apologized, but she stroked his cheek affectionately.

"Don't apologize for having once felt something you no longer feel, Miguel. I just had to know. That's all."

Miguel spotted a dead frond on a palm tree. Nothing would bring it back to life, but it clung to the trunk, fused to it. And yet it was nothing but an inert, lifeless remnant. When the municipal gardeners pruned the tree, it would be relieved to be freed from a dead past. He was almost feeling sorry for himself, but Carmen rescued him from that fate with a joke about old people and their yearnings. They continued walking in step to the taxi stand, where they said their goodbyes, promising to meet up again, not to let time get in the way of what little they once had in common. But as Carmen climbed into her cab, they both knew they'd never see each other again, that sometimes two lives come into contact for one magic moment, never to be repeated.

Why was she listening to that song now, so many years later? It had been Louise's favorite; the morning of the accident, she'd been singing along with Frank Sinatra at the top of her lungs. Helena had never wanted to hear it again after that day. Scent and sound can bring us back to the past, memories flooding us unexpectedly with a certain aroma or song. Helena had been sitting on the balcony of her hotel room that night, gazing at the deserted beach, when the song on the Muzak reached her as she worked her way steadily through the contents of the minibar as the pile of butts in the plastic ashtray continued to grow. Helena was thinking of Louise and scratching the scar on her leg with one fingernail. She knew she was wallowing in self-pity, feeling abandoned with Miguel off on his date with Carmen.

He deserved this. Didn't everyone? To find answers and see the dream he'd deferred for so long finally fulfilled. Deserved to live a long life and find peace at the end of it, find meaning in everything, a love that made sense of the life he'd lived. So why wasn't she happy for him? They'd made an agreement; this was the end of their trip together. Miguel had reached his destination, and now she had to decide whether to carry on to her own invented yet indispensable destination, which could be Malmö or anyplace else. No one would know the difference. If she died here, overlooking a beach lined with identical lampposts and sickly palm trees, no one would even notice she was gone. Miguel. He would. Helena wanted to believe that.

There was a knock at the door. Helena glanced at her watch in surprise. It was almost three in the morning. She searched the bed for her pajama top, put it on, and opened the door. And there was Miguel, handsome and awkward, maddeningly silent, with a different sort of glimmer in his eye, a rebellious glint. Helena's glance fell to the bottle of cava in his hand.

He smiled and raised the bottle.

"Aren't you going to invite me in?"

Helena stared at her friend. Something about him was different. There was a new keenness in his expression, and a steady desire in his beautiful eyes. He'd taken off his glasses, the knot on his tie was loosened, and he smelled vaguely of alcohol. She stood to one side to let him in with a theatrical flourish. Miguel walked to the center of the room and looked around, his glance stopping at the table on the balcony covered in miniature bottles of booze and cigarette butts. He set the cava on the dresser and walked to the window. Helena closed the door and walked over to stand to his right.

"Do you want to tell me how it went?"

Miguel shrugged.

"It went exactly the way it needed to go."

"What does that mean? You should be up to your eyeballs in Viagra, giving it your all right now. If you're here, something went wrong."

Miguel tilted his head toward Helena. He was a little nervous and didn't understand why. Or, rather, he understood only too well the reason why. He'd had time to reflect on his feelings on the way over, on the lightness he felt after leaving Carmen, on the urgent need that hurried his steps, the closer he got to Helena. He understood exactly what had prompted him to stop at a Pakistani-run corner store to buy the bottle of cava and why he'd knocked on Helena's door without even stopping at his own. He knew what he wanted and finally dared to take a step toward it. He wasn't going to let love letters stand in for reality anymore. Miguel was tired of collecting mementos to evoke memories later. He wanted to experience them here and now. Truly, he had every right to expect much more of himself.

Quickly, he stroked Helena's hair, and this was so unprecedented as to seem downright audacious. He wanted to shrink from her curious, perplexed look but something stopped him. This time, his fingers carefully reached for the curve of her chin, and then rested near her lower lip.

"I've lived my whole life without having the courage required to just be myself. I don't mean to say that I was a coward when I decided not to take things further with Carmen; that wasn't what I wanted, it never was. I liked my life at the bank, and with Águeda and Natalia. But I think I lacked the intelligence, the vision, and the courage to make the most of each day. And then suddenly, when I no longer expected anything, you appeared, shrouded in that mist that surrounds you. So real, so close, and it's like I want to be surrounded by that mist, want to touch it, breathe it."

Helena hugged herself. Suddenly she felt both warm and cold at the same time.

"Well, well, well . . ." she murmured, moving slightly away and fixing her gaze on the seafront promenade, where a cleaning truck advanced slowly, its orange lights casting a circular pattern as it drove. "No one has ever made a such a metaphorical pass at me before; that is what you're doing, right? Making a pass at me?"

But Miguel didn't lose his nerve. He wasn't thinking about whether he'd be rejected or accepted. He was simply, for once in his life, trying to be himself, express his thoughts freely, without fearing that he might come off as ridiculous, or weighing his words and gestures. He'd already wasted too much time, almost all the time he had.

"Suddenly I'm too bold? You're the one who accused me of being insipid."

"I can think of two possible reasons for this sudden emotional release. The first is that Carmen rejected you, and now you're coming in search of a placebo so as not to waste the Viagra you took in anticipation of the heroic deeds you might perform. The second, no less plausible, is that you drank more than you're used to, and wandering down the empty streets, you suddenly felt nostalgic, old, and alone, and decided I feel the same and that two lonely old souls equals one companionship. I'm sorry, but you'd be incorrect in both cases."

Miguel had learned to interpret Helena's faux ennui and knew what her phony sarcasm and ironic comments hid.

"I didn't take anything, and I certainly don't think we're two old folks who need to cling together to keep from drowning. Neither of us is like that. And it's true, coming here I did realize something. I might have realized it sooner, in Madrid, or the day of your friend Marqués's funeral. I don't know when it happened, but while I was having dinner with Carmen, telling her about you, I realized that there's something between us, something that's been there all along."

Helena blushed slightly. She could no longer hide behind her usual dodges.

"And what's that?"

She didn't need an answer and Miguel didn't give her one. He hadn't predicted how things would go, didn't know what he'd do when she was right there in front of him. He simply stopped thinking, and that was a revelation. His hand reached out, he slipped it just below her ear, and pulled her to him, her lips to his. And it was marvelous, being in the here and now, lips parted, half in surprise and half in desire. Feelings. Growing slowly, not with the abruptness of youth or the irrepressibility of desire. Feelings were what had grown steadily between them.

Helena closed her eyes and let herself be carried away by Frank Sinatra's voice, accompanied by Louise, singing along over the sound of the car's engine as they raced along the curves of Tarifa at top speed.

Fly me to the moon, and let me play among the stars.

24

Barcelona

Darkness can be flattering. Lying in bed, Helena had no desire to turn on the light yet. They'd made love in the dark not because they were afraid of seeing what they already knew—that they were old and so were their bodies—but to delight in the miracle of fingers and mouths. They pretended to be shadows, sensing each other, laughing at themselves and their shadows. It didn't feel to either of them that hours had gone by, and yet the weak light of daybreak was slowly filtering into the room, bringing them slowly back to a less ethereal state. Miguel leaned over Helena, kissing one of her dark nipples. She shivered and let out an exhausted laugh. Their smells blended together in the sheets, creating a new and different one—that of their union, of them both, erasing the impact of the past.

"I wish I'd met you earlier," Miguel said, sounding remorseful. Suddenly he'd felt wounded, vaguely intuiting the men who'd formed part of this chemistry of smells.

Helena sensed this and pulled away cautiously.

"Ah, retrospective jealousy."

He shook his head and leaned on the pillow.

"That's not what I meant; it's something else . . ."

Helena jumped out of bed to look for her cigarettes. Miguel stared admiringly at her beautiful legs and buttocks, no longer firm but still delicious. She realized what he was doing and let him observe her, smiling naughtily before climbing back into bed with a lit cigarette. At one point in the night he'd had fun counting her freckles.

"Okay, then, what do you mean?" she asked, pulling the sheet up to her chest.

Miguel gazed admiringly at her neck. He had little experience with women. With the exception of that weekend with Carmen, he'd never been unfaithful to Águeda, and no one had come before her. But something told him that Helena was and had been exceptional in many respects, including as a lover. He blushed almost apprehensively, recalling his surprisingly insistent erection and the things they'd both said and done until just a few minutes ago.

"I've just been through the most intense time of my life."

Helena winked. She looked beautiful with no makeup, her hair disheveled and face clearly exhausted.

"Don't go too far over the top or it'll sound like charity."

"I'm being serious, Helena. These months we've had together, what happened with Natalia, your help...and last night..."

Helena turned onto her side, resting the cigarette hand on her hip. Her eyes filled with tenderness. She was so close to Miguel that their two morning breaths became one, absorbing each other's words.

"Are you insinuating that we're not just two horny friends? This wasn't a one-night stand?"

Miguel looked at the hotel room—the disheveled sheets on the bed, their clothes jumbled on the floor, the open balcony door, the smell of cigarettes heavy in the air, the empty cava bottle and glasses—like an intruder; he was filled with premature nostalgia.

"I could be this man, the man I am right now, all the time. I could really do it, I can feel it—be happy, intensely alive. I could acknowledge what I feel, call it love."

Helena scooted a bit higher on the pillow. Her eyes focused intensely on a tiny hair on Miguel's shoulder. She felt filled with intense warmth. Something inside her was growing increasingly excited.

"And what would be wrong with that?" she dared to ask.

Miguel turned to her, quiet, on the brink of something that hadn't happened but would. A shadow projected over the joyful present, snatching it away.

"I think I may have taken a lifetime to discover the man I am, but within two years, maybe sooner, I won't even remember him. Alzheimer's will devour these moments. I won't even know that this happened. It's so cruel, the idea of finding something, relishing it for an instant, and forgetting it forever."

Helena looked startled. She looked for the ashtray in order to buy herself a few seconds, to compose her expression, and then turned back to Miguel and curled up in his lap.

"I'll be your memory, Miguel. I'll remember for the both of us."

ater, when Miguel fully woke up, Helena's side of the bed was cold. The daylight streaming in was bright and he heard the sounds of people strolling up and down the promenade.

Miguel stretched, feeling he hadn't slept so well in years. Of course, his whole body hurt—the genital region in particular—but he was filled with renewed energy. He put on his pants and went out to the balcony. Helena was leaning over the railing, the ever-present cigarette in one hand and a cup of coffee in the other. She'd showered, and when Miguel walked over and gave her a kiss on the neck he could tell that the aromas of the night had been substituted by a pleasant soapy smell. Helena had put on a long, flowing dress that clung to her legs in the sea breeze.

"Are you off in space?" he asked, noting her pensive look.

She pulled the still damp hair from her face.

"I was thinking about how similar and yet different every seashore is. It's paradoxical, the way I'm petrified of the sea and yet always feel the need to have it within reach."

Something had happened between when they'd fallen asleep in each other's arms and now. Helena wasn't the same. Miguel could tell. Did she regret what had happened? That possibility gave him a slightly queasy feeling. He didn't want the hours they'd spent to seem clichéd in the cold light of day, didn't want to feel that their words and expressions no longer held the same significance. She sat down on the wooden bench behind her, lifted her skirt above her knees and massaged the scar on her leg.

"All that exercise is taking its toll. I'm no longer so skilled at acrobatic sex," she said, poking a bit of fun at herself and the night they'd spent together.

Miguel acknowledged the comment with a brief grimace.

"Is that all it is? You seem different this morning."

Helena remained pensive, gazing out at the beach, now full of sunbathers and umbrellas, people selling canned drinks from coolers. It reminded her of Tangier, where similar vendors sold homemade ice cream that she used to love. She remembered her intense curiosity on seeing Muslim women covered head to toe walk to the waterfront and wet their feet, in a section of the beach cordoned off from the men. And naked boys leaping in the waves as their sisters looked on enviously from the sand. These were the sorts of things she'd told Louise over that fateful summer, and now all of it—the memories, the present, images of childhood, flashes of her night with Miguel, traveling with Louise—was part of a sequence that overlapped again and again. As if time were circular rather than a straight line.

"There's something I have to tell you, Miguel. Something about my past that you need to know. Or that I need to explain. Something that happened thirty-two years ago."

t had been difficult to convince Walter that her trip to Spain was absolutely vital to her professional career. He found it odd that the company Helena worked for would suddenly deem her services essential in Andalucía.

"You're always complaining that they don't value you, and now out of the blue they want you to go away for a whole week?"

"And that's exactly why I can't say no."

"Just like that? With no planning, no nothing? What's so urgent?"

Louise was so urgent. After David caught them in bed together, things had gone into overdrive. Helena had tried to speak to her son, explain it to him, but David had refused to discuss it outright. *I have no idea what you're talking about.* It was like he'd convinced himself that he hadn't seen what he'd seen. But Helena was worried. The fear that David might decide to spill the beans to his father hung over her head like a sword, and she had no way of knowing when it might fall. That was the reason she told Louise they had to stop seeing each other, at least as lovers. Helena was confused about her feelings, but she wasn't going to risk the stability of her family or the security her situation afforded her.

At first Louise tried to talk her down, saying that David wouldn't say anything, that he liked Louise too much to do that. *Besides, he might not actually have seen what you think he saw.* Helena became furious. *You were there, you saw the shocked look on his face just like I did.* And Louise fired back, her own fury growing in turn: *Well, I guess you'll have to choose your priorities, Helena.*

They stopped seeing each other for a few weeks. Louise moved into a small apartment in Shepherd's Bush, which really pleased Walter, whose daily run-ins with Louise had turned into his only form of communication. But Helena thought about her all the time; and even though she tried to accept the new situation that she herself had occasioned, she couldn't stop thinking that she deserved a little happiness too. Without intending to, she vented her unhappiness onto Walter and David, making veiled accusations against them for being the cause of her misery, arguing over the silliest things, provoking situations that enabled her to unleash her bitterness.

Finally, one morning Helena took Walter's car and drove over to Shepherd's Bush.

They slept together and all of their anxiety dissolved, but once their physical urges had been satisfied, reality reared its head once more, like a boulder between them. Louise curled up in bed, hugging her knees, her beautiful long legs on display as she stared into space. She was still sweating and her skin was covered in scratch marks and red blotches when she told Helena that the time to decide had come. She spoke slowly, as though weighing each word carefully. There was no turning back: Helena could be with Louise or have her old life, but not both. *I need time,* Helena responded as she fastened her bra, her back turned. It sounded like the same old dusty excuse, a way of attempting to defer yet again.

That had been half a lifetime ago, but Helena could still feel Louise's eyes like a slap in the face in the darkness of that modest bedroom, the cold glint in her eyes when she told her to open the nightstand drawer and Helena found two tickets to Spain, plus hotel reservations. *One week. Give me seven days, Helena. Then decide.*

"It's strange to truly discover a country you thought you knew, holding hands with someone who gives you a new perspective on yourself. The countryside and Louise seemed to join forces on that trip, defining my happiness, showing me what life could be like, if I wanted it. There were endless clear skies and violet dusks; hours spent in little bars in the remote villages of Serranía de Ronda; days spent at little tables in a church square watching women who looked like they were from a Spain trapped in the past walk by, in permanent mourning. I remember the lazy way dogs walked up in that heat to drink from the fountain and the games children played, drawing on cobblestones with chalk; private conversations over *cortado* coffees that slowly went cold; chatting with old folks who smelled of cheap cigars and anisette; rolling cigarettes in shop doorways; holding hands under the tablecloth at a restaurant in Cádiz, staring at each other, our silence full of passion even when we were surrounded by people on Calle Larios in Málaga. I remember a Buñuel movie we went to see, sitting close in the last row, making out in the dark, and the amazing magical day we bumped into the poet Rafael Alberti in a used bookstore, leafing through the complete works of Juvenal and Persius in Latin. Neither of us had the nerve to approach him despite knowing so many of his poems by heart. We spent the rest of the afternoon reciting them, thrilled."

"Didn't Walter suspect anything?"

"I called him every night from the hotel where we were staying. I'd lose track of my lies, pretending tedium, complain about work, about being bored, tell him I wanted to come home. I suspect he didn't believe me, but he was putting off something that was starting to take shape in his mind that he wasn't ready to confront. I asked to talk to David but he was always sleeping, or studying, or spending the night at a friend's. My son didn't want to speak to me, and I took his silence like an accusation that made me feel dirty, like a bad mother and an even worse person. But there was Louise to pick up the pieces and put me back together again, always full of plans for the following day. Going to some forgotten church to see an El Greco mural, or to a baroque palace, an antiques market. She was unrelenting, filling every moment so I'd have fun, to keep me from thinking. And the nights of sex, we hardly slept. But more than the sex, and even better, was what came after the orgasm. Tenderness that lasted for hours, touching each other in silence, our feet entwined under the sheets, stroking each other's faces, breathing so close, staring into each other's eyes without blinking or speaking, on the same pillow. And then we got to Tarifa."

They made it to the sea, and it was like reaching the end, which was also a new beginning. Tarifa, with its furious winds lashing the waves and the land, clearing her heart of doubts, pushing the brave forward and the fearful back. Helena found a moment of peace—which she needed to find what she was looking for—in the pure smells and colors. She asked Louise to give her a few hours alone so she could find herself, figure out who she was. She wandered through the dunes of Playa Bolonia, ate at a beach shack, and visited the ruins of Baelo Claudia. Then she sat on the wet sand to gaze out at Africa.

"I hadn't been that close to the geography of my childhood for years. But when I reached my hand out toward Africa, I realized my arm was too weak a bridge for the ghosts of Thelma, Enrique, and Abdul to get from one shore to the other. There they were, clinging to Tangier, stubborn and silent, looking at me like a stranger. So far away. So impossible to get back. I looked around and felt lost and alone, rootless, tossed to the shore like garbage. A piece of rotting wood. I cried so much I thought I'd never cry again. I was wrong."

Just then a young Scottish guy with sun-kissed skin approached her, sat down, and offered his silent company without asking questions. He held out a joint, and they smoked quietly for a time, staring at the horizon. Only later did they laugh politely, striking up the kind of conversation people have to avoid silence with a stranger. He was friendly, had a lovely accent that brought back memories, reminded her of home. He wore a loud bathing suit and had a surfer's body, with long, very blond hair, and dark freckles circling his blue eyes like a leather cord with fake sapphires. He invited her to party with friends around a bonfire, and they drank, smoked some more, ate fried fish, and then headed off to where some small boats were tied up. He recounted with passion the trips he'd taken and his interests. And Helena smiled and knew right then that she'd never have a different life. A short while later, amid the beached boats, she sat astride him, riding him, her back to the twilight and to Africa, to her entire past, she made a decision: she would go home, to Walter and David.

"That night, I went back to the hotel lacking all dignity, the guy's semen still inside me. I wanted Louise to see me that way, to smell someone else on me, I wanted say: 'This is who I am. You have no reason to stay with me.' Louise was waiting for me on the steps. She was smoking, despondent, as if she'd just taken part in the massacre of the innocents. She looked up and her eyes stopped at my shoes, which I held in one hand. Louise didn't dare look any higher. She knew what had happened without my saying a word. She nodded heavily, took one last drag of her cigarette, and flung it away. And then she gave me the terrible news. 'Walter phoned. He left a message at reception; the girl who took the call couldn't speak English for shit, but it sounds important. You should call him.' I ran to the phone. It was almost two in the morning, but he answered on the first ring. He must have been waiting by the phone. He sounded exhausted and was brusque with me. 'You need to come home immediately. David's had an accident. It's serious.'"

She still got the same empty feeling in her stomach even now, recalling it: the horrified expression, silent, hands shaking so badly she dropped the receiver, which dangled from the cord as Walter spoke on, Helena unable to hear him. She remembered the receptionist's voice, asking if she was okay, remembered turning to see Louise, frozen, her expression a mix of disappointment, concern, pain, and sadness.

"There were no flights to London from Cádiz. The closest one was going from Málaga via Madrid the following afternoon, but I didn't want to wait, or hear Louise's thoughts on it. I had to leave immediately. I needed to get moving, create the illusion that I was already on the way. I took a quick shower, and overcome with disgust, scrubbed my body, which had just been licked by a stranger. Then I threw my things into the suitcase as Louise gazed on in silence. 'I'm not going,' she said. I knew that was the end for us, but at the time it hardly mattered. I wanted to call a taxi, but she insisted on driving me to the airport. We'd say goodbye forever there."

Helena shook her head slowly, staring into space.

"The country air smelled of fertilized crops, lights twinkled in the foothills. I remember the landscape like a curtain that had been drawn, you could intuit the shapes beneath it. I remember the narrow road that had no shoulder or dividing line, the hot wind in my face, and speeding— though not fast enough. What I really wanted was to fly, to bridge the distance, eliminate it, steal every minute from the hours. My son needed me, and I wasn't there."

They raced through empty towns, Helena urging Louise to drive faster. On their way out of one of those spooky, deserted ghost towns a pack of mules was on the right side of the road. They were tethered to a rope held by a sleepy-looking boy dressed in black and accompanied by two emaciated dogs zigzagging back and forth across the road. The car headlights illuminated the back of the last mule in the pack, which was white. Like the burro in Juan Ramón Jiménez's *Platero and I*, Helena thought for a minute, even though in the book Platero was a donkey. The mule startled, pricked up its ears, and cocked its head. And though this may not have happened, Helena could have sworn the animal saw its life pass before its velvety eyes. Like two big puffy black buttons that had been sewn on, reflecting the car's headlights.

She didn't have time to scream. It all happened very fast, but at the same time, so slowly: Louise swerving to avoid the mule, one of the dogs frozen in the middle of the road, another swerve, and then the car leaving the road, flying through the air—finally, flying. It seemed light, like a feather, as they soared beneath a star-studded sky, surrounded by silent mountains and the silhouettes of pine trees like night watchmen. Then crashing into the hillside, the car rolling down the slope, their bodies hurled together by the impact. And suddenly stopping, like a wake-up call, their fall broken by an enormous boulder. Then the sound of a creek and up above, in the distance, the pitiful howling of a gravely injured dog.

"I woke up three months later in a Málaga hospital. My condition had been too serious to sustain a trip to England. And the first thing I saw was Walter's pale, gaunt face. It took me a minute to recognize him. He wasn't the one who told me what happened, not at first. The doctor was the one to say that I'd been in a coma, that it was a miracle I'd survived the accident. He showed me X-rays of my broken bones, told me about the operations, my leg being reconstructed. 'Very lucky indeed,' he said, patting my shoulder before leaving me with Walter. Imagine what it's like to close your eyes, and when you open them up three whole months have gone by."

"That must have been awful."

"For three months, I didn't exist. You wake up and feel like the world has an advantage over you. It took a while for my memory to return. They told me that was normal, that it would all come back. I wish it hadn't. I wish I'd never woken up, had been given the gift of amnesia. The very thing you, Miguel, fear most would have been a blessing to me. The first thing I found out was that Louise had died in the accident. The initial impact of the crash broke her neck. Walter had arranged to have her body sent back to England. That was how he found out about us. He had the decency to pay for a plot in Stoke Newington cemetery with a nice marble gravestone. By that point, Louise's family had wanted nothing to do with her for some time."

Miguel didn't suppress his desire to stroke her arm.

"It must have been awful to find out like that."

Helena remembered the look on Walter's face. It was empty, a premonition of the emptiness they both inhabited from that moment on. She often wondered if Walter wished that she'd died in the accident too, wished he didn't have to be faced with all the questions that he never asked. He could have become a lonely old widower with no need to confront the neighbors shaming him, his colleagues' comments at the university, or students' jokes. For quite some time, the whole thing had been all over the tabloids. It had all the makings of the kind of scandal Brits love: just the right amount of sex, deceit, and tragedy to capture the headlines for a few weeks. The unfaithful wife of an esteemed professor, a second-rate lesbian actress, an elite girls' boarding school... and a teenage son who died in dramatic circumstances.

Miguel startled.

"Died? I don't understand. I thought your son lived in Malmö?"

People's faces express not only what they have, see, and recognize. They also express absence. And that was what Miguel saw in Helena's eyes at that precise moment: a darkness so huge, so dense, it tormented her heart. A look so fragile it could break with a simple snap of the fingers.

"David died when I was in a coma. Walter told me when I woke up. David had been playing with his friends, hanging from a bridge as he had other times, and he fell. A concrete pillar broke his fall. He lost consciousness and drowned. The irony of it. My mother almost drowned me, and my son was swallowed by the Thames. While I was off playing fugitive, like my father, my son was dying, just as part of me had died on that beach in Tarifa. I was screaming in pleasure while he was screaming in terror. Later, they told me he hadn't suffered. A lie; a painkiller. How could anyone who dies with their whole life ahead of them not suffer? They plied me with tranquilizers and strapped me down to keep me from screaming and attacking myself, scratching and hitting. I slept, but when I woke up my son's death was still there, squeezing my chest, like steel claws digging into my heart. I hadn't dreamed it, and there was Walter, in a chair at the foot of the bed to remind me of it, telling me with his silence. I asked him to let me see the body, but he said it had been impossible to wait for me to wake up to bury him. That was his way of saying I didn't deserve to say goodbye to my son. I hated him desperately, intensely, with all my heart—the same hatred he professed for me from that moment to the end of his days. No one who hasn't been through something like that could understand how much mutual hatred unites two people. It took another three months for me to be released from the hospital so I could go back to England. When I landed in London, the first thing I did was visit my son's grave. He was buried under a huge willow tree in a small plot in Highgate. It got the morning sun, there was a small flower bed that a gardener tended regularly next to it. The gravestone was tasteful, covered in fresh bouquets of flowers, notes from school friends, and objects that had special meaning to him. There was also a photo—a picture of his girlfriend, who neither Walter nor I knew anything about. Everyone else seemed closer to him than I had ever been. They were at his funeral, cried for him, said a few words, threw handfuls of earth onto the coffin, maybe laughed over some shared joke. And I hadn't been there. I felt like an intruder, like my son didn't want me to be there on my knees, crying for him."

Helena turned to the beach and used a hand to shield her mouth as she lit a cigarette. Out at sea, beyond the yellow buoys, a group of people on the deck of a sailboat jumped and dove into the water. The sun was shining and the seagulls that slept on Barceloneta rooftops and in the cathedral spires at night now flew overhead, keeping an eye on them.

Miguel shook his head.

"But . . . what about your trip to Sweden, your phone calls to David on the computer . . .?"

Helena blew smoke and rubbed a thumb across her forehead. She pursed her lips and cast a sidelong glance at Miguel.

"I'm a pathetic old woman, too lonely to accept loneliness. When I moved to the old folks' home after Walter died, Director Roldán told me about a program run through some kind of Swedish NGO that was aimed at providing support and companionship to elderly people who had no families. People offered their time in exchange for the chance to practice their Spanish. When I saw David's profile, I was interested because he had my son's name, and I thought that if my David had lived long enough, he'd have looked like him at that age. And I've grown fond of him, told him things I'd never told anyone until today."

"But then, why this obsession with going to Malmö? He's not even really family."

Helena shrugged and hugged herself, rubbing her elbows.

"It wasn't just for him. My father died in Malmö in 1978. When he got out of prison he went in search of Abdul and found him living in an immigrant neighborhood there. I have his address and I've got the painting my mother made of Abdul, so I thought I'd go see him."

Miguel couldn't believe his ears.

"That's absurd, Helena. 1978? You don't even know if Abdul still lives there. He could have died a long time ago. And even if he didn't, what would be the point of meeting him and showing him your mother's portrait?"

Helena turned calmly to Miguel.

"That man destroyed my mother's life, my father's life, and my life."

Miguel didn't agree; the way he saw it, everybody hurts themself in their own way. But he refrained from saying as much.

"So what are you hoping for? Answers? Revenge?"

Helena shook her head slowly.

"What were you hoping for when you took your mother's ashes to the Valley of the Fallen? What brought you to Barcelona to see the woman who wrote those letters? I just want to see his face, feel his presence, confront the reality of my childhood memories."

Helena held out her cold hand and took Miguel's warm one. She needed his help to guide her through this maze. If she got too far off track she wouldn't be able to find her way back.

"Now you see who you slept with, Miguel, the kind of woman you claim to be in love with."

Miguel looked into the distance. Summer was right there, with its incorruptible joy. It was as if people had signed a truce with their sorrows. Why not them too? The sea breeze helped, so did people's laughter, bright colors; everything was so clear and simple. He looked up into the sky and saw the contrails of planes taking off and landing at Barcelona airport. Miguel remembered how invisible it all was up there: there was no sorrow but no joy, it all had to be imagined from a plane window, where nothing could be truly experienced.

"I've got an idea. Come with me," he said suddenly, moved by an impulse.

"Where?"

"Down to the sea."

elena stopped short when she felt the water on her feet. "I can't do it."

Miguel looked at her, a smile on his face. He took off his shoes and rolled his pants up to the knee. Then he held his hand out to Helena once more.

"Trust me."

Trust meant ceding fragility and fear to another, closing your eyes and putting yourself in their hands. Trust was an act of faith, courage, and idiocy. But Helena trusted.

She let Miguel lead her into the water, and when the warm sea swirled around her dress, she didn't stop, despite the fear. She walked a little farther, guided by Miguel, and then like the Muslim women of her childhood, sank into the water until they were both submerged up to their heads. Miguel helped her float, her face in the water, his hands under her belly more solid than ground.

"I'm not going to let you go. I'll never let you sink," Miguel said.

And Helena believed him.

25

Barcelona, two weeks later

ook at those fuckers; they're having a blast."

"Gustavo, please. I'm begging you."

"Do you think he's sleeping with her? I do, I bet the old man can still get it up."

He turned to Natalia and grinned. Without his fake teeth, Gustavo had become a grotesque caricature of an attractive man. His eyes were bloodshot from all the coke.

"How does it feel to think about your father screwing some other woman? Sure didn't spend long mourning your mother, did he?"

They saw Miguel and Helena move through the glass-front restaurant and then disappear behind a curtained window, becoming two shadows who could only be imagined.

"What are we doing here?" Natalia asked. She regretted not having deleted her father's WhatsApp messages—he'd told her which hotel he was staying at in case she decided to forgive him. Over the course of the past few months, his messages had changed in tone. They had gone from dark and imploring to determined and loving. It was as though now that he'd left the residence behind, her father was evolving as he traveled. And Natalia suspected that the woman who was with him had had a lot to do with the evolution.

Sitting in the car, Gustavo tensed his whole body and banged his fist twice on the steering wheel. He fixed his gaze on Natalia, exhausted and immobilized by her size.

"What do you think we're doing? Saying hello to my father-in-law, talking to your father like nothing happened. Water under the bridge. I'm going to forget all about the weeks I spent in the hospital, and about this," he said, pointing to his left knee.

The beating Ivan and his friends gave Gustavo had destroyed his leg, but in the end, everyone gets their just deserts. Luckily, while Gustavo was hitchhiking, almost to the French border, the truck driver who'd picked him up near Junquera decided to stop for coffee, and Gustavo saw news of the accident on TV. So that little fucker and his friends couldn't touch him now. And that was when he got hopping mad and decided he wasn't going to let things go. He was going to fuck Miguel up bad. Stick it to him where it hurt the most. It wasn't hard to find Natalia.

Over the course of the months they were out of contact, she'd gotten fat as a pig; pregnancy had left her deformed, but he could still give it to her from behind. And no way was that rape: after all, she was going to be the mother of his child. She belonged to him and always would. The time for prevaricating was over: no more letting her go to work, go out, use her phone without supervision. He was convinced the whore had been sleeping with some other guy in that time, and though she denied it even after he'd smacked her around, he knew he wasn't crazy. There had been nothing incriminating on her cell phone, but he did have a stroke of luck. The half dozen WhatsApps Miguel had sent Natalia were a compendium of imbecility, totally pathetic. A bunch of bullshit about putting the past to rest, his mother's ashes, the ghost of his father. The old man was off his rocker; he'd even gone to Barcelona to find some chick he'd screwed thirty years ago. Now that was faith! It was so idiotic he laughed out loud.

"I'm going to teach you both what the real world is like."

From the balcony, the city was a blanket of light, twinkling like a candle. Miguel was in bed reading a travel magazine, classical music playing in the background. Helena leaned over the banister and smiled. She'd get used to this music, just like she'd get used to not smoking in enclosed spaces when he was around, drinking a little less, and holding her tongue a little more. She was even excited about this new trip, which was real and rooted in the present—a vacation Miguel had begun planning with the enthusiasm of a schoolboy talking about his class trip.

"What about Australia?"

Helena squinted her eyes without turning around because she was still a little embarrassed for him to see her naked joy. She'd go to the North Pole if he asked her to.

"Isn't there anyplace farther?" she asked, just for a laugh. "I think it's great that you're not afraid of flying anymore, but that's almost twenty hours in a plane, and you won't be able to get off if you suddenly panic."

She thought about the past two weeks. Ever since Miguel had tried to teach her to swim, things had changed so much. It was as if the best things in life had all been saving themselves up for those fourteen days. Helena thought she would never again feel a shiver of pleasure on lacing her fingers through someone else's as they walked down the street, or feel so calm while seeing herself floating in the reflection of someone's eyes. She, who'd sworn she would never care about anyone again, felt warm and tender while making Miguel take his medication, was patient when he got befuddled, and if he seemed not to remember that he'd told her something just a few minutes earlier, she didn't become alarmed or condescending. Sometimes, when she found Miguel staring absently at a wall, she feared what was to come but made sure he didn't realize. And when the inevitability of where he was headed was too much to bear, she went out, saying she needed to buy a pack of cigarettes, and cried on a bench, then dried her tears and returned with her best smile on her face.

She almost never looked at the rolled-up portrait of Abdul at the bottom of her suitcase and had given up on the idea of going to Malmö. There was no need to, not anymore. Somewhere deep inside she could tell she'd begun to forgive her parents and was even beginning to forgive herself. She found herself able to show Miguel pictures of Louise and David, and evoke good memories, tender moments, laughs they'd had. The past was slowly being healed by large doses of the present. And as far as the future went, well, it didn't exist for them.

Even the sex was surprising. There were warm, unexpected aspects to it. They were learning about each other but had no desire to show off, took their time with no need to pretend to be anything but what they were. They spent countless hours simply cuddling and touching, affectionately as well as sexually, and when they played games they'd blush and giggle, because behind the kidding lay desire. Sex was sometimes placid and other times anxious; they played, slept, held one another, started all over again.

If only time had stood still, and they didn't see, hear, or feel anything but what they had right then.

Natalia could no longer remember the first time Gustavo hit her. She tried, thinking back over the slaps, kicks, and insults, trying to find the first time, but it was hopeless. It was like it had never been any other way. She tossed and turned uneasily; the bed was narrow and had creaky springs and a smelly mattress. She raised her head to look over Gustavo's shoulder as he slept, and pondered the idea of jumping out the window. Or creeping into the bathroom to grab scissors from the vanity and stab him in the neck. Her jaw ached and her eyelid was still swollen. But she let her head fall back on the pillow, stared at the damp-stained ceiling, and wondered if her child could hear the screaming, crying, and insults. She was trying to keep the baby safe by resting one hand on the half-moon of her belly, whispering beautiful things. Sometimes she'd place headphones on her stomach so the baby could listen to music. The sounds of traffic entered the room, and somebody was walking around in high heels on the floor above them, dragging a chair.

Natalia thought about her father and the woman she knew nothing about, except her name. She wondered how to warn them about what Gustavo was going to do, but he'd taken her phone and wouldn't let her near a computer or even let her go outside on her own. Gustavo was planning to kill her father and then bury her and her unborn son, she was convinced of it. That morning she'd passed a young woman in the hallway of the hostel. They'd exchanged glances and Natalia had begged her for help—silently, because Gustavo was with her—but the woman had looked away, slightly ashamed. It was impossible that people didn't hear them, but everyone acted deaf and blind. In the next room, someone turned up the volume on their TV, and Gustavo stirred restlessly. He opened his eyes and sat up, turning his back to Natalia without so much as glancing her way. Before, at least she had the consolation of his regret, the fragile calm derived from promises like *It won't happen again*, though sooner or later it always did. But now there was not even that. Gustavo scratched his balls, rubbed his injured knee, and grunted like a dog reminding himself why he was so full of fury to keep the rage going. He went into the bathroom and closed the door. Gustavo liked to do his business in private, but he always took his phone with him. Natalia sat on the bed and observed the slanted light coming in through the blinds, which had come off their track and couldn't be raised or lowered. She didn't know what time it was; past twelve, at any rate, she was certain of that. There was no longer any regular schedule for meals, work, or sleep. The only routine was Gustavo's presence and his unpredictable mood swings. Natalia heard the shower go on and trembled. She looked at the nightstand with remnants of coke and her credit card—now almost maxed out—cigarette butts on the purple carpet, his underwear. She knew what came next. If only she could open the blinds wide enough to slip through and jump the four floors to the ground below. If she was lucky, she'd survive, her baby would survive; an ambulance would come pick them up, the police would be called. If she could at least warn her father.

Gustavo stood under the shower's boiling jet, letting the stream of hot water pound his shoulders. It loosened up his muscles and helped him think. This was the best part of the day, waking up dazed and dragging himself to the shower, leaning his forehead against the tiles. Sometimes, it felt so good that he got an erection and had to deal with it immediately. But today there was another side to his pleasure, one no less exciting. Today he was going to take Miguel down, and he'd finally decided how. He'd thought about using a hammer, breaking his bones one by one before crushing his skull, or strangling him with his bare hands so he could watch the old man's eyes pop out of his head. Or pouring flammable liquid on him and then setting him on fire and watching him run like a human torch. None of it seemed awful enough, but in the end, he'd opted for a more conventional but effective method. He turned off the water when it really started to burn and took a deep breath. Yes, today was definitely going to be a good day.

Gustavo walked out of the bathroom naked, with an erection, steam coming off his body. He smiled upon noting Natalia's fearful expression. Finally, he'd made her see that there was no escape for her. It took him a minute to find the revolver in his duffel bag. It wasn't in particularly good shape, but he'd made sure it could do the job. He went to Natalia and enjoyed watching her shrink, pathetically holding the pillow before her like a shield.

"Did you know that even though Spain is one of the world's biggest arms exporters, it's extremely hard to get a gun and ammo without a license?" he asked the air, wielding the pistol in Natalia's face, flicking her bangs with the barrel's sight. "Of course, anything's possible if you've got money. Hiring someone to leave you crippled, for example. I could do that, too, pay a few hundred euros to have some back-alley thugs break your father's back with a chain. But there's nothing noble in that, is there? Sending someone to do what you don't dare do yourself, that's for cowards. And your father deserves better than that. He deserves to have me look him in the eye when I shove this down his throat and pull the trigger."

elena had rushed out to buy cigarettes so quickly that this time not even Miguel could pretend he didn't know the reason behind her sudden escape. He was getting worse and there was no point denying it.

How long had he spaced out this time? Twenty minutes, maybe longer, and he had no clue what had happened in that time, except that he'd soiled himself and ended up sitting on the bathroom floor with his legs covered in filth. Helena had found him and brought him back, and Miguel had been so disconcerted that he didn't even have the presence of mind to keep her from cleaning him up. She'd joked about it, but this time Miguel hadn't followed suit and instead fell into an obtuse silence that he still hadn't broken. He was waiting for her to come back from her supposed trip to get cigarettes with a smile on her face, as she had the other times.

"I'm fucked, aren't I?"

His father had returned weeks ago, and although he hadn't told Helena about it for fear of alarming her, in a way he was glad to have him near. His father's unreal presence was comforting. This time he was in a wide-collared black shirt with the sleeves rolled up past his wrists, and black work trousers. He was barefoot, and Miguel asked facetiously if the wardrobe department in purgatory—he'd decided that that was where his father lived—had no shoe budget. Then he shook his head, annoyed with himself.

"I'm sorry, I've been with Helena too long and it's starting to show."

His father smiled and walked over to the balcony railing, spread his arms, and held out his hands. It was a beautiful morning. His shirt rippled in the sea breeze like a pirate flag, and he looked like he was about to rise up and levitate. Instead what he did was capture a little of the breeze in his fists and slide his hands into his pockets.

"Aren't you going to say anything, Father?"

There was a knock at the door. Amador looked at him sadly. He wished he could be sick instead of Miguel, wished he could do that for his son; it was what any father would want, the power to inscribe or erase things in his child's book of fate. But he couldn't, and his presence was as useless as it was inevitable.

"It must be Helena with her dose of nicotine. That didn't take long."

It wasn't Helena.

It took Miguel too long to react, and by the time he realized what was happening, Gustavo had already pushed him into the bedroom and closed the door behind him. Gustavo looked unkempt, he was dirty and smelled bad. The man was visibly high, his sunken eyes twitching nervously as he glanced around, nodding in approval.

"Nice room. Nothing like the rathole your daughter and I are living in."

Miguel backed up until he hit the bed, without taking his eyes off Gustavo. He felt more surprised than afraid.

"What are you doing here?"

Gustavo looked at him with an amused expression. He took a step toward Miguel just to watch the old man shrink.

"Visiting my father-in-law. What's wrong with that? We're family. Plus, I'm bringing a message from your daughter." Miguel looked side to side, uneasily, as Gustavo pulled a cell phone from the pocket of his jean jacket. "Make yourself comfortable, grandpa. You're going to like this," he added, pushing Miguel down onto the bed.

Gustavo showed him a video. It was Natalia, sitting in a chair in front of a filthy wall. She was plainly terrified, dressed in dirty pajamas, her hair disheveled. She kept touching her cheek with her right hand as the left one rested nervously on her bulging stomach.

Miguel felt a shiver of excitement. That was his grandchild growing in her belly. He heard Gustavo's voice say "Go on," and then Natalia began to speak unsteadily, faltering. She was like an automaton, like someone on one of those videos terrorists and kidnappers make, where they force their victims to make a statement that nobody believes but that is painfully humiliating and demoralizing to the person and their families.

"I want you to know that I agree with Gustavo about what's going to happen now. What you did to him, to us, can never be forgiven or forgotten. He's the man I love, I want you to know that. I'll be by his side always, come what may. I hate you, I renounce you as my father, and your grandchild will never hear your name or know anything about you, except that you were despicable. I want you to die knowing that no one will remember you unless it's to spit on your memory."

Gustavo turned off the video with an unhinged giggle.

"Nice, huh? Not very convincing, I know, but that was the best I could get out of her in three takes. Your daughter isn't very good at monologues, honestly. She does better at faking orgasms so I'll leave her alone."

Miguel was trembling, clenching fistfuls of bedspread in both hands, and felt like he couldn't breathe.

"Why are you doing this? What kind of animal are you?"

Gustavo straightened up. He pulled the revolver from the back of his waistband and smacked Miguel in the face with the butt. The blow sent him flying back against the bedspread. Miguel began to bleed profusely and whimper. Gustavo stepped back, shaking his head. He began walking in tight circles, furious. Adrenalin coursed through his body, making him even more anxious. The gun shook in his hand. He shouted and tried to destroy everything in reach. His outburst lasted several minutes, and then he was calmer. Gustavo looked at the broken lamp on the carpet, the painting wrenched from the wall, and the overturned phone he'd hurled from the nightstand. He picked up a chair and sat on it backwards, the gun between his legs as he gazed at Miguel's bloody face. Miguel was using one end of the bedspread to try to stanch the bleeding.

Gustavo pulled out a joint and lit it. He rubbed his injured knee and felt his anger surge, felt it flowing under his skin. Not because of the attack Miguel had ordered but something that began far earlier, an autonomous fury that fed on any offense, real or imagined. It was something that had caused terrible, unending anguish since he was a child. He should have stopped it at some point, back when he had the power to control the monster growing inside him, but now it was too late. He was no longer able to see himself with any perspective. Hatred was his master. Gustavo was mentally disturbed, a failure, a sick wounded animal who sickened and wounded anyone he could. The only way for him to make sense of his life was by making others miserable. The weak were his victims of choice, and he only attacked when there was no doubt he could defeat them. That was how he'd met Natalia back at university. She was pretty but also full of complexes, thinking that her good looks forced her to live up to the expectations projected on her. Insecure, unsatisfied despite her clear success, a brilliant student, she was too smart not to see that her education was something she used as a shield to hide behind.

And yet, Natalia had disarmed him at first. She told Gustavo that what he saw in her was just a mirror, that he was the insecure one, the one who'd been undone by his reputation as a good-looking rebel, someone special. His reputation forced him to act ever more erratically, be more and more extreme, it made him a victim of the image he himself had cultivated. It was Gustavo, not her, who was unhappy, isolated, phony; he was the one who hated himself, not her. Natalia, like his previous girlfriends, was just a projection. Her cutting but honest speech had an impact on Gustavo; she fascinated him. None of his other girlfriends had spoken so frankly yet hopefully. Natalia, unlike the others, was strong enough to pull him from the pit of depression he'd secretly been in since adolescence. She saw further and deeper into him than anyone ever had.

At the time, Gustavo was listening to Rachmaninoff and thought it made him special. He was the only one in his group of friends who liked classical music, and he decided he'd impress Natalia by taking her to a concert by some Hungarian pianist with an unpronounceable name who was going to interpret the Piano Concerto no. 3. It all went well at first. Gustavo watched Natalia from the next seat, registering her amazement, excitement, thoughtfulness, and passion, which indirectly made him amazing, exciting, deep, and passionate. It was like Gustavo was the composer, or at least the pianist up there, playing onstage. But after they left the concert hall, it all fell apart. As they walked by a dark alley, Gustavo felt the urge to celebrate his victory. He'd gotten an erection, which was rare even back then, and wanted his just deserts after taking Natalia on this unforgettable date. They'd been going out for three weeks and still hadn't gone all the way. This was the moment. But Natalia was reserved, returned his kiss half-heartedly, and though she let him touch her breasts through her top, refused to go any further when Gustavo tried to pull down her pants. She was tired, she said, and the alley was dirty. She wanted it to be different, to be special. To Gustavo it sounded like a bunch of excuses, and they echoed in his head like rocks falling into a well: boom, boom, boom. Suddenly he was no longer the special, sensitive, educated man he'd been a moment earlier. Natalia's refusal made him feel awkward, dirty, vulgar, rejected. Just some horny guy, and it made him furious. Things got worse when he pulled down his underwear and grabbed Natalia's hand, forcing her to masturbate him. He came instantly, and seeing the semen on his fingers made him want to kill her for having made him feel so despicable.

They stopped going out for a month, but then she told him that she missed him, and he apologized for having acted like a monster, and it seemed like things were back on track. They slept together that very night, but Gustavo couldn't shake the feeling that Natalia was just going through the motions, doing what she saw as an obligation. This kept him from getting a decent erection, which exasperated him even more. Was the understanding look she gave him actually mocking? When she said it didn't matter, was she being empathetic or condescending? Gustavo got even more upset when she decided to masturbate in front of him. He called her a whore and told her to go.

But she didn't leave immediately, and she should have. Should have gotten dressed and walked right out of his life, never to return. Instead of seeing the signs, however, she held him and cried and apologized for her tactlessness, saying it was all her fault because she didn't know what she was doing, that it was all due to her inexperience. So they did it again, and this time Gustavo managed to ejaculate. The role playing was what had excited him—him dominant, her submissive. Making her feel bad, and guilty, and then forgiving her afterward. They both accepted it, and from then on, Gustavo knew that Natalia was his. It was thrilling. Not the sex but the feeling of power he got by controlling her, watching her go home heavyhearted, dragging her feet, not understanding why she let him treat her that way, sensing that it was a trap and yet falling back into it, over and over.

Now it was too late. Natalia had become an amorphous object with no identity of her own, just some heap locked in that room in the pension, huddled in a corner between the bed and the wall, waiting for his return and any small consolation, a kind word she'd lap up like a dog. And the game would last exactly as long as it took Gustavo to tire of her, smash his toy, and go find another one.

"There's something I want you to know, Miguel. I'm going to kill you, and then I'm going to go back to the pension, fuck your daughter one last time, and then shoot her in the face. I've thought about it a lot, done the math, and it doesn't add up. Something tells me that the child she's carrying isn't mine, regardless of what she claims. I'm sure that slut lied to me."

"You're insane!"

Gustavo nodded. Sure, maybe he was. Or maybe he just saw things clear as day and had the balls to do something about them when nobody else dared to.

"I wanted you to know that, so you can think about what awaits your daughter and grandkid as you die."

They both heard the door open and turned to look. Helena stood in the doorway in her sunglasses, a plastic bag in each hand. She wore a pretty, sleeveless mauve dress that showed off her shoulders, and she'd been to the hairdressers. She looked much younger. And her lipsticked smile was the same as ever. Upon seeing a stranger with a gun, however, and Miguel's bloody face, it morphed into a look of incredulity, and she tried to cry out. But the sound of two shots drowned out her scream.

It seemed unreal. The shots had popped like two fire-crackers, and the bloodstain on Helena's mauve dress looked at first like a pinprick. Even the bags fell from her hands in what looked like slow motion, spilling their contents—a bottle of red wine, a carton of cigarettes, and a magazine—onto the carpet, which muffled the impact. Helena's body was thrust backward but did not immediately collapse, held for a moment between the open door and the wall. The bloodstain grew quickly, dark and viscous on her belly and then dripping down her legs. Then suddenly things sped up: her eyes rolled back in her head, her arms dropped, and she fell forward, just inches from Gustavo, who seemed shocked at what he'd done. For a second he stared at the revolver without grasping that it was true—if you pull the trigger of a loaded weapon, it fires, and something happens. Not in your imagination but in real life. Panic, instinct, the urge to leap into the void and finish what he'd started, all suddenly impelled him to act. He had to get rid of any witnesses to what he'd just done.

Gustavo turned with the gun but Miguel was not where he was supposed to be. He'd moved left just far enough to bring the bedside lamp crashing down on Gustavo's head and make him stumble. Gustavo fired again, blindly this time, and felt another blow to the face, harder this time. They struggled. The old man was strong, he realized; it was the strength of desperation. Miguel screamed for help as he tried to get the gun off Gustavo, who felt a vicious bite on his hand, let out a yelp, and dropped his weapon.

"Did you bite off my finger?" he squealed, astonished, backing up in horror and staring at his hand, which he held at the wrist. Gustavo tripped over Helena's body and fell. He tried to get up, but Miguel was aiming the gun at him.

Miguel's arm trembled and it was impossible to make it stop. His eyes saw nothing but Helena, facedown, the bloodstain beneath her expanding, now soaking the carpet. He called her. Again and again, but she wouldn't answer.

And then he fired.

PART SEVEN

August 2014

26

Barcelona

n August, the posh neighborhoods above Avenida Diagonal were practically deserted. It was hard to find an open outdoor café anywhere near the gynecological clinic, hard even to find a *café con leche* and decent croissant. Natalia was still smoking despite her doctor's recommendations.

"The doctor said everything is fine, Papá. The baby and I are both fine. Miguel will be born healthy, I promise."

They didn't talk much about what had happened weeks ago. It still hurt too much, but at least they had each other in their lives again.

Natalia had told Miguel that the baby would be named after him if it was a boy; she'd been planning it the whole time, she claimed, though Miguel suspected she had only said it to cheer him up a bit.

"Let's hope the baby takes after you and not me. In fact, I'd be thrilled to have a granddaughter."

Helena's funeral had been rough, and the questioning he'd been through with the police after Gustavo's arrest hadn't made things any better.

The shot Miguel fired had only grazed Gustavo's arm, so the public defender claimed it was self-defense. That was what the police believed, but the fact of the matter was that he'd tried to shoot Gustavo through the heart and only missed because he'd never had a gun in his hands before.

Natalia stirred her *café con leche* with a melancholy look.

"Gustavo told the police what happened in Sevilla. They questioned me, but I told them he was lying."

Miguel nodded without replying. She reached out and touched his forearm.

"Papá, I'm sorry for everything I put you through. I'm sorry I was so blind, and so unfair."

Miguel stroked his daughter's cold fingers.

"None of this is your fault, I want you to remember that, Natalia. It's Gustavo's fault, and I hope he rots in jail."

She closed her eyes for a moment and leaned back in her chair. When she opened them back up, her eyes glistened.

"I'm sorry about Helena. She must have been an extraordinary woman. I would have liked to meet her."

Miguel played distractedly with the crumbs of his croissant. He hadn't even tasted his coffee. He gazed absently at his daughter, not wanting to say the word *dead*. That would be like accepting that she wasn't coming back, accepting the fact that when he went back to the hotel she wouldn't be there, smoking on the balcony or stroking Louise's flask.

"She taught me to fly."

Natalia had no idea what her father meant, but he made no attempt to explain.

"Can I have a cigarette?"

"Since when do you smoke?"

"Since now." He ignored his daughter's shocked expression and helped himself, then summoned the waiter and ordered a gin. A double.

Natalia couldn't believe her eyes.

"I don't think you should be drinking in your state."

Miguel smiled. What was his state? Now he wished his Alzheimer's was more aggressive, that it kept him from remembering anything or feeling any pain. Sometimes, sitting on the toilet, he wept at how terribly lucid he felt. All he had to do was sit among Helena's things: the suitcase with her dresses in it, which he stroked as if it was the skin of her ghost; her cigarettes, which he smoked alone since they made him feel she was closer to his lips; the postcards from her father, which she stored in a box tied with a ribbon, and read every night. He spent hours contemplating the portrait of Abdul, which he would lay out on the bed, recalling everything Helena had told him about her life. A life he'd encountered too late.

"I couldn't help her. I couldn't. I was so far inside myself..."

A municipal street-cleaning truck rumbled down the deserted avenue. Jets of water shot out from either side and a dog chased alongside, leaping through the water and biting it joyfully.

The waiter brought his gin. Miguel reached into a pocket and pulled out Helena's flask, with Louise's inscription on it.

"Could you fill this?"

"What do you need that for?"

He looked at Natalia and shrugged.

"Reserves for the trip. I hate flying, so this will help."

"We don't have to fly. We can drive or take a train back to Sevilla."

Miguel stroked his daughter's cheek. He was happy to see her finally free, picturing a future for herself and the baby. For as long as he was able, he'd be at her side, but there was something else he needed to do first.

"I'm not going back to Sevilla with you. I'm going to Malmö."

H elena would have liked Vikingagatan. Everything there was impeccably manicured, like the set for a film where everything turns out perfectly in the end.

Actually, Miguel corrected himself mentally, she wouldn't have liked it at all. It was too fake, like the campaign billboards he'd seen lining the freeway on the drive in from the airport, with politicians' faces digitally manipulated to make their teeth whiter, their hair darker, their wrinkles and blemishes minimized. The cab driver pulled up in front of a house.

"Can you wait for me? I'll only be ten minutes."

The house was identical to every other one on the block: a two-story A-frame with a small front yard, low wooden fence, vegetation that gave off the smell of wet grass and mildew, a walkway paved with beige tiles, and a wicker chair by the entry. The window beside the front door was vibrating from the music being played inside, something sounding like modern pop music that Miguel couldn't identify. He clacked the door knocker twice. After a few seconds, he heard footsteps coming down a staircase. Someone pulled back the curtain over the window and a woman's face appeared, giving a questioning look.

"Can I help you?"

Miguel didn't understand the woman, and he asked if she spoke English. She said no but he carried on anyway, asking in English to speak to the homeowners. She gave him a searching look, then finally motioned for him to wait there, and closed the door. After a minute the door opened again. This time a rather tall man with glasses and a beard stood there.

"What can I do for you?" he asked in perfect English.

"I suppose you must be David."

The man nodded warily.

"I'm Miguel Gandía. I've come from Spain. You won't have heard about me, but I've heard about you. I'm a friend of Helena's."

He looked doubtful, and for a second Miguel feared things were going to go worse than he'd imagined; the man didn't even remember Helena's name. But to his relief, after a second, he reacted, surprised but also happy.

"Helena, of course! Please, come in."

Miguel walked in and saw a foyer crowded with stuff—children's toys, a coatrack full of jackets, a bicycle. It smelled good, like lavender air freshener.

"Thank you, Fatima." The woman nodded and swiftly, silently walked back toward the kitchen.

David led Miguel into his office and asked him to have a seat.

"Wow, this is really a surprise. But any friend of Helena's is welcome here. How is she?"

Miguel sat on the edge of a chair and looked around: photos of the kids, of his wife, a couple of Staël prints, and a dozen or so books in various languages. He smiled on seeing Lorca's *The House of Bernarda Alba* in the original Spanish beside a small charcoal drawing of the writer's face.

"Marta did that. She worships Federico—that's what she calls him, like he was family. In fact, she was the one who urged me to sign up for the support program where I met Helena. We talked a lot about literature, poetry in particular, though I have a feeling Helena prefers Auden. But if you're a friend of hers, you already know that."

Miguel nodded with a smile.

"'In headaches and in worry / Vaguely life leaks away, / And Time will have his fancy / To-morrow or to-day.' 'As I Walked Out One Evening' had been her favorite poem lately. She recited those verses all the time, I think as a kind of premonition. Helena died, David. She died a few weeks ago. She'd been planning to come see you; she wanted to meet you and your family in person. I don't know if you realize how much you meant to her. In a way, you were like a son to her."

David was visibly upset. It took a moment for him to stop waving his hands around and shaking his head.

"That's terrible. She was such an extraordinary woman, such a sharp sense of humor. Her way of looking at things always got a smile out of me. Marta and the kids and I were hoping to visit her in Tarifa. What happened? She seemed so strong, so healthy..."

Miguel didn't want to go into details, so he lied.

"Heart attack."

What would she have made of this encounter with reality? This man, this house, this city? Would she have been disappointed?"

For a minute neither of them spoke, and it was as if now that the news had been broken, Miguel's presence was pointless, burdensome even.

"And you came all the way from Spain to tell me?"

"Not exactly. I came to Malmö for a different reason, but I think she would have liked for me to come say hello, to meet you."

Just then the woman who'd opened the door walked in to say she was leaving. She must have been the cleaning lady.

"Thank you, Fatima. See you tomorrow."

The woman glanced at Miguel out of the corner of her eye. After she'd left, David asked for details about the funeral. He was friendly, but it was clear that this was none of his concern. After a few minutes, he clapped his hands to his thighs, seeming to feel awkward.

"I'm really glad you came to tell me. It's terrible news. But I'm afraid I have a meeting in a few minutes."

Miguel nodded. He felt strange there now. His mission was accomplished, and the meter was still running. He needed to get out of there, to breathe. When he said goodbye to David somewhat coldly, David too seemed relieved to put an end to this unusual encounter.

As he passed the bus stop, Miguel saw Fatima sitting there, staring absently at the sky, and wondered at how similar their destinies were. Sometimes he felt that people were mysteriously connected without ever realizing it. Though he didn't know this woman, would never run into her again, seeing her so alone on the bench at that bus stop—evasive, as if she was trying to escape the world—he felt he understood her pained expression, her inability to comprehend so many things, and her profound silence.

27

Malmö

Although it was far too late, the police eventually returned Yasmina's body to Fatima. She'd been profaned; the excuse they gave was that sometimes the dead revealed things about their death if they opened them up and examined their viscera. Fatima turned up at the funeral parlor barefoot and stood there without bowing or showing exaggerated signs of grief. The women who'd come to help would have reprimanded her if she did, because as the Prophet says, "Every soul shall taste death," and death is not the end. To complete the ritual, though it was now pointless, she closed Yasmina's jaw and smoothed her right hand down her daughter's face, simulating closing her eyes. She covered Yasmina's body with a cotton cloth so that those present could not see it. Next Fatima began the ablution for the dead, reciting the words: "Whoever bathes the dead and keeps their secrets, Allah shall forgive and bless." First, she washed her stomach, then rinsed her mouth and nose, and finally bathed her entire body, beginning at Yasmina's head and working down to her feet. If her head hadn't been shaved, she would have combed Yasmina's hair and perfumed it, following custom. The women removed the wet cloth from her body and proceeded to shroud Yasmina. They wrapped a skirt around her thighs, dressed her in a simple white camisole, covered her face with a veil, and wrapped her body in two cotton sheets that had been tied together.

The authorities wouldn't let them transport the body to the cemetery without a casket, so a simple unadorned box was selected and then lowered into the grave, with Yasmina's body resting on its right side, leaning eastward, toward the qibla, while the imam, in the classical Arabic of the liturgy, recited verse 55 of sura 20 from the Koran: "From the earth We created you, and into it We will return you, and from it We will extract you another time."

By midafternoon, it was all over. Fatima, visibly exhausted but holding up, accepted the community's condolences, and though she would have liked to spend a little longer by her daughter's grave, marked by a very simple headstone, she kept to tradition and left with the women in the cortege. Her daughter was no longer of this world. And though she pretended otherwise, nor was Fatima.

The couple she worked for was very kind to her. They were good people and overwhelmed her with their affection and concern—even the children seemed to intuit her fragility and behaved themselves. David insisted repeatedly that she take the rest of the week off, but Fatima wanted to get back to her chores, return to routine, with the excuse that she needed to keep busy. The truth was, she didn't want to go back to the Rosengård apartment and face her father. The teachings of the Koran and the sunna expressly forbade criticizing, cursing, or insulting the dead, but Abdul—despite considering himself a true believer, going to the mosque every Friday, following the precepts, and being ludicrously pious—had refused to attend the funeral, telling anyone willing to listen what he thought of his granddaughter. He branded her as impious, one of Sture's whores, a slut, a source of shame to the family. "The day will come when the world will be destroyed and Allah will bring up the dead for judgment," the imam reminded Fatima when she turned to him in pain, desperate for consolation. "Then the truth will be known. Meanwhile, your obligation as a daughter is to honor your father, even if he is wrong." Shut up and await the final judgment, that was what she was being told to do. But she'd been silent for too many years, and what she'd thought was obedience and respect for her father had only been cowardice. Her silence had made her complicit in the most horrific aberrations, led her husband to commit suicide and her children not to be born, and she herself to lose Yasmina before she'd actually died.

Deputy Chief Gövan had paid her a visit. He'd been friendly and seemed truly upset at Yasmina's death. The investigation was moving quickly, and everything pointed to Sture. The deputy chief had promised to do everything in his power to send the man to jail. From that moment on, Fatima didn't let a day go by without listening to the news on the radio, watching it on TV, or reading the paper. But weeks went by, and Yasmina's murder was back-burnered. The elections were approaching, and politicians' statements—including one by the deputy chief, a self-proclaimed hero ready to tackle people's mounting anxiety—took up all of the program time. The media whipped up a generalized sense of danger, and it rooted in people's minds. There were disturbances in Rosengård, murders in Gothenburg, a Jewish cemetery defiled in Stockholm, gangs of Albanians attacking truck drivers . . .

But nothing about Sture. The cops had interrogated him, but he'd strolled out of the police station with a self-satisfied smile, surrounded by the best criminal lawyers in the country. He'd even had the gall to make a statement for the cameras, expressing support for the Swedish Democrats and presenting himself as a simple business owner who'd been the victim of reverse racism. A significant number of those in the crowd had actually applauded. After seeing that, Fatima lost heart. Gövan wasn't going to make him pay for her daughter's death and neither was anyone else.

She had to do something.

Abdul had retreated inside himself.

What would become of him now? That was all he could think as he finished the cup of hot chocolate Fatima had made for him.

"Why did you take so long to come? Were you going to leave me on my own?"

Fatima was changing his bedsheets. They had dried feces on them. She'd hardly said a word and avoided her father's inquisitorial look.

"I've been busy with Yasmina's funeral rites, and I have responsibilities to the family I work for."

Abdul shot her a fierce look. He didn't want anyone speaking of Yasmina in his presence and had made that very clear.

"You need to quit that job. You have to take care of me now, that is your obligation."

Fatima sighed despondently, then balled up the dirty sheets and carried them to the utility room by the kitchen, her father following close behind.

"Did you not hear me?" Abdul insisted.

Fatima lost her patience and dropped the dirty bundle. She inhaled deeply, one hand on her belly, but didn't dare turn to face her father. It was absurd, but after all these years she was still afraid of him.

"If I don't work, how do you think we're going to get by?"

"On my pension," Abdul responded flatly.

Fatima bowed her head. They both knew there was no way they could survive on her father's pension. She bent down to pick up the dirty sheets, opened the washing machine and stuffed them in. She wanted to leave the utility room, but her father was blocking the door.

"What's the matter with you? You haven't said a word since you walked in and you won't even look at me. You have no right to cry over her. It is your duty to forget her and to care for the living. That is what the Prophet says."

Soon you'll be one of the dead, too. We all will, Fatima thought. And she wasn't ashamed of this thought, was ashamed only at wishing it so as soon as possible. She dropped her hands and sat on the stool. In that position, her father, standing above her, looked even taller and more fearsome. But Fatima didn't care. Something inside her had cracked, and it was going to grow into a gaping hole that could never be repaired as soon as she began to speak, to say what she'd kept quiet all those years. And if that condemned her, it would be up to God to decide whether to forgive or punish.

"The police are sure that Sture's responsible for Yasmina's murder, but they don't have enough proof. Inspector Inga called me. She seems like a good woman. She's very interested in the case, but she needs help. You could tell them what Sture did in 1978. I've heard those kinds of crimes have no statute of limitations."

Abdul's dark eyes, which so unsettled her when he was younger, grew wide as saucers and then hardened. But his expression lacked the conviction it had back then, and he was unable to intimidate her. Not even by raising his hand as if to strike her. Fatima held his gaze, challenging and stony, until he dropped it, trembling uncontrollably.

"I don't know what you're talking about."

Fatima grabbed the hand that had so often beaten her when she was a girl. That was how he'd taught her when she was young, just as it was the way he'd been taught himself, as had his parents and grandparents. Men had no need for words; force was enough. But her father was no longer a man.

"You have to do it, Father. They'll believe you. I'll go with you, I'll tell Gövan what Sture did to me for years, tell him about the abortions. You owe it to your granddaughter. We're the ones who condemned her."

"I don't owe that whore anything. Or you."

"Then I'll go myself. I'll tell them what you did, how you looked the other way every time he raped your daughter, and then your granddaughter."

Abdul winced pathetically. His eyes twitched, searching for an escape, but Fatima held his wrist firmly. His daughter had never dared to speak to him that way, or to grab him forcefully, to cause him pain. The imam was right, the whole world was losing its mind, the foundations crumbling. If his daughter revolted against him, what was next?

"Get out of this house. You are no longer my daughter."

Fatima stood and faced him, the monster who'd clutched her heart in its claws her whole life. She was so filled with sorrow and rancor that it took all her strength not to collapse. When she spoke, her voice was trembling—but not out of fear. Tears as big as stones rolled down her cheeks, and she did not wipe them away.

"You let Sture rape me. Whenever he wanted. For years. And every time I got pregnant, you forced me to abort. You, so self-righteous, kept your mouth shut and looked the other way. The only reason you let Yasmina be born was because Sture insisted when he found out I was having a girl and threatened to kill you if anything happened to her."

Abdul thrashed in an attempt to free himself of his daughter's grip, but rather than let go, she squeezed tighter. Furious and desperate, he shook his head.

"You can't speak to me this way, I'm your father."

"Of course I can, you selfish bastard! You saw your cowardice reflected in Yasmina, but do you know what I saw in her different-colored eyes? In one I saw my daughter—innocent, good, full of life. But in the other I saw Sture on top of me, saying he wanted me, biting my neck, touching my breasts *right there* in that room, with the door closed while you and my husband sat in the living room watching television!"

Abdul collapsed. His flaccid, fleshless lips opened and closed like a fish out of water. A string of spittle hung from the corner of his mouth and then fell onto his dirty sweater.

"You don't understand . . . I . . . There was nothing I could do. I had to save the family."

The filthy walls of the wretched apartment where they'd been trapped like animals. No papers, no money, no knowledge of Swedish, no one who could or would help them. No phone, no electricity, no running water. The whole family slept in shifts, on the same mattress on the floor, and everything reeked of fermenting misery, rats, and roaches. The only one to offer them any help at all was Sture. And his help came at a price.

"You paid his price and then some. And when Yasmina started to grow and Sture became obsessed with her, he just took her like she belonged to him. He snatched her from me and none of you did a thing."

"She was never my granddaughter!"

"She was my daughter. I hated my own daughter because I wasn't allowed to hate you, so by hating and punishing her, I punished you and hated you, and my husband, and Sture. And I kept my mouth shut and let it happen all over again. And now he's killed her."

Fatima dropped her father's hand without even realizing she'd left fingernail marks on his flaccid skin. She tried to move, to get out of the narrow utility room that forced her to be suffocatingly close to her father. She walked into the kitchen and looked around like she'd never seen it before. Then she went to Yasmina's room but didn't dare enter. Instead she stroked the closed door and turned. Abdul stood at the end of the hall, an ancient ruin, an old man who should have left this world long ago but was still pitifully grasping at the straws of his life with tenacity.

"I wish you'd never brought me to this country."

"It was for the good of the family."

"The family? My mother hated you as much as Grandfather did. Did you know that? She was afraid of you and felt sick every time you came back from one of your trips. She was disgusted by your body, by you touching her when she knew you'd been with that officer. Every day she prayed for your death, for you never to return from that trip around Europe when you ran off with him. And when you came back, she wasn't happy, and neither was I. No one in the village was. Your whole life has been infected by selfishness and vanity, you never had any love to give anyone but that Spaniard, and even him you betrayed. Twice."

"Dear God, Daughter. You're killing me."

"God, yes, pray to God as much as you like, beat your chest, scratch your face, rip out your hair. It will all be in vain. You'll leave this earth bearing the hatred and contempt of everyone who knew you, and it will be soon. You're right to be afraid. Men will not forgive you and neither will God. There will be no forgiveness or clemency for us, Father. You need to make amends for what you did to Enrique Pizarro. And if you won't talk, I will."

Fatima walked out, slamming the door and leaving her father alone. Suddenly, the place was empty. The apartment that had always been so tiny and cramped, where the only privacy possible was in his bedroom, was now silent and huge. The memory of that night in 1978 when Enrique turned up at the door of this same apartment was indelible. It felt as if he was still there, gazing at him. Without warning, the past invaded the present, coming to demand his attention, to collect on an unpaid debt. Enrique didn't even bear a grudge against Abdul. He'd come—as if time had not passed—in search of understanding, answers he was prepared to accept, as one does with someone he truly loves. Not one reproach, not one complaint. At least not at first. Until he realized Abdul would give him nothing—not a kind word, a gesture of affection, or any sign of repentance.

"Out, damn ghost!" Abdul shouted, batting the air as if to scatter the cobwebs of his mind, which was playing tricks on him. He was a changed man now, he'd found God. And God forgives all, including the past. It had taken him a lifetime to gain the respect of the community of the faithful, and the memory of Enrique was not going to bury his efforts under useless nostalgia.

Why had he let Sture sully his hands with blood and sin? Because Enrique Pizarro would not leave. Every day he prowled around outside Abdul's building like a homeless man, following him down the street, begging, imploring—demanding—that they get back together.

"You should never have come, Enrique. You should have stayed in Spain," Abdul moaned.

Enrique had built a makeshift refuge in an alley, out of boxes and discarded objects. He survived by begging, and drank away almost everything he earned in his new profession. When Abdul walked to Friday services at the mosque with other men from the community, he'd see Enrique out of the corner of his eye and pretend not to, picking up the pace. But Enrique would approach, in front of his friends: *Do you know what they do to men like me in prison? They raped me, beat me, pretended to hang me in my cell. The guards spread rumors about me, telling other prisoners I was a stool pigeon, a queer turned whore who would have sex for cigarettes. And I endured it all, because I love you, Abdul.*

"Sture was the only one who could free me of you. Can you understand that? You asked for it," Abdul shouted into the empty space, seeing Enrique in the shadows.

The scandal reached Sture, who knew everything that went on in the neighborhood. Though he was under thirty back then, Sture had already become the man he would be. Everyone feared him. *Is it true what that drunkard's going around saying?* Sture already had his eye on Fatima, and though Abdul didn't know for sure and didn't want to find out, he believed that Sture had already slept with his daughter. Abdul vehemently denied Enrique's accusations but Sture didn't believe a word of it. When it came down to it, he didn't actually care whether it was true or not. *I can help you. It's no good for you to have someone spreading that kind of rumor in the neighborhood, and now that we're friends, it's no good for me either.* Abdul saw the skies open above him but refused to see the trap being laid beneath his feet.

"All I wanted was to teach you a lesson."

But Sture didn't teach lessons. He found permanent solutions. He threw out a number, one clearly impossible for Abdul. It would take a lifetime to repay. Abdul let some strangers beat and kick Enrique half to death, then agreed without hesitation to deliver the coup de grâce when Sture put a gun in his hand and smiled mockingly, instructing him not to stand too close or he'd be spattered by brains.

If he did as Fatima asked and confessed all, he'd be forced to leave the neighborhood, move to another city; he'd lose everything he'd worked so hard to build: respect, irreproachability.

"Don't give me that look, you bastard." In the darkness of the apartment, he saw Enrique's eyes as he'd fired. His beautiful green eyes, staring at him through the blood running down his forehead and covering his face. He'd stared with no rancor, no hatred.

Abdul looked around. This was all he'd fought for. Eighty-six years, to end up alone in a fake leather chair, dressed in dirty pajamas, stinking, done for, a frayed blanket over spindly legs with no thighs or buttocks to speak of. His bare feet were bony, his toenails long, his hands on the worn armrest no longer doing what he asked, moving spasmodically without his permission. He, who had seduced men and women alike, who'd had everything he ever dreamed of back in his village, in fact had nothing. And he never had. It had always all belonged to Sture.

He tried to get up to go to the bathroom and felt a sudden stabbing pain at the back of his neck, followed by intense heat that spread throughout his head.

"What's going on?" he spluttered. A strange tingling crept across his right cheek. It was all happening so fast that it felt like a burn. The corner of his mouth drooped. He was afraid.

Abdul tried to call out and realized, in horror, that his tongue would not move, would not respond to his orders. The phone, he thought. He had to get to the phone and call Fatima. He took a step blindly, unable to focus his eyes. Dear God, please, he whimpered, feeling for the support of a chair. His hand touched only air, and Abdul collapsed, falling flat on his face.

28

Malmö

On the other side of the bridge, the last ferry arriving from Denmark blew its foghorn into the darkness like a mournful portent.

Gövan was almost certain no one had followed him to the site, not far from where he used to meet Yasmina, but he looked around cagily nonetheless. When he was certain, he got out of the car, walked through the headlight beams that cast his shadow onto the wall of an abandoned paper factory, and sat on the Škoda's hood to wait. He disliked the squalor of the place, the nocturnality that it forced him into, the danger that something like this entailed, now that it was all so close to turning out perfectly. Someone might see him. It would be easy to recognize him now that he was on the news every day, and if anyone did, there would be no way to justify being there at that hour.

A few months ago, none of that would have mattered to him; he'd been infatuated with Yasmina. Now it was hard to look back and not laugh at how sincerely he'd professed his love, at his pathetic puppy-dog eyes, the urgency with which he took off her clothes. Gövan still thought of her with sorrow, but it was dwindling. He no longer saw her everyplace he went, at all hours, nor did he have the oppressive anguish of guilt or the fear of being caught. It was only on returning to places they'd gone together, like this, that he thought of her and was hit by a vague sense of grief. Things could have turned out differently, he told himself with utter conviction. Fortunately, the present imposed itself like a tyrant, leaving no time to look back at the past. True, sudden bouts of melancholy would unexpectedly overcome him sometimes. He'd be making love to his wife, for instance, and out of nowhere feel his stamina abandon him, and his wife would say he seemed absent; or in the middle of a party committee meeting, while debating electoral strategy, he'd respond monosyllabically to questions, not really paying attention.

He had excuses—the pressure of the murder investigations, the responsibility of being so close to a seat in Parliament, the never-ending interviews, and all that public exposure. Everyone was very empathetic, hoping for the best outcome.

Everyone but Inga, the chief forensic inspector of Malmö, who kept badgering him with questions and theories about the phone number Gövan had promised to look into. For the time being, he'd managed to dodge her, but he knew the chief inspector. Inga was the kind of person who wouldn't let things go. Conscientious and methodical, she didn't stop until she got answers to her questions. And lately she had too many of them. A few days ago she'd gone too far, asking Gövan innocently—and he was convinced that it was feigned innocence—if the place by the lake where Yasmina's body had been found wasn't the same place Gövan and his sister used to play.

"How did you know about that?"

She stared at Gövan intently, as though reading his mind, and reminded him that he'd told her himself, back when they were going out, in one of those regrettable bouts of sincerity that creep into pillow talk after making love.

"No, I'm sure it's not the same place," he'd replied a bit too quickly.

Judging by her reaction, Inga wasn't too convinced. She was starting to ask questions about Yasmina and her clients, the bars and clubs where she hung out. It was just a matter of time before she found someone who could tie Yasmina to him. So the deputy chief had taken the additional step of suggesting to the inspector general that Inga be transferred, perhaps to a remote region in the north where her suspicions would fade away once she was far from any ears that were prepared to listen. Inga herself had provided the perfect excuse for his request: she'd been the one who pushed the hardest to have Sture detained, and at the end of the day, the Turk's arrest and subsequent media appearance had been a humiliating defeat for the Malmö police force. The judge had taken less than twenty-four hours to free Sture, stressing how weak the evidence presented against him was. Someone had to pay for that mistake, and Gövan was discreetly maneuvering to have all fingers point to Inga.

Fatima was another loose end. Gövan had underestimated her. Yasmina's mother had turned out to be very combative indeed. As if to make amends to her daughter now that it was too late, she was constantly in the media demanding justice for Yasmina, doing the rounds on TV shows, holding up a photo of Yasmina like a prayer card where her daughter was the saint, even turning up in person at the station on a near-daily basis demanding to know how the investigation was going. The whole situation might have gotten out of control if Gövan hadn't leaked parts of the family's past. Finding out that Yasmina was a prostitute, that Fatima herself had aborted several times under strange circumstances, that her husband had committed suicide, and her father was part of a radicalized Muslim community had undermined the support of the public, which had at first been quite sympathetic. Abdul's stroke had been a final lucky break. Even if the old man knew something, there was no way for him to open his mouth now. Plus, Gövan had used his influence to get him into a clinic, paid for on the public's dime, and subtly made Fatima see that this helping hand was contingent on her attitude. She was to stop attacking the police and criticizing their inefficiency, stop insisting that resources weren't being dedicated to finding her daughter's murderer because she was Muslim and lived in Rosengård.

She couldn't bite the hand that fed her and expect to keep eating. Reluctantly, Fatima seemed to get the message, and though she didn't stop making demands, she did become less belligerent and tone it down. It was a matter of time before journalists and the public alike forgot about her.

Free and clear—almost. The one remaining thread was the hardest one to cut, the real danger. The one person who could screw it all up. Gövan wasn't fooling himself. He knew there was nothing dignified about the hot muck he had stepped into. He shouldn't have panicked and killed Yasmina to begin with, but there was nothing to do now but plow forward, no matter what it took. He wasn't about to renounce the life he had or spend the next twenty years in prison.

Gövan saw headlights coming down the path, and stood tensing his muscles. Ready. He clenched his fists inside his jacket pocket and began to walk toward the car that pulled up next to a graffiti-covered wall. A few yards away, he stopped and waited.

Sture got out of the car. They weighed one another up from a safe distance. Neither of them trusted the other. They knew each other too well, hated each other too much. They'd been playing cat and mouse for years, crossing paths again and again, biting and scratching but never managing to knock the other off balance.

Sture stared at Gövan with infinite hatred.

"I have to congratulate you, deputy chief. Or should I call you a member of Parliament? I see the polls put you in a clear victory for Sunday's elections. Scania's constituents are lucky to have someone of your valor, though you'll have to give up police work, an irreparable loss for the citizens of Malmö. Let's hope your successor is up to the task."

Sture recalled the first time Gövan had arrested him in a raid. He wasn't yet known as the Turk, he was just one of the goons in the service of his uncle Sigmund, the one who ran the business back in the seventies. Gövan was a rookie at the time, a new recruit who wanted to prove himself to the veteran officers, so he smacked Sture and then threw him into a glass wall at a brothel in full view of the hookers, the clientele, and Sigmund's other thugs. He still had a ringing in his ear from that smack.

Gövan wasn't in the mood for nonsense.

"You know why I called you, Sture. The material Yasmina told me about—the photos, videos, and recordings. What are you going to do with them?"

Sture tilted his head back and gazed at the starry sky. August nights were the most beautiful of the year, in his view. When he saw the heavens so full of stars, it made him realize how absurd everything down on earth was. Death, violence, drugs, kids, marriage, grudges, he and Gövan... They'd be old men soon, lose their teeth, and still they'd keep snapping their jaws at one another pathetically to defend their stupid conquests. He knew this, and yet couldn't force himself to veer from the script.

"I have to admit, your bumpkin look, the whole country-boy thing, made me underestimate you. But you got everyone to believe I was the one who killed Yasmina. Your setup—arresting me, parading me before the cameras until the courts turned you into Mister Clean—that was very good. Must have brought in some incredible returns."

"You killed the guy at the port, you're responsible for the decapitation in the park. You went too far with your appalling spectacles."

Sture nodded, cracking a slight smile.

"I had to send a message to my friends in Ankara. We can't let a bunch of foreigners come here all cocky and think they can impose their ways on us now, can we? I confess that in that particular case there was a personal element, I admit it. Though it's kind of ironic for me to be here making excuses to you. After all, you killed too, and yours was personal as well, right?"

Sture approached Gövan, and their silhouettes merged in the headlights of both cars.

"You didn't have to kill her, you know. We could have come to an agreement, which after all is why you called me. You didn't have to kill her, but you shattered her skull with a rusty ax, because you could. Did you hate her? Did she wound your sense of manhood? Betray your feelings? She told me you were falling in love with her, that you were going to leave your family, your privileged life . . . Poor, naive little girl. You were never going to do any of that, were you?"

"You know nothing about me."

Sture nodded.

"That's true. But I knew a lot about Yasmina, far more than you can imagine. And I know that she was falling in love with you, that if you'd honestly been on her side and not just lied and fucked her, she'd have betrayed me in the end."

Gövan winced. He didn't want to contemplate that possibility.

"She was just one of your whores. She did what she did because you ordered her to."

Sture flared his nostrils and inhaled deeply. He thought about the gun tucked in his waistband. Had a quick debate with his rage and calmed himself down. That wasn't the way to do it; he was no longer an impetuous kid. He knew how to fight, and when and where.

"You're so blind, deputy. Yasmina was much, much more than one of my whores."

Gövan studied Sture's face and saw that Yasmina's death was affecting him personally. This wasn't just about the two of them, or losing a possession, or a strategy that had failed. It was like he'd lost something close to him and felt guilty about it.

"The goods—what do you want in exchange for them?"

Sture narrowed his eyes for a second, and Gövan relaxed, recognizing the voracious predatory look. This was someone he could make a deal with.

"I want what Yasmina told you: unrestricted access, my face to disappear from the investigation, and our cooperation to extend beyond Malmö. In your new post, business opportunities that could benefit us both will increase exponentially. We'll keep appearances up, but let's be honest, deputy, we need each other. We both know we could destroy one another, kill each other or have each other killed, but neither of us wants that. See, when it comes down to it, we're pragmatists, you and me. It's business."

Gövan didn't trust any of this. He had no intention of launching his political career with a sword of Damocles over his head, but getting rid of Sture now would be a strategic mistake of incalculable measure. Gövan had to bide his time, cement his power, and then distance himself. He took an envelope from his inside jacket pocket and handed it to Sture.

"A gesture of my goodwill: these are the open investigations against some of your men. Everything we know about your drug distribution networks, the drops, your contacts at the port..."

Sture let out a low whistle, took the envelope, and tucked it away.

"This is going to save me some serious headaches. I appreciate it. I don't think we'll be seeing each other again, but we'll be in touch." With that, Sture turned and walked back to his car.

"Wait! What are you giving me in exchange?"

Sture cocked his head with a sly smile.

"I'm voting for you on Sunday, MP."

When he was a kid, Erick dreamed of being a hero, like one of the Portuguese soldiers who fought in Angola, like the one in the photo his grandmother kept on her bedroom dresser but never talked about. Or maybe one of those gold diggers in the Jack London novels he liked, or even—why not?—a famous soccer player like Zlatan Ibrahimović, who'd just scored two goals against Ireland on

Sweden's national team. Anything to avoid being cooped up at home, studying on Saturday afternoon, and listening to his mother prattle on about the importance of higher education. He didn't want to be an entrepreneur or spend his days in an expensive suit, going from one office to another with a leather briefcase, but his mother refused to listen. And that was what they'd fought about, again. That, and the fact that she'd sided with Sture after Erick called him a murderer, getting slapped so hard in return that he'd ended up with a split lip. And Erick was her son, her flesh and blood.

His mother had knocked on his door repeatedly, but Erick refused to open it. *She's just like him*, he thought, lying in bed, his lip still swollen. Erick hated Rosengård and the restaurant; couldn't stand the yellowed picture of Omar Sharif on the wall or his mother's onion-smelling hands; detested Sture's ridiculous mustache and the people who sat at the tables covered in red-and-white-checked cloths. He hated his room, which was small and cluttered, hated his school and his friends, books and the French Revolution.

He couldn't breathe. He was drowning and everyone refused to see it. He didn't even want to sit at his computer looking at dirty pictures anymore, or chat on social media. All he wanted to do was lie in bed all day with a pillow over his head. Curl up into a ball and disappear into dreams of him and Yasmina.

After he'd seen her dead, on TV, Erick stopped thinking about her to get excited; the idea of it now embarrassed him and seemed sick. Instead he just listened to songs she liked and watched videos of her favorite singer on the internet. She looked a little like Yasmina, though Yasmina was prettier and had two different-colored eyes. He missed seeing her walk into Old Sweden with that determined look, swishing so rhythmically that Erick couldn't help but imagine her body under her clothes, wild and passionate. Sometimes she'd flash him a smile, and he clung desperately to it, grasping at straws. And when they chatted briefly about stuff they both liked, Erick felt like he had already become the man he'd one day grow to be—a man who could tell her everything he felt, and everything he was willing to do to get her out of the sordid world she hated.

One time she kissed him on the lips. Just thinking about it was enough to give him a huge erection, but he refused to touch himself. He didn't want to sully the memory: it was a fleeting kiss, her lips just brushing against his after a conversation in which he confessed that he'd been stealing from the register for ages, saving up to buy two tickets to New York. *Why two?* she'd asked. And he told her, gazing at her dolefully, one for him and one for her. She'd given him a tender look and stroked his hair. *I wish you were older, or I was younger.* Erick knew what she meant. But ten years wasn't that much once you hit a certain age. Ten to twenty, sure, that was a lot; fourteen to twenty-four, maybe. But she could go out with someone who was twenty, couldn't she? *Twenty to thirty's no big deal, right?* That was when she'd nodded and given him a kiss. He wanted more, but that promise was enough. Because you don't just kiss someone if it doesn't mean anything, not on the lips. That's what he thought. And now Sture had killed her, he was sure of it. The old man had spent all afternoon talking about her, running his mouth, half-drunk, taking little sips of whisky. Yasmina this, Yasmina that, I loved her, I killed her. His eyes were all glassy and his mouth drooping as he leaned on the bar. *Yes, I pushed her to do it, I killed her. It started the minute she was born, just like with her mother.* Those were his words. Erick, at the end of the bar, looked up from his geography book and stared at Sture, not understanding what he meant. He knew that Yasmina's mother was alive, he'd seen her on TV holding up a picture of her daughter and asking for possible witnesses to come forth if they had anything that might help the police investigation. But the essence of what Sture had said stuck with him: that he'd killed Yasmina. And on one corner of his page, over the physical map of Europe, he wrote down the number that appeared under Fatima's picture, the one for the police hotline. Sture realized that Erick was looking at him and reached over the bar to grab him by his shirtfront.

"You! Little bastard. You were in love with her, weren't you? Like everyone else."

The words flew angrily from his mouth, spittle hitting Erick in the face. "You poor, stupid wimp. I would never have allowed it, do you understand? She was too much of a woman for you. For every asshole in this fucking neighborhood."

It was at that point that Erick thrashed to break free of Sture and screamed that he was a murderer, furious not just for Yasmina but for himself, for all the contempt he'd borne for years and the way Sture looked at him like a cockroach stuck to the bottom of his shoe, crunching with every step.

Sture straightened up and gave Erick a backhander. But Erick wasn't afraid this time, as he had been so many times before. He held Sture's gaze and wielded the knife he'd been holding. *Touch me again and I'll cut you, I swear.* First Sture gave him a shocked look, but it quickly morphed into a hurtful laugh that grew and grew until he finally threw his head back for air and inhaled deeply. Then he stopped sharply, flashing a look full of hatred and scorn. *Go on, you little shit. If you had one drop of my blood in you, you'd have slit my throat by now.* Erick hesitated, still gripping the knife firmly. *Do it, you sissy! You think I killed the woman you loved? Do it. You'll never get another chance.* But Erick lost his nerve, and Sture snatched the knife from him and held it to Erick's eye, totally apoplectic. *Do you know what it feels like? You don't have the balls, do you?* Then he threw the knife and walked off. *Now run and go cry to your mama*, he said without bothering to turn around, kicking the door on his way out.

Erick got out of bed and looked in the mirror. His lip stung, and the knife had left a mark under his left eye that looked like a mosquito bite. The knife was on his desk.

Sture used to bring Fatima here sometimes. He liked to stroll along, feeling the pebbles under his feet, imagining he was a regular person with everyday concerns and ambitions. Someone who'd never do anything beyond the pale. Now the neighborhood had become gentrified, colonized by young middle-class couples fleeing the bustle of downtown. On Sundays you'd see them walking with their kids out by the new pier, strolling along the wooden board-walk that went out to the beach, or having a drink or snack in one of the cafés, making the most of the sunshine. Back then it had been a depressed fisherman's neighborhood. It was where Malmö ended, and Sture and Fatima would sit on the rocks, smoke, and talk about things. This was where she'd told him she was pregnant—again—but that this time it was a girl. He still didn't know why he'd been so excited about it. Maybe because, for a minute, he'd thought he could become a different man—escape the life he led, put his arm around Fatima like they were just a normal couple, forget that she was in fact afraid of him, that she was only there be-cause Abdul had forced her. Yasmina had liked it there too. Half-jokingly, she'd say that one day she was going to buy one of those attic apartments with a tiny window and a view of the bridge. Sture would buy her a sandwich and a soda and they'd sit on a bench, like father and daughter. Sometimes he even felt like that's what they were.

"I should have bought her that damn apartment."

Now it was election Sunday, and the boardwalk was de-serted. At this time of the evening, people were gathered in front of the TV watching the ballot count. He pictured Gövan at party headquarters, flanked by his wife and kids and the party faithful, anxiously awaiting the second they could unleash their euphoria and proclaim victory. He'd no doubt have prepared a short, emotional speech and would appear on the balcony, waving, his family by his side. Happy. Feeling like a winner. In an hour, two at most, Gövan would become a star, out of reach, in a different galaxy. And from the heights of his Olympus, the first thing he'd do would be take care of Sture. Sture was sure of that. What Gövan had given him—names, reports—was chump change, bait so that Sture would be sidetracked until the final blow came crashing down on his head.

But Sture was going to outsmart him. He checked his watch. That other cop, Inga, would be there soon.

The deal she'd offered was fair—or it was what he'd expected, at least. There would be no pardon, no strings pulled, not with her. She was one tough cop and had made herself perfectly clear: no deals with the prosecutor, no blackmail. *The best you'll get is extenuating circumstances for cooperating with the police, possibly a reduced sentence.* She'd also said he could choose a prison close to Malmö and ensure a visitation schedule that would allow Raquel to go see him regularly. Crumbs, that was what the chief inspector of forensics had offered in exchange for the intel Sture was prepared to offer up on the deputy chief. But it was better than waiting for the hit Gövan was sure to put out on him. *I'll need proof*, Inga had insisted, tough as nails, refusing to take his word for it when he said that Gövan was the one who'd murdered Yasmina. And yet Sture got the impression that his phone call hadn't surprised her and that in a way she already suspected as much.

The proof was in his backpack. Enough to destroy Gövan, destroy every part of his life, leave nothing untouched.

He hadn't told Raquel what he was planning to do. She'd have flat-out refused, would never understand his rationale. Maybe he didn't understand it himself. Sture had lived this way his whole life—running, chasing, never questioning what he was doing. The world needed people like him to make it real, make it painful. He'd never experienced anything else, and he didn't complain about it. He'd always known this moment would arrive. And it wouldn't be the first time he went to jail, though there was no doubt that it would be the last. But he was going to take the deputy chief down with him, and everyone would know why. Sometimes defeat and failure can be a sweet comfort.

He spent ten minutes skulking around the piles under the pier. It looked surreal in the moonlight. In the distance, lights from the bridge and boats twinkled. His world, his universe, was there. He rummaged for a cigarette and his lighter and then realized that he must have left them in the car. Turning, he glimpsed a shadow spying on him from a few yards away. The boardwalk lights were in his face, making the figure's outline indistinct.

"Who's that?"

The shape advanced, hands in the pockets of a leather jacket. Sture narrowed his gaze.

"*Erick*? What the fuck...?"

That was all he had time to say. His brain processed what was about to happen a split second too late.

Suddenly, a knife jabbed deep into his neck.

He tried to protect himself with his hands, but Erick thrust the knife down to the handle. Sture felt its cold blade ripping through him. He reached for Erick's hand but couldn't stop him from yanking the knife out and plunging it back in again, this time into his chest, stabbing with brute force, over and over, again and again, until the blade broke off.

29

Cemetery, outskirts of Malmö, one week later

t rained the day of the funeral. A horde of black umbrellas
paraded before Raquel, in full mourning attire but refusing to cry, standing tall and dignified.

To her right, Erick—flanked by two plainclothes officers—
was the one attracting all the attention. As a minor, he was
exempt from handcuffs.

Off to one side, behind the swarm of umbrellas, stood
Inga, watching. Once Sture's grave was sealed and the pro-
cession began to dissolve, she nodded and made a gesture,
signaling the officers to allow a brief exchange between Raquel and her son. Erick was crying.

"Don't cry. I don't want anyone to see you looking weak.
You're a minor, there are extenuating circumstances. You'll
get out soon, and I'll be waiting for you."

Erick let his mother hug him and felt the warmth of her body through the wet coat she wore. He'd never been so afraid, not even when he saw Sture stare at him with that fierce expression and grab for his legs as he lay dying.

Raquel pulled away from her son and held his shoulders.

"I won't let anything happen to you. Ever. Do you believe me?"

He nodded, then meekly allowed the police to lead him away. Raquel followed with her eyes until he got into the police car. He waved from the back seat and she waved back, and only after the patrol car had begun to drive off did she succumb to her emotions and begin to sob.

"Raquel, I'm so sorry about all of this."

She dried her tears and turned to the inspector. They'd spoken several times since Sture's death. Inga kept pressuring her.

"If anything happens to my son, if they touch one hair on his head, I'll hold you responsible!" she replied vehemently.

Inga shivered in her trench coat, in part from the rain, which was soaking her, and in part because she took Raquel's words as the threat that they were.

"He'll be in good hands. But we could make things go more smoothly. Have you thought about what I said? I'm sure the night Sture died he had a backpack on him, and its contents are very important to us. But your son is still claiming he knows nothing about a backpack. I think he's lying to me."

"I know nothing about it. I've told you a dozen times already."

Inga was convinced Raquel was lying too. She'd been the one to call emergency services when Erick told her what he'd done. And her call was made from the same place Sture died, which meant that Erick had called his mother, told her what he'd done, and she'd gone to meet him. Later, however, she claimed that she'd been someplace else. It took the first patrol car fifteen minutes to get to the scene. That was more than enough time for Raquel to have made the backpack disappear, and with it the proof that they needed to incriminate Gövan—proof that Sture had been planning to give her.

"Are you sure?"

Raquel shot Inga a defiant look. Someone approached with an umbrella. Inga recognized it as one of Sture's men. *So she's in charge now.* Inga cocked her head to one side, heavyhearted. The cycle would never end.

"I understand. If you want to talk, you know where to find me."

Gövan was having a hard time getting used to the tedious dinners where nobody actually said what they really thought or laid their cards on the table. The world of politics could be far more coldhearted than the world of the streets, and Gövan had to learn its rules. From time to time, his wife reached out under the table and touched his leg to remind him he wasn't alone, and Gövan gave her a grateful smile.

A waiter approached and whispered something in his ear. Gövan nodded gravely, cleared his throat, and touched the tip of his napkin to his lips.

"I'm afraid I've got an urgent phone call. If you'll excuse me...I'll be right back." His wife shot him a questioning look, but he patted her shoulder reassuringly.

He recognized Sture's wife out on the terrace, smoking and gazing at the luxury SUVs parked in the restaurant's circular driveway. Deep down, he was thankful to Sture's bastard: Erick had freed him from a thorny problem. And he had no intention of creating any new ones. It wouldn't do to have someone see the next member of Parliament being friendly with the wife of a known criminal.

"What are you doing here?"

Raquel turned and gave Gövan a careful once-over. She'd pictured him taller, more attractive. Of course TV makes everything seem better, truer than it is in real life.

"Do you know who I am?"

Gövan looked around cagily.

"Of course I do. And I'll ask you again. What are you doing here?"

Raquel didn't do things like Sture. Her husband loved to play little games, speak in riddles, but she was direct. The sooner things were clear between them, the better it would go for everyone.

"I know you killed Yasmina and I know why."

Gövan's face constricted.

"I have no idea what you're talking about. I understand that you're in a difficult situation and I respect your sorrow. But that doesn't give you the right to come here and start making absurd accusations."

Raquel didn't bat an eye.

"Don't do that. Don't try to pull one over on me. I'm not one of those reporters who fawns all over you. I've seen the pictures and the videos, I've heard the recordings. And your colleague, Inspector Inga, is pressuring me. I'm guessing Sture had an agreement with her and was about to snitch on you. What's to keep me from giving her the goods?"

Gövan was genuinely shocked. He hadn't imagined that Inga would go so far. He tried to feel the situation out cautiously.

"If you're so sure I killed Yasmina then what are you doing here with me when you could be giving her the proof?"

"I don't trust cops. And I came to propose a deal."

Gövan looked around cautiously before speaking.

"What kind of deal?"

"Sture told me you two had reached an agreement, that you were going to collaborate in the future. I want the same conditions. I'm in charge now. And I promise not to make trouble for you—no more dead bodies, no scandalous decapitations in children's parks. I like to be discreet. In exchange, I'll give you all the proof Sture had on you."

Gövan examined Raquel carefully. What did his instincts say? *Kill her. She's going to be trouble.* But not now, not with so much buzz, so much in the news. He had to buy some time—a few months, a year. However long it took for things to die down and people to forget about this story. The prudent thing would be simply to tell her to leave, but if it was true that Inga was behind all of this, he couldn't take the risk. He had to kill Raquel soon, tonight.

"Let's just say I accept. What kind of guarantee are you offering me?"

Raquel opened her hands as a sign of goodwill.

"I've got a lot to lose and very little to gain. Plus, I have a better reason than Sture did to honor our agreement."

"What reason is that?"

"Erick. I want my son home in less than a year."

Gövan shook his head.

"Not possible. The law is the law. Your son killed a man."

"You killed Yasmina, and yet here you are, having dinner at a fancy restaurant with your wife and rich friends like nothing ever happened. Isn't that what power affords? Not money or influence, but impunity. If you want the proof, you'll have to get my son out."

Gövan pretended to be weighing things up. After a long pause, he nodded.

"I can give it a go. I have a few friends in child prosecution services. You'll have to give me some time."

"That's not good enough. I want you to promise, here and now, that you can do it."

Gövan felt himself growing impatient. Stupid bitch. Why couldn't she let it go?

"All right. I'll get your son out," he agreed.

Raquel seemed satisfied.

"One more thing. Don't underestimate me, deputy chief. I'm smart, and I'm not weak. I'm almost thankful that you killed that bitch Yasmina. I'm going to help you, Gövan, and you'll help me. Agreed?"

Gövan nodded. He heard his wife's voice, calling him.

"Give me your number. I'll call you tomorrow, Raquel. I'll have news about Erick. And bring the proof. I think we'll get along just fine."

When Raquel returned to the car, her legs were trembling. She leaned back against the seat and closed her eyes, trying to calm down. She was going to need nerves of steel for this.

The following morning, Raquel got a message from Gövan. He told her to meet him in a park on the outskirts of town, by the freeway. She drove Sture's SUV quickly, her pulse throbbing in her temples, her heart pounding. She was thinking about Erick, about the future that the fortune-teller had promised for her son. And she was willing to take the risk. Although Raquel arrived five minutes early, Gövan was already there, sitting on the hood of his old Škoda, calmly smoking. He raised an arm in greeting, tossed his cigarette off in the distance, and approached with his hands in the pockets of his overcoat. Smiling and overconfident.

"I've got good news," he announced the moment Raquel stepped out of the car. "My prosecutor friend told me that Erick will be able to get leave in a couple of months. And by the end of the year, he'll be home. Free."

Raquel's face lit up.

"How did you pull that off?"

"We all do each other favors, everyone owes everyone in this world. Do you have the proof? I want to be done with this as soon as possible."

Raquel took a small backpack from the back of the car and handed it to Gövan. She bunched her hands into fists to keep him from seeing them tremble.

"Now what?"

Gövan opened the backpack and examined the contents. He nodded, visibly relieved.

"Now, you go back to your life and I go back to mine. Like nothing had happened. But first tell me one thing. Exactly what does Inga know?"

Raquel swallowed. She hadn't imagined it was going to be this difficult.

"She thinks you killed Yasmina because you were afraid the girl could tie you to Sture. Her guess is that you got nervous and made a terrible mistake."

Gövan's face hardened.

"Inga doesn't know shit. You and I know what kind of person Yasmina was, right? You said so yourself last night: you hated her as much as I did. Yasmina was like poison, she got into your blood. She was clouding my vision, steering me off course. Do you know I almost believed her? For a minute, I thought she actually loved me and that it was possible to give it all up, go back to being the Gövan I used to be, before the police force and politics and all this crap. That's why I split her skull with that ax. She closed that door, reminded me that you can't trust your emotions. Your emotions trick you."

"You don't have to give me all the details. All I want is my son home. I've got to go."

Raquel went to open the car door, but Gövan grabbed her wrist as she reached for it.

"Did you really think this was how it was going to go? I'm sorry, I can't take that risk."

He grabbed Raquel's neck. Strangling her would be easy. She struggled, tried to scratch his face, eyes open wide, but Gövan overpowered her with a knee to the stomach and she folded up like a broken accordion. "Don't fight, this will be quick." He held her to the ground and sat on her, his hands still around her neck. Raquel's blouse came open, and suddenly Gövan saw it. Involuntarily, he let up on the pressure.

"What the hell is that? You're wired?"

Simultaneously, he heard footsteps running up behind him, voices shouting. One of them was Inspector Inga's.

The paramedic who examined Raquel in the ambulance said she was fine. Just a few scratches that would fade in a couple of days. Inspector Inga sat beside her on the cot.

"You did the right thing, Raquel."

Raquel pulled out the mic hidden inside her bra and handed it to Inga.

"Are you going to get my son out?"

Inga looked away, staring out the ambulance window. Gövan was being put into a patrol car, hands cuffed behind his back. Another officer held the backpack with Sture's proof.

"Anything's possible . . ."

30

Malmö, late August

The old lady had eyes in the back of her head and knew everything that went on in the neighborhood. Her face was old in a way that looked totally decrepit.

"No reason to keep knocking, there's nobody there. Who are you looking for?"

Miguel gazed at her half-hidden face as she peered from a crack in the door next to the one where he stood. He couldn't understand a word she said.

"Abdul, I'm looking for Abdul," Miguel said, pointing to the door he'd knocked on. He raised his voice, as though rather than speaking a different language, the woman was hard of hearing. He thought she was about to slam the door in his face when a girl of fourteen or so appeared behind her, giving him a curious look.

"You're looking for Mister Abdul?" she asked in passable English. Miguel nodded, hopeful. "He's not here. They took him away a few weeks ago. He's in the hospital, in Västra Hamnen. Do you know where that is?"

Miguel shook his head and was grateful to the girl for writing down the address.

Back on the street he saw that his taxi was still there, parked in front of a shuttered restaurant called Old Sweden, which had a For Sale sign up. Nearby, a group of young men spoke loudly, so they could hear one another over the blaring rap they were listening to on a huge radio. A bit farther on, a very young woman pushed a little girl with short, stiff braids on a swing. A car with tinted windows crept by, and then, reaching the roundabout at the end of the street, sped off and began honking its horn.

The taxi driver lowered his window with a stern expression on his face.

"It's not a good idea to hang around here if you're not from the neighborhood. The place is full of *blatte*. Understand? *Blatte*. Blacks, Arabs, riffraff."

Miguel was troubled by the comment. He glanced at the buildings all around: clotheslines with laundry hung out to dry, satellite dishes, doors with bars over them. Climbing into the back seat, he gave the hospital's address.

The taxi driver was listening intently to the radio. While he drove, he tilted his head as if to hear better, and turned up the volume.

"Is something going on?"

The driver shrugged.

"Nothing that should surprise me, at this rate," he said in English. "The Malmö police just arrested an old deputy chief who'd been elected member of Parliament for Scania in the most recent elections."

"Wow. I didn't think that kind of thing happened here."

"This guy had us totally fooled, pretended to be all hard-line with criminals, promised to rid the city of these rats," he said, indicating the people on the sidewalk, "and it turns out the bastard was a murderer. He killed a girl from this very neighborhood, a hooker. Not that I care about *her*, you understand. Step on one and a hundred more come crawling out of the cracks, but fuck, a police officer mixed up in that? And one with a political post, at that. This country is going to the dogs. In the last elections, I voted for Löfven's Social Democrats, but no more monkeying around. Next time I'm voting for the Sweden Democrats. I like Söder, he's got the right idea. I mean, fuck, we're a small country, under ten million, and we just keep taking in all the trash that nobody else wants."

"I guess your ten million compatriots don't share your views."

The cab driver shot him a look the rearview mirror.

"Where are you from?"

"Spain."

The taxi driver narrowed his eyes. Spaniards, Portuguese, Italians, Moroccans, Kurds, Turks, Albanians. No doubt they were all the same to him.

"Could you pull over here?"

The cabbie furrowed his brow.

"The hospital's over by the old docks, a long way from here."

"No matter. I'll take a bus, or walk. I wouldn't want my filthy Spanish ass to sully your precious taxi."

Not everything had stopped, it just looked that way. On the inside, he was still intact. From his chair by the window, Abdul kept an eye on things. He heard the sound of people's voices, watched the expressions on their faces, and interpreted their hand movements. Everybody assumed he was just a smoldering ember, part of the furniture, dusty and silent, but he was still writhing inside, alert to the signs, to the impossibility of communicating, moving, or speaking, rendered desperate by his frailty. Abdul's mind no longer governed as it should; he ordered his body to do things and his body did not obey; he'd been subjected to the indignity of being shunted around by the nurses like a plant that's in the way, of sitting in his own reeking filth when he soiled his diapers and they took too long to notice.

But his mind could still fire. At times a spark of lucidity came over him, and he saw those around him as enemies, intent on burying him before his time. He stiffened when Fatima arrived—emotional, exhausted, silent—and she hardly spoke to him. Abdul would try to force his vocal cords to express rage, but the most that came out was an incomprehensible gurgle, which led to coughing attacks that turned his cheeks red and made his eyes go bloodshot. Fatima would stare at him pitilessly, vacantly, and then give him a sip of water and wipe the slobber from his chin. An hour later, his daughter would leave without saying goodbye, kissing his forehead, or taking his hands to warm them in hers. Abdul was cold all the time, especially his hands and feet. It emanated from his brittle bones, seeped through the pores in his dry skin, filled his nose with frost, and made his tongue go stiff.

That's why he sought the sun that filtered in through the window. When it sank down behind buildings, he even got cold in his cheeks. He'd shiver, thinking the cold was actually death, and imagine his body curled up in some dark grave, covered by a shroud, dirt filling his mouth, his nose, his eyes. So far from life. He shook his head uneasily, desperate to escape the shadows that surrounded him like a pack of dogs awaiting the final moment.

"How are we feeling today?"

Abdul heard a voice at his right ear—the offensively childish, ridiculous tone of a nurse whose breath smelled of menthol cigarettes. An impostor, patting his bony shoulder. She knew he couldn't reply, yet she asked anyway. Stupid harpy.

"You've got a visitor! He's come from very far away to say hello to you. I'll leave the two of you alone for a bit."

The nurse spun his wheelchair, moving him away from the benevolent trajectory of sunlight and before a stranger, who observed him in curiosity. Abdul tried to protest and insist that she wheel him back to the window, but all that came out was a pitiful, strangled whimper.

Who was this stranger standing there, staring at him like he was a museum piece?

Miguel gazed attentively at Abdul. His thin hair had been combed to one side, and someone had doused him in a sickly cologne. He'd been shaved too, and was clad in a droopy green-apple-colored robe in a vain attempt to indicate a state of health and hygiene.

"I brought you something." Miguel opened the cylindrical tube strapped over his shoulder and spread the contents out before Abdul, watching his eyes for a reaction. There was nothing left of the old fervor in his dead, watery eyes, which stared straight ahead, tear ducts leaking. You'd never even guess they were the same person.

"Do you recognize yourself? I'd say Thelma was very generous in her interpretation."

Miguel glanced around the spartan room, devoid of furniture except for the bed and a metal table that held medical supplies. The bare walls, painted light gray, seemed a reluctant greeting, not welcoming or inviting anyone to stay too long. A transitory room, a simple stopover before the final destination.

"I think it would look good right here. You don't mind, do you? I asked the nurse for some thumbtacks."

He realized that despite the old man's stiff unmoving body, Abdul could follow him with his eyes, which he managed to direct, albeit falteringly, in the direction he wanted. Miguel hung the portrait on the wall and wheeled Abdul's in front of it.

"You can hear me, can't you? You understand everything I'm saying. You don't fool me. I don't care if you pretend to hide in there." He pointed to Abdul's eyes, which had sunk deep in their sockets and made him resemble the skull he'd soon become. Cunning eyes, despite his apparent composure.

Abdul opened his mouth slightly, the tip of his tongue poking out. He made a baleful sound, which Miguel interpreted correctly.

"The past. Yes, that's all past. Like the half-closed shutters on this window; that's what you'd like, isn't it? A room to walk out of, only a tiny bit of light coming in, a painting in the dark that can't be seen clearly. Something to be forgotten."

Abdul tilted his head to look away from the canvas with his face on it, now hanging on the wall. Miguel forced him to look at it.

"Mirrors are a problem. That's why there aren't any in this room. People see their reflections in the mirror, and sometimes they don't have the guts to look into their own faces. They feel disgusted by themselves. We can fool others for a lifetime, but we can't fool ourselves, not if we look and really see. No one can stand the secrets they find in their own reflection, the murmuring they sense in the eyes looking back at them. I've brought you a mirror, Abdul."

Abdul's pupils dilated, his eyes glimmered. The vein in his neck swelled and throbbed with his pulse, his mouth opened and he let out a horrible, rasping whimper.

"Sin? No, just evidence, Abdul. There's the man you could have been, and here you are, the dregs that remain."

For the next hour, Miguel recounted Helena's life to Abdul in detail, telling him about the girl who watched her own mother commit suicide after she'd tried to drown her. He showed him and read to him each and every one of the postcards Enrique had sent his daughter, described their encounter in London, when Enrique got out of prison, spoke of Helena's inability to love Louise without feeling guilty. He spoke of the regret and remorse she felt over her son David's death, and, finally, in a subdued romantic tone he wasn't even aware of, he recounted his last few months with Helena and their mutual discovery of freedom and desire, and love.

"She wanted to come here and tell you these things herself. She wasn't looking for revenge. All she wanted to do was tell you that the circle had closed, that she was at peace with herself and that all the ghosts now belong to you. For years, Helena questioned that portrait and got no reply, but she doesn't need it anymore. You do. There are so many questions you never wanted to ask, and answers you're not going to like, Abdul."

Under his brows, Abdul's eyes had dried out before the portrait, withered by fear, and he couldn't avert his gaze from those other eyes, the ones painted by Thelma, in which he saw not only his entire past but also what the desiccated future had to offer him.

Before he left, Miguel took one last look at Abdul: his bowed chin, lolling head, and mouth hanging open, a thick line of drool falling onto his shoulder.

Thirty thousand feet, that was their altitude. Best not to think about it. The engines' muffled drone helped calm his nerves, evidence of the fact that, counter to any logic he could fathom, man had learned to fly. It still astounded him that something so heavy could glide so smoothly atop the channels of wind that it felt like they weren't moving at all but simply suspended above the clouds by invisible cables.

"Would you like something to drink?"

Miguel thanked the flight attendant but declined the offer and turned back to the window to concentrate on the marvel he was witnessing. In the distance, at one corner of the horizon, an undulating blanket of cloud had been pierced by the sunlight, making it shimmer with various colors, like stained glass.

"That's a storm," the flight attendant said.

Miguel couldn't believe his eyes; on the other side, the sun was shining. The flight attendant nodded and gave him an indulgent smile, the way you might an astonished child.

"We're flying above the rain."

The world was down there, silent and impassive. But he could hear none of its commotion, its stress, the strange sounds and echoes of life. Rain was falling on fields, cities, houses, buildings, animals, rivers, mountains, and invisible people—some running for cover, others embracing it wholeheartedly. Leaves were turning green, ports were getting choppy, boats rocking impatiently. Highways were glistening, gardens soaking up drops, fences around farms weathering the storm. It was raining in the Sevilla airport parking lot, where Natalia was waiting for him, maybe even against the window of Abdul's room, on Helena's grave, and the funeral niche of her friend Marqués; raining on the Thames, in a ditch by the side of the road in Tarifa, on a beach in Tangier, in the peaks surrounding the Valley of the Fallen, between the tree roots and rocks where his mother's ashes lay. Perhaps even ghosts were getting soaked in the shower.

He conjured up one of the few beautiful images he had of his father. It wasn't actually a memory of the man himself but his smell, lingering on a coat that his mother made him put on one winter. Miguel recalled his hands inside the pockets—their lining was coming unstitched—the dry crackly smell of an Extremadura winter, the vague scent of olives from the olive oil factory, and straw on the jacket's collar. Those were the smells of his childhood, of his father. Of hard dirt and sprawling fields and low skies, paths fading into the olive groves, sheds and corrals that stank of wet straw when it rained.

And he recalled, too, that the shower caught him in the field and he covered his head with the coat and, when he got home, found his mother trying to bail water that was knee-deep by using a rag she wrung out into a bedpan, as the damp wood gave off a thick humid smell. Then his mother saw him in that coat, the sleeves too long for his arms, and she smiled, as though seeing not him but his father; she came over and folded back the cuffs so his hands poked out and then took them in hers and blew on his fingers to warm them, and dried his sopping hair with a piece of cloth that smelled like her. All of those smells mingled together, and something wonderful overcame him in that coat, a warmth that had nothing to do with the fireplace.

"Are you all right?" the flight attendant asked.

Miguel nodded yes, wiping his cheek with the back of his hand. The world was what it was, so much larger than him that there was no way to understand what it all meant. All he could grasp was that it was fading quickly, ebbing away, and with it all of the affronts and sorrows and joys. Some people scrunched their eyes shut and covered their ears, hiding from life altogether; others suffered in silence, bearing it like a cross they never even turned to see, and a few—very few—actually learned to live before it was too late.

"It's beautiful, isn't it?" the flight attendant asked, gazing at the distant rain as the pilot announced their initial descent into Sevilla's airport and asked the passengers to buckle their seat belts.

Miguel smiled.

"It is, it certainly is."

EPILOGUE

Tarifa, three years later. June 2017

Time has passed leaving no trace. Slowly, the wicker basket of his memories has come unwoven and there is no way to patch the holes they leak out of.

All that's left are random images that appear and disappear at will, no context or connection, and a vague sense of nostalgia for something lost that Miguel can't put his finger on. He spends hours unaware of time passing, on the same bench at the seafront promenade, in the same silence, with the same peaceful calm in his eyes, gazing out over the sea.

The distance he sees cannot be perceived by others; finding things, going beyond what can be seen, has become his mission. He's been told he lives in the past, but it's not true. For Miguel, the past is present. And it's a present that is all landscape, because he can no longer distinguish reality and has entered the truth of the present moment, has realized that they're the same thing. Moments woven together with silk thread, like larvae in a cocoon, still blind but hoping to see. All true and yet remote at the same time. The woman who crouches down and ties his shoe and speaks sweetly and tells him that she's his daughter. She helped him put on his navy blue suit and matching tie this morning. Miguel likes his suit. It makes him feel good. And he likes sitting on this bench in the sun, too, even when the wind is blowing, like today. The wind has a smell, yes, it smells of iodine. And he likes to watch the swell of cresting waves as they curl over themselves before crashing heavily onto shore. He used to be able to come on his own, but for some time now he has needed help and a cane because his legs sometimes forget how to walk.

"Okay, Papá, there you go. Laces nice and tight, how you like them."

Miguel nods timidly, slightly confused. He feels ashamed and afraid to ask what her name is again, and when they met, and where. She seems to know him well. Miguel feels something unites them, that they are somehow similar and identify with one another.

A little girl runs up. Her hair is a mess. Miguel is startled by her momentum.

"Hello, Grandpa. Look, I got shells." She shows him the palm of her hand: shells, water, sand. She speaks patiently, as though prepared to repeat herself as many times as necessary. Miguel smiles and glances up at the woman. She smiles too, but you can tell that she is tired and disconsolate.

Miguel lets the frizzy-haired, green-eyed girl touch his face. He shrinks when she touches his mouth and eyes and kisses his cheek, leaving a trace of childhood on his old man's skin.

He watches them walk out to the beach, empty today because the wind has picked up. Miguel stirs uneasily. He's afraid they will forget about him. These days he's afraid of everything, all the time.

Sometimes he forgets about his body, which has shrunken to nothing, skin and bones, and trembles in fear when someone helps him shower or get dressed. He allows his hair to be combed, his face to be shaved with fresh-smelling cream that leaves his skin silky, his neck to be sprayed with cologne. And then, seeing himself in the mirror, he's struck with painful intensity by the fact that it's all coming to an end, here and now. And so is he. And then he forgets.

In his pocket is a slip of paper. He finds it by chance when reaching for a cigarette. He took up smoking late, he knows that much. Lighting cigarettes reminds him of something, brings a happiness that he cannot trace to its origin, which is lost in the desert of his memory. This morning, on waking, he wrote down a word with great urgency so as not to forget. A name.

Helena.

He moves his mouth and says it aloud, very slowly, as though his mouth were full of sand.

Helena.

He listens to it echo in his head, waits for a reply, but all that comes is the void, like footsteps on a cold marble floor.

The wind, furious, rips the paper from his fingers and carries it away in its own invisible pocket. Miguel watches it fly off, twirling and spiraling as though the name on it were alive.

He takes short puffs on his cigarette and feels the calm beating of his heart, ever slower and weaker. It's an irregular, arrhythmic beat, with long pauses; it's extinguishing.

"It will all be okay, Miguel. Don't be afraid."

He looks to his right and there, beside him, is his father, gazing at him so tenderly that it warms his heart. His father is someone that he does remember, clearly. It seems natural for his father to be there, because there no longer is a supreme, immutable order to anything. Time is like a jumbled collection of photos flashing before his eyes like shadow puppets.

"Where's Mamá?"

"She's waiting for us."

And now he remembers, though he doesn't know it's a memory. Because it's actually happening.

Miguel, in short pants, looking up at the man with big eyes and strong hands, the one who smokes cigarette butts he finds on the ground. The same man who says "You have to behave and take care of your mother until I come home." The man who sits beside him and puts an arm over his shoulder and pulls Miguel to him and smells of damp wood, dry fields, and old straw. The man who has flecks of tobacco in his pockets, and when he smiles it's like his teeth are the window that's open when they come home at night. *Take off your shoes, you two, they're all muddy, and wash your hands in the basin or no dinner for you.* That's the voice of his mother, in the kitchen with her apron on, her hair pulled back in a bun, the white skin of her neck showing. His mother, vigorously stirring the pot on the woodfire stove. And the two of them, father and son, winking and joking quietly at the basin, arm to arm: the man's arm strong and hairy, the boy's white and freckled, skinny; both with their sleeves rolled back, both with their hands submerged in the basin's cold water. Their hands, touching beneath the surface of the water as it grows cloudy with mud.

Miguel touches his chest. It hurts. Feels as though it's being squeezed by a claw.

His father takes his fingers and kisses them.

"It will be over soon. The pain will pass. You rest."

A boy's fingers, dirt under the fingernails, bitten down to the quick. Hangnails that sting and that his mother treats with hot water and salt. Miguel is holding a doll of wood and cardboard, a soldier that his father made for him on the eve of Twelfth Night, when Christmas presents are exchanged. That and an orange, left for him by Melchior's page. Nuno— the dog who went blind when a guard fired buckshot into his eyes, the dog they adopted because it broke his father's heart to see him roaming the streets of Almendralejo—sniffs the orange and gives it a little bite. His father laughs and says dogs don't know how to peel oranges.

He's so cold. His father's arm grows and he takes refuge in its embrace, like he used to when it rained in the fields and they had to stop searching the ground for fallen olives, and his mother waited at home for them with the fireplace lit, cooking *migas*. It's raining cats and dogs and they run, laughing, to the house, his father first, in the big coat he likes so much. Miguel's foot gets stuck in a ditch and he twists his ankle. He falls to the ground, which is soaking wet, and his father picks him up and consoles him.

"Don't cry, it's nothing. Falls like this happen all the time. You fall and you get back up, again and again."

They go home in the rain. His father carries him, kisses Miguel's head, which is shaved because he keeps getting lice and all the town "barber" does is shear sheep. Miguel feels his father's scratchy beard on his ears and the warmth of his hand on his cheek. Calloused hands, mountains erected by hard work.

He wants to go to sleep, curled there against his father's chest, in his arms, protected as he's carried home; forget the baking July afternoon in the olive grove and the swifts circling overhead that were startled by the sound of the church bells, before the first shots were fired, the ones that brought the war and took his father away.

"You can't remember that. You hadn't even been born."

But Miguel does, he remembers it. And he remembers being a baby, his mother's breast calming his cries and his father running through the furrows following Nuno's bark to hunt a rabbit. And long before that: he remembers his very first cry, his mother sobbing as she gave birth, the light he saw when he left the womb, startled from a dream that was peaceful but make-believe, remembers being brought into a world of blood and viscera; and the cold, the cold of life, hitting him for the first time. The same cold he feels now.

"Everything comes and everything goes, Miguel."

He lets himself be rocked in his father's arms and drifts off to the smell of his old clothes. And as life ends, he remembers why he wrote that name down when he woke up this morning.

Helena.

CREDITS

Epigraph on page ix from *Gilgamesh: A New English Version*, translated by Stephen Mitchell. Copyright © 2004 by Stephen Mitchell. Published by Free Press, a division of Simon & Schuster, 2004.

"Young Folks" lyrics on page 235 by Peter Bjorn and John. Copyright © Sony/ATV Music Publishing LLC, 2006.

Poetry excerpt on page 265 from "Evening Calm" by Ivan Bunin, translated from Spanish by Lisa Dillman.

Poetry excerpt on page 399 from "Late Ripeness" from *Second Space: New Poems* by Czeslaw Milosz, translated by the author and Robert Hass. Copyright © 2004 by Czeslaw Milosz. Translation copyright © 2004 by Robert Hass. Used by permission of HarperCollins Publishers.

"Fly Me to the Moon" lyric on page 484 by Bart Howard, 1954. Original title, "In Other Words." Copyright © T.R.O. Inc. Poetry excerpt on page 530 from "As I Walked Out One Evening" from *Another Time* by W. H. Auden. Copyright © 1940 W. H. Auden, renewed by the Estate of W. H. Auden. Published by Random House, 1940.

VÍCTOR DEL ÁRBOL was born in Barcelona in 1968 and was an officer of the Catalan police force from 1992 to 2012. As the recipient of the Nadal Prize, the Tiflos Prize, and as the first Spanish author to win the Prix du Polar Européen, he has distinguished himself as a notable voice in Spanish literature. His novel *A Million Drops* (Other Press, 2018) was named a Notable Book of the Year by the *Washington Post*.

LISA DILLMAN has translated a number of Spanish and Latin American writers. Some of her recent translations include *Such Small Hands* and *A Luminous Republic* by Andrés Barba; *Signs Preceding the End of the World* and *A Silent Fury* by Yuri Herrera; and *A Million Drops* and *Breathing Through the Wound* by Víctor del Árbol. She teaches in the Department of Spanish and Portuguese at Emory University in Atlanta, Georgia.

Also by **VÍCTOR DEL ÁRBOL**

A Million Drops   Translated by Lisa Dillman

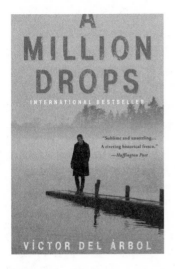

"Defies categorization, pulling
together the best elements
of historical fiction, psychological
thrillers, and literary character
studies." —*Washington Post*

"Del Árbol, a gifted storyteller, keeps
the pages turning even as he probes
the dark, compromised souls of
his characters." —*Chicago Tribune*

"Succeeds as historical fiction,
a thriller, and a detective story."
—*Library Journal* (starred review)

NAMED A BEST BOOK OF THE YEAR BY THE *SEATTLE TIMES*,
WASHINGTON POST, AND *CRIME READS*

An intense literary thriller that tears through the interlocked histories
of fascism and communism in Europe without pausing for breath.

Gonzalo Gil is a disaffected lawyer stuck in a failed career and a strained
marriage, dodging the never-ending manipulation of his powerful
father-in-law. The fragile balance of Gonzalo's life is pushed to the limit
when he learns that his estranged sister, Laura, has committed suicide
under suspicious circumstances. Resolutely investigating the steps
that led to her death, Gonzalo discovers that Laura is believed to have
murdered a Russian gangster who killed her young son. Suspenseful
and utterly absorbing, *A Million Drops* is a visceral story of enduring love
and revenge postponed that introduces a master of international crime
fiction to American readers.

▟▙ OTHER PRESS

Also by **VÍCTOR DEL ÁRBOL**

Breathing Through the Wound   Translated by Lisa Dillman

"Del Árbol's *A Million Drops* was one of 2018's most complex and powerful thrillers. His follow-up, *Breathing Through the Wound*, cements his place as one of the most exciting voices in contemporary European noir." — *CrimeReads*

"The reveals provide multiple gut punches that require readers to reevaluate their assumptions...Noir fans will get their money's worth." — *Publishers Weekly* (starred review)

NAMED A BEST INTERNATIONAL CRIME NOVEL OF THE YEAR BY *CRIMEREADS* **AND A BEST BOOK OF THE YEAR BY** *POPMATTERS*

An engrossing psychological thriller that traces a widower's descent into the seedy underbelly of Madrid.

Eduardo Quintana's life lost all meaning when his wife and daughter were killed in a tragic accident. The once-renowned painter wallows in grief and guilt, subsisting on alcohol and drugs, not caring if he lives or dies.

But when a grieving mother asks Eduardo to paint a portrait of the man who killed her son, he finds himself drawn to the unusual commission. He alone understands her need to look deep into the soul of the man who changed her life forever, and he alone can help.

As Eduardo sets out to discover what it takes to know a killer, he is pulled deeper and deeper into Madrid's criminal underworld, where mercenaries, prostitutes, murderers, and thieves are all entangled in a dangerous and deadly web, in which nothing, and no one, are as they seem.

⊞ OTHER PRESS